POWER
INITIATES

By
RICHARD ROSS

BOOK 1 OF

COSMIC
ENDEAVOR

POWER INITIATES

RICHARD ROSS

CONTENTS

Chapter 1

INAUGURATION

Record Dates: 347.412 – 347.428 PGST

"I GOT IT!" YELLED THE young man as he fought to catch his breath, approaching her house.

"You got what?" Illandra yelled back, tucking a black strand of hair that had fallen out of her sloppy ponytail. He had called her some time ago saying he was on his way, but her patience was about to run out. Even though it was early spring, it was so cold that Illandra had to wrap her hands in the sleeves of her fuzzy green robe and stuff them in the pockets just to keep them warm. "Did you run all the way from the Stacks?"

The Stacks got their name from the small cubed houses that were stacked upward on each other to save space. They were the least-desired residential areas of the planet Galilei. Only those who couldn't afford a normal house or a spot in one of the three newly built megastructures lived there.

"It was more of a brisk walk," he panted as he approached the corner of her driveway. "My mom is still working the graveyard shift."

"That's like ten miles." Her eyebrows lifted in surprise.

1

"You hate running."

"Tell me about it." He grabbed the pillar at the end of her vehicle port, using his hand to prop himself up. He lifted a leg to jump over, but only made it about a foot before giving up. "A little help, please?"

The fence was only about a meter high. Normally, he would have just hopped over it. "Fine, fine." Illandra started down the path to let him in. The young man took off his light-gray jacket and threw it over his shoulder as he waited to be let in. His green shirt had patches of dark where the sweat had been absorbed from his body. Even the waves of his long brown hair were being dragged straight by the sweat dripping from them.

The sun rising blinded her as it peeked out from behind the megastructure to the east. Even though it was still under construction, the monolith had already eaten an hour of sunlight from the morning at Illandra's house some miles away.

She waved her hand over the panel for authentication. The fence responded by lowering itself to let him pass. "What's got you so worked up, anyway?"

"I got it!" he said, whipping an envelope out of his back pocket.

It was the fourth envelope Illandra had seen in her life. Only official documents were delivered through the mail system these days.

Illandra snatched the paper from his hands and started to inspect it. It was a little damp from the young man's sweat, and had a smell that almost made her want to hand it back.

"Is this what I think it is?"

"Yep." He smiled. "You're not going to believe it."

The adhesive on the back of the envelope had already been torn. "You opened it?" Her teeth clenched so hard, pain shot up her jaw. "We were supposed to open them together."

"Sorry." He pursed his lips. "I couldn't help myself. Did you get yours?"

"I don't know!" Illandra gasped. She slapped the letter on his chest and jogged to the mailbox to check. Her brown slippers made a whoosh sound as they skirted along the pavement. She placed her thumb on the slot. The box opened to reveal a hollow, empty container.

She sighed and reluctantly closed the container. "Come on. Let's go inside. Give me that." She plucked the envelope back out of the young man's hand as she walked by. She stretched up onto her tippy-toes and puckered her lips. He still had to bend down to complete the kiss.

As Illandra continued into the house, she pulled out the small digital card from the envelope and pinched the corner to display the message that it held.

"Dear Race Allard…" She started to mumble as she read the letter. "Thank you for submitting your citizenship application for the United Galactic Republic. Blah, blah, blah…" She skimmed farther down. "…application accepted…like to congratulate and welcome you as a full citizen with the rights and responsibilities that go along with it… You will find your citizenship ID card enclosed." She froze just inside the door. The sweaty young man bumped into her. "As you well know, all citizenship cards are color-coded based on the testing scores of your citizenship-aptitude assessment test. Based on your results, you have been issued…" She was unable to control her jaw as it dropped upon seeing the words. "That's impossible."

"No, it's not." Race pulled the card from another pocket, reached over her shoulder, and held it near her face.

Illandra responded with a loud shriek. Before Race could cover his ears for protection, Illandra snatched the card from his hand. The card was transparent with a green stripe embossed with the name "Race Allard" in white letters running across it. A unique identification number was embossed just below.

Stomping noises came from the floor above as an older man and woman came charging down the stairs.

"What's the matter, sweetie?" said Illandra's mom.

"Is everything okay?" added Illandra's father.

"Look." Illandra held up the green card she had snatched from Race.

"Oh my god," the parents said as they dashed to get a closer look.

Their concern quickly turned to shock as they eyed the rare treasure.

"I don't believe it," said the father as the mother beat him to the card. "There are only a couple of green cards handed out every year. Sometimes none at all."

"Your mom must be so proud," said Illandra's mother as she handed off the card to her husband to finally give him a look. She went to give Race a hug. The young man put up a hand to stop her about the time she stopped dead in her tracks after catching a whiff of his strong odor. Illandra's mom was wearing a red suit with a skirt that neither of them wanted to ruin.

"Sorry, it was a long run to get here," Race explained. "She hasn't made it home from the graveyard shift yet. I'll tell her later when I see her."

"Well, you should be very proud of yourself, son." Illandra's father returned the card to Race and congratulated the young man with a fist pump to his shoulder.

"Thank you, sir," Race said, taking the card back and stuffing it into the back pocket of his jeans.

"You know you can call me Frank, Race," Illandra's father insisted. "Now, if you'll excuse me, our ride should be here any minute." The father bent down to give both of his ladies a kiss on the cheek before returning back upstairs to retrieve their luggage.

Illandra exchanged an impressed look with her mother.

"He's never asked me to call him by his first name," Race observed as he watched Illandra's father disappear.

Illandra pulled a small metallic cylinder out of her pocket to check if any of her friends had mentioned anything about receiving their cards.

"Please, make yourself at home, Race." Illandra's mother invited him to sit on one of the pearl-white leather-like couches in the living space. "Would you like something to drink?"

"That would be great," Race said, taking a seat on the edge of the couch so as not to mess it up with his sticky body.

Illandra's mom spoke the command to turn on the holovision to try and make Race more comfortable before she disappeared into the kitchen to fetch Race a drink.

"Looks like everyone else got their cards, too," Illandra told Race as she read the news. "They're talking about meeting up at the Hangout later on for reveals. We should head over," she said, looking up at Race.

"Do you want to go?" Race asked. "You haven't gotten yours yet. Won't you feel a little out of place?"

Illandra caught her mom looking nervously at her purse on the couch. "I don't think that will be a problem," Illandra replied. "Besides, it doesn't matter what color mine is. You're going to be the center of attention, Mr. Green Card."

Much to her surprise, Race had a huge smile on his face. Everyone loved to receive a little praise now and then, and Race was no exception. "All right," he replied, "you'd better get ready."

Illandra's father returned from upstairs, pulling a couple pieces of luggage behind. "Ride's here."

"Can I help you with anything?" Race offered, standing up.

"I got it," said the father as he pulled the suitcases out the front door.

"You know, the house's AI has been acting up again. If you could take a look at it while we're out, I'd really appreciate it," Illandra's mom said as she returned to Race with the drink.

"Of course," Race said, taking the glass and helping himself to a large gulp before setting it down on a coaster on the glass coffee table at his feet. He walked down the hall where the access panel was stored.

"See us out, sweetie?" Illandra's mom asked of her.

The two ladies went outside to find Illandra's father and the chauffeur sticking the luggage in the back of his luxurious floating car. Illandra's mom turned to her and put a hand of each of Illandra's shoulders. It was almost like looking into a mirror from the future, from the coal-black hair to the light-brown eyes, even their short stature. "Marry him," she told Illandra.

"MOM!" Illandra grabbed her chest to keep her heart from jumping out.

"Honey, he's a green card. All the doors are going to just open up for him. He's going to be famous. Girls are going to throw themselves at him, literally." Her mother's head shook in explication. "You need to lock him in before some other woman comes and steals him from you."

"Aren't you and Dad always telling me I don't need a man to be happy and successful?" Illandra corrected her mom while pointing a stern finger at her.

"Of course." Her mom smiled. The two shared a hug while bits of laughter bubbled between them.

Illandra's father came back to retrieve his wife so they could depart. "No parties," he told Illandra sternly, "and be good."

"Aren't I always, Daddy?" Illandra said as she innocently wrapped her arms in front of her, batting her eyelashes to melt his heart.

"Of course, sweetheart." He chuckled, giving her a good-bye kiss on her forehead and embracing her in one last hug.

"We should be home in a week or so, honey," Illandra's mom interrupted.

"Before you go," Illandra said as she stuck out the palm of her hand. "Give me."

"Wha...I don't know what you're talking about," her mom said defensively, tightening the grip on her purse.

"You checked the mail early this morning and hid my acceptance letter in your purse." Illandra squinted accusingly at her mother, pushing her open palm closer.

"I...I..." Illandra's mom stuttered nervously as her eyes failed to meet Illandra's gaze. "Oh, I hate it when you do that," she fumed, stomping one foot on the ground. She opened up her purse and started sorting through its contents in search of the letter. "I swear you're a mind-reader sometimes."

"No, just a mom-reader," Illandra responded, with her empty palm still waiting.

"You were out late last night," Illandra's mom protested as she pulled out the magical envelope and handed it over. "We were leaving this morning. I just wanted to have some time to celebrate after you opened it."

"You can watch me open it before you leave." Illandra snatched the envelope from her mother and quickly ripped the short side open. She pulled out the accompanying note and put it aside before diving back in, her hand searching for her card. Her parents watched anxiously as she quickly snapped her arm up from the envelope, prize in hand.

The family gasped in unison as their jaws dropped in awe.

"Wow," gasped the driver, breaking the silence that followed. "Not every day you get to see a green card!"

"Holy shit!" Illandra exclaimed. She ran back toward the house to show Race before realizing she hadn't properly said farewell to her parents. She rushed back and gave them both a quick kiss on the cheek.

"Bye, Mom. Bye, Dad. Have fun," she hollered over her shoulder as she dashed back into the house.

"I think I fixed the AI," Race's voice came from the hall. "Just needed a little reboot."

Illandra's face collided with his chest as they met at the corner. She almost fell to the floor as she bounced off of him.

"Look." Illandra held out her matching green card, almost knocking him over.

"Oh, my goodness," Race said, taking it from her to compare to his.

"I know," she exclaimed. "I'm going to go get ready so we can get to the Hangout." Her nostrils flared as she caught the scent of Race's sweat. "After we get you home; you need a shower and change." She tried to fan the smell away with one of her hands as she headed upstairs.

* * *

Race held the door open for Illandra, who then proceeded to drag him in behind her. The place was ablaze with chatter from all the overcrowded tables of newly initiated citizens showing off their different-colored citizenship cards. They were quickly waved down by one of Illandra's friends from nearly halfway down the room. As they pushed their way past the crowd, they could see most of their fellow graduates' cards in hand, while others' lay on the tables in front of them. All the cards were identical to the couple's cards, but instead of the green strip cutting through the upper half, most of theirs were the abundant yellow or blue. A few orange cards were lying around for some of the lower achievers that still wanted to partake in the festivities. The only color not represented was the shaming purple card. Any recipients were obviously too embarrassed to make an appearance at the gathering.

"What's it looking like?" Illandra questioned as she finally reached the table.

"Not bad," replied the friend that had waved them over. She started to point around the table and announce what each person had gotten.

"Where's Jasmin?" Illandra asked when the round of information was finished.

A few of the party members rolled their eyes just hearing the name. "Over there," one of the girls snarled, pointing to the far corner of the room. "The red cards have gathered. I'm surprised they found a table big enough to sit them and their egos."

"Red, huh?" Race said, trying his best to become a part of the conversation.

"Let's go congratulate her." Illandra nudged him with a nod of her head.

"Wait," the guy in the middle of the table said. "What did you two get?"

Illiandra responded with only a wink before disappearing back into the crowd. Illandra and Race continued to navigate the mosh pit as they made their way to the back of the diner.

"Jazz," Illandra called to her friend as she squeezed past a couple of towering crowd members. "We heard the news! Congrats!" Illandra gave Race's hand one last tug to get him through the blockade of people before letting it go.

A girl with long blond hair jumped up from the table to embrace Illandra and they excitedly danced back and forth. Jasmin was only a little taller than her, but Illandra still had to tilt her head up a little bit to not be smashed by Jasmin's shoulder. "Isn't it exciting?" Jasmin exclaimed.

"Yes," Illandra said, releasing her friend's embrace. "Very impressive."

"Hey, Race," a guy stuffed into the table's corner called out. "You come to join all the cool kids?"

"Sup, Reggie." Race nodded back across the table. "Not sure if I'm cool enough for you guys. I hear this is the red-card table."

Race and Illandra knew several of the students from their school. They had shared a couple of the school's advanced classes together. They must have assumed that just because they were in some advanced classes, they would also be red cards.

"What?" exclaimed Reg. "I thought for sure that you'd be a red. Hardly any of us could keep up with you."

"You practically taught the advanced calculus class," another table member stated.

"Sorry to disappoint, guys," Race apologized, trying to keep the smirk from breaking the surface.

"What about you, Illandra?" Jazz interjected. "You got a red, right? You were great at debates and psychology."

"No," Illandra answered, shaking her head in disappointment. "Unfortunately, I didn't."

"Okay, now I don't believe either one of you. Show 'em," Reggie demanded, calling them forth with his hands.

Illandra looked up at Race. She could tell that it was taking almost everything he had to keep from ripping the card out of his pocket to show everyone.

"All right," Illandra replied. "Help me up, Race," she said as she stepped up onto the seat Jazz had recently vacated. She took Race's outstretched hand for support as her right foot joined the other on top of the cushioned booth. She placed her other hand on her neighbor's shoulder to stabilize herself. Even with the added height of the seat, Illandra stood barely a foot taller than her fellow graduates.

"Excuse me, everyone," Illandra called out, taking control of the room. The loud roar of the crowd quieted down a soft whisper. Even the waitresses stopped what they were doing to turn their attention to Illandra. She always did have a way of working a crowd. "Sorry, I just thought I'd speed up this process a bit. I'm just going to call out a color," she continued. "If that's your card, raise it up and show it off."

"Let start at the bottom and work our way up. Any purple?" Everyone started to scour the room for cards.

"I didn't think so," Illandra reported, not seeing any show of hands. "What about orange?"

Again, heads started to turn in search of the area, this time catching a few people holding their cards sheepishly over their head. "A couple of you," Illandra observed, looking over the crowd. "Not bad. All right, who has yellow?"

A large group of hands shot up over patrons' heads with yellow-striped cards. "Good job," Illandra complimented while scanning the room. "Okay, what's next? Blue?"

The yellow cards dropped from above the crowd to be replaced by a sea of blue cards. A proud holler from their holders joined some of the cards' appearances. "Awesome, guys," Illandra congratulated. "Okay, let's see those prized red cards." She reached both hands down to the party she had crashed.

The people sitting at the table next to Race and Illandra shot up their hands, adding a large roar so as not to be outdone by the previous group. "Impressive," commented Illandra. "You guys were always the best. Great work." She turned her attention back to the crowd. "Did I miss any?"

"Not unless you think someone got a green card." Reggie chuckled as he put his card back down in front of him.

"Good point, Reggie," Illandra thanked him. "Do we have any legendary green cards?"

Illandra looked down at Race's dancing blue eyes as the two of them reached into their pockets to find their treasured cards.

In unison, they both pulled out their cards and held them proudly above their heads, letting out a proud howl for all to hear. Their shouts were nowhere near as loud as the rest, but the silence that fell before them made their whoops seem louder than everyone else's combined.

The faces of most of the occupants were locked in position as they tried to understand what had just happened. As quickly as the noise had stopped, it suddenly turned into a bombardment of questions as each person tried to get the couple's attention.

"I hope you can get used to this," Illandra said, looking down at Race with her hands on his shoulders. She was starting to like the view from up here. It wasn't often that she got to feel like the tall one.

"I guess I'm going to have to." Race smiled back as he put his hands on her hips to help her down.

*   *   *

The next couple of days were an adventure for the couple. They were the hit at all the graduation and acceptance parties, and Illandra was pretty sure that they had been invited to just about every one of them. Illandra had noticed that her mom's premonitions were starting to come true. Every time she left Race alone for more than a couple minutes, she'd come back to find herself having to shoo a flock of girls attempting to gain Race's favor.

Race was trying to adjust to his newfound fame. While he was coming to find himself enjoying all the attention, he quite often found himself out of place, especially when Illandra wasn't by his side. When the two were together, Illandra's presence was enough to keep him relaxed him enough to enjoy the celebrations.

Beyond the parties, the two spent a large amount of time trying to avoid the local news crews. It hadn't taken long for word to get out about the "Green Couple" and several reporters were anxious to interview the two. Race and Illandra did their best to avoid them, even breaking into Illandra's own home late one night. When they were there, the two held up in one of the secluded rooms with almost no windows so the paparazzi wouldn't know of their presence.

"Are you going to be all right?" Illandra asked Race one night as they sat next to each other in the barely lit room.

"Of course." Race laughed, trying to put on a brave face. "What wouldn't I be all right about?"

"Tomorrow's the big ceremony," Illandra replied. "We get sworn in as full citizens."

"It's just a bunch of standing around," Race said dismissively.

"And lots of people," Illandra added. "And I bet all these cameras following us are going to be there as well." She could feel Race start to tense up beside her. "Relax." She grabbed his hand to calm him down. "I'll be there with you the whole time."

"Then why are you getting me all stressed out about it?" Race complained loudly.

"Shhhh," Illandra quieted him, covering his mouth. "You're going to let them know we're inside."

"Then why did you bring it up?" Race managed to mutter through his clenched teeth.

"Because I wanted you to be prepared," Illandra whispered. "Forget I brought it up." Illandra dropped her hand from Race's mouth and repositioned herself on the floor a little. She tried to focus her attention back to the movie playing on the holovision they had moved into the room.

"Sorry," Race said, breaking the awkward silence. "I guess I overreacted."

That was one thing that always worried Illandra about Race. Race was always quick to apologize for anything, even when he was in the right.

"Don't worry about it," Illandra whispered back, repositioning her head back on his shoulder.

"You ever wonder what it would be like?" Race's thoughts started to go where they usually went. "Just to take a ship and leave it all behind?"

"That's your dream, not mine," Illandra said, digging around in the bowl of fluffy snacks, trying to find a piece she liked. "I'd go crazy without anyone else to talk to. Besides, you couldn't survive too long by yourself."

"Probably," Race sighed disappointedly. "Someday I'm going to get my hands on my own ship, and then I'm going to run away from all this. Take some time to discover me. What do you think about after initiations? Have you given any thoughts to what job you're going to pick?"

"Kind of hard to know without seeing the list," Illandra said. "Something without too much training, I hope."

"No joke." Race laughed. "I think we've had enough school."

"What about you?" Illandra asked, looking up at his face with the light from the movie dancing over his face.

"I don't know," Race answered. "Something tells me that we're not going to have as big a selection to pick from as we'd like."

"What do you mean?" Illandra's brow scrunched up

puzzled. "We're green cards. We'll probably have too many options to pick from."

"I don't think so," Race replied. "I mean, I know that's how it's supposed to work. Something just tells me that it's not going to happen for us."

Illandra felt the nagging in the back of Race's mind as if it were her own, forcing her to sit up to look him in the face. "Explain," she demanded flatly.

Race sighed as he looked to the ceiling for the right words. "I just overheard some people talking the other day about tensions within the government's relations between the Consortium and us," he tried to explain. "When I heard it, it just made me feel that they were going to use that as an excuse to push us into a special job."

Such predictions were laughable, but Illandra knew better than to doubt Race's ability to draw intangible lines between events. More often than not, his weird sense to web together random bits of information was good enough to lead to some startlingly accurate predictions.

"So what is it exactly you're trying to get at?" Illandra questioned carefully. It was now her time to be the tense one. "We're at least going to be together, aren't we?"

"I don't know," Race said, dropping his head, hoping one of his curls would fall and keep him from looking her in the eyes.

"But you don't think so," Illandra read Race's reaction.

Race did his best to turn his head up and look at her directly. Unable to bring himself to speak the words, he bit his lip and shook his head from side to side before once again

17

staring down at the floor.

"That's bullshit!" Illandra exclaimed, jumping to her feet. "That can't happen! That won't happen! They can't break us apart," she said, defying his prophecy, and then took to pacing the room, waving her arms up in the air. "You just watch, we're going to be together forever."

Illandra continued her rant for some time before sitting back down next to Race. "So what?" Illandra said, finally running out of the energy needed to continue her protest.

"Well, we can at least stay in touch," Race suggested.

"That's true." Illandra nodded her head in agreement. "Just because we'll be on different planets doesn't mean we still can't keep in touch."

"And when we're able to, we can work on getting back together."

"What if you find someone else?" Illandra questioned.

Race laughed at the thought. "How am I going to find someone? I'd actually have to socialize."

"You found me," Illandra complimented, and she spun onto her hands and knees and prowled seductively up Race's arm to give him an array of kisses.

"No, I didn't," Race said between kisses. "You're the one"—kiss—"that found me." Kiss. "So if anyone is going to find someone else"—kiss—"it's probably you."

Illandra stopped the wave of kisses and sat down on her heels. "Who could ever take your place?"

"I'm sure plenty of guys are willing to try," Race scorned.

"Is that jealousy?" Illandra mocked as she teasingly pushed him by the shoulder, forcing him to use his other hand to keep her from knocking him completely over.

Race's cheeks turned a bright red that glowed even in the dim light. "No." He tried to cover the faint smile creeping through his lips.

"You are," she teased him, forcing him over and jumping on top of him.

"Well maybe if you stopped giving me reasons," Race joked, crossing his arms protectively in front of him, "I wouldn't have to be."

"How can I be guilty of you imagining me with someone I haven't even met?" Illandra said playfully, giving him a big kiss. "Is he cute?"

"What happened to no one being able to replace me?" Race laughed.

"I was just hoping you knew of someone who might live up to my standards," Illandra toyed.

The two slowly forgot all about the movie as their playful kisses gained a little more passion. Before they could get too far, Illandra was forced to jump off of Race as something between them started to vibrate violently. "Uh, now who?"

Race dug into his pocket to pull out a small cylindrical device. "It's my mom."

"Have you told her yet?" Illandra questioned, helping him up so that he could answer the call.

Race quickly shook his head in response to the image of his mother. "Mom?"

"Race!" an image of a woman said as her face showed up a couple of inches above the device.

"What's going on?" he asked as he got up to pace around

the room a bit.

"It's crazy around here! There are reporters everywhere. Is it true?"

"I did ask, but Illandra hasn't answered me yet," Race answered. "I'm thinking a fall wedding. We'll have to figure out the details after our continued education courses, but then we'll settle down, buy a house, the 2.5 kids, and all that good stuff."

"Stop being a smart-ass," Race's mom responded over the phone. "You know what I mean."

"Yes," Race answered, still enjoying the clever remark he had come up with, "it's green."

"Oh my goodness!" Race's mom squealed, causing her holographic image to break up into bits of static for a second. Race had to beat on it a couple times to get the image back to being visible. "Where are you?"

"I'm over at Illandra's," Race answered. "We boarded ourselves up in one of her rooms to get away from the reporters. She got a green card, too."

"I heard!" Race's mom exclaimed, causing another fit of static to dance across the screen. "Your parents must be very proud, Illandra. Congratulations."

"Thank you, Miss Allard," Illandra called out so that his mom could hear her. "They were very happy about the news."

"Why don't you come down to the store, Son?" his mom begged. "I really want to see your card. I'll sneak out the back really quick so you can show me."

"All right," Race answered. "I'll be down in a bit."

"Okay," Race's mom replied. "I'll see you in a few. Love you."

"Love you, too." Race fidgeted with a button on the side of the cylinder before the device finally shut off.

"You really should get a new comm," Illandra told him as he shoved the device back into his pocket.

"You know how much work I had to do just to afford that one," Race reminded her. He let out a little moan as Illandra sneaked up under his arm to snuggle up beside him to give him a farewell hug. "Do I have to go?"

"Stop being a baby," Illandra scolded him. "She's your mom."

Race let out one last sigh before Illandra let go of her embrace. The couple exchanged one last kiss before Race picked up his jacket and headed to the window. He slid the window open as quietly as possible, and stuck one leg out into the dark abyss before taking a seat on the sill. "Don't forget to lock up," he warned before disappearing into the darkness altogether.

Illandra grabbed the remote and resumed the movie, but she only made it a couple of minutes before she lost interest and turned it off altogether. She wasn't even paying attention to it in the first place. The only reason she'd been watching was that it hypnotized Race.

The house started to feel creepy as the shadows inside started to match the darkness she had just sent Race off to. Illandra could feel the hollow void starting to close in around her. "I hate being alone," she whispered to the darkness. A thought sprang into her mind that shattered the dark void. She quickly made her way to the kitchen, turning on as many of the lights along the way as possible. She could feel the stirring of the small crowd outside the house. The coffee pot started to hiss and moan as she flicked the switch on it. She continued to the front door, where she flipped on a couple more switches for the outside lights.

Most of the crews were scattering for their cameras when Illandra peeked out the window. Standing to the side of the door, well outside the crowd's view, she opened the door and pushed it open.

"I just put on a pot of coffee," Illandra called to the mob. "You're welcome to come in and have a cup with me, but no cameras."

She could hear several of the individuals mumbling to each other as they tried to figure out what to do.

"Once this door closes, that's it," Illandra called to them one more time. "Better hurry up and make up your mind. Ten… Nine… Eight…" The sound of several people wrestling with their belongings made it to Illandra's ears as they hurriedly secured their belongings. The last of the crew came through the door as Illandra closed it behind them. Illandra counted the mob, the majority of whom were young men slightly older than herself, way outnumbering the few women in the group.

"I hope we have enough cups," Illandra said as she turned to lead them to the dining area.

*　　*　　*

Illandra was already darting through the crowd of people trying to make her way to Race. She was still shaking the last of the haziness out of her head from her late night socializing. Luckily, the ceremony hadn't required her to be too conscious, just a lot of standing around, repeating the oath after the ceremony leader.

The groups had then broken up and funneled through several lines where they were to get their availability lists. Illandra was shocked by her list. Race had been correct when he predicted that they would only have a limited number of choices. She was still trying to decide how she felt about her opportunity, but it seemed a logical choice to follow in her family's profession. She had assumed that Race had gotten the same letter, but she could almost feel his outrage from across the crowd of people.

"What!?" she heard Race's voice say while she tried to weave through some of the crowd. "How is that possible?"

"I'm sorry, sir," she heard a man answer him. "I don't make them. I just hand them out."

"This can't be my list, though," Race demanded. "I'm a green card!"

Illandra finally broke through the last of the crowd between her and her objective. Race was fuming as he towered over the man in the chair operating the list.

"Race," Illandra called to him, hoping that she could defuse him before he actually lost his temper. "Calm down! What's going on?"

"Look." Race steamed as he handed her a small piece of paper.

Illandra grabbed the paper from his hand and started

to read it over. She was able to read the entirety of the list in one word. "Military!" she yelled, reading the list. She slammed the paper on the small desk in front of the man, almost mimicking Race's previous outrage. "This can't be right?"

"I'm sorry, miss," the worker reported once again, his hands shaking as he wiped the sweat from his brow. "That's what printed out. I don't make them. I'm just here to make sure it works properly."

"Have you seen the color of this card? It's obviously not working properly," Illandra scolded as she grabbed Race's hand and stormed off. They walked over to the next table. The people waiting in line had all stopped, focused on the outraged couple's display.

"Excuse me," Illandra said, cutting in line. She turned Race and held out her hand. "Card." Without a word, Race took out his card and handed it over to Illandra. She took the card and placed it in the slot specially designed to read it. She then put Race's hand on the biometric reader to confirm his identity. "Please print it," Illandra asked the operator as nicely as she could.

The lady quickly pushed the console, which prompted the printer to eject another small piece of paper. Illandra snatched the list before the operator even had a chance to move to grab it. She lowered it in disappointment. "Whom do we talk to about this?" Illandra demanded through locked teeth.

The lady turned and pointed to a flight of stairs toward the back of the building. "The district manager's office is back there. He should be able to help you out, miss."

"Thank you," Illandra said, already dragging Race in the direction pointed out to her.

The crowds instinctively parted, creating a path for Race and Illandra. They climbed the stairs to the director's office, where the receptionist greeted them and had them take a seat while they waited.

As the time passed, Race's rage started to turn into despair. "What am I going to do?" he cried. "I'm not a fighter. I don't even like to exercise. Running is for people that are being chased. That's not my style. How am I supposed to be a soldier?"

"We're going to fight this, Race," Illandra claimed, biting her nails while trying to decipher what was going on. "If nothing else, you can always decline admission."

"No certified company will hire me, which means no job, period," Race exclaimed nervously, pacing around the room. "No voting rights, not even allowed to own property. Practically no rights at all. I might as well go live in the outer colonies."

"Oh, it's not that bad," Illandra lied. "You might like the pirate life. I can imagine you with a peg leg and an eye patch." The outskirts weren't real pirates, no matter how much they liked to refer to themselves as so.

"Don't forget the talking parrot." Race chuckled as he plopped into the chair next to Illandra. He let out a depressing sigh as he sunk into the chair. After a moment of silence, he realized he wasn't the only one with a problem. "Did you get your list?"

Illandra pulled her hands out from under her chin to hand him a folded piece of paper. He grabbed the equally short list from her hand, and opened it up to read its content.

"Political relations?" Race said, sitting up. "They want you to be a politician?"

"So it seems," she replied.

"Not what I expected," Race said. "But not something that you'd be bad at."

"Yeah," Illandra answered shortly. "It's an interesting choice. Not sure how I feel about it."

"I'm sure your parents would be happy that you are following in their footsteps. It's better than military," Race retorted with a low chuckle.

"There is that." Illandra chuckled back. "Hey," she said, straightening in her chair, "wouldn't that make me your boss?"

"No more than usual," Race responded with a hint of a smile breaking through the corner of his lips.

The stubby director turned out to be useless. All he could tell them was that the government had "exercised special privileges" to lock in both of their availabilities. He couldn't tell them anything, as their records were classified beyond his clearance. Illandra yelled out some choice comments about the man's lack of hair before they were forced to leave without a resolution.

Race did his best to accept his position and explore his options. Illandra supported him by accompanying Race around to the different recruiters. Several of them were unable to promise him anything substantial, while others promised him everything. Illandra could easily tell that most of them were lying to try and get Race to sign up and would not be able to deliver on their promises.

Ironically, they found the most reliable person in the most unlikely place. "Will I see combat?" Race asked the same question he had asked the other recruiters.

"Possibly." The recruiter started pouring himself a beverage. "I'm not going to tell you no. There's always the possibility. If your test results are high enough, we can guarantee you something with a low probability, if that's what you like. But you never know where you're going to find yourself. You might be working on a general's terminal on some distant planet, and all of a sudden, the place comes under attack by mutant lizard soldiers. Unlikely, seeing as military studies on animals have been outlawed since before galactic travel, but you never really know what to expect. I can't guarantee that any more than I could guarantee you not getting mugged walking out that door."

"What jobs do I qualify for?" Race asked.

"Let's find out," the recruiter said, joining them back at his desk. "Let me see your citizenship card."

Race pulled the card out from the inside pocket of his jacket and handed it over to the soldier. The recruiter admired the card before sliding it into a slot in his computer. He made a few motions to the hovering images while sipping from his cup with the other hand. He put his cup down on the table and reached up to grab the corners of the hovering image and angle it toward the two of them.

Race looked over the list, which was much more generous than the one handed to him before.

"I can only guarantee you one of these major categories," the recruiter said, pointing to the headings. "Find one that has a good grouping you like, and we'll take it from there."

Race's knee started to bounce anxiously as he eyed the list of possibilities. "Race," Illandra interrupted before he could blurt out a decision, "can we have a moment outside?"

"Huh?" Race said, his attention snapping from the endless possibilities before him. "Oh, sure."

"Take your time," the recruiter said, taking Race's card out of the terminal. "Here's your card in case you decide to run off."

"What is it?" Race asked when they were outside the lobby. "Don't tell me you don't trust him."

"Actually, he seems to be completely trustworthy," Illandra said, passing her judgment. "It's just…are you sure about this? These guys have a reputation for being pretty intense. This isn't the most laid back of the branches."

"Easy is boring," Race responded quickly. "Besides, how bad can they really be?"

"I'm sure you'll find out," Illandra answered. "I just want to make sure you're confident."

There was a moment of silence as Race ran through the facts one more time in his head. "I hate to say it, but I think this is the right option," Race concluded. "I feel I can make a real difference this way."

"Okay," Illandra replied. She reached out and opened the door for Race. "If you're sure."

"I can't believe I'm going to do this," Race said, taking

one last breath, and shaking out what bits of nervousness he could. He walked through the door and looked the recruiter in the eyes. "Sign me up."

"I knew you'd make the right decision," the recruiter said. "Welcome to the United Republic Space Marines."

Chapter 2

TRAINING

Record Dates: 347.432 – 347.761 PGST

RACE WAS STILL TRYING TO understand the full weight of his decision to join the Space Marines. Once he had signed the contract, minutes passed faster than the beats of his heart. He had spent the first two weeks traveling back and forth between his home and the recruiting center, going through all sorts of physical exams to ensure that he was fit enough for duty. Illandra scowled at him every time he left. There was at least one huge argument. She was too busy meeting with her own counselors to plan her future. He had done his best to support her, but the enchantment of her career only made him despise his own career placement more.

Then he was gone, on a planet as alien to him as almost any other. Oppenheimer was considered a very special planet to the government. It was completely dedicated to military training, operations, and research. Not only did the Space Marines conduct their training there, but each of the different military branches had an array of bases scattered across the planet. A lot of times, they shared the different training facilities and conducted several exercises together, more often than not against each other.

Race had landed on a nice urban part of the planet. It was a little colder than home. He guessed this part was closer to an early fall season compared to the nice spring he had just left. Some of the trees were beginning to show the speckled red leaves of fall.

The recruits were herded into an off-white building, where they had their heads shaved, and traded in their clothes for some military camouflage. The recruits were then loaded up with several shots to bring them up on their immunizations. The final part of the enrollment process involved binding a military sensory unit to the recruits' forearms. The process was quite painful, as a metallic cylinder was surgically implanted through the recruit's arm.

Race's model was noticeably different than the other recruits'. The metal didn't contain any of the stains or tarnish of the others, and there was some additional hardware registered in the system he discovered when he compared it to some of his squad's sensors. He guessed it had something to do with his green card, as it matched another recruit that was specifically called out during installation. Race came to find out that the other recruit was a fellow green-card recipient named Henry Straum.

The recruits were given the remainder of the week to rest so they could recover from the sensory implantation. Then the real "fun" started. The Marines were introduced to their drill instructors and their new residence, an open bay full of bunk beds. The recruits were bunked according to their card colors, setting Henry and Race together at the end of the bay.

Most of the recruits' time was spent either exercising or training. Race constantly found himself fighting for breath in the beginning, but he continued to push himself until he could keep up with the rest of the troop. Once their bodies were in top shape, training turned to combat and weapons handling. That was when they started to get more familiar with the units attached to their arms. Inside were materials stored in a liquid state. When the Marine activated a weapon from the device, the biosensor used the metal to construct it from a predefined schematic. This process could also be used to construct the more common tools as well, greatly aiding any stranded soldier.

As much as they focused on their physical development, they also trained in non-combat disciplines, including medical usage, substance analysis, and terrain mapping. On one occasion, they were even allowed to use the biosensor's communication system to call home. While the arm units could be controlled via touch sensors, most people used the speech recognition for the interface.

The weeks had started to blur together when Race and the others were herded into a large auditorium to be issued the last of their weapons. At the front stood one of their drill instructors, sharply dressed in their normal attire. In front of him was a table with a couple of weapons laid out.

"Listen up, recruits," yelled the instructor, causing the chatter in the room to cease. He reached down and picked up the larger of the two weapons. "This is the M23B2 multi-functional rifle. It has many forms and uses, much like your hand-to-hand weapons in your arm units.

"Level-1 weapons are non-lethal, usually used for peace-keeping missions such as riot control and escort duty. They include pulse and stun blast.

"Level-2 weapons are deadly-force weapons and are designed for life-or-death situations. Like your biosensors, level-2 options cannot be used without a proper security command. This is a signal from the company commanders before entering a combat situation. Government officials can also issue level-2 weapons in emergency situations. The main weapon for this mode is a semi-automatic pulse rifle with a 300-meter effect range, which you will all become experts at using before you leave. With the laser targeting and scope, there's only one philosophy: 'If you can see it, you can kill it.'"

Several of the Marines in the auditorium let out a loud bark in response to the instructor's motivational line.

"You like that, don't you," hollered the drill instructor, a broad grin on his face as he enjoyed showing off the weapons. He laid the large rifle on the table in front of him and picked up the smaller handgun. "If you liked that, you're going to love this. The SDK1700, or sometimes called the Sidekick. Has most of the same functions as the M65 but is designed for closer ranges, about fifty meters. It's ideal for close combat and clearing out buildings.

"Both firearms link to your biosensors, which you can use to select the desired modes. This also keeps anyone else from firing your weapon. They both use the same standard energy clip, which can also be set to overload for a small explosion. It will also notify you when the energy pack is running low, so you can replace it and get back to what's really important! Killin'! Oorah!"

"Oorah!" roared the students in unison. Race refused to join the cheer. Taking a life never seemed like it should be a sport to him.

"Let me show you what it can do," said the drill instructor as he took his position to one side of the stage. He called for some of the other Marines in the front row to move a sectional wall into place on the other side of the stage.

"I need a volunteer," the instructor called out to his audience. "Where's Allard? Front and center, recruit!"

Race was already getting up from his seat when the instructor called his name. Race and Straum were commonly called upon for demonstrations, even by the instructors from other platoons. More popularity from his green card that Race felt he could have done without.

The instructor motioned for Race to take a place up against the wall. When both Race and the instructor were in place, the instructor lifted his arm to his face and commanded the firearm for automatic fire. The rifle dropped to point toward Race as the instructor pulled the trigger.

Race instinctively brought his arms up to protect himself from the array of projectiles that leaped for him. He could hear several gasps from his fellow recruits as he closed his eyes in preparation for the impact.

"As you can see, these weapons will not fire if they detect a fellow Marine in the line of fire," Race heard the instructor's voice say. "We don't need you numbskulls killing your own team members out there, so we eliminated it. Let me make this clear. This does not give you a reason to stop practicing proper weapon safety."

Race was too busy examining himself for holes to pay attention to the rest of the speech. He breathed a sigh of relief, finding everything was as it was supposed to be. He was about to head back to his seat when he noticed something peculiar with the static sheet meant to catch the energy shots. Most of the traces were as expected. As Race continued to examine the traces that came closest to hitting him, he saw that they veered off at an odd angle, almost like they had ricocheted off of something. Race was about to stick his finger in one of the shots when the drill instructor grabbed him by the shoulder.

"Didn't you hear me, recruit?" the instructor yelled, spinning Race around. "Are you okay?"

"Sir, yes, sir!" Race hollered back, taking one last glance at the anomaly.

"Then you're dismissed."

Race had to fight the urge to stay and continue to examine the shots, but he knew better than to invoke the wrath of any of the instructors. He quickly gathered his composure and rushed off the stage back to his seat.

* * *

Several alarms were going off while two soldiers scrambled to flip the switches in the cramped consoles to disable them. "What was that?" yelled one of the soldiers to the other.

"Whatever it was, it was off the charts!" exclaimed the other scrambling soldier. "You got anything yet?"

"Looks like it's one of the new guys," the first soldier called as he quickly motioned one hand through the air to flip through several images floating in front of him. "I'm trying to pull the data from his unit now. Better call the general."

"I'm already here," a highly decorated soldier said as he slid in from the back entrance. "I was in the area when the alert went through. What happened?"

"We're still trying to figure it out. It's one of the new greens, sir," answered one of the soldiers with his attention still focused on the controls. "It's a little early. They haven't even started him on any training yet."

"General Vyson, sir." The other soldier jumped from his desk and grabbed a digital pad to show his findings. "I'm looking at the brain functionality retrieved from his biosensor. It's not in the area he tested positive for." The soldier hit a couple buttons on the interface as he approached the central column of the cramped room. A holographic image of a brain projected from the display in the center of the room. "His test identified him as a possible precog, which would have been in the thalamus area," he said, pointing to a highlighted point on the image. "Instead, it showed up more in the mid cerebellum area. We've never seen anyone with functionality in that part of the brain before."

The general passed around the image as he examined the information presented. "Pull up the results for citizen 773 Alpha 9 Tango Charlie 1," the general ordered.

"Yes, sir," said the soldier, vigorously tapping away on his interface. The brain image shrank down to about half size and another image of a brain hovered in the center of the room next to the other one. "There," he said as he turned back around to join the general, comparing the two results.

"Look," the general said as he practically attacked the display. "They overlap. This might be the clue for identifying her ability!"

"Sir, I got the footage from the auditorium. You're not going to believe this," the other soldier shouted excitedly.

"Let me see it," ordered the general. The floating brains quickly vanished as a render of Race being shot at started to play over the screen.

"Weapon-safety demonstration?" the general asked after doing some quick calculations in his head.

"Appears so. Look at this, though." The soldier drew a square with his hands over an area on the screen. "Repeat, zoom, slow to fifty percent."

The image obeyed the command and zoomed into the section outlined. "As you can see, the line of fire goes along here, but when the rounds approach the point where the safety engages…"

There was a small flash on the screen barely noticeable to the human eyes.

"What did I just see?" asked the general as he watched the display, his fingers trying to re-cycle the image to the beginning.

"I'm not entirely sure yet, sir," confirmed the other soldier. "I've got weird readings all over the place. We'll have to run some further tests, but I think in the panic, he may have created a telekinetic force field to protect himself."

"A kinetic? We weren't even sure they existed." The other soldier's face whitened in shock. "In a precog? Is it possible?"

The general took a moment to ponder the possibility. "Gentlemen, I want to be there before he starts the experimental training," he stated firmly.

*　　*　　*

When the recruits were too tired to exercise or train, they usually found themselves attending a class of some sort. For the most part, Race found it to be pretty standard. They had several history classes covering the history of both the United Galactic Republic and the Space Marine Fleet. It went back to the creation of the transdimensional drive, an engine capable of warping space and time for faster-than-light travel. Its discovery rushed in the era of space exploration, and was deemed so monumental that it called for a reset of the calendar year back to zero.

To help fund the new space age, several countries united to create pre-galactic nations in an attempt to pool resources. The former United States became the first major entity to emerge, supplemented by Canada and Japan to become the first United Galactic Republic, the largest of three great space governments. Most of the remaining countries merged into one of two other entities, the Great Euro-Alliance, formed by the nations of the former European Union, and the Imperial Consortium, consisting of mostly East Asian countries.

The remaining countries that wished to join in the space

endeavor ended up applying for statehood in one of the three established governments. A few countries tried to form their own space program but never made it much farther than Earth's solar system before burning out and abandoning for other successful programs. Some countries, like Australia, didn't even bother with space travel, even when faced with the high number of citizens lost to imigration.

Near the end of the second new decade, the three empires had a summit to establish the exploration boundaries of each galactic entity. The first border was set using the line between earth and a large nebula to separate the United Galactic Republic and the Imperial Consortium. The remaining borders were put into place, allowing for equal expansion between the different nations in proportion to their size and available funding, the largest chunk going to the Republic.

The Geneva Convention was expanded to include the terms for handling first contacts with alien races and colonization of other worlds. There hadn't been any public contact with any intelligent aliens, but per the convention, a representative from each of the three governments was required for any negotiations, and any contact was required to be reported immediately.

Planetary colonization called for new rules to protect any planet that might someday produce intelligent life. Depending on the ecosystem, a planet could be colonized up to roughly 60%, but colonization was unrestricted for uninhabited planets, where rare materials sprang life to several mining colonies. Lifeless planets suitable for terraforming went through the decades-long process to be transformed to suit human life and allow for full colonization, like Earth's closest relative, Mars. These terraformed planets were what made up the majority of the planets colonized by the human race over the past centuries. As each government expanded, more planets were found to transform and colonize.

Even though the transdimensional drive helped to spark humanity's ability to travel from system to system, the journeys could still take several weeks. Much of the galaxy was still unexplored as mankind slowly leapfrogged its way into the cosmos.

The United Republic's military was a mesh of the pre-galactic armed forces. The United Galactic Republic took the militaries of each nation and shuffled them together, creating the United Republic Armed Forces (URAF). The initial entity was created from the naval and air forces, later augmented by the armies and any existing national guards. The only military force that wasn't absorbed was the Marine Corps. Many presidents had fought the congressional branch on keeping them separate, but they were able to hold out and keep the Marines as a separate, distinct branch of the military. The president kept them as his emergency-response force, free of congressional red tape. The Marines held their distinct autonomy with a separate name and mission but were still subject to the laws and regulations of the URAF.

*   *   *

As the recruits' training continued, their daily exercise started to take effect and their bodies transformed. Race could barely recognize himself in the mirror anymore. Before joining, his friends referred to him as a string bean for his tall, scrawny shape. Now his body bulged with new muscles as a new strength started to build in him. Race wondered if they were adding some special supplements to their food, or maybe some of it was hidden in their initial immunizations. Regardless of where it came from, he liked the results.

The more their bodies developed, the less time they spent in the classroom environments. Their training started to focus on more combat training, making use of the recruits' new physique. They spent a few weeks on various hand-to-hand combat techniques, which also included gaining proficiency with several different weapons.

Race found himself paired up with Henry for most of the exercises. On occasion, they would mess with some of the other recruits if they had aggravated them, but both Race and Henry enjoyed the extra challenge of facing each other that none of the other recruits could provide.

When the rest of the squad had downtime, Race and Straum were often taken for further extensive training. The few exceptions to this came during the weekly downtime on Sunday mornings when the recruits had free time to write home and relax.

The past weeks' training had been both physically and mentally exhausting. Race decided to use his free time by doing absolutely nothing on the bottom bunk of his rack. The chatter from the neighboring bunks kept him from completely sailing off to dreamland.

"Who are you writing this week?" asked the recruit Race

had come to know as Painter.

"Oh, I thought I'd write my girl," answered the other. They called him Lus, short for Lucero.

"What's with those two?" asked another recruit, joining the others. Race could sense the finger pointing at him through his closed eyes.

"They're probably really tired," answered Lus as he continued to scribble. "They've been getting back pretty late from whatever training they do."

"Hey," the newer recruit said, kicking the bunk and sending a wave of vibrations through the entire bed. "What do they take you guys out for, anyway?"

"Stupid shit, mostly," Race replied without opening his eyes. "Scenario evaluations, pattern projections."

"They seem pretty fond of locking us in a room and telling us 'Don't get hit' while they fire a bunch of small balls at us," Straum added from the top bunk.

"Like tennis balls?" asked one of the guys.

"No," answered Race, still trying to be relaxed. "They're about the size of tennis balls, but they're a lot more solid, and hurt like hell when they make contact." Race lifted his shirt up to show a large bruise on his abdomen that caused most of the guys to tense up.

"Ouch," sympathized the recruit farthest to his right. "What's the point of all that?"

"You got me," Straum answered. Race could hear him folding up the letter he was writing to put it into an envelope.

"How come I never see you writing any letters, Allard?"

Painter tried to change the subject.

"No one to write," Race replied.

"I know that ain't true," Straum said, jumping down from the top bunk. "I've seen that picture of the little hottie in your footlocker." Straum went to the front of the bunk where two broken chests holding the Marines' personal belongings were stored and flipped open the top. "See, right here."

Race shot out of his bunk and barged past the recruits to close his chest. He was too late to keep Straum from grabbing the picture of Illandra he had stuck to the lid.

"That's your girlfriend?" said one of the guys as he passed the picture along, drooling.

"Was," Race corrected, making an unsuccessful swing for the picture.

The group of recruits looked curiously at Race.

"She was my girlfriend," Race clarified, trying not to remember their last moments together.

"What happened?" asked Straum, handing over the picture as he became aware of the emotional attachment it held.

"We went our own separate ways," Race explained as he put the picture back into its place in his footlocker. "She was another green card." Race finally gave in to the awkward silence. "But her job assignment was government relations. We probably won't even see each other again, let alone be in the same solar system. She had to let go, to move on. She had more important things to do than get dragged down by me."

"I'm…sorry, bro," Straum said, offering his condolences. "You should probably get rid of the pictures. You don't need those memories weighing you down."

"She may be a lot of things, but she will never weigh me down," Race replied. "I wanted her to move on. I never said I was ready to."

Before Straum could respond, their drill instructor entered the squad bay. "All right, recruits," he hollered, making his presence known. "Break time's over. Straum, Allard, you've got special playtime. You know where to go. The rest of you, grab your gear."

Race was used to being taken off for special training with Straum. Most of the exercises involved them attempting to survive almost hopeless scenarios. Some of them had the recruits overtake an enemy stronghold. Other exercises pitted the two against each other, which they both found delightfully challenging. They enjoyed their versus challenges so much, they would spend countless hours discussing their strategies to prepare for their next encounter. Every clash saw their strategies become more and more complex as endless countermeasures were compounded for their opponent's actions. The same strategy could never be used more than once, as the two prodigies were quick to learn their lessons and adapt their strategies to prevent the other's from succeeding again. The two gained so much experience against each other that the exercise where they worked in cooperation rarely lasted beyond their opponent's setup stage until a united victory.

Other exercises involved increasing the duo's awareness and response time. One of the more popular methods involved the two dodging projectiles shot from automated turrets. This training usually took place after a short required meditation period, which the two couldn't help but loathe. Although they couldn't stand it, Race came to find that the meditation did help him clear his mind and helped to prepare him for the testing, which in turn cut down on the number of bruises he returned to the barracks with. After about a month of toning their reflexes, they had become so good at dodging the projectiles, Race and Straum felt that they could almost sense where the projectiles were going to be.

It was some time later when Race found an actual application for these skills. An exercise pitted Race's entire squad against another unit in a combat scenario. A large field was staged for the practice, the units placed at opposite ends of the field. Along the area, several objects were placed as debris to mimic a combat zone. Things didn't start off so well for the recruits, as mere minutes into the exercise, a quarter of their squad had already been taken out.

Race ran across a small open section, sliding into cover next to Straum. "Something's wrong here."

"No kidding," Straum replied, checking the corner for possible aggressors. "Who are these guys?"

"I don't know, but they're too damn good to be recruits," Race answered while swapping the battery clip that powered his rifle. "We need to change tactics…fast. Three o'clock."

Straum was already aiming toward the direction when some soldiers came out of hiding and fell to the ground, disabled by two short blasts of his rifle.

"Any ideas?" he asked as he took cover back with Race.

Race pulled up a map of the area on his biosensor. He examined it for a second before having to react to another soldier that sprang to assault them. "Lucero, Painter," Race called to his fellow recruits using the comm in his helmet. "I'm sending you two locations; grab anyone you can and fall back to the nearest one. Aim your rifles into the center and shoot anything that moves."

"Roger that," the two recruits' voices came back at him.

"So what's the plan?" asked Straum as he waited for someone else to come around the corner.

"We're going to flush them out," Race replied, setting his rifle on his knees and resting his head on the back of the debris providing them protection. "Give me a minute."

"You're doing that now?" demanded Straum.

"Shhhhh," Race hushed him. "You know this takes quite a bit of concentration."

Straum was about to yell at Race for his impeccable timing, but another wave of attackers forced his attention once again to survive the encounter.

The gunfire made it hard for Race to concentrate on emptying his mind, but he pushed himself through the noise and cleared his consciousness into the void-like state. Once he was there, he moved to the next stage, where he tried to open himself to his surroundings. He was aware of everything from what seemed like a bird's-eye view, becoming aware of every soldier on the battlefield. The more Race concentrated, the more details he became aware of. Not only could he see the soldiers, but he could also see the sequence of actions, even the next ones to come.

He could see the troops closing in on his position, his partner becoming overwhelmed by the sheer numbers. Almost as if having an out-of-body experience, Race watched himself take out his sidearm from his leg holster and trade it to his left hand. With his right arm, he grabbed his service rifle and stood up to face the attackers. Their attention on Straum, they didn't have time to react to Race's swift counter-attack. The men dropped to the ground as Race's deadly accurate shots caught them off guard.

Race started to walk down the battlefield, leaving Straum behind. "Take a minute." Race stopped Straum from following him. "Catch up when you're ready."

Straum looked at Race for a second before nodding his acknowledgment and following Race's meditation routine.

Race started his advancement into the enemy-controlled area. Still seeing things from his omniscient perch, he dissected the enemy force like a surgeon's laser scalpel. He tucked his sidearm between some of his protective jacket's straps to quickly grab a partial magazine and set it to explode. He threw the charging explosive over the wall and pulled his sidearm back out.

There was a rush of panic as several of the soldiers reacted to the threat. Most of the soldiers that survived the blast were quickly shot down by the sudden appearance of Race turning the corner. The two soldiers that managed to escape the onslaught ran straight into Straum coming out of his meditation and joined their comrades for a cozy nap in the dirt.

The attacking soldiers were now on the defensive, and

scrambled to set up a defendable area. Those that poked their head out to check on their opponents were shot by the deadly duo advancing upon them. The remaining members of enemy soldiers tried to regroup and perform another assault, but in their attempt to storm the area, they ended up tripping over each other as they were shot instantly upon leaving the safety of their cover.

Those that saw the foolish efforts of their fellow squad members tried to retreat, unknowingly walking straight into Race's fellow recruits waiting in ambush.

"Cease fire! Cease fire!" signaled the end of the exercise over their comms. "Unload! Show clear!"

The firearms of all the recruits went dead as the order was issued. The recruits pulled the power clips out of their rifles and lifted them up for the inspectors to see they were properly disarmed.

Almost like waking from a dream, the enhanced awareness started to fade as Race stepped back into his body. While some of the instructors went around checking weapons, the rest of them started to make their rounds to reanimate the fallen soldiers that had lost during the exercise.

"Hey, Captain. I thought you said we were fighting recruits," Race heard one of the opposing soldiers say as he was helped to his feet.

"They are recruits," responded the officer helping him up. "Still have a month left, I believe."

"No way," said another soldier, adding his opinion. "They seemed like fresh meat at the beginning, but those two over there got crazy good way too fast."

"Yeah," the soldier that started the conversation said. "They feed the recruits special-ops food now? Not many recruits can take on us recon that easy."

Race's head shot up in surprise. He couldn't think of any possible reason why his unit would be forced to face a recon squad. Race turned to address the recon soldiers, but before he could take a step toward them, his drill instructor called out to him. "Let's go, Marine."

The mistake in title shocked Race. "It's recruit, sir."

"You more than proved yourself today," his instructor answered his unasked question. "I doubt any of them would dare call you a recruit," he said, pointing to the amassing group of recon soldiers.

* * *

"Amazing," commented General Vyson as he watched the mock battle play out from an observation post overlooking the field.

"I'll say," said the man sitting to his side. "After about the first five minutes, I thought for sure I had that bet won."

"Me, too," laughed the general in response. "They really are something."

One of the soldiers in charge of monitoring the recruits entered the perched hideout. He saluted the general and his guest, as was custom, before handing him a stack of papers. "Still using paper?" the general's friend mocked.

"Data can always be intercepted or recalled," the general answered as he started to flip through the report. "Not so easy with shredded and burnt paper."

His friend nodded in consent to the general's foresight.

"Their readings are higher than any other we've seen, sir," the Marine reported. "Jackson believes that pitting them against each other has advanced their abilities exponentially."

"I'd say that's a good assumption, considering they just destroyed a platoon of URAF recon soldiers," commented General Vyson, still sorting through papers.

"One of the better ones at that," the general's friend added, shifting in his chair to get a little more comfortable. "So what's next?"

"I don't know," the general answered. "Even our most seasoned commanders can't last more than ten minutes against them in the simulations. Most of them are refusing to participate anymore."

"I doubt that will be much different than the other combat units on the planet when they get word of this," his friend added.

"I don't know how I can push them any further than I already have." The general sighed.

"You don't happen to have any more greens like them you can bring in, do you?"

"None that will be available before they graduate," the general responded, putting down the stack of papers. "Looking at these readings, I think they're beyond most of them, anyway. We're in uncharted territory here," he continued as he stood up to pace around. "For the first time, we have two precogs, and by pitting them against each other, they've advanced further than a single one would over a lifetime. I honestly don't know how much more I can safely push them without putting their lives in danger."

"Not to mention we hardly know anything about the one's second gift," whispered the soldier.

"What?" The general's friend sprang up attentively in his chair. "One of them has dual gifts?"

"Yes," General Vyson said, looking angrily at his subordinate. "However, that's extremely classified."

"Sorry, sir." The young soldier looked down nervously.

"What is it?" asked the general's friend, anxiously waiting for the news.

"We're still not a hundred percent sure," stated the general, "but we think he's a possible telekinetic. And before you ask, I can't tell you any more," the general said, cutting off his friend just as he opened his mouth to ask a flurry of questions.

The host slumped back down in his chair, disappointed.

"I guess we'll just have to find a way to challenge them after they're in the fleet," the general sighed.

"Maybe it's time to start thinking about where you want to assign them," suggested the general's friend.

"Would you like me to pull up a list of openings, sir?" asked the subordinate.

"Do it," the general said, dismissing the lower-ranking individual.

*   *   *

Race finished up the remainder of his training as scheduled. There were a couple more heavily challenging events, but he managed to complete them with Straum's assistance. Before they knew it, it was graduation time. There was a giant ceremony, where the newly inducted Marines showed off their coordination to all the attendants.

Straum and Race were given awards for their achievements and a meritorious promotion. The rewards almost made Race appreciate all the extreme challenges he had gone through over the past months.

When the ceremony finished, they were granted some time off to return home and visit family.

Race's trip home was rather uneventful. His mom was still working awkward shifts, but she did make some time for them to spend one day together. Race was able to visit a couple more friends before having to leave. Most of his fellow graduates from school had moved off-planet to follow their own career goals. Race felt a rift between himself and the few friends that had remained on the planet, the changes he had experienced in the past couple months making him feel even more different than before. Race was almost happy when his break was over so he could continue his new life.

Race found his new assignment very exciting. It was to be his first time on a space station, and it was located near the nebula border between the United Galactic Republic and the Imperial Consortium. Race's ship docked with the station and he was met at the landing platform by a few other soldiers who escorted him to his new assignment.

"Welcome, Lance Corporal Allard," greeted his new commanding officer as he reported in. "I'm Captain Jenson. I'm the commanding officer here at SORD. Anyone tell you what you're going to be doing here?"

Race wasn't accustomed to having a superior talk to him without bellowing commands. He greeted his new commanding officer with a firm salute. "Thank you, sir. I was told to report here, nothing else."

"Not too surprising," the captain mumbled, returning the salute. "We're an experimental special forces unit. We work with civilian scientists to create new technologies and test them in combat. Kind of surprised to see a Marine fresh out of boot camp. You must have some amazing connections, or some of the most impressive scores in the past decade to get this as your first assignment." The captain started flipping through Race's digital record, looking for the answer. After scrolling through several pages, he dropped the datapad to his desk. "Well, that would explain it. Let me see it, Marine," he said, looking intently at Race.

"Sir?" questioned Race.

"The card, Marine. Let me see your citizenship card."

Race hit the release button on his biosensor to eject his citizenship card and handed it over to the captain.

"Well I'll be damned," the officer said, staring enraptured at the card. "Welcome aboard, Lance Corporal. I have a feeling you'll fit right in."

Chapter 3

ΛCΛDEMY

Record Dates: 347.512 – 349.011 PGST

THE WAIT WAS ANNOYING. EVEN worse, the school had already given Illandra a mountain of homework to do. She hated the idea of being left behind while almost everyone else in her class had already left the planet to start their school. Race hadn't left her on the best of terms, either. He had decided to pick a fight and a poor excuse to break up with her. By the time she realized what he was doing, he had escaped from the plant to go to his training. She admired what he was trying to do; the very thought of it actually made her appreciate Race almost as much as it made her want to strangle him.

When the thought of it stormed annoyingly through her mind, Illandra often noticed that one of her course books soon found its way into one of her hands to distract her. While it wasn't the most interesting way to spend her time, it did keep her from having to answer any questions from her parents. Every time she looked through one, Illandra couldn't help but remember the feeling she got when her counselor issued them to her. They seemed like simple sample tests, but Illandra felt that there was something more to them. Luckily, she didn't find much of the work difficult. The psychology studies felt basic and seemed to be common sense to her. Her father's service in the government made her pretty familiar with most of the proceedings.

The only thing that she had to spend time on were the sections on galactic history, which went into way more detail than her high school course. Some of the information was intriguing, most was boring. The primary subject of the material seemed to be the effects of the transdimensional drive on the human endeavor to colonize the stars and the Tri-Galactic Border.

There also seemed to be an endless amount of content on the newly discovered mineral dentarite, the cornerstone of the modern technology. Dentarite could be used to make several different alloys, and usually enhanced or gave new properties to materials it was mixed with. Gold became so conductive that it could pull electricity from its surroundings. When used with hard metals like steel, it made the metals several times harder, making titanium indestructible and the desired material for the hulls of spacecrafts.

Dentarite alone was a great material for building starships. Because of its rarity, the expense bordered on insanity. There were only a couple known locations of the rare metal in its purest form, most of which were located on a Euro-Alliance planet. The next best source was the Gum Nebula border, where it was commonly gathered by independent mining vessels and resold to the Republic and Consortium.

And just when Illandra thought she was about to finish

all the material, her counselor issued her yet another mountain of school material. When it came time for her to board her transport for the university, she decided not to make use of the ship's slumber chambers for the three-week journey. Instead, she took up in the ship's small dining area, because it was the only area with enough space for her to spread out her multiple datapads she randomly cycled through to keep from one subject boring her too much.

As was customary for longer trips, the rest of the passengers were deep asleep in their pods. The only other people on the ship that weren't sleeping were the ship's crew, which usually rotated in groups of three to pilot the ship. Illandra enjoyed most of the crew's company when they had a chance to come around for something to eat. It was a nice change from the mountain of data she had been shifting around.

"Still hitting it hard, huh?" The young pilot named Carson that Illandra had been admiring since she boarded the ship startled her. Illandra looked at the time of one of her pads. She hadn't even been aware of how late it was, time for the pilot's shift to start. Illandra did her best to smile at the young man with the curly hair as he made his way around the tables of the small dining area for his pre-shift coffee. Illandra quickly made sure her hair wasn't out of control while the pilot's back was to her, almost regretting not doing something more than the now-customary ponytail. "I don't think I've seen anyone attempt to go through that much material before. What are you going to school for? Doctor?"

"I'm not even sure anymore," Illandra said, putting down her datapad for a welcome break. "I don't even think any of this stuff counts for credit."

"That's a lot of material to go through just for fun." The pilot smiled at her as he finished adding his customary condiments to his drink. Illandra tried her best not to let his bright smile make her melt in her chair. "How many more years you got?"

"Three, I believe," Illandra answered, strategically moving some of her pads so that the young man would have to sit across from her. "I haven't even started yet, so…"

"You haven't even started and you're already a book drone?" the pilot said. "Such a tragedy. College should be all about fun, exploring new things and such, not burying yourself in a bunch of books."

"Well, there's not much of that I can do here, is there?" Illandra questioned, waving her hands around the dreary ship. "Besides, the more of this I do here, the more time I'll have to do all that when I do get there."

"Eh." The pilot shrugged, trying to push a stray black lock of hair into place before taking his post. "I guess that's one way to think of it. What are you studying, anyway?" The pilot picked up the datapad off the top of Illandra's stack and turned it on. "Advanced psychology? That doesn't sound very entry-level to me."

"Well, I aced all the other ones," Illandra said, trying to figure out which datapad to go through next.

"How do you ace a book?" the pilot asked, setting the pad back down on the table and taking a sip from his cup.

"There's a test at the end of each book," Illandra replied. "They're even timed."

"That doesn't sound right," the pilot said, confused. He picked up the datapad again and made a gesture with his hand to scroll to the end of the book. He didn't make it that far into the question list before drawing his conclusion. "This isn't a practice test."

"Then what is it?" Illandra asked, just shy of picking up her next datapad.

"I couldn't tell ya," said the pilot, getting up from the table, "but it's almost time for my shift. You should probably finish up and get some rest, though. We land in a couple days, and if you've never entered a star system, you're not going to want to miss it."

"Can I ask you a question?" Illandra asked. There had been something about the pilot that had bothered Illandra ever since she first met him. The mystery was further enhanced by the fact that while even the ship's crew cycled through the slumber chambers, the seemingly young pilot refused his chance and remained active the whole trip.

"Go ahead," the pilot said, making one last self-check before reporting in.

"The pilot crew's rotated twice through the sleep chambers since we launched, but you've been on each crew. How come?"

The pilot took a deep breath. His skin started to turn pale thinking about Illandra's question.

"I'm sorry," Illandra apologized. "I didn't mean to pry."

"No, no," responded the pilot. "It's okay. It's just not a question I get asked often."

"Forget I asked," Illandra said, sweeping up the datapads

to cover her embarrassment. "It's obviously none of my business."

"No," the pilot repeated himself nervously, recalling something he had obviously tried to forget. "It was about ten years ago, one of my first flights. I was piloting a freighter ship, much like this one." He sat back down at the table to continue his story. "There was an accident. Most of the ship's crew were killed. I was the only one that survived, stuck in my pod. You know how the chamber is supposed to be like a deep sleep, kind of a dream state?"

Illandra nodded her head in acknowledgment, as afraid of what the story might reveal as if she were listening to one of her friend's ghost stories while out camping.

"Well, in the accident, my chamber was damaged. The REM module broke." Carson spoke so softly that Illandra struggled to hear him.

"That's the part that puts you in a sleep-like state, right?" Illandra hoped she remembered that correctly.

"Yeah, I was fully aware of my surroundings, but my body was still stuck in suspended animation."

"That's horrible," Illandra gasped. "How long were you stuck there for?"

"Almost seven years," the pilot said, trying to steady his hands as he took another drink. "Seven years of not being able to move. It wouldn't have been too bad, but some of the alarms went off, so I had to just sit there listening to the darn beeping noise."

Illandra's hands trembled slightly as she vividly imagined the horrors the pilot had gone through. "I'm so sorry."

Illandra choked on the words after a brief silence.

"Don't be." The pilot smiled once again, excusing himself from the table. "Not like you could do anything about it. Besides, that's why the captain was so anxious to hire me. Not too many people want to stay up for an entire ride. It's fewer people he has to hire for rotations. Anyways, I'd better report in," the pilot said, getting back up from the table and leaving Illandra to the dark thoughts he had revealed.

"Well, I'm going to have nightmares tonight," Illandra sighed, picking up her datapad once more to distract herself.

The pilot had been right about one thing. The experience of entering the planetary system was quite remarkable. He allowed Illandra to come up to the pilot deck to experience it. The ship passed several of the system's planets on its way in. Illandra watched doe-eyed as tiny specks of light became unimaginably large upon their approach. She'd then run to the rear of the ship to see them turn back into tiny specks in the ship's tail, then run back up to the front to repeat the proces.

The last planet that started this process didn't finish it. The ship slowed down as the planet started to grow in appearance, and then made for one of the two moons orbiting the planet. They landed and the ship's passengers departed to the moon's surface with the crew shortly behind them. Illandra grabbed her belongings and made her way to the shuttle station, where she caught a ride to the planet below. The school had sent someone to pick up her and some of the other arriving students to take them to their dorms. She had barely put her stuff away when she was summoned to see the dean. He welcomed her to the planet and quickly took all the datapads from her and put them into a bin for processing. He was a short man, not much taller than Illandra.

"You did all the tests at the end, correct?" the dean asked her while starting the process to read them all into his system's database.

"Yes, sir," Illandra answered, getting comfortable in the chair the dean had offered her. "Nothing too difficult."

The dean looked at Illandra, almost blown away by her statement. "Those were some of our toughest tests."

"I'm sorry." Illandra tried her best to sound apologetic, even though she didn't feel the need. "I just didn't find them that challenging."

The dean gave her a stern look. Before he could open his mouth to scold her, he was interrupted by an alert from his computer. It was obvious that the dean wasn't satisfied with her apology and Illandra feared he would find an excuse to yell at her. Her mind was already looking for counterpoints to argue with him on while he started reviewing the information on his system. Illandra hoped that whatever the message was would be enough to distract him from his previous thoughts.

"Well, Miss Illandra," the dean said, finding his humility. "It looks like you passed all the CLEP exams with flying colors. Counting your advanced classes from high school, we should be able to skip at least a year's worth of classes. I'll have your counselor revise your schedule. If we can get you on an accelerated schedule, wave some electives, et cetera, et cetera, with any luck, we'll have you out of here in two and a half years," the dean continued. "Maybe less."

"Thank you," Illandra replied, the words almost stumbling out of her mouth. Not knowing what else to do, Illandra excused herself and went back to her dorm room.

*   *   *

The surface of Plato was covered by massive megastructures, many of which Illandra caught sight of from the planet's moon from approach. Each university was its own megastructure, a vertical city reaching to the stars. Plato was a planet dedicated to education, thus named after the Greek philosopher and founder of the first institution for higher learning.

Illandra's first semester of education was pretty standard, other than the fact that she had received a double load of classes to keep her busy. Luckily, she was able to get a good reading of what each teacher wanted and was able to direct her efforts efficiently enough to not be overburdened with the workload.

What little free time she did have she usually spent in the student lounge, socializing with her fellow students. On the weekends, she would try and go out with her roommate and her new friends. Sometimes it involved taking in some of the local sights. However, the other girls were a little more interested in the next big party rather than the planet's attractions.

The second semester was much easier for Illandra, as several of her classes veered away from the traditional lecture method to more open-ended styles. Illandra constantly found herself in the middle of scheduled debates and mock negotiations. The course change gave Illandra a much lighter load of homework, allowing her to actually have somewhat of a social life, although she did still spend large amounts of time as a bookworm.

"What are you doing?" Illandra's roommate asked her one day while Illandra was doing some research.

"Professor Trace expressed a horrible idea about some 20th-century government that drove me nuts," Illandra answered, scrolling through her research.

"And?" asked one of her friends that was currently sprawled out across her bed. She was using some equipment to change the color of her nails in an attempt to find something that matched her dark skin.

"I'm looking for something to change his mind," Illandra answered.

"You definitely need to get out more." Illandra's roommate laughed.

"Or a boyfriend," teased her friend.

"No kidding." Illandra's roommate joined her friend on the bed to check out the color she had picked. "There're so many guys lining up. I don't know why you don't just pick one."

"Or two," added her friend.

"I have a boyfriend, thank you very much," Illandra said, shutting off her datapad. *Even if he doesn't want to admit it*, she thought to herself.

"What?" squealed her roommate, jumping up from the bed. "How come I didn't know this? Is that who this guy is?"

She ran over to Illandra's projector of memories and cycled through to a picture of a young man Illandra kept.

Illandra squinted at the picture, her eyes strained from all the reading she'd done recently. "Yes, that's him," she acknowledged. "Race."

"He's kind of cute," her roommate complimented.

The other girl quickly rolled off the bed to also check out the picture. "He's very cute," she added, making Illandra a tad jealous.

"I like to think so." Illandra smirked. "I doubt he looks much like the picture anymore, though. The Marines shaved off all that hair the moment he got there."

"A man in uniform?" asked the visitor with a sly smile creeping onto her lips. "We should go visit him."

"You know, I'm not judging, Lan," Illandra's roommate said, using the nickname she had given her, "but I thought you'd be more into the intellectuals. Why are you with a common soldier?"

"That common soldier happens to be another green-carder," Illandra said, crossing her arms smugly.

"Really?" Illandra's roommate said, surprised.

"We definitely should go visit him," repeated their friend.

"Oh, stop it." Illandra laughed, throwing the nearest harmless object she could find at her flirtatious friend.

*   *   *

Illandra got a weird feeling one day while studying in the student hall. She suddenly felt really anxious, like she was trying to find something. What made it weird was that she felt like it was herself that she was looking for, and the feeling was coming from somewhere else. Illandra tried to put the feeling out of her mind, but it nagged at her so much, she had to go outside to get some air. Illandra barely made it a couple steps out of the student center when she ran into her frantic counselor, and source of the phenomenon.

Her counselor attempted to remain calm and greet Illandra before quickly dragging her off. They ended up in a private room with a table and some chairs. In the corner was a holovision playing what Illandra mistook as a movie at first.

"Now, Illandra, this might seem a little different than what you're used to, but I just want you to remain calm and relaxed. This is just a little test of your studies," said the counselor as she motioned Illandra to take a seat in one of the chairs. "On the screen, some actors are going to be playing out a scene where terrorists have infiltrated a government building. They haven't made their intentions known yet, but we do know that they have hostages. What we want you to do is tell us everything you can about the situation and what you think it would take to resolve it. Remember, this is just a simulation."

"A pop quiz?" Illandra played along, smiling innocently.

The counselor's stress level dropped slightly as she thought Illandra had accepted the explanation. Illandra knew then that it wasn't a test.

Illandra focused on the footage being played in front of her. She looked each individual over, attempting to get a good read on them. It was easy for her to find out who the leaders of the band were, and that most of them were radicals. Many of their fellow terrorists could barely keep their weapons steady, a sure sign they had gotten more than they had asked for. This only helped to reconfirm her deduction; actors wouldn't be this scared in a simulation.

Illandra turned her attention to the peace officers. As she looked at them, she could tell they were afraid for their lives, genuinely terrified. She could feel it almost as if she were in the situation. Her blood started to boil as she turned to confront her counselor.

"Well, do you have anything?" interrupted a voice from the back of the room.

Illandra turned to see a holographic image of a military officer standing behind her.

"They're radicals. All they want to do is spread fear and a polluted message," Illandra answered as she tried reading the new man. "They'll probably kill all the hostages and themselves before they're done. These two over here are the ones you want to focus on," Illandra said, pointing the two out on the projection. "They're the ones that have been designated to kill the hostages if anything looks bad. These guys over here are the leaders; a good portion of them will probably give in if you take them out pretty fast. Unfortunately, they probably won't know much. You'll probably be able to piece together enough to get this guy here to talk if you can keep him alive." Illandra pointed out another man on the display.

"Are you sure about that, Illandra?" asked the military officer, examining the men that Illandra pointed out.

"Yes. I am," she replied with a stern look as her jaw tensed. "And next time you want my help with something, I would appreciate it if you didn't lie to me and tell me it is a scenario when real people's lives are on the line."

A smirk snuck onto the general's face that he tried miserably to hide. "I didn't want you to feel pressured," answered the officer, "or guilty for any consequences."

Illandra walked over the general to look him eye to eye. "You've followed me enough to know that I'm never wrong on this type of stuff," Illandra answered with a voice that cut the decorated officer down to her size. "And I'm a big enough girl to accept any consequences I might be responsible for." There was some noise from the holo-unit that caused Illandra to turn and look at it. She could see the assault team moving into place on the holoscreen to execute her suggestions.

"Now, if you'll excuse me, General, you're dismissed." Illandra waved her hand through the officer's image, causing it to flicker in static as the signal was disrupted, preventing the officer from making any comments or response to the situation as she walked through him and out the door.

"Wait," said the counselor, failing to stop Illandra before she disappeared down the hall and out of sight.

*   *   *

"That was absolutely amazing, General," stated a soldier.

"Yes, it was," mumbled General Vyson as he sorted through another stack of results. "She's impressive, even for being so inexperienced."

"I've never seen anyone read a holotransmission so readily, let alone a pathic," the young man said, poring over charts. "She was clearly reading those people light years away. She read that situation like a book, right past the whole test thing!" The general stopped and turned to the soldier, his face still a little red from his embarrassment from the encounter. "Sorry, sir."

The general raised his finger to scold the young man, but put it down with nothing to say and returned to his trek down the hall of their facility. "How is her advancement?" mumbled the general as he changed the subject.

"So far, she's right on schedule," the soldier said, scrolling over some data on his datapad. "Unfortunately, she still has a long way to go before she graduates, even with the accelerated schedule you've put her on. You know, it's too bad we don't have another pathic to pair her with. Maybe we could have accelerated her advancement like the precogs."

The general came to an abrupt stop so quickly that the soldier following him almost ran into him. He stood silently as the idea churned in his head. "That's a great idea, Sergeant!"

*   *   *

It was nearly three weeks after Illandra's little incident with the general when she was summoned back to the counselor's office. Against her better judgment, she decided to go see what she had to say. As she walked through the halls, she could see a large number of students running around frantically as some great news seemed to be spreading amongst them.

As she approached the administrative building where her counselor's offices were, she noticed some new faces sticking out. Their rugged frames and scowls made her feel they were security related. She entered the building and took the stairs to her counselor's floor. As she reached to open the door, she was surprised to find it open before her.

"Well hurry up, lass," came a mysterious voice from the other side of the door. "We don't have all day now, do we?"

Illandra went through the door and turned to see the stranger that had opened it for her. She instantly recognized the older man in front of her. He was one of the most famous people in the Republic, almost as famous as the president himself. His gray hair and his grayish half-suit marked the importance of his position.

"Ah…" Illandra stuttered out, "I…"

"It's okay, lass," the old man teased, patting the top of her hand with his well-manicured one, "your speech will return with time. I know perfectly well who you are. Now, why don't we have a seat?"

The instructor led Illandra over to her counselor's office, where they sat at the round meeting table.

"Illandra," the counselor greeted, "I'm very sorry about last time. I was against the whole thing, I never wanted to…"

"Don't worry about it," Illandra interrupted. "I understand."

"Now that that's out of the way," the older man said, "on to business, shall we?"

"Yes." Illandra finally retrieved her ability to communi-

69

cate. "Congressman Martin, or do you prefer Doctor Martin?"

"You are a keen one, aren't you," said the old man, looking slyly at Illandra. "My friends call me Tony. I hope we'll have the time to make it that far. I've been going over your progress with your counselor here, and I must say I'm very impressed."

"The government's most important congressman came all the way here to check up on my progress?" Illandra asked, folding her arms in front of her.

"Us green cards have to stick together," Anthony replied with an added wink. "But no, that's not why I'm here. I've been asked to do some guest lectures here at the university. While I'm here, a mutual acquaintance of ours has asked me to stop by and offer some assistance to you."

Illandra stopped to think about whom he was referring to. Only one person came to mind. "The general." Illandra smiled as it dawned on her.

"Yes." Anthony smiled back.

"I hope I didn't bruise him too much," Illandra said, starting to enjoy her conversation.

"He's tougher than he looks," Anthony said, waving his hand out in front of him as if brushing it away.

"So just how are you going to help me?" Illandra asked. She knew that she should be on her guard with this man, but she somehow felt awkwardly at ease with him.

"I'm glad you asked," Anthony said, almost jumping out of his chair. "First off, since you can no longer trust your counselor, you'll now be dealing with me. Ms. James here will still handle most of your logistical stuff, but from now on, all of your stuff will now go through me.

"Second, there will be some changes to your schedule. We'll be adding an additional class to your schedule. One that meets once a day and is taught by me, where we'll discuss several things, like that terrorist attack you handled so well."

"And how many other students will be in that class?" Illandra asked.

"None," the old man answered shortly.

There was a long silence as everyone patiently waited for Illandra to respond. Her eyes wandered around the table looking for signs of a practical joke. There were none that she could find.

"When do we start?"

It didn't take long before most of Illandra's free time was being monopolized by the great Anthony Martin. She found herself doing all sorts of weird tasks. Quite often, she was put in a room with a complete stranger and asked to determine as much as she could about them without even being able to talk to them. Other times, they'd watch live holovision and attempt to do the same thing. After a couple months, Illandra and her new mentor were almost inseparable.

"You're doing very well, Illandra. I'm impressed with your progress," complimented Anthony as they sat down for a lunch break after one of their more intense training sessions. "You'll make a fine representative some day."

"Thank you, Tony," Illandra said, sitting down with him and stuffing a large helping of food into her starving mouth.

"I still don't understand the whole point of all this, though. No offense, of course. I just don't get what it is you're trying to teach me that I haven't already learned in class. It just seems like a waste of both our time."

"Knowledge and experience are two totally different things," Anthony explained, taking a small scoop of food from his plate. "An artist could spend several years in a classroom listening to a teacher lecture on the importance of different brush techniques, but it won't make a lick of difference until he picks up a brush and develops the skills for himself."

"So what type of skills are you teaching me?" Illandra said, swallowing her massive lump of food. "How to read people?"

"The short answer is yes. But it's…complicated." Anthony hesitated while putting down his utensils.

Alarmed by her mentor's uncertainty, Illandra also put down her spoon and reached out her hand to comfort him. And then it dawned on her. "You mean it's classified," she blurted.

"What?" Anthony shot up from his seat. He looked down at their joined hands before quickly pulling it away protectively to his chest. "How? You shouldn't be able to do that yet."

"Do what?" Illandra questioned, puzzled at what was going on.

"You…" Anthony stopped himself before looking around the crowded room. "Come with me."

Anthony stood up from the table and started to walk out

of the room. Illandra looked down mournfully at her food. The morning had been so busy that this had been her first chance to eat, and it was probably going to be a while before she was able to eat again, but she knew whatever she was onto was very important. She quickly shoved several scoops of food into her mouth and grabbed the food that she could hand-feed herself and followed her mentor out of the busy building. He took her back to one of their training rooms and locked the door behind them. He removed a wall panel and hit a couple buttons on it. Illandra could hear several mechanisms in the walls and door.

"What was that?" Illandra asked, almost scared of what was going on.

"Security measures," Anthony answered. He motioned for Illandra to a nearby chair. "Sit, please."

Illandra awkwardly moved around the table and silently sat down.

"Relax," he said, trying to calm her. "You'll understand soon enough. Tell me, how much do you know or remember about your citizenship entry exam?"

"Other than the nightmares it gave me?" Illandra chuckled. "Not much, really. Basically, they tested math, science, language, you know, the basic skills."

"What was the last exam?"

"Ehhh," Illandra said, puckering up as if she had just eaten some sour fruit. "The stress test. That one was horrible."

"You're half right," confirmed Anthony. "It is horrible. But it wasn't a stress test. You see, the intense stress has a way of activating different parts of the brain. In the room, there are several sensors monitoring brain activity. You can't even see them, as they're practically invisible."

"What's the point of that?" Illandra said, leaning back defensively in her chair. "They wanted to see how much of my brain I was using?"

"Not quite," Anthony said. She wasn't used to this side of her new mentor. His normal playfulness meant to keep people off guard had been replaced by this serious person in front of her. It didn't do much to ease the tension. "They wanted to see what parts of your brain you were using."

Illandra stared at him, confused, silently waiting for him to explain further.

"Okay, the average person only uses certain parts of the brain for certain functions. For instance, this part right here," he said, pointing to the left side of his head, "is used for analytical reasoning. This part over here is where you store long-term memories," he said, pointing to the back part of his head. "And this part here, which both you and I have a large amount of activity in, is used for mental readings like empathy and telepathy." He stopped for a minute to let it soak in.

The very suggestion of it made Illandra's mind start to whirl. While completely impossible, it almost made perfect sense. "You mean I'm… I can…"

"You do it all the time, just look at all your exercises. How often do you know what someone's reaction is going to be, how they feel about something, sometimes even knowing the exact words they're thinking. I'm sure you know when something is bothering someone, even when they do their best to hide it. It's because, as an empath, you can feel a person's emotions as if they were your own."

Illandra was still in awe of the possibility, her mouth hanging open, awestruck by what she had just heard.

"Well, maybe you weren't ready," said the doctor, shaking his head down in disappointment.

"No, no, no," she replied, reaching out across the table. "So what you're saying is that the rumors about psychic testing in the citizenship testing are true? Is that why I got the green card, because I can read people's minds?"

"Well, not so much their minds, more so their feelings. You'll probably be able to pick up rare thoughts here and there like you did with me just now. You shouldn't be able to do that yet. It takes several years of empathic development before that's even possible. Yet here you are, almost instinctively developing it."

Illandra took a bite out of the food she had managed to hold on to. With her mouth full of food, her brain nibbled nervously on the information. Her mind started to replay several memories that suddenly made sense. Her mom trying to hide her card. The freighter pilot and his experience in the failed sleep chamber. Race, she mentally sighed. Race always tried his best to put on a show, but always felt so different. "And what about Race? He received a green card. Can he read minds, too?"

"No. He'd be here, too," concluded the professor. "Where did he end up going?"

"Military," Illandra snarled. "Space Marines."

"Ah, one of the fun ones. Let me see, an extremely lucky

guesser, able to connect completely random events together. Ruins all the movies by figuring out the plot before it's revealed. Amazing reflexes." Anthony leaned in close. "Almost like he can see the future," he whispered.

"Nooooo," she said in wide-eyed disbelief.

"They call them precogs, short for precognition," Anthony said, leaning back in his chair as his charming smile started to reappear. "They're usually very distant from others. It's because they take in so much information at any time. Everything around them is moving as part of a giant machine, like the inside of a giant clock tower, watching every cog and gear turn in perfect synchronization in every direction, all the time," Anthony said, acting out some detailed explanation with his hands. "At least that's what I gathered from the few that I've met. It's hard to comprehend it, really. You and I can come close when we can be overburdened by everyone else's emotion in crowded areas. I guess that's another difference between them and us; emotions are just part of the machine to them, like variables in some elaborate equation. They're usually pretty guarded. You probably wouldn't have been able to get that close to him had it not been for your own powers."

Illandra was sure that something in her brain was about to break trying to come to terms with everything being presented to her, but she could tell from reading her mentor that everything he was saying was true. The fact that she was "reading" pretty much confirmed what he was telling her.

That brought up another good point. "You have a calming effect about you when you're dealing with people," Illandra stated, bringing her observation to light. "Is that because you read people to know what to present them with, or because you're projecting the calm onto them?"

Anthony suddenly shot up in his chair, his playful nature once again abandoning him. "I really shouldn't be going into this," he said awkwardly, covering his mouth. "I've already said too much."

"You project it." Illandra jumped to her feet, drawing the conclusion on her own.

"It's an open door; traffic can go both ways. Now, Illandra, please," her mentor pleaded, grabbing her hand to pull her back to her seat. "You can't go off practicing this stuff on your own. It can be very dangerous. You can hurt, possibly even kill someone. That's why I'm here to guide you."

Illandra could feel the seriousness in the congressman's warning. She attempted to restrain her excitement as she allowed herself to be pulled down. "So how much can we read from someone?" Illandra asked once she had found her calm.

"A sentence at the most, maybe an image or flash of a memory," Anthony answered, once again bringing himself back to being at ease. "Although if you manage to touch the person and they're willing, you can get quite a bit more. Here, give me your hands." Anthony put his hands up in the middle of the table, his palms facing Illandra.

Illandra shoved the last bit of food into her mouth and wiped her hand on her blouse. She placed her hands up next to his.

"Okay, now imagine a door. The door is the entrance to

your mind. Now, open the door and allow me to enter."

Illandra did as she was requested, opening herself to her professor to allow him into her thoughts.

"Now, close your eyes. If there's something you don't want me to see, just imagine putting it in a box and closing it." There was a pause as they closed their eyes, trying to concentrate. "Ah, there's Race. Tall fellow. I bet that hair is gone. Is that really what you kids are wearing nowadays?" There was a brief pause while Anthony tried to gain a reading in her mind. "The two of you had a serious conversation before he left. Doesn't seem like it ended on a high note." He let out a slight chuckle. "Good for you, girl. I wouldn't let him get away with that either."

"Let's move over here," he said, making a mental shift. "Looks like family memories. There are your mother and father... They seem familiar. Have I met them before? I see she tried to take your card with her."

"Empty," Illandra said, interrupting her professor.

"What?" he said, opening his eyes to look at her in shock.

"So many things you wish you could have done better, even though you've done so much. You still feel great sorrow for those that you haven't been able to help. Your wife is a beautiful woman, but you've been having troubles reconnecting ever since..."

The professor snapped his hands back, breaking the connection. "How did you do that? I never gave you permission to read me!"

Illandra looked around, dazed, doing her best not to fall out of her chair. "I'm sorry. I didn't... I..."

"It's okay, I just didn't expect it," said her mentor as he tried to regain his composure. "I'm sorry, I shouldn't have pushed you so."

"No!" exclaimed Illandra. "That was amazing, show me more!"

"In time, lass," sighed the congressman. "In time."

*   *   *

"About time. I've been trying to call you for the past hour," exclaimed Anthony as his holographic call was finally put through. "You're never going to believe this."

The torso of General Vyson was projected into the room. He was currently wearing just a T-shirt with his short gray hair in a mess while rubbing his barely open eyes. "Calm down, Anthony, it's only the third cycle here. What's going on?"

"She's amazing, Zack, simply amazing," Anthony said, taking off his custom-decorated half-robe. "We were eating when she reached over the table, grabbed my hand, and picked up a surface thought. Then we were doing an exercise. I was reading her mind, and at the same time, she turned around and read me. Life-trained pathics struggle with that."

"What are you doing showing her that stuff?" screamed the general's image, suddenly becoming alert. "You know that's prohibited!"

"She's powerful, Zack. It was only a matter of time before she would have ripped it from my mind on her own. This isn't like those two boys you got over there in boot camp.

You can't just shoot a bunch of things at her and expect her to tell you how they feel. She can't work on skills she doesn't know she has, and if it isn't done properly, she could seriously injure someone, including herself."

The image of the general looked down while he contemplated his friend's insight. "So what do you suggest?"

"Experience is still the best teacher, but we need to make sure that it's controlled, too. I can continue to teach her here for a little longer, but she's advancing too fast for any program we have in place. Once she's done here, I suggest you assign her to my staff and let her follow me around for a bit, give her a chance to practice reading people and let me keep an eye on her."

"Any idea where you're going next, Anthony?" replied the general.

"I have a few small assignments, but the president is sending me to the Taurus Space Station. He's been getting some suspicious reports from the other side of the nebula."

"That's great. There's an opening in a tactical RND unit there. It's a little intense for a first assignment, but we were thinking about sending one of the boys there to see how their abilities developed."

"One of the boys is named Race, correct?"

"Yes," answered the general, looking suspiciously at Anthony. "He appears to be the stronger out of the two. How do you know about him?"

"He and Illandra were high-school sweethearts before entering the Republic," Anthony answered. "Do you think you could assign him there? We might be able to use him to help better her skills."

"I can probably arrange that," the general answered. "You might be able to help him, as well."

"Help him?" The congressman stopped in his tracks.

"We think he might have dual gifts," the general stated. "We have some footage of him possibly creating a telekinetic field. We're not sure how he triggered it, or how to develop it without possibly killing him, but if you can find a way to guide it out of him, it might help us figure out how to identify, handle, and train it for future occurrences."

"You're kidding me," Anthony said, plopping into his chair. "Not only do I find probably the strongest pathic to date, but now you're telling me we've got the first dual-gifted psychic?"

"If you think that's impressive, you should see him in action," said the general, smiling.

"How does this happen, is there something about their home planet?" asked Anthony.

"We're investigating all possibilities," asserted the general confidently, "but right now it's looking to be pure coincidence."

"Very well. I'll see what I can do with the boy when I get there," the professor said as he reached over to press the button to end the conversation.

"Anthony," interrupted the general, keeping him from hanging up. "How are you hanging in there?"

"I think I'm going to be all right," the doctor said, smiling.

The general looked at his longtime friend, examining

him for any fault in his statement. Finding none, he returned the doctor's smile. "Good to have you back."

*   *   *

Over the next couple of months, Illandra spent even more time with Congressman Martin. Now that the big secret had been revealed, they were able to be a little more direct in her training. Anthony had brought in several of his staff that were aware of their gifts to use for Illandra's training, and the more they practiced, the easier it became.

In no time, Illandra was able to start reading people with very little effort. As her mentor had taught her, the ability to touch her targets greatly amplified the readings she was able to receive. With a little concentration, she was even able to see flashes of past memories, almost as if she was reliving them herself.

As her abilities developed, however, the need for touch became almost irrelevant. She surprised her mentor by starting to tell him who was in the practice room before they even entered the building. This, of course, spurred a long, tiring discussion on the importance of control.

Then came the basics of self-defense from other pathics, the most common of which involved imagining a strong material and wrapping it around her mind. With enough practice, even Anthony wasn't able to penetrate her thoughts. An unfortunate incident where Illandra had sensed him trying and pushed back so hard it sent him tumbling out of his chair had made him stop trying altogether.

With her accelerated schedule and the extra credits she

had gotten from her time with Congressman Martin, Illandra finished her university training in a record one and a half years. She even managed to graduate with honors. After the ceremony, Illandra was given a brief vacation to go home before reporting to her first assignment. It was no surprise that Anthony had pulled some strings and gotten her added to his staff. Illandra was excited at the idea of following her mentor around the galaxy, not to mention what other marvels of the new world he might introduce her to.

Her trip home had something else to reveal, too, as Illandra sat with her mother one day.

"Race stopped by some time ago," stated Illandra's mother. "I gave him your address. Did he write?"

Illandra felt a brief moment of disappointment as she let out a brief sigh. She had really been looking forward to seeing him again. "No, he must have gotten distracted. Did he have anything interesting to say?"

"Not really. You're not going to believe this, though. There was another green card with him at boot camp. Isn't that amazing? Three green cards in one year! What are the odds?"

"That's amazing." Illandra faked being impartial to the news. Now that she knew what a green card really meant, she was even more amazed at the findings. She had to fight the urge to tell her mother what it meant and all about her new abilities.

"You don't sound too enthused," said her mother, smirking.

"I'm sorry, Mom. I'm just really exhausted right now.

Did he say where he was going next?"

"I didn't catch the name, dear. I think he said he was going to some space station."

Illandra's father came down the stairs to join the two. "How was school, Illy?" Her dad called her by her nickname that only he was allowed to use.

"It was good, Dad," she replied, kissing him on the cheek as he joined them. "We had a surprise instructor, a guest celebrity. Doctor Anthony Martin. I actually got to spend a great deal of time with him. I'm even going to be a member of his permanent staff."

"That's amazing, Illy," exclaimed her father. "He's a great guy. I got to work with him a couple times when I served. How is he doing?"

"Pretty good," answered Illandra. "Still a great guy."

"Oh, that's good to hear," interjected her mother. "It was so sad to hear about his son."

"His son?" asked Illandra.

"Oh, it was tragic," said her mom. "It was about five years ago, wasn't it, honey?"

"I think so," confirmed her father. "He was a green card, too, just like you and Martin. He was on some mission on the Spertanian Station when it was attacked by some radicals."

Illandra was finally able to complete the thought she'd had several months ago when her mentor had first taught her to use her power. It was the loss of his son that was the source of all his pain.

*   *   *

After her vacation was up, Illandra was back on another space flight on her way to meet up with her mentor, this time as a member of Anthony's staff. As she got to know him more, she caught on to his naming conventions. She could tell how close someone was to him just by what name they addressed him by.

With her new position came new responsibilities, as well as new requirements. She was now forced to wear a uniform. Unlike Anthony's, which closely resembled a loose suit, her uniform was tight and constraining. It was mostly white, with black and gray accents. The belt of the uniform turned the excess material in the jacket into a tight skirt around the top of her thighs. She could often feel the skirt fighting with the uniform leggings for which one got to be closer to Illandra's skin.

Anthony had Illandra accompany him around several places in the galaxy as he met with different officials, and she sat in on several private conversations. But Illandra's most exciting time came when they got to visit the galactic government's capital planet of Einstein, where she was even allowed to sit in on a Galactic Senate session. She was caught more off guard by the fact that several of the senators already knew her by name, and several of them made an effort to talk to her.

Anthony later informed her that the green card she had received gave her a good chance of holding some sort of office someday, and the politicians were most likely trying to get on her good side while they still had a chance.

There were several closed-door meetings on their journeys, and it was very rare that any of Anthony's staff got to sit in on them, including Illandra. From the few meetings that she was a part of, it was obvious something major was disturbing many of the people.

Then the day came when their errands took them to what was supposed to be a base of operations for the next several months, the United Republic Border Station Taurus. Illandra stood anxiously near a window of the ship as they approached the space station.

"I don't think I've ever seen you so anxious," came the voice of her mentor behind her.

Illandra jumped as she was startled by the sound of his voice. With her new awareness, she usually felt people coming before they even entered the room. Anthony had still managed to find a way to sneak up on her every so often.

"I didn't feel…" She hesitated. She was sure that she hadn't left herself that open.

"You don't have to be a mind-reader to always know how someone feels. Besides, I think you're projecting to half the ship right now. Everyone's pretty antsy."

Illandra let out a nervous laugh. "Sorry."

"It's okay, lass," laughed her mentor. "You're still learning. Remind me later, we'll work on creating barriers for keeping your feelings from getting out of control. I've come to enjoy the effect you have on people, keeping them all in a good mood. Now I see I probably should have taught you some restraint. Just try and remain calm and try thinking of this room as a box holding your emotions in here."

Illandra closed her eyes and took a deep breath.

"Ah, look," interrupted Anthony, "There's Taurus now."

"Where?" Illandra exclaimed, throwing herself against the barrier between her and the emptiness of space. She watched as the magnificent structure came closer into view. The glare of a far-off star gleamed off the metallic shell of a structure. She had felt herself being tugged to the station for some time now.

"I always thought it looked like a giant egg myself." Anthony pursed his lips.

Anthony's observation caused a slight laugh to bubble to her surface. Her mentor was correct; it did kind of look like a giant boiled egg that had been sectioned and spread out. Even so, the stations overshadowed the ships orbiting around it. As their ship approached the station, she was able to make out assorted tube-like structures connecting the different sections together, as well as some of the ships. There were even smaller ships flying in and out of the missing sections.

"It will do," said Illandra, smiling and giving Anthony's arm a small hug.

Chapter 4

REUNITED

Record Date: 349.011 PGST

Race had merged well with his new unit at the Strategic Operations Research and Development unit, usually pronounced S(w)ORD for short. The people in his unit had a great sense of humor, and they accepted him as part of their family very quickly, even with the great difference in their rank and time in service. It was sheer luck that one of the other members had retired recently, leaving an empty spot for Race to slide into. From what he could gather, people usually didn't get a spot in SORD unless they had some distinguished military background. Race could only assume that his green card had some play in that decision.

Race was no longer required to wear his presentation uniform. Instead, he was allowed to wear his rough passive camouflage, which consisted of pants, a T-shirt, and a rough blouse. The pants and blouse were covered in small checkered squares, about half a centimeter each. His clothes could change color to match their surroundings, but usually remained gray on the station.

Besides Race and his commanding officer, Captain Jenson, there were three other members of his unit. The most senior member was Staff Sergeant Konway Reece, a skilled Marine that contradicted most stereotypes. He possessed extensive knowledge in several fields thanks to his experience in the vast array of different projects in his many years in the SORD unit. His age wasn't that apparent; a few streaks of gray flowed through his brown hair, making it appear almost blond in places. Race was pretty sure the staff sergeant wasn't too far away from retiring himself; he'd overheard him talking with some of the other team members about how he looked forward to the day when he could retire with his wife.

While being the most experienced Marine, he was still no match for the combat expert of the team, Sergeant Zain Amyas. A true Marine in almost every sense, Zain was an expert in almost every form of combat, from hand-to-hand to long-range tactics. The only thing Race had found deadlier than Zain's hands was giving him a firearm. Able to disassemble and reassemble almost any weapon in mere seconds, Zain was by far the most effective Marine on the team. Zain was commonly put in charge of most tactical missions, even above Konway, his senior, although the two had a long-time agreement of working together when planning the team's strategies. In appearance, Zain was massive compared to the rest of the team; he had a shoulder span almost twice the width of Race's own. Race often wished he had the sergeant's good looks, up to the perfect part in his blond hair.

The last member of the unit was the fiery-tempered Sergeant Annette Keegan, the only woman on the team. Annette had only been on the team for a couple years herself before Race had arrived. Her vehicular expertise had earned her a spot on the team, being able to drive almost anything with a control panel attached to it. It didn't come as much of a surprise when Race discovered that she came from a family with a long line of engineers that had developed many of the ships and space stations currently in use. She had earned her reputation by defeating many of the so-called "experts" in all types of races and dogfights, which had earned her position in SORD. The only thing hotter than her temper was her lush red hair, which was usually balled up in the customary bun for many military females.

Race enjoyed his new group of friends. Despite their wide rank and age differences, Race quickly earned his status as an equal among the team during the first couple of missions, and the differences soon rarely came into play. The difference in rank only became obvious when the Marines found themselves in official settings, when they were forced to follow procedures. Even then, Race was often allowed the same courtesies as his fellow teammates.

Their branch of SORD was located on the bottom-most section of the United Republic Border Station Taurus, which had been dedicated entirely to their research. Much of this area was a testing section about the size of a football field that could be made to simulate different climates and conditions, such as a hot room to simulate desert conditions, and its opposing cold room. The Marines spent a good portion of time in this area, either testing equipment, conducting training exercises, or just doing their daily fitness routines.

The area that was left over was used as labs for research. Race's team bounced around to all the different departments reviewing and helping with the various projects, often conducting tests and offering feedback. A lot of times, they were assigned to projects themselves, especially any based off of their suggestions.

As much as Race loved to play in the labs, they were still a special-operation unit and heavily called upon. Since Race had joined the squad almost a year ago, the team had been sent on several missions. Luckily, Race's extensive training from boot camp had prepared him for the position. His abilities were quickly tested, and much of his squad had come to trust his judgment without question.

The Marines' duties kept them fairly busy, but they always tried to come together at lunchtime to enjoy each other's company.

Race was followed to their normal spot in the middle of the cafeteria. As usual, most of the crew had cleared out and headed back to their duties. There were a couple gatherings of people dispersed, most of whom were in the military uniform.

"Dude, this new program is so cool." The massive young man whose uniform was barely able to contain the hulk-like muscles sat down at the cafeteria table. "They've guarded the biosensor program for so long, I can't believe you talked them into letting us mess with it, Race."

"I know," replied Race as he joined his blond friend. "I just can't believe you spent all this time turning yours into an arcade."

"Yeah, well, at least I'm not trying to be some virtual pimp, dickhead," Race's friend countered.

"Hey, Bella's not like that," Race said defensively, hugging the sensored arm to his chest. "He didn't mean it, Bella."

The screen on his biosensor flickered to life, revealing a crude polygon-constructed face. "Zain is probably disappointed that is not your goal; I bet he wanted to be your first customer." Race smiled as he pressed a display to dismiss the digital woman.

Zain tried to his best to contain his laughter while pushing the food around on his plate with his utensil. "Why you gave her such an attitude is beyond me."

"I didn't," Race said, also digging in to his food. "We only added a little subroutine to allow for some personal growth. You know, try and make her a little easier to relate to. It's probably going to be removed before launch. She only acts this way when she's around you."

"Hey, guys," a sandy-brown-haired man said as he joined them at the table next to Zain. "You giving Bella a hard time again?"

The two men laughed as they greeted their friend. "You know how this fool is, Konway. I think he's jealous because she doesn't like him."

"You sure you didn't program her that way?" replied Konway as he started to dig in to his food.

"Shhhhh," Race replied with a mock whisper, "I thought I told you not to let him in on any of my secrets."

"Hey!" exclaimed Zain as the other two broke into laughter.

"What's so funny?" interjected the redheaded woman as she joined the boys at their usual table.

"Konway is giving away my secrets about Bella," Race said, attempting to make room for the newcomer.

"What?" The woman smiled. "That you can't even program a woman to like him?"

The two men howled in disbelief at the woman's roasting of their comrade and congratulated her with a round of high-fives with some roaring laughter.

"Looks like Bella's not the only woman you have problems getting along with, Zain," said Konway, laughing.

"Yeah, but this one doesn't come with a mute button," Zain retorted, earning his own set of victory high-fives from the table.

The group quieted down as they started to enjoy their meals. "So how is Bella's development, Race?" asked the redhead between bites.

"Great, she's to the point where she's monitoring almost all the sensors in the lab at once. She even detected a small leak before the lab's sensors did. Jonathan and I are going to start working on getting her to interface with other devices and reviewing some of her subroutines, see what we can clean up to increase her performance. It's a pain in the ass trying to get an AI to run on such a limited platform; it's nice having one of the most renowned AI programmers on your team. How's your project going?"

"Eh," she said, sulking. "Eddie's been a great help, but we're still nowhere near test flight. We're having a heck of a time finding an efficient steering method that doesn't use too much fuel. The magnetic-field generator is nice, but it just takes too much space and power reserves for such a small vessel."

"You know, you might want to dissect a torpedo and see what kind of guidance system it has," Konway suggested. "I believe it's some sort of gyroscope, the circular rotation helps cause resistance in zero gravity and atmosphere, so you can have some sort of force to maneuver off of."

Annette looked up as she started to roll it around in her head. "That might actually work," she said after a long moment of silence. "Hey, give me a hand," she ordered, standing up from her seat. Race and Konway offered their hands, which she accepted so she could step up onto the table. Once atop the table, she started peering around the mass of people in the cafeteria. "Eddie!" she yelled across the room when she found who she was looking for. "Remind me when we get back, I got an idea for the navigation system!"

A slightly embarrassed gentleman across the room acknowledged her shout as discreetly as possible.

"How about your project, Zain?" asked Konway as their friend came down from atop the table.

"It's going okay, I guess. It's not really too much different than some of the training programs out there; we're just trying to run it off the biosensors. Should make tactical training a little easier, and since it's on the biosensors, Marines can run simulations anytime they want."

"You're actually doing something useful," commented Annette. "I'm surprised."

Zain replied with a sarcastic smile. "You know, Race,

once you get Bella to interface with a comm-visor, you can have her put on a little show for you," he said as he started to dance and unbutton an imaginary shirt.

"You guys need to stop trying to create virtual babes and get yourself a real woman," Annette replied, disgusted by Zain's display.

"You volunteering?" laughed Konway.

"Please," she said, breaking into laughter, "like they could handle this."

"Actually," Zain said when the crew's laughter died down a little, "I've had my eye on the waitress over there." He motioned off to the side. The rest of the table attempted to look inconspicuously at the girl cleaning up the tables Zain had pointed out. "I think I'm going to go ask her out."

"Go get her." Konway nudged him.

"You think?" Zain asked.

"Yeah." Konway once again tried to push him into action. "She wants you."

"All right," Zain said, stacking his stuff onto his tray while standing up. "I'm going in."

Zain started to make his way around the tables toward the young woman. The remaining members of the party scooted in closer to whisper their comments.

"This is going to be good," Konway whispered. "He doesn't stand a chance."

The crew watched as Zain approached his target. Caught off guard, the young waitress jumped when Zain announced himself. The two started to talk as the crew watched on.

"What line do you think he's going with?" Race whispered.

"It doesn't matter," Annette answered, "they all suck."

The group was suddenly cut off by the young waitress's jaw dropping followed by her hand shooting up to slap Zain on the face before storming off. The slap's echo roared with the team's laughter through the area.

"How'd it go?" Konway asked, still trying to stop laughing.

"I think she's the one," Zain said, rubbing his red cheek.

"She seems like a keeper," Race said, trying to wipe a tear from his eye.

The screen on Race's biosensor once again flickered to life, displaying the image of the woman from before. "You only have ten minutes before you need to report back for duty."

The group of soldiers let out a few curse words as they stuffed their faces with a few last morsels from their plates while getting up. The team darted off toward the cafeteria's exit, running past several bystanders trying to find a place to eat their lunch. The squad successfully navigated the perils of their favorite eating area with little difficulty, and soon all four of them were cramped into a confined room.

"Level 7559," stated Konway as the doors to their transport closed on them. "I think we're going to have to take the service tunnel," he said to the rest of the crew.

"Really?" Zain whined. The tunnels were a small network of shafts that ran through the stations for maintenance. They were so small, Zain's wide shoulders had once gotten stuck in one. He had hated them ever since.

Moments later, the doors to their elevator opened as the group exploded into a passageway full of people. The soldiers charged the pathway, trying to make it to their next destination, dodging past several crowds of people, apologizing as they blasted by. Farther down the hall, another set of elevator doors opened to greet the oncoming Marines.

Race stopped just outside, looking around for something that had grabbed his attention. Annette, who had been following closely behind him, grabbed Race and pulled him into the elevator behind her before the doors had a chance to close.

"Why'd you stop?" Annette huffed as she tried to catch her breath. "You want to be late?"

"No," replied Race, also trying to catch his breath, "I just had one of those feelings."

"Uh-oh," huffed Konway. The team had come to rely greatly on Race's instinct. In the past few months that he had been with them, his gut had saved the Marines on more than one occasion. It even earned him a meritorious promotion to corporal, granting him a rank closer to his coworkers'.

"It's different, though," claimed Race. "It's not like 'danger,' more like…I don't know."

The team exchanged a questioning look. "We should still check it out," said Annette, interrupting the many gazes. "We'll let the captain know when we get back. Get ready, we're almost to our level."

"Careful," cautioned Race, "watch out on your right."

"One of these days, you're going to have to let us in on how you always seem to know that," replied Zain.

"I wish I knew," Race answered just as the lift dinged, letting them know that they had reached their level.

The squad braced themselves to launch out the door. Once the lift stopped, they flew out the door and down the hall. Despite Race's warning, Zain still almost ran into a couple of servicemen a few feet away from the elevator as he rushed out. The Marines ran all the way to the end of a hall, which appeared to be a dead end. Konway was the first to reach the end; he had taken a tool out of his biosensor and started removing some of the restraints holding a panel to the wall.

"I hate the service tunnels," stated Zain as he crawled into the confined opening.

"Stop whining!" yelled Annette as she crawled in behind him, giving him a helpful push.

Konway entered the tunnel last as he closed the entrance behind him. The unit crawled to the next junction of the narrow tunnel. Zain took a deep breath as he prepared himself for the next phase. Then, one by one, the members of the group slid down the next tunnel. The tunnel twisted and turned several different times as it took the team to their next destination. Some parts reminded Race of a large tunnel slide he had long outgrown.

Like clockwork, each member pulled their own tools from their biosensors, which turned into large discs. With a spoken command, they all placed the discs onto the wall of the service tunnel. Giant magnets in the discs grabbed the wall and jerked them back, slowing their descent. The speed of the group decreased rapidly and they came to a stop inches away from the closed exit.

"I hear the captain," stated Zain, suspended upside-down in the narrow shaft. Bracing himself with his feet and a little help from Race, just above him, he released his tool from the wall. With another command, his tool transformed again so that he could use it to remove the tunnel entrance. He removed a couple of pieces holding the cover in place and slid the door to the side, revealing a man pacing around in the room below.

"They're late," commented the man to himself.

"We're not late, are we?" whispered Annette.

Race looked up at his biosensor, which intuitively displayed the current date and time. "No, two minutes early," he answered.

"The captain always keeps his clock five minutes ahead," informed Konway.

Zain shushed the group from below, trying to prevent them from blowing their position. They didn't have to wait long for the pacing captain to walk out of the room. Zain let himself slip out enough to where he could touch his reformed magnet to the ceiling of the room. Using the mounted handle, he swung into the room, the rest of the team dropping in shortly behind him.

Zain quickly closed their access route as everyone started grabbing what they could to make them look as if they'd been there waiting. Their commanding officer returned down the path outside the waiting room. Looking through the window, he noticed the team now inside the room. He was forced to take a second look in disbelief upon seeing the room he'd left vacant just seconds ago. "What are you guys doing here?" asked the man as he barged through the door.

"Thirteen hundred hours, sir," answered Konway as the team snapped to attention and saluted their commanding officer. "This is where we're supposed to be."

"I was just in here," he exclaimed, not being able to decide which Marine he wanted to yell at. "I was watching the only entrance in here, so I know you guys didn't come in there."

"We've been here for a while, Captain," answered Annette. "Corporal Allard had something he wanted to investigate so we tried looking for you in the labs for permission. When we couldn't find you, we came back here for the scheduled report in time."

"Is that true, Corporal?" asked the officer, now focusing on Race.

"Yes, sir," answered Race, trying to hide the fact that he had just caught his breath a couple of seconds ago. "Something seems to be trying to get my attention, but it doesn't feel threatening like usual."

The captain looked intently into Race's eyes, trying to determine if he was lying. "Granted, but take a shadow," he consented. "And report anything suspicious."

"I'll go," volunteered Annette.

"Fine," snorted the captain, turning to leave. "The rest of you, back to work."

In unison, the group released a large sigh of relief. "Bella, I thought I asked you to notify me when we had twenty minutes left, not ten," scolded Race to the unit around his arm.

The screen once again flickered to life to display the digital face. "I thought I told you not to mute me in the middle of a sentence," replied the image, leaving its wearer with a dumbfounded expression.

"You sure you didn't model that thing after a real woman?" asked Konway, patting Race on the shoulder as he walked out the door.

"'Cause if you did, you hit it right on," noted Zain, dodging an elbow from Annette as he walked out.

Race and Annette left notes for the lab teams before heading out to investigate Race's earlier disturbance. Since they weren't in any hurry this time, they were able to use conventional methods of travel. They took a few elevators to get them back to where Race had first felt the unusual sensation. When they got there, the two started to look around, trying to catch a clue of what had triggered the strange feeling.

"This would be easier if we knew what we were looking for," commented Annette.

"There's a service console over there; let's see if we can get anything out of that. Bella, interface," Race directed to the device on his arm as he approached the communication station on the wall. He took his arm and stuck it in a round opening on the panel, but not before noticing that he had been cleared for level-two weapon usage. "Captain must be worried," he commented.

Annette looked down at her armband to see what Race had noticed. "With a record like yours, I don't blame him."

The console recognized Race and granted him access to several of the station's logs. Race started pushing buttons on the terminal, searching for possible sources, mysteriously poking away at different options trying to figure out what it was he was looking for. It wasn't long before he found himself looking through a list of the station's docking logs.

"I don't know why you don't just use the audio interface," commented Annette.

"Because I don't know what I'm doing, and I don't want others to know what I'm doing," he mumbled. "Also, I'm not so fond of listening to myself talking to walls. Got it," he yelled as he pulled his arm from the system. "Docking Platform 77B," he said as he darted off, Annette on his tail.

The two were once again running through the open corridors, zigzagging around people as they tried to get to their destination as fast as possible.

*　　*　　*

The ambassador's private ship was small enough that it was able to land in one of the cutout sections of "the egg" station.

Illandra's ship had finally docked with the space station Taurus. It seemed as though she had been waiting forever just for the clamps to secure so they could finally start disembarking.

Her mentor led the way out for his staff after they were given the signal by the deck supervisors. The entire crew was all dressed in their best attire, a requirement of working with Anthony, as he always expected them to be prepared for a good impression when leaving their ship.

"Ambassador Martin," greeted an elder man in a clean-cut uniform that seemed to demand the attention of most of the bay staff. "Welcome to the United Republic Border Station Taurus."

"Admiral Casten," Anthony replied with a warm smile on his face. "A pleasure to see they actually put someone intelligent here for a change."

The two smiled as they exchanged a firm handshake and patted each other on the shoulder. "I trust your flight was good?" asked the admiral.

"Yes," answered Anthony, "it went pretty well. I'm sure most of my crew is exhausted from such a long trip. I, however, would love a bite to eat if you don't mind catching up with an old friend. I'm sure we have much to talk about."

"Your quarters are prepared; I've brought some of my men to help your staff to their rooms. If you like, we can head down to the Destiny Star." The admiral signaled his men as they sprang to life and helped grab the luggage. Everyone then proceeded down the long tunnel leading back to the station.

"It's still there?" asked Anthony, his face brightening.

"Of course. Best food this side of the galaxy," answered the admiral. "I think they even have your special table ready."

"Oh, good," replied Anthony.

The metallic band wrapped around the admiral's forearm chirped to get his attention. "Excuse me, Ambassador," said the admiral, bring his arm to where he could see the display. "Go ahead," he said into the band.

"Admiral," said an officer who had appeared on the digital display, "that corporal from SORD is at it again. He's heading your way, Docking Platform 77B to be exact."

The admiral let out a silent curse before barking orders at his men, who quickly formed a protective barrier around the ambassador and his staff. The guards un-holstered their firearms from the sides of their legs as the metallic armbands transformed into large shields to give an added defense to the people behind them.

"Why did you call it in?" A voice reached out from the past from far down the corridor. "I told you it wasn't a threat."

"Well, do you know what it is yet?" echoed a woman's voice in response.

"No," answered the male's voice as its owner sprinted past the end of the corridor. Illandra could swear there was something familiar about the man's face that flashed by.

A woman with red hair appeared to be chasing him but stopped at the end of the hall and whistled. "You passed it," she called, motioning him back to the hallway. There were a couple of squeaks as the young man turned around to join his friend. Once the two met up, they continued their jog down the corridor to meet up with the group of soldiers protecting Anthony and his associates.

"We're getting close," the man said to his friend.

"Corporal," called the admiral as the pair came close, "what's the situation?"

"Admiral Casten!" the young man shouted, quickly snapping to attention and saluting his superior officer. "I'm sorry, sir, I keep telling everyone there's no danger, but they just won't believe me."

"Then what is it?" questioned the admiral.

"I don't know, sir; something seems to be calling me here, but I don't feel threatened," explained the soldier. "I don't understand it myself, sir. All I know is that it's something really big."

Illandra had been trying her hardest not to explode from excitement as she recognized the young man approaching. She calmly pushed her way between two of the shields meant to protect her. "I think I can explain, Admiral," she stated, doing her best to sound calm. "The corporal and I are good friends. I sent him a notice I would be in the area; he must have forgotten some of the more important details."

"Illandra?" gasped the young man, almost as terrified as he was excited. He then turned to the admiral. "I'm sorry, sir."

"Ah," interjected Ambassador Anthony, "so this is the young Race Allard I've heard so much about. I thought I recognized the lad. Would you care to join us for a bite, Corporal?"

"I'm sorry, Ambassador," answered the embarrassed young man, trying to shake off the shock of his predicament, "but I…"

"That wasn't a request, Corporal," said the admiral in a deep, commanding voice.

"Uh." Race hesitated. "Yes, sir."

"Super!" Anthony clapped his hands in enjoyment. "I know this great little place on E deck. Illandra, can you please help the rest of the staff get to their quarters? I'll be up shortly."

Illandra was startled back to life. The last thing she wanted was to be separated from Race after finally finding him.

"I'll be there shortly," Anthony cut her off before she could object, "and I'm sure Race will come to see you after his shift today."

Illandra fumed a little, but it wasn't wise to fight with her mentor in front of the soldiers. She grabbed the bags she had dropped and the group was escorted away by their military guards.

"Now for you, young lass, what is your name?" asked Anthony of the woman who had accompanied Race to greet them.

"Sergeant Keegan, sir," she answered with a salute. "It's an honor to meet you, Ambassador Martin."

"Thank you, lass," said the ambassador with a smile. "Could you do me a favor and let your CO know that I'm going to be borrowing Corporal Allard for a bit? I promise to have him back within the hour."

"Yes, sir!" she answered. She gave the admiral a quick salute before leaving the area the same way she had come.

As the sergeant passed Illandra's crude formation, she gazed intently at Illandra. Illandra could feel the confused emotions swirling around in the sergeant, all seeming to center on Race.

"Well, that should only make things slightly complicated," Illandra whispered to herself.

*　　*　　*

Soon the landing bay had been cleared and the three men were on their way to the diner. They arrived to find it almost empty, a couple members of the staff wandering around cleaning already spotless tables. The owner came to welcome their long-missed friend the ambassador and took him to a special seat, having reserved it for their arrival. The ambassador took off his overcoat and put it on the back of his chair while Race and the station commander got as comfortable in their uniforms as they could. They ordered a round of drinks.

"I feel as if I've known you for most of your life, Race," opened the ambassador once their waiter left to get their drinks. "Illandra said she messaged you that she was coming, but I don't think she even knew you were here. Is that true?"

"She may have," Race answered, rubbing the back of his neck, "but I don't recall getting anything from her, sir. We haven't talked since I left for boot camp."

"So then how did you come to be on the docking platform?" Anthony asked curiously, perched on the edge of the table.

"It's funny, sir," Race stated, trying to find a place to put his hands to keep them from distracting him. "I just kind of felt like I had to be there."

"I may be old, lad," laughed the ambassador, "but you don't have to rub it in calling me sir all the time. Doctor Tony will do."

"Don't let him fool you, Tony," interrupted the admiral as the waiter arrived with their drinks before being waved away, none of the group ready to place their order. "Corporal Allard has only been here for a short time, but he's already caught three fugitives, apprehended a few loads of illegal contraband, and I think he almost stopped the space station from blowing up once."

"It wasn't anything special," Race said, feeling his cheeks starting to warm up. "I'm sure the station's sensors would have caught the mechanical failures before she blew up."

"Was it this same feeling that helped give you such a good record so far?" asked the ambassador, taking a sip of his drink.

"Pretty much, sir," answered the timid soldier. "It's just a gut feeling I get, there's usually been a sense of…" He hesitated for the right word. "Danger. I've come to learn it's better not to ignore it when it kicks in. But this time, I had the feeling I had to be there, just without the pressure. I tried to tell everyone that everything was okay, but I guess my past experiences made everyone think elsewise."

"Indeed, lad," erupted the ambassador. "You caused quite the panic on the landing bay." The ambassador paused for a second as he looked the young man over. "So here's a question for you. You've been here…" He extended a hand to the admiral, hoping he would fill in the blank for him.

"Almost a year, I believe," helped the admiral, enjoying his fizzy beverage.

"A year?" gasped the ambassador. "Such a distinguished record for a soldier's first year? Yet you're still only a corporal?"

Race chuckled a bit. It had been no small feat to get the rank of corporal within his first year of service, but to think that he could have jumped higher seemed preposterous. He had received his promotion to corporal shortly after he'd reached the station, where most soldiers would just be getting promoted to the previous rank.

"Well, Ambassador," the admiral interjected on Race's behalf, "he's already been meritoriously promoted once in the past six months, so I don't have the authority to promote him again. He'd probably be a shoe-in for the boards, but the next one doesn't happen for another couple months."

"Well, isn't that a shame," commented the ambassador sourly. "And what about the challenge?"

The challenge system had been put into place nearly a hundred years ago when the commandant of the Marine Corps came up with the deranged concept to keep his troops in top condition. If a Marine with a lower rank had an issue with a direct superior commanding Marine, he could challenge the superior for his rank. This kept the higher-ranking Marines in shape in case a lower-ranking member decided to challenge him. It also kept the high-ranking Marines honest and forced them to treat their subordinates with respect. Respected Marines rarely challenged their superiors. The clause was still active, even though it was almost never used.

"I really don't think that's a good option for me, sir." Race hurried to dismiss the idea. "My unit is pretty small; I think it would just cause unneeded turmoil. I have a really good rapport with my fellow soldiers; I don't think I should be attempting to steal any of their ranks."

"That's pretty insightful for such a young man," said the ambassador admiringly. "Anyways, I'm sure I've taken up enough of your time. The admiral and I have plenty of things to discuss. It's best you return to your duties. And don't forget to come by tonight; I know Illandra has been looking forward to seeing you for the longest time. We're in…" He again waved his hand to the admiral.

"Government Estates, Section Delta," the admiral filled in.

"Thank you, sir," Race said, standing up from his seat and shaking both men's hands. "It was a real honor to meet you, Ambassador Martin."

"The honor was mine, lad." He reached out his hand to shake that of the young soldier.

Race accepted the outstretched hand, following it with a salute before leaving the table and disappearing from the restaurant.

"Quite remarkable," commented the ambassador. "So young in his abilities, but already so strong. I could almost feel the gears turning when I peeked inside his mind. I just can't help but wonder, did he sense her, or did she call him?"

"You're the expert in that field, Ambassador, not me," said the admiral, smiling. "I don't think it's going to be too long before you have to tell him about the card, though."

"It's not my call," said Anthony, flustered. "You're probably right, though."

"So what is an important man like yourself doing out

here in the corner of the known universe?" the admiral asked, discreetly changing the subject.

"Well, we've been receiving reports of strange behavior from the IC on the other side of the nebula. I'm here to keep communication open between the two sides and pray that a war doesn't erupt."

"I didn't know that praying was part of your job description," laughed the admiral.

"It's not. I added it when I found out who was in charge of this station." The ambassador laughed as the two went on to enjoy their meal.

*   *   *

Even though the doors were automatic, Annette still managed to find a way to make a huge amount of noise as she stomped through them back into the SORD headquarters. Needing time to gather her thoughts, she continued past her normal lab and down the hall to the storage room where she normally went to fume.

"What happened?" Zain asked as Annette steamed past him. "Everything okay?"

"Yeah," she mumbled shortly. "Everything's fine." She barged through another door, creating some more noise on her way out.

Zain followed her down the hall, stopping to knock on the window to Konway's lab to get his attention and motion him into joining them. The two rendezvoused and followed Annette's path to find the redhead pacing up and down the aisles, chewing on her fingernails.

"Uh-oh. What'd you do?" Konway asked, picking a spot they judged was safely away from their emotional friend.

Zain held up his hands innocently. "Not a thing. She came back like that."

"All right. Cover me, I'm going in." Konway took a deep breath and slowly stepped toward his raging friend.

"Right behind you," Zain replied, taking a step in the opposite direction to prepare for an escape.

"Annette, what happened?" Konway said, approaching Annette. "What did you and Race find?"

Annette's pacing accelerated slightly. "Some woman from his past," she muttered, spitting out a piece of a nail she had bitten off.

"Dude, she's all yours," commented Zain as he turned to make a break for the door.

Konway lunged to grab Zain's giant arm and forced him to sit on a stack of boxes. "Don't even think about it. I had to deal with her last time she was like this. It's your turn."

Zain took turns looking between Annette and Konway blocking his exit. His odds were not looking good. He let out a long sigh of defeat. "Well, this should be interesting."

The comedic performance of her teammates over-whelmed Annette, forcing her to forget what was bothering her. "You guys are dorks," she said, shrugging off some of the tension.

"So." Konway began to slowly approach Annette. "Tell us what happened, from the beginning?"

Annette quickly recapped the story of how the two had found their way to the launch bay and run into Illandra.

"That doesn't sound good," Zain said.

"Sounds like an ex, right?" asked Konway.

Zain nodded in agreement to his friend's question.

"What do you think this means for you?" Konway asked Annette.

"I don't know." She sniffled. She dragged herself over to a near wall and used it to brace herself as she slumped to the floor. "I thought we were getting along pretty well. I'm sure he was going to ask me out soon."

The two men exchanged a sympathetic glance before joining their friend on either side of her on the floor. "You know, no one is saying they're going to get back together. He hasn't even mentioned any of his past girlfriends since he got here," Konway said soothingly. "He might not even be interested in her anymore."

"You know, I hate to ruin the optimistic twist you're trying to put on the situation, K," Zain started, "but there're two things I need to say. First, just because we can see that you like him doesn't really mean that he sees it. He's only been here a short while, and I've seen several girls around the station flirting with him. Let's face it, he's clueless. Even if a woman practically throws herself at him, he'll just catch her, help her up, and go on his way."

"Like that waitress at Lucky's that is always giving him extra dessert," added Konway.

"Perfect example," thanked Zain, pointing at the imaginary fact in front of him. "Or that MD trying to get him to come back every couple days for a follow-up."

"You guys aren't helping," Annette said through grinding teeth as a hint of her temper started to flare up.

"Sorry," apologized Zain. "What I'm saying is, he's a smart kid and all, a great Marine, but the boy doesn't know zip about women."

"Ain't that the truth." Konway rolled his eyes in agreement.

"What's the second?" questioned Annette, slumping in response to the disappointing truth her friends had brought up.

"Well, try not to take this the wrong way," Zain said, already lifting his hands to defend himself, "but I'm not sure he even considers you a woman."

"Hello? Boobs!" exclaimed Annette as she grabbed her chest and juggled her womanly possessions so that everyone could see.

"Well, physically, yes, you're a woman. But think of how you act when you're around us. You're always cracking rude jokes, you're an awesome soldier on the battlefield and…"

"And you won the burping contest last week," interrupted Konway.

"Yeah, that too," chuckled Zain as he continued. "Anyway, what I'm getting at is that when you're with us, you act like one of the guys."

"And these uniforms don't do anything to accentuate the twins," helped Konway.

"For sure," agreed Zain. "And since we're such a close-knit group here, he probably sees you more like family, like a sister."

"Or brother," Konway joked.

Annette gave Konway a quick jab with her elbow while hiding a little chuckle. "What can I do?"

"Well, the first thing you have to do is change Race's perception of you," answered Konway.

"You're going to have to wear a dress," Zain said. "Something revealing, or at least something that's going to show off your curves."

"I'm not wearing a dress!" she panicked, trying to get up and away from Zain's suggestion.

"Then you might as well just start helping them plan the wedding," concluded Konway, reaching up to put a hand on Annette's shoulder to prevent her from running off.

"Fine," she agreed, allowing herself to be pulled back down. "What's the second thing?"

"We have to get you out of the friend zone," concluded Zain. "We'll have to put the two of you together in situations that just make him think, 'Hey, this isn't too bad.'"

"So you guys are going to help me with this?" she questioned hopefully.

"Of course, you're like a brother to us," joked Konway.

"Thanks, guys," she said as she gave them both a large hug.

There was a sound of a door closing in the hallway outside the file room. The group could hear someone greet Race as he walked down the hall outside their location.

"The first thing we need to do is get more information," Konway suggested after the moment had passed.

"Definitely," agreed Zain. "Annette, give him a little bit and when he's alone, go check on him. Take your top off, too."

"What?" Annette gasped, shocked at the suggestion.

"Just your cammie top, leave your undershirt on," Konway clarified. "But tuck it in tight."

"Oh," Annette said, relaxing.

"Actually, I meant the whole thing." Zain leaned over to correct Konway. "But I guess that will work."

*   *   *

After running into Illandra in the afternoon, Race had decided to work late to try to give himself time to think about how he should handle the situation. If nothing else, it would provide an excuse for him not showing up to see her early enough for them to actually do anything and not be forced to spend too much time together.

"I know that look," Race heard the soft voice of his female co-worker come from behind him.

He turned to see Annette leaning casually in the doorway. It took a couple of seconds for Race's eyes to focus on her instead of on the code of his holodisplay. She had taken the jacket of her uniform off, exposing a womanly figure he had been almost oblivious to. Her fiery hair had also been let down from its customary bun, dropping into luscious curls down the side of her face. Race couldn't help but stare at this alluring woman standing in the doorway. He was curious about how she had gone practically unnoticed all this time.

"Yeah," Race said, rubbing his eyes in an effort to take them off his coworker, "I'm just trying to debug the last bit of this code before heading out."

"I know it's only been about a year since you got here, but I know you better than that," Annette said, brushing a curl behind her ear. "You've been distracted ever since you got back from meeting that representative girl. You knew her?"

"Illandra," Race moaned, rolling his eyes. "We dated in high school, but we broke up before I left for boot camp. Our lives were going in two completely different paths. I was pretty sure we were never going to see each other again."

"But here she is," Annette concluded, crossing her arms in front of her.

"Yeah," Race mumbled in agreement, "here she is."

"Do you think she wants to get back together?" Annette asked, her shoulders tensing slightly.

"I don't think so," Race answered mournfully. "We kind of left off on a bad note."

Annette left the door and walked across the room to grab a chair not too far from Race. She spun the chair so the back was facing Race. "You want to talk about it?" Annette said, straddling the chair.

"No, thanks," Race said, grateful for his friend's concern. "You watch my back enough in the field, you don't have to put up with my personal crap, too."

"You're wrong on so many counts," Annette chuckled, shaking her head slightly, her curls bouncing with the slight movement. "I can't even cover it all right now. I will tell you that any unit that works in life-or-death situations as much as we do is as close as any family, and we will always be there to watch your back, both in and out of the field."

117

"True story," commented Zain as he passed by the door carrying a load of boxes, heading for storage.

"Stop listening in!" Annette yelled, waving her fist at Zain through the glass window between them.

"Sorry," Zain yelled back, almost out of view. "I'll leave you two lovebirds alone."

Annette picked up the nearest object she could off the counter and threw it at the window, hitting where Zain would have been.

"See," Annette said, attempting to get comfortable, once again straddling her chair, "it's like the brother I never wanted."

"You know that was a six-thousand-credit laser torch, right?" Race asked, trying to keep his smile from getting too big.

"Oh, shit!" Annette jumped from her chair to check the device she had thrown.

*   *   *

Race did one last self-check before making the dreaded march to the section of the station where Illandra was staying. Because of the sensitive nature of that section's residents, Race was required to check in with the security detail before being allowed into the area. Luckily, Race was familiar with the guards and they let him pass right through.

Unlike the areas reserved for the station's soldiers, which were just a bunch of corridors with tiny rooms, the suites of the executive areas all surrounded large open meado areas for visitors' families to play and socialize in. They were even covered by fake synthetic grass to give them a planet-like feel. Race passed through three of these areas before coming to the one where Illandra was assigned, one of which was occupied by a small family playing around.

He took a deep breath and reached for the alert button to let her know that he was here. His finger stopped inches away from the button as the door suddenly slid open to reveal Illandra standing there. She was no longer wearing her profession-suited skirt from earlier, but instead a pastel skirt that went all the way to her feet with a string of flowers going down one side. Her top was covered by a loose white blouse whose short sleeves exposed much of Illandra's arms and contrasted against her hair, giving it a certain pop Race couldn't help but admire.

"You sure took your time," Illandra said, staring at Race through narrow eyes. "Why are you still in your work clothes?"

"Sorry," Race laughed nervously. "Lost track of time at the shop."

"Well, do you want to get something to eat?" Illandra asked him, her tone almost easing up on him.

"I think most of the stuff in this sector is closed," Race answered, looking around.

"That's okay," Illandra said, reaching back behind the door to bring out a couple of containers, "I figured you'd try and make up some crappy excuse about working late to get out of seeing me, so I got us some takeout. You still like Italian, right?"

Race eyes widened with anticipation as he practically

lurched for the outstretched container, oblivious to the fact that he had just been called on his poor excuse to avoid the encounter.

"There's a table over there." Illandra pointed over to the corner area of the grotto. She exited her quarters and let the door close behind her. The two of them walked over to the area she had designated, where Illandra punched on a side console to have a round table with stools slide up from the ground.

The two sat down at the table and opened their food containers. Race started to swallow his food in enormous bites faster than he could possibly enjoy it.

"You can slow down." Illandra laughed at him. "It's not going anywhere."

"Sorry," Race said, covering his overstuffed mouth. He grabbed the napkin out of the utensil kit and wiped his mouth as he attempted to properly chew and swallow his food. "Bad habit I picked up in boot camp. It wasn't uncommon for the instructors to give us a couple of seconds to eat our food. You learn to inhale your food pretty quick."

"And how much time do you have now?" Illandra asked, taking a bite of her food.

Race checked the time on his arm sensor. "A couple of hours or so," he answered.

The two went back to eating their food in an awkward silence. This time, Race tried to eat at an almost normal pace. He still finished his plate long before Illandra was even close to finishing hers. His eyes started to roam around the room, looking for things to distract him.

"Illandra," Race started, "I just wanted to say…"

"No you don't," Illandra cut him off.

"Huh?" Race questioned, stupefied.

Illandra quickly swallowed the bit of food still in her mouth and wiped away substance on her lips with the disposable napkin. "You're going to say that you're sorry, but you're really not," Illandra clarified. "You really thought what you were doing was with the best intentions, even though you were doing it in the most asinine way possible."

Race looked confusedly at Illandra, baffled by her inside knowledge. "I, ah…"

"Thought that with such different assignments, we'd never see each other again," Illandra finished. "You didn't want me whining or pining over you, so you thought you'd piss me off so that I would get over you faster and move on to the next guy."

"All right," Race cut in, "that's getting…"

"Annoying?" Illandra interrupted once more, trying not to laugh. "I'm sorry. I guess you weren't the only one that picked up some bad habits."

Race couldn't help but smile across the table. She knew him so well, no matter how hard he tried to trick her. "So now what?"

"Well," Illandra started, "I can almost forgive you for being a jerk, I know you didn't really mean it."

Race let out a sigh of relief.

"However," Illandra said, before Race could get too comfortable, "what I can't forgive is that you would think that I would be so weak as to pine over you for years and years."

Race was trying not to laugh. He admired how little she had changed in the time they had been apart.

He could tell that his laughter was a little contagious, as it was starting to peek through Illandra's smile. "And…?"

"And I know it's been a while, we've both been through a lot, so instead of picking up where we left off, I suggest that we work on rebuilding our friendship and getting to know one another again. You can work on repenting for your actions, and we'll take it from there."

"So…friends, then?" Race asked, making sure he understood where she was coming from.

"For now," Illandra said, closing the top of her food container. She brushed out the wrinkles in her blouse and picked up her stuff and started to head back to her quarters.

"Where are you going?" Race asked.

"I still have to unpack," Illandra explained. "Not to mention I have a very busy day tomorrow. I'll see you on Friday, 1900 hours. You're taking me to a movie. Don't be late." Before Race could respond, the door to her quarters closed behind her, cutting him off.

The display on Race's sensor kicked on, displaying the rough image of the AI program contained within. "I like her," said the program.

Race quickly hit the sleep button on his wrist unit, not interested in a conversation. "Yeah," he still felt the need to answer, "me, too."

Chapter 5

OPEN CONFLICT

Record Date: 349.163 PGST

EVER SINCE ILLANDRA HAD ARRIVED on the station a couple of months ago, Race's head felt like it was going to explode. Whenever she was around, it seemed like all his attention was expected to be on her. Doctor Anthony had also called upon him on a couple of occasions to help with some random things, usually under the pretense of providing security. Luckily, most of their time was monopolized by their respective duties, and the two were frequently visiting the nearby systems or conferences. It almost seemed to Race that the time went too quickly while they were gone. No sooner had Race been able to break away from the two new residents of the station than his teammates started to push to spend more quality time together. Between Illandra, his friends, and completing his project for SORD, Race barely had a moment to himself.

With any luck, that was about to change. Race's project had made several leaps and bounds over the past couple of months and was almost completed. Like most AIs, Race's had been designed to monitor several sensors and anticipate its owner's needs, but this was the first AI to run on such a small and resource-limited platform. Because of the need for such a compressed code, the team needed to develop a complex array of multifunctional algorithms. So far, they were able to repurpose many of the unit's algorithms so Bella could interface with virtually any peripheral. A couple of tweaks and she could use it to decipher most spoken or written languages. The same algorithms were even able to be applied to hacking computer systems and mainframes, which was part of where she networked much of her resources from. With some further tuning, any soldier could have an expert hacker with them whenever they got into trouble.

The programmers Race worked with had been letting Bella run rampant over the past couple of weeks to fully test the latest updates, and they had received high praises in return. Race's commanding officer had been so impressed that he had requested a working demonstration to the review board ahead of schedule. He was anxious to move the project to the next phase. If successful, the AI system would be deployed to a small group of soldiers for further testing and eventually moving on to full deployment.

Race had so many mixed feelings about that outcome. While he was excited about progressing to the next step, it came with a certain amount of regret. Since he had been the project initiator, he had been able to volunteer his biosensor for a testing environment. There was the possibility that the personality he had grown attached to would possibly be deleted. Race had always known that this was a possibility ever since he had first proposed the idea as a simpler way of interfacing with the program, but now that the time was almost upon him, he really didn't want to say goodbye to his dear friend.

Illandra had tried to convince Race to go out with her tonight, as had his fellow teammates, but he had canceled on them to do some last-minute testing—or at least that was his excuse. In all honesty, he had just wanted some time alone.

Race was rummaging through several of his datapads scattered over the room while Bella used a holographic unit used for conference calls to alter her appearance. She was currently using the unit as a means to manifest her upper torso instead of being restricted to the small display on Race's biosensor.

"I hadn't remembered making you so…big in that area," said Race, pointing at the hologram's chest area.

"I increased their circumference by five centimeters," replied the semi-transparent torso. "After hearing your conversation with Zain, I thought you would prefer them this way."

Race's face turned a bright color of red that he tried to hide behind his hands. "Bella, please do me a favor and disregard all conversations regarding a woman's appearance between the guys and me. As a matter of fact, don't even listen to us when we're talking about that. Why don't you see if you can assimilate some of the fashion periodicals from the galactic net or the station's library? Avoid anything extreme, though."

"Conversations erased," she replied. "Do you wish me to decrease their size as well?"

"Please!" begged Race. "I'm starting to wonder if I gave you too much freedom with your appearance," he said as he returned to organizing his notes.

Race was busy reviewing several of Bella's statistics when a sound from the hallway door caused him to jump. To his knowledge, he was the only person authorized to be in the facility this late. Given the security procedures of SORD quarters, it was very unlikely that it would be someone that wasn't allowed there. Race still felt the urge to investigate the noise. He went to the door to his lab and poked his head out. The hallway was poorly lit, but he could still make out the shadowy figure of a woman at the end of the hall.

"Who's there?" Race called down the hall, almost sure of the answer.

The figure was concentrating so hard on not tripping over their own feet that they were startled by Race's voice. "Holy crap, you scared me," came the voice of his fellow Marine as she grabbed her chest.

"I had a feeling it was you," Race responded. "What are you doing here, Annette? I thought you guys were going out?"

"We were," came the familiar voice as she came into the light, igniting the color of her hair, "but after you canceled, Zain decided to go after the waitress he's been chasing for the past month. And you know Konway's married, so just the two of us is a little weird for him, so we just called the whole thing off. I was on my way to the O' Club when they called. I figured you'd still be here working so I thought I'd check and see if you needed anything. Knowing how you get so busy you forget to eat sometimes, I brought you something."

There was something about his teammate's concern that made Race feel a little warm. It wasn't something he was accustomed to with Illandra. She was so dominant that most of the time, he felt he was just being dragged along for the ride.

"If you'd rather be alone, I can go," Annette said, starting to turn for the door, misinterpreting the silence.

"No." Race stopped her. "Some company would be nice right about now."

Annette smiled, tucking a long, curly lock bashfully behind her ear. Annette began to walk down the hall at a steady pace. Race had never seen Annette in heels before, and the way she tried to keep her balance showed she probably hadn't worn them much more. The light set off several sparkles in a stunning ivy-green dress that wrapped loosely around her athletic body, complementing the glow of her red hair. Race could barely contain his astonishment at the beautiful woman he was just seeing and had known for over a year now.

"I don't think I've ever seen you wear a dress," Race blurted.

"I haven't worn one in ages." Annette blushed. "I don't even know what possessed me to buy it. Maybe I was just hoping to get someone's attention tonight. Do you like it?" Annette said, stopping to give the dress a little twirl for approval.

"Jeez, Annette," Race apologized, suddenly feeling bad

about his decision to abandon his friends. "I didn't know you were looking... You look so...amazing. I feel like I wasted all your effort."

"Well, it's not a total waste," Annette said, resuming her trek to the lab. "You got to see me."

Race was in the middle of blushing when Annette suddenly stumbled forward into him, requiring him to catch her before she planted her face on the floor.

"Sorry," Annette said, "been a while since I've worn heels, also."

"Are you okay?" Race asked as he helped Annette regain her balance.

"Yeah, just take this before I drop it, too," she said, handing Race the bag with the containers of food in them before entering the lab. Annette was so embarrassed that she couldn't even look in Race's direction, her face almost matching the color of her hair as she tried to hide it.

"How about we get you off those feet for a bit?" Race said, trying to help his friend not feel so bad about her spill. He put the bag on one of the counters as he started to fumble around the room to stack some things to make an area for Annette to sit on. "There," he said, presenting his construction.

Annette used her peripheral vision to look over at Race's creation. "Why don't I just use one of the chairs?" she said, the confusion displacing some of her frustration.

Race looked over at the line of chairs along the wall that the staff used for their daily operations. "Well, I guess you could," he tried to joke, when he really wanted to slap himself. He quickly moved his poor excuse for a chair out of the way to make room for a real chair, then grabbed the chair and set it across from him so she could sit. As Annette sat down, Race noticed that she wasn't as frustrated with herself, probably the only good outcome of his own airheaded blunder. At least that softened the embarrassment for him a little.

"They didn't have much in the main hall," Annette said, attempting to get comfortable in the chair without exposing too much of herself with the dress. "I hope you don't mind what I picked out."

"It doesn't matter," Race responded, cracking open the container. "I'm too starved to care right now."

"How's the testing going?" Annette asked, trying to find something to talk about.

"Testing is running at optimal performance," said the image of Bella, reappearing on the hologram unit she had been using. "Greetings, Sergeant Keegan. How are you doing? I love your dress."

"Are you two in the mood for scaring me today?" Annette said, grabbing her chest, shocked by the program's sudden appearance.

"Wait," interrupted Race, "what did you change, Bella?"

"I have assimilated complete publications for several different fashion periodicals from the public library and adjusted to meet current trends. My lashes are now a millimeter thicker, my hair is now three centimeters longer with added highlights. I've increased the pixilation of my texture map by..."

"Wow, wow, wow," interrupted Race, waving his hands in front of him. "On second thought, I don't want to know."

Annette tried unsuccessfully to hold in her laughter. "When did you start letting her play with her appearance?"

"When I started letting her play with the holographic imaging," Race explained. "She wasn't happy with the base low-res model we made her, so instead of me rebuilding something hi-res, I just unlocked some of the files and let her make her own."

"You know, I've been dying to ask but didn't want you to get teased even more by the guys." Annette peered over the detail of the hologram. "Why did you decide to model her after a woman?"

"Well, we could have kept it neutral." Race picked up a random object to keep his hands busy while he explained. "But then everyone would have been like, 'Well, what is it,' you know? Kind of hard to relate to, also. So I figured I had two possibilities. First, I base the AI on a female, everyone ends up ogling her, and then they make fun of me not being able to get a real woman."

"If that's the good choice," Annette teased, "what was the bad one?"

"The second was to make it a guy, and have everyone question my sexual preference and ability to pick up one," Race noted, causing Annette to almost choke on her food. "Are you sure you're okay?" Race asked, patting her on the back.

"I'm fine." She laughed, trying to regain her composure. "So how much can she do?"

"More than we thought she'd be able to," said Race, smiling. "You want to see something really cool? What's your favorite song?"

"'Last Time Around the Moon' by the Blazing Comets," Annette responded without hesitation.

"That was surprisingly quick," Race observed. "I always took you for a Blazing Comets fan. Bella!" Race jumped excitedly from his chair to address the hologram. "Remember that little training exercise I had you practice the other day?"

"Are you referring to when I used the different devices to simulate the 23..."

"Yes, yes," interrupted Race, trying to keep her from spoiling the surprise. "Why don't you show Annette?"

"Beginning calculations. Please remain quiet during the discovery phase." Bella's image on the holo-unit flickered a few times before finally disappearing. An awkward silence filled the room as Annette waited impatiently for Race's surprise. Growing anxious, Annette was about to ask a question, but Race held up a finger to cut her off, reaffirming Bella's request to remain silent. A loud clatter cut the silence as almost every device in the room sprang to life, making every possible noise imaginable.

"What is she doing?" Annette yelled, plugging her ears with her fingers.

"Learning," Race yelled back, also attempting to muffle the noise. "Remember when I told you that most of Bella's power comes from her copying parts of her subroutine to spare resources on devices around? With each one she copies to, she exponentially increases her processing power. A lot of these devices have some sort of audio chime or something. You ever hear of a junkyard band?"

As quickly as it started, the noise disappeared. The room went deadly quiet. A couple more seconds passed before the holographic image of Bella reappeared on the conference unit. "I believe I am ready to proceed," she greeted.

"Execute," Race nodded his approval.

A repeating click started to play out a rhythm on a device sitting on the counters near the couple. Slowly, more and more items began to join in, each adding a unique blend to the ongoing tune. The excitement grew as the music picked up. Race and Annette couldn't help but start dancing in their chairs. Almost without thinking, Race stood up and offered his hand to Annette.

Annette looked up at him, confused by his gesture.

"The only reason you're not dancing at the O' Club is because I canceled and everything fell apart," Race explained. "Let me make it up to you."

Annette bit her lip, attempting to resist the temptation. She looked down at the heels on her feet. She quickly took them off before accepting Race's hand and joining him in the last couple of minutes of the song. Bella even took over the lights to alter their colors, almost giving the lab the full club experience. When the song came to an end, Annette and Race shared a large amount of laughter before returning to their chairs.

"That's just amazing," Annette said, catching her breath and grabbing her shoes. "How did she do that?"

"We were discussing different ways to reuse some of

her algorithms when one of the guys suggested repurposing some of her language and sonar routines," Race said, eager to share his story. "I was trying to figure out a way to test it when I had the idea to have her use her device interface routines to scan everything for what kind of noises they made and reassimilate them into a constructive pattern."

"And what better pattern than my favorite song?" Annette concluded for him.

"Exactly!" Race exclaimed. "But don't tell anyone, please. I don't think they'd like to hear I've been using high-tech military equipment for our personal musical enjoyment."

"Your secret is safe with me," Annette said, using her finger to cross the exposed section of her chest just over her heart. "So how much more do you have to do?"

"I think I'm just about done," Race said, looking around the room. "I just keep thinking that something's going to happen tomorrow and throw off the whole thing, you know?"

"It's your first presentation," Annette reminded him, putting the dreaded heels back on her feet. "Of course you're going to be nervous. I've already been through a couple of them. I assure you, it doesn't get any easier. I'm sure you'll do fine, though. If something happens, you'll find a way around it, you always do. We'll all be there too, just in case you need us."

"Thanks," Race said. The words helped, at least a little. "I guess I'd better at least try and get some rest. You need help getting back to your room with those shoes?"

"Please." Annette rolled her eyes, taking Race's hand to

help her up.

Race quickly sorted his datapads into a neat pile before the two started to make their way toward the living quarters. The halls were nearly void of most people, the laughter of Race and Annette echoing through them as they exchanged jokes and witty remarks. Fearing Annette might take another tumble, the two remained close together so that Race could catch her if she stumbled. This caused their arms to constantly brush against each other, and Race came to find that he didn't mind the feeling of his partner so close to him.

"Well, I think Bella's awesome, and you're going to be great tomorrow," Annette said as the two approached the door to her room.

"Thanks," said Race. "That means a lot."

"You know, it's still early, you want to maybe get something to drink?" she offered.

"I shouldn't." Race laughed nervously. "I have an early day tomorrow. Double-checking everything and getting ready for the demonstration. I really should try and turn in. Maybe some other time, though?"

"Sure." Annette smiled. "Well, we'll be there to cheer you on tomorrow, but I'm sure you'll do great."

"Always got my back, huh?" Race smiled, placing his hands behind his back so as not to keep awkwardly playing with them.

"I'll see you tomorrow." Annette turned to enter her door, but before entering she turned back around. She reached out and wrapped her arms around Race's chest and placed her head gently on his shoulder. "Thank you for the dance," she whispered into his ear before disappearing into her living quarters.

*　　*　　*

"Oh," growled Annette as the door closed behind her, "put a rifle in my hand, I kill a man at 500 meters. Put a control stick in my hands, I navigate an asteroid field better than most computers. Put a dress on me with some heels, I become a blabbering idiot that can't walk!" she exclaimed, removing her shoes before throwing them across the room, breaking one of the heels off with her bare hands before sending it flying. She went into the bathroom while practically trying to rip the dress off of her.

"That bad, huh?" questioned Konway, who was lying on the floor while he played with a controller in front of the holo-unit in Annette's room.

Annette's head shot out from the bathroom to see her two friends lying on the floor of her private quarters playing video games. "How did you guys get in here?"

"We never left," answered Zain, playing with a similar controller next to Konway. "What happened?"

"It was horrible," Annette fumed, ducking back into the bathroom to finish ripping the dress off and to find something to cover herself with. "Everything that could have gone wrong practically did. I couldn't even walk down the hall in those stupid heels without tripping. I would have landed on my face if Race had not caught me."

"See, I told you they'd work," Zain said, nudging Konway with his elbow.

"It couldn't have been all bad," Konway said.

"Well, no…" Annette smiled as she came out of the bathroom tying a bathrobe around her waist. "He was actually kind of sweet."

"Oh really?" Zain said as he and Konway paused their game to get up from the floor.

"Do tell," Konway said, pushing for details.

"Well, after seeing me all dressed up, he felt bad that I didn't get to go out, so he had Bella put on some music and we danced," Annette reminisced.

"Aww," Konway and Zain sighed almost in unison.

"Our little girl is growing up," Zain teased. "It seems like yesterday she was putting on her first dress."

"It was yesterday," Konway clarified. "That's when we bought it."

"I know," said Zain, wiping an imaginary tear from his eyes.

Ever since Annette had gotten home, something had been off about her quarters and she had been trying to figure out what it was. "Did you guys go through my stuff?" she asked as she noticed one of her dresser doors half open.

"Stay focused, girl." Zain jumped up and grabbed Annette by the shoulders to give her a little shake. "What happened next?"

"Nothing," Annette said, pushing Zain off of her. "We came back here. I gave him a little hug and thanked him for the dance and came inside."

"He walked you home?" asked Konway hopefully.

"Yeah," Annette answered.

"Aww," the boys sighed once again in unison.

"He had to with those heels I was wearing," Annette said through clenched teeth. "I probably wouldn't have made it home on my own."

"First dates can be so magical," Zain said. "I still remember mine and Jadzia's first date."

"You mean the time she slapped you, threatened to report you to your CO, and told you if you ever talked to her again that she'd file a restraining order against you?" Konway asked.

"Yeah," Zain said, having a moment of his own. "The good old days."

"On the plus side, it looks like we're starting to open him up to the possibility of dating you," congratulated Konway.

"His perspective is definitely starting to shift," Zain agreed.

"Great." Annette rolled her eyes. "All I have to do is wear outfits that turn me into an airhead and lose the ability to walk in a straight line."

"Sounds about right." Konway nodded his head in agreement.

"Can't you just shoot me instead?" Annette pleaded, falling into one of the chairs.

"You'll be fine," Konway assured her. "You only have to be a bimbo for a little bit, just long enough to attract his attention."

"Fine," Annette huffed. "Anyway, you guys better get going. I need to figure out how I'm going to salvage that dress I just ripped up. Check the hallway, though, make sure Race doesn't see you leaving."

"Okay," the boys sighed as they started to head toward the exit. They used the peeping camera to scan the outside corridor before opening the door. As the two left, Annette grabbed Zain by the arm, preventing him from leaving as she outstretched her other hand accusingly at Zain. Zain returned an innocent expression as he tried to dodge her unspoken charges. After a couple more tries to attempt to free himself, he reached into his pocket to pull out a pair of socks he had stolen and return it to its owner.

"Why socks?" Annette looked at him confused.

"It was for a bet," Zain explained as Annette pushed him out of her room and locked the door behind him.

*   *   *

Race had been going back and forth between Konway's and Zain's rooms for about twenty minutes when he decided to give up and head back to his own residence. Miraculously, as he turned the corner, he barely avoiding bumping into them.

"There you guys are," Race cried out, relieved.

"What's the matter?" Konway asked.

"Can we talk for a minute?" Race asked. "Like seriously? It's kind of a personal matter."

"You bet," Konway said, concerned, placing his arm over Race's shoulder. "There's a spot just over there where we can sit." He pointed.

The trio made their way over to a small social area that had been set aside for the soldiers. Zain and Konway took a seat opposite Race to hear what he had to say.

"What's bothering you?" Konway asked as they got comfortable.

"It's Annette," Race answered as he rubbed the back of his neck, slightly embarrassed.

"Oh?" Konway asked as he and Zain sat up straight.

"Yeah," Race continued, struggling to explain the situation to his friends. "She came by the lab tonight because we all canceled on her. She brought me some food, and I was working and…"

"And…" the boys said, waiting intently to hear Race's side of the story.

"I don't know," Race said, standing up to pace around nervously. "We danced a little. If I didn't know any better, I'd say it was a date."

"You little rascal, you," Zain teased, attempting to defuse the stress a bit. "What was she wearing?"

"Oh my god, you guys wouldn't believe it." Race's face brightened as he remembered the apparel. "First time I'd ever seen her wear a dress, and it was amazing."

"Hot?" Zain asked for clarification.

"Hawt," Race answered dreamily, rolling his eyes.

"So what's up?" Konway interrupted Race's daydream. "You thinking of asking her out?"

"No," Race said, quickly dismissing the idea. "Well…" he said, stopping suddenly in his tracks.

"Ahhh," Zain said as the two moved to the other side of the table to be closer to the action, "you're not sure."

"That's what you wanted to talk about," Konway concluded.

Race gave a quick nod to his two friends. "I mean, I'm supposed to be working on getting back together with Illandra, but things are so different between us than they were back then. And I really had a nice time with Annette."

"Didn't you say Illandra just wanted to be friends?" Zain asked, listening intently.

"Yeah," Race answered, resuming a slow pace, "that's what she said, but that's not what she meant."

Zain and Konway exchanged a confused glance, waiting for Race to enlighten them.

"Illandra can say one thing and mean a totally different one and make them both apparently clear at the same time," Race explained. "She said she wanted to be friends for now, but what she meant was, 'I'm going to have some fun torturing you before we get back together.'"

"Sounds like too much effort if you ask me," Zain replied.

"What about Annette?" Konway asked, trying to steer the conversation back to the original topic.

"I don't know. It'd be weird, right? I mean we're so close, all of us. Wouldn't it be weird if all of a sudden we started dating?"

"I don't think it'd be that weird," Zain answered. "I mean, Konway and I have been here forever. Now the two of us, that would be weird. You've barely been here for a year, and Annette not much longer."

"What Zain is trying to say is that we just want you two to be happy, and if that makes you happy, we'll find a way to work through it."

"But she doesn't even like me that way, does she? And what if things don't work?" Race said as the questions kept rolling through his mind. "What if it's a complete disaster? Then we'll still have to see each other every day. Work together. Wouldn't that just be awkward? And stressful?"

"It could," Konway confirmed. "It is a risk with office relationships. But it could also turn out very good."

"Let me ask you this," Zain interrupted. "How did you feel with Annette last night?"

Race stopped, the dreamy smile starting to creep back onto his face. "It felt…nice."

"And Illandra?" Zain asked.

"It's all right," Race said, snapping out of his daydream. "I mean, it's great. Illandra's just one of the few people that really gets me, you know. It can be hard for me to talk to people sometimes, but with Illandra, I don't even have to say anything. She gets me. Then there are times where it doesn't even seem like it matters. Like I'm just being dragged along to do whatever she wants."

"My advice?" Konway said, putting a supporting arm on Race's shoulder as he got up. "Don't worry about it right now, you have a big presentation tomorrow to get ready for. Just don't be so quick to close the door on any possibilities without giving them a proper chance. You just might miss out on something great."

Race looked down as the wisdom of Konway's words sank in. "Thanks." Race nodded, tapping his friend's shoulder with a fist. "I'd better go get some sleep."

"You bet," Konway said as Race turned and left his two friends.

The two soldiers watched as their friend walked off down the hall to his quarters. "This is going to be harder than we thought," Zain commented once he was sure Race was out of range.

Konway moaned sourly in agreement.

*   *   *

The crew of the *Blitzkrieg* was hard at work mining their little section of the great asteroid barrier, hoping to make their quota for this session's deployment.

The Blitzkrieg spent most of its time in the belt searching for sizable deposits of dentarite to collect that were small enough to tow back for processing. The crew was looking forward to their nearing break so they could head back home to the families.

At least that was the plan before some strange readings started coming over the sensors.

"What is it?" asked the small ship's captain of one of his crew members manning a console.

"I don't know, Capt'n," replied the crew member. "The interference is pretty heavy in this part of the nebula, it looks like a ship. A big one, too, I'd say military."

"What?" screamed the captain as he jumped out of his chair. "Out here? See if you can contact them. While you're at it, see if you can relay our position and readings to the nearest border station."

The young operator's hands were ablaze on the console

attempting to execute the captain's orders as fast as he could. "Attempting relay now, sir, but with the interference, it's hard to tell if it's getting through. No response back from the vessel yet."

"What in the world…" the captain started to ask as a huge ship came through the fog-like nebula.

"Sir, I've received an acknowledgment from the ship," exclaimed the operator, "but I can't make any of it out, it's all garbage."

"Put me on," the captain said. When he received the crew member's signal, he addressed the approaching ship. "To the incoming ship: This is Captain Malone of the mining vessel *Blitzkrieg*. You have entered a neutral area and are in violation of the Tri-Galactic Territory Act. In accordance with the treaty, you must remove yourself from the nebula and return to your section of space."

"Very well done, sir," congratulated the console operator.

"I've got my moments," chuckled the captain helplessly.

The console flared up as more threats were detected "Sir, two more ships have appeared on the sensors," called the young man, panicking. "I think they're getting ready to fire!"

"Get us out of here!" yelled the captain.

*   *   *

Race was exhausted from a night of endless tossing and turning when he reported into SORD the next morning. It seemed he had just fallen asleep when his alarm went off. His crew checked in with their CO before reporting to their stations, where Race and his partners started setting up for their presentation later that day. Still feeling the pressure, Race continued to demand test after test, assured there was still some bug in the system.

It wasn't too much later before Zain came and literally pulled Race from his team. A few moments later, they were inside one of the simulation training areas they commonly used for practice.

"Here, take this," Zain said, tossing Race one of the testing firearms they used in their simulations.

"I don't have time for this, Zain," Race said, passing the rifle back to his friend. "Something is going to happen to ruin this presentation, I have to figure it out beforehand."

"Your head's about to explode, and I'm guessing you didn't sleep all night. If you don't blow off some steam right now, one of those geeks is going to start a fight with you, and then you're probably going to kill the poor little guy because you're a deadly killing machine and he's a puny little nerd," Zain explained, almost yelling at Race. "Now, take this."

Race stopped protesting and reluctantly took the firearm from Zain. "Fine. What are we doing?"

"Boktoran swarm." Zain smiled.

"Just the two of us?" Race whined, dropping his arms.

"We got this," Zain said, trying to calm Race. "Just take the right side, kite 'em if they get too close, and take out the fliers first. If you get in trouble, holler and I'll help you out."

"All right." Race submitted once again. "Just hold on a second." Race put his firearm between his legs for a second while he took a moment to rub his eyes, trying to remove the strain they felt. He then removed the top of his uniform and hung it near the door. When he was done, he slapped himself a couple of times to get the blood flowing. He re-armed himself and nodded to Zain to start the simulation.

Zain hit a button on the terminal that triggered a timer to start counting down in the middle of the room. They moved into position in the center of the room. When it reached zero, the chamber came alive as hundreds of holographic critters suddenly inhabited the area. The insects of Boktoran were notoriously agile creatures with a thick exoskeleton covering most of their canine-sized bodies. When threatened, they could roll their bodies up into a protective ball. This made them very difficult to injure, let alone kill. The combatants had to be extremely accurate with their shots.

Zain and Race wasted no time opening fire on the wave of large bugs moving to devour them. The only advantage they had was that the insects stopped to devour their wounded. Even then, it wasn't long before the two were on the run as they attempted to put as many obstacles as possible between them and the giant bugs. Sometimes they had to use the butts of their weapons to smash the bugs' heads in or kick a rolled-up bug like a soccer ball.

The two had been at it for nearly ten minutes when the simulation was abruptly cut off. They turned to see Annette by the terminal. "Come on," she said, a certain amount of seriousness in her expression that sent shivers down Race's neck.

"What do you think that's all about?" Zain said, bracing

his hand on his knees in an attempt to catch his breath.

"I don't know," Race said as he put his weapon away in the slot next to the door, "but I think we're about to find out why my presentation isn't happening." Race grabbed the top of his uniform to put back on as he headed out.

The captain was waiting for them as they came running in. "About time!" he almost yelled as they entered the room.

"What's going on, sir?" asked Konway as the last of the team finished funneling into the overly tense room.

"Get ready to deploy," their commanding officer said. "A couple of unknown ships have breached the nebula and are heading this way. The President is sending some G-class Stingers this way to investigate. Admiral Casten has asked that we join the *Puller* and intercept the incoming ships. Get your stuff and report to docking tunnel A-5. We leave in three hours."

The Marines exited the office without hesitation and made a quick stop by the labs to inform their civilian counterparts that they were being called away. Most of the scientist already knew what had happened and were prepared for the Marines' departure. Several had rushed to give them some of the experimental equipment they had been working on to take with them. Then they were on the way to their rooms to pack what belongings they could take with them.

*   *   *

The past couple of months hadn't been anything like Illandra had planned out. Quite frequently, Anthony had taken her off Taurus to some nearby planets for special conferences. The time she was able to spend on Taurus, she was constantly helping Anthony entertain diplomatic guests to the station and not able to spend as much time with Race as she had hoped for. The little time she did get, she always had to fight to break him away from his friends. Not only did she have to fight with Race's friends for his time, but her mentor had also become very good at coming up with excuses to pull him away from her.

Race's friends had been a crude bunch, and their sense of humor was just a little too much for her to handle at times. She did appreciate the bond that had developed between them, though, especially knowing how hard it was for Race to open up and make new friends. Unfortunately, this bond of theirs made it hard to determine their true feelings for the female member of Race's team. Their training as an elite task force had also given them greater control over their emotions, so it was entirely possible for them to ignore their emotions, or sometimes act totally against them when the situation called for it. Because of this, Illandra found it extremely difficult to get a good bearing on all of Race's friends.

Illandra was strolling around one of the artificial groves attempting to plan the next stage of her and Race's involvement together when she was struck by a sudden overwhelming emotional outpour of several of the station's crew. Following Anthony's training, she quickly sat down and attempted to focus on her breathing while trying to wrap a mental barrier around her head and shield herself from the mounting anxiety. It was no surprise when her phone went off. She took one of her hands that was trying to keep her head from exploding to reach into her pocket to answer the device.

"I was afraid of that," Anthony said, quickly examining Illandra through the holo-imaging device as she set it on the ground to grasp her head once again. "News is spreading pretty fast. Are you okay?"

"I'm coping," Illandra said, rocking back and forth on the floor. "What's going on?"

"Trouble," Anthony stated. "I can't explain over the phone, but I need you to pack your stuff. We're leaving in a couple of hours. Meet us at docking station A-5, where we'll board the *Puller*. Try and pack light, but get everything that's important, I don't know when we'll be back again."

"I'll see you there," Illandra said before hanging up the phone. She continued to rock herself for a little longer while she gathered the last of her strength to fight the outpouring of emotion. Once she was pretty sure she had it together, she got up and headed back to her room.

On her way, she passed by a small group of high-rank-ing individuals. Failing to fight the urge, she temporarily dropped her barrier to try and read their thoughts to get a clue of what was going on. She got a couple of images of ships in the nearby nebula before she had to reconstruct her barrier. Unfortunately, she also got one very clear word from the officers: "War."

*　　*　　*

Admiral Montana of the U.R.S. Puller had gathered his guests to meet with him in his ship's conference room before taking off. The four Stingers had just entered the station's orbit and were moving into the formation along with the two other ships already stationed at Taurus.

Race had been surprised to see Illandra and Doctor Martin had also joined the crew of the *Puller* for the mission. He suspected they were along to attempt a diplomatic resolution to whatever situation was playing out. Above the center of the large table floated several holographic images from the conference rooms of the other ships. As Race understood it, this was to be their last briefing before heading to confront the oncoming threat.

"All right, everyone." The admiral spoke up, quieting the room. "Some of you might have heard the stories about a mining vessel going critical in the nebula not too far from here. The truth is, it was no accident. Before losing communication, the ship relayed a message to the local border station, including all its sensor readings. There was a lot of interference, but we were able to piece most of it together. Take a look." The admiral signaled one of his subordinates, who started playing some haunting footage that replaced the images from the other ships.

For the first time, everyone in the room was able to see the incoming threat and how easily their weapons had torn through the small freighter. Several people turned away, not being able to stand the grim sight, while others tightened their fists in frustration.

The display finished and the holograms returned to display the crowded rooms of the other ships, reflecting the same feelings of the conference room aboard the *Puller*.

"We think they're trying to use the interference of the nebula to hide their approach," the admiral stated. "Does anyone want to point out any observations before I start?"

"I'm not too familiar with too many IC ships," said one of the captains from his holographic image, "but those don't look like any of their standard models."

"He's right," Annette said, pushing through some of the crowd to get a closer look at the footage. She squatted between the two chairs closest to the image and took control. She restarted the footage and forwarded it to where she could get a good look at the incoming ships. "But there's definitely some ICS designs in there. Like here and here. If I didn't know better, I'd say they'd cut and pasted parts of a battlecruiser with something else to make these things. Looks like they've reinforced most of the hull. I'm not too sure about these weapon systems, though. They have to be pretty high-tech to cut through the hall of a mining ship. Have you guys seen anything like it before?" Annette said, trying to look at Konway and Zain through the crowd.

"Something seems familiar about it," Konway said, stepping a little closer to get a better look, "but I can't seem to place it."

"Remember that PXR project we did a couple of years ago?" Zain said, more serious than Race had ever seen him.

Konway's eyes widened, recalling the experiment. He quickly dashed over next to Annette and examined it intently. "You might be right."

"What's a PXR?" one of the members in the room asked.

"Plasma Experimental Railgun," clarified Konway. "It

was an experiment that we were working on. You know the concept of a railgun? Accelerating particles to almost light speeds?" Konway asked, waiting for the man to nod his acknowledgment. "Well, imagine replacing the particles with a superheated stream of plasma. Plasma alone is dangerous enough; speed it up to light speed and not much it can't cut through."

"Like the double-layered hull of a mining vessel," Annette gasped, looking back at the footage.

"Exactly," Konway said, not looking too thrilled at the footage himself. "We had to discontinue the project because it was just so impractical."

"I thought it was because you almost cut the station in half?" Zain added without breaking his intense expression.

"That too." Konway brushed off Zain's attempt at embarrassing him.

"Very impressive," interrupted the admiral before returning his attention back to the rest of the room. "I'm not sure how many of you are familiar with the Special Operations R&D unit from Taurus, but in less than five minutes they've come to the same conclusion as the team that's been reviewing this for the past several hours.

"We're fairly certain this is only the advanced wave to test our reaction and defenses," the admiral continued. "Even if we manage to repel them, there might be several more ships coming through right behind them. We're going to have to find a way to outmaneuver them. With any luck we can slam them so hard and fast, the Consortium will think twice before sending any more ships into Republic territory. I need all ships to coordinate our tactics with Commander Everett here on the *Puller*. Everyone run a full systems check and prepare to engage. We leave in about thirty minutes," finished up the admiral. "Does anyone have any questions?"

A cold silence answered the admiral's question.

"Very well. Dismissed," he said, bringing the conversation to a close and turning off the holographic display.

Everyone started to find their way out of the overstuffed conference room. "Corporal Allard," called the admiral before Race could escape out the door, "a word, please." Race turned and attempted to dodge the wave of people trying to leave the room. Once he finally made it, they waited for everyone else to vacate the room so that they could speak in private. "Some of your training videos managed to make their way into my hands not too long ago. I must say you're an extremely talented strategist."

"Thank you, sir," Race said respectfully.

"Even though your team has already proved their worth, the only reason that any of them are even here is so that you can help coordinate our defenses against the Consortium attack."

Race almost lost his composure. "I'm sorry, sir. Me?"

"Yes, Corporal," answered the admiral, "you. However, I'm sure you can see how disruptive it might be to have a corporal running point during such an important operation."

"Yes, sir," Race responded appropriately, trying to determine what point the admiral was getting at.

"Now, if you were a sergeant, things wouldn't be that

bad. That being said, I'd like to remind you that while you're here, your unit is going to be attached to STF 266, and I've heard that there might be a sergeant or two in need of an attitude adjustment. I'm sure you'll find several of them preparing for combat on the docking bays. If you happen to attain the rank of sergeant by the time we are ready to head out, I will allow you to assist us when we arrive."

"Th…thank you, sir," Race said, tripping over his own words.

"Dismissed," the admiral said. The two exchanged the traditional salute, which was immediately followed by Race running out of the room.

Race's friends were waiting for him outside the room when he came running out.

"What did he want?" asked Konway as the three joined their friend in flying down the hall.

"Ah, man, why do we always have to run everywhere?" whined Zain.

"You're not going to believe it," Race replied as he flew down the hall.

The group funneled into an elevator as it closed behind them. "Computer," Race commanded. "What levels are assigned to STF 266?"

"Sections 89A through 89F," replied a digital voice from the computer.

"And where are the security areas in those sections?"

"What's going on?" asked Annette as she caught her breath.

"Their main security center for that section is 89B," answered the computer.

"I need to gain a rank, and quick," answered Race. He turned his attention to the lift sensor above the door. "Take us to section 89B."

"How do you plan to do that?" asked Zain.

"The challenge," Race said with a grim tone. "Bella, I need you to scan all personal files on all the sergeants and staff sergeants for the special task force unit 266 on board this ship. Find out which ones have the most complaints and demerits."

"Personal files are restricted," Bella replied. "Would you like me to hack into them?"

"That won't be necessary," Race replied. "Just send a request to Admiral Montana; I'm pretty sure he'll grant you access."

"Very well," Bella said, disappearing.

Race yawned as the stress of the day started to catch up with him. Feeling he had a moment to rest, Race closed his eyes and attempted to lean against the wall while waiting for a response.

"You're not planning on challenging one of us?" Annette asked, breaking an awkward silence.

"What?" Race jumped awake. "Not you guys! I couldn't. While we're on the ship, we fall under STF 266."

"You can challenge anyone in their ranks!" Konway said excitedly as the plan suddenly became clear to him.

"You sure you're up for it?" Zain questioned. "You look pretty tired to me."

"I need to." Race yawned again. "The admiral wants me

to run point on the defense strategy when we engage, but he thinks me being a corporal might be too disruptive. He'll only let me do it if I'm a sergeant."

"Why you?" Konway asked, almost insulted that he wasn't picked for the job.

"Part of my extracurricular training, I guess," Race answered, fighting another yawn. "Straum and I were constantly getting pulled out for engagement training. Land, sea, air…"

"And space," Konway added.

"Mhmm." Race nodded. "I still get called for them every now and again."

"Is that what they call you off for?" Annette asked.

"Yup," Race answered shortly.

"Explains why you're so skilled in the field," Zain complimented.

"I'm not too sure I like this," Annette objected. "We don't even know what we're up against here, and you're already exhausted as it is. How are you supposed to fight some random guy, then defend against an experimental invasion fleet?"

"It's only three ships," Race said, leaning back against the lift's wall. "Besides, I can do combat strategies in my sleep."

"You might just have to," Konway responded, disappointed.

"Listen." Zain motioned his friends closer so he wouldn't have to talk as loud. "I'm the fighter. I'll go with Race and make sure we get the most pathetic sergeant we can find for him to challenge. Why don't you two head down to engineering and see what little hints you might be able to pass along to the chief engineer to get some extra oomph out of this ship."

Race's biosensor buzzed to life, waking him back up as Bella appeared on the display. "I've received permission from the admiral and have sorted through the ship's personnel files," she responded as Race started to look through the list.

"Destination reached: Section 89B," the computer interrupted as the doors opened.

"Here we go," Zain said as he and Race exited the lift, leaving their friends behind.

*   *   *

"Does it have to be him?" pleaded Race as he watched a tall young sergeant belittle a group of soldiers running practice drills for the upcoming battle. "His shoulders are twice as wide as my whole body. What is he, seven feet tall?"

"And a real dick, too," added Zain. "He shouldn't even be allowed to wear that uniform, let alone the rank. Treating his subordinates like that at a time like this, he should be instilling confidence."

"You think I can take him?" Race asked, questioning his skills.

"Not a chance," Zain answered. "They're Special Forces, they practice combat almost as much as us."

Zain's comment was enough to shake Race awake.

"Just kidding," Zain said, putting him at ease. "I just needed to get your adrenaline going for a second. Here, take this," Zain said, handing Race a drink he was mixing up.

"What's this?" Race asked, taking the glass.

"It's my pre-workout supplement," Zain answered. "It'll help wake you up a little, give you some extra energy."

"Nothing illegal?" Race questioned, catching a whiff of the foul odor.

"Naw," Zain assured him. "Just make sure you drink a lot of water afterward."

Race gulped down the drink, his face puckered from the taste. "Oh my god, that's awful."

"You get used to it," Zain replied.

"Really?" Race questioned, not sure how anyone could ever get used to such a horrible thing.

"No," Zain answered, "not really. Give it about fifteen minutes and you'll be ready to run a marathon."

"All right," sighed Race. "So what's the plan with this guy?"

"He's got a pretty short temper," Zain observed, watching their target throw some boxes around as he yelled at one of his troops that had dropped some equipment by mistake. "I'm sure picking a fight won't be that hard. Just question his authority a couple of times, get him to throw a punch at you. That should give you enough reason to issue a challenge."

"All right," Race said. He then held his hands up to his mouth to amplify his voice. "Maybe if you didn't push them like pack mules," he called to the fuming sergeant.

The sergeant stopped hollering at the man he was berating to turn slowly and face Race. "Stay out of this," he yelled, pointing at Race.

"They're men, not machines," Race explained. "You

should be instilling confidence at a time like this, make them feel they're going to live, not making them want to give up and die."

"Not bad," Zain whispered.

The sergeant boiled in anger, his face turning a steaming red as he marched over to Race. "You got a problem with the way I treat my men?" the sergeant said through clenched teeth.

"Yeah," Race challenged as he stood tall in opposition to the sergeant, barely coming up to the sergeant's mouth. "If you keep degrading them like that, they're going to give up on you the moment you need them most. This isn't boot camp; you don't need to break them down any more. You need to build them up, make them ready to face any adversary."

"Well, last time I checked, I'm a sergeant, and you're a corporal, and if you don't like it, I suggest you get the fuck out of here."

"Why? You don't like being made to look like an idiot by a junior Marine?" Race asked.

"That's it," the sergeant said, grabbing Race by the collar and pushing him back into the wall.

"Sergeant," Zain interrupted with a deep, commanding voice, stopping the sergeant from assaulting Race any further.

"Staff Sergeant," the sergeant said. "I was…"

"I saw," Zain cut him off. "I've been here the whole time."

"I…uh…" the sergeant attempted to explain.

"Corporal," Zain said, addressing Race as the sergeant

let go of Race's shirt and backed away, "this sergeant has assaulted you. Would you like to file a complaint?"

"No," Race said, straightening his uniform. "I'd like to challenge him for his rank?"

"What?" the sergeant yelled, surprised.

"That's your right." Zain ignored the sergeant's protest. "As a senior ranking member of this unit, I hereby authorize this challenge in accordance with the military law."

Both Race and the sergeant's biosensors lit up as the challenge procedures were initiated.

The lights on the corridors started flashing, directing them to the nearest challenge station. The two combatants followed them with the remaining soldiers trailing behind to view the spectacle.

"Any advice?" Race said, bouncing around, feeling the energy of Zain's supplements.

"You've got to be careful," Zain coached him from behind. "Like I said, he's still Special Forces. He can mess you up as bad as you can him. His anger is a little more focused on you from the walk over here, but I still think you can use it to force him to make a mistake. Just whatever you do, don't let him hit you; he'll probably knock your head right off."

"Thanks," Race said.

"Good luck," stated his friend as he gave him a pat on the back, sending him into the arena.

The arena was a small area with several platforms in it. Most of the platforms were small and crescent-shaped, standing a couple of feet off the ground. There was also one large round pillar about the size of a table just off the center of the area. The object of the challenge was to run around the different platforms and try and knock your opponent off; the first one to touch the ground was declared the loser, and automatically demoted one rank. If the winner was the lower-ranking soldier, that soldier would be promoted a rank.

The two combatants were given a pair of giant cushioned pugil sticks. They were also given a few items of protective gear to wear for safety during the fight. When they were finished, each man took their place on pillars on opposite sides of the arena and waited for the fight to begin.

Usually, Race would have let the big man take the center pillar and taunted him until he became frustrated and started chasing him, but Race's half-hour deadline was rapidly approaching. The buzzer went off as the challenge was started, the small crowd bursting into a large roar as they cheered the two competitors on.

As was expected, the large man immediately tried to dominate the large round pillar. Race was rushing toward the same area to meet him. The two men approached the high island within seconds of each other. The sergeant tried to combine his momentum with a massive swing as he aimed for Race's head. Race prepped for his attack and ducked under it as he felt the swish of air on the back of his neck. His opponent attempted to reform his attack into a backswing, which Race blocked with the center of his weapon.

The soldier pulled back his weapon, trying to reposition for another swing, but before he could do anything, Race was able to twirl his stick to give the sergeant a quick jab to the face, knocking him off balance.

Race launched his attack, taking advantage of his dazed opponent. He rotated his legs to get a better swing. With one fluid movement, he spun around in a full circle, his weapon clashing with the soldier just regaining his balance. The force of the collision sent the sergeant stumbling back off the platform. Losing his footing, the oversized giant fell to the floor, ending the match.

Race was already ripping off his padding before his opponent even hit the ground. Race waited long enough for the system to clear him before jumping down from his pillar. He grabbed the top of his uniform and he was soon dashing out the arena door.

Zain joined him as they ran down the hall, where they bumped into Annette coming out of the same elevator they were trying to jump into.

"What happened?" Annette asked, trying to catch up to the guys that had just passed her.

"Let me introduce you to Sergeant Allard," Zain said, stopping just outside the lift door.

"You did it?" Annette said excitedly. "Congratulations!" Annette jumped over to Race and gave him a huge celebratory hug.

Race looked uncomfortably over to Zain. The combination of sleep deprivation, Zain's energy drink, and the rush of adrenaline from his fight left his mind too clouded to know what was going on. Zain shook his head and grabbed one of Race's hands and put it on Annette's back to complete the exchange.

"Listen, I'm going to stay here," Zain stated after Annette let Race go, "see what I can do to help get these soldiers back on track."

"All right, we'll catch up with you after the attack," Race said as the doors closed.

The elevator doors opened to reveal the bridge of the U.R.S. Puller. Race stepped out and saluted. "Permission to come aboard, sir!" he bellowed.

"Ah, Sergeant Allard," greeted the ship's admiral as he turned in his chair to face him. "How nice of you to join us. And you brought one of your fellow squad members. Why don't you both come in and find some place to help out. We're going to need all the help we can get by the time this thing is over."

Chapter 6
INVASION

Record Date: 349.164 PGST

THE TENSION ABOARD THE *PULLER* was intensely thick and bore through Illandra's mental barrier. Despite all the training with her mentor, Illandra was barely able to keep herself from running down the halls of the ship screaming like she had gone insane.

After their brief meeting with all the other ships, Anthony had taken Illandra and the ship's senior staff to a secure room, where he gave them some more detailed background information on the situation.

Behind closed doors, Anthony revealed to the leading officers how intelligence had been gathering some suspicions of a secret government coup by a terrorist party identifying themselves as the Cenari. He explained how several government officials were radically converting to the following practically overnight. Any opposition had a talent for disappearing without a trace.

The discussion turned to the motions passed in their legislative branch. The new movement pressed that the Imperial Consortium had been a victim of the Tri-Galactic

Territory dispute and received a useless piece of space while the Great Euro-Alliance and the United Galactic Republic had received areas with more precious resources. Most of their rage had been misdirected at the Republic, spending a large amount of their resources to try and stop relations with the United Galactic Republic. Most people thought that the Consortium was after minerals rights to the nebula; others suspected they feared a secret alliance between the Alliance and the Republic. Whatever the excuse, they were so intent on breaking ties with the Republic that they were even trying to block all transmissions to the Republic, making it harder for their opposition to rally support.

Once the briefing was complete, everyone went back to the bridge before preparing for travel. Illandra and Anthony had been given an empty station off to the side to keep out of everyone's way. Each of the ship's stations were broken up into a round console, in which two to three soldiers sat at chairs mounted on a rail that allowed them to circle the inside of their station rapidly. The functioning stations circled that command station in the center of the room, where the admiral sat elevated above the other stations. From his perch, he could quickly turn his chair to view the other stations and talk to the operating soldiers. Within the command station were two other stations directly in front of the captain. One was a two-seated console for the pilot and copilot. Illandra had no idea what the other station was for.

Illandra and Anthony had been offered a place in the Communication station behind the admiral. They were here to talk to the Cenari, after all. The two had taken a quick lesson in the station's operations before being turned loose. Anthony had quickly grown bored and started kicking his chair around a section of the rail that was not being used by the other members.

"These chairs never get old," her mentor said as he slowed to a stop, bumping into her seat. "Are you okay?" Anthony whispered to the young woman privately.

"I think so," replied Illandra as she massaged her temples. "Things are a little overwhelming, but I'm managing."

"They are, even for me," agreed the elder man as he patted his protégée reassuringly on the shoulder. "Just do your best to clear your mind and focus on your barrier."

The door to the elevator opened and Race stepped onto the bridge, where he requested the ship's captain's permission to come aboard. The captain acknowledged his presence and invited the spirited Annette to join as well, much to Illandra's disappointment. Illandra had come to notice that it was hard for Race to go anywhere without the young girl following him like some stray puppy.

Race joined the tactical officer as he had been instructed while Annette quickly kicked the copilot out of his station and took control of the navigation console. The young redhead took to the console with almost lightning-fast hands as she tweaked it to her liking. Illandra was impressed at Annette's mastery of the control unit, no matter how hard she tried not to be.

Illandra tried to turn her attention back to Race. Her mixed emotions about the young woman only seemed to enhance the ones trying to push through her barrier. Race fought sleep with constant yawns breaking through their steady conversation. One time, she even caught him resting propped up against the back wall, seconds away from a deep sleep. Things weren't looking too bright if Race really was expected to be the savior of the fleet, as everyone had secretly planned.

There was something else that she had noticed: the admiral had called Race a sergeant and not a corporal. Luckily, she currently shared a station with the communications officer.

"Excuse me," Illandra said, sliding next to the officer in charge of their station with a flirtatious smile. "What's your name?"

"Lieutenant Ramirez, ma'am," the officer replied as he looked up to meet her gaze.

"Do you know that Marine over there?" She pointed to Race, who was mimicking some ships with his hands.

"Sergeant Allard?" the communications officer said. "I've heard of him."

"Wasn't he a corporal just an hour ago?" Illandra asked, thinking back to when they'd first boarded the vessel.

"Yes," the office stated, starting to share some of Illandra's confusion, "I believe he was."

"How does someone gain a rank so quickly?" Illandra asked.

"There are a couple of different ways," the comms officer replied. "I could check the ship's logs if you like?"

"That would be great." Illandra smiled at the young man.

Illandra could feel Anthony's smile as he overheard her

prying conversation with the comms officer, even without seeing his face.

"Here it is," the comms officer said, pulling up the info on the inner panel. "It appears he challenged one of the STF security Marines."

"Challenged?" Illandra asked.

"It's an old practice, hardly ever used anymore," the officer stated. "Basically, a way of handling a disagreement between two soldiers. If the junior soldier wins, he gains a rank; the loser gets demoted."

"So if Race would have lost..." gasped Illandra, turning to look at Race.

"He'd be a lance corporal again," the officer confirmed. "That might have even cost him his position at SORD."

"Isn't that a little risky, then?" Illandra questioned, still almost in shock at the possible risk he'd faced.

"You know the lad better than any," interrupted Anthony, making a silent implication of Race's secret skills. There was also a hint of her mentor's involvement in the event.

Illandra turned her gaze to Race only to discover that he was looking curiously at her, a tinge of jealousy in his eyes over her conversation with the communications officer. She gave him a quick wink to spring him back to life, and he went back to planning out scenarios on his terminal, slightly embarrassed to be caught staring.

The rest of the trip was slow. Illandra grew anxious waiting to put the experience behind her. There wasn't much for them to do but wait as the ship flew through subspace, and Illandra could feel the nervousness that was currently occupying most of the crew members' emotions. After roughly an hour of travel, the small fleet reached its destination. All six ships fell out of the slipstream and took up a formation in preparation against the oncoming assault.

"How much longer until they exit the nebula?" asked the ship's admiral.

"It's hard to be certain with all the interference, sir," reported the science officer. "I'd guess another twenty minutes."

"All right," the admiral said, straightening his posture. "Red alert. Everyone to their stations. Lieutenant Ramirez, open a channel between the other ships and have them set to broadcast it to all crew."

Illandra slid back over to give the communications officer his space as he sprang to action, pressing several buttons on the terminal in front of him. "You're live, sir."

"Thank you," the admiral said. He cleared his throat as he prepared to address his fleet. "This is Admiral Montana of the United Republic Ship Puller addressing the fine men and women serving in this fleet. As you all know, we are about to meet up with three unknown vessels coming through the nebula border between the Imperial Consortium and the United Republic. No one is really sure what they want or why they're here, but I do know one thing. I would hate to be in their shoes when they come out of that nebula and seeing a bunch of warships sitting here waiting for them!"

There was a faint cheer as the admiral's speech sent a small rush of confidence through the fleet. Illandra was happy to finally have some positive emotions to latch onto. She was even able to let down her barrier a little bit and take some of it in.

"I don't know what the next few moments might hold," continued the admiral, "but I know that there will be lots of stories of how the crew of this fleet made the Consortium run back home, crying about how we broke their new, shiny ships. Now, I want you to take a look at your fellow crew members and know this: each of us is relying on you to do your job as much as you are on us, and I have no intention of letting any of you down. Let's stick together and show the Consortium what it means to come into Republic space without an invitation. Now then, if you'll excuse me, I need to inform someone that it's going to take more than three hyped-up ships if they want to move into this neighborhood."

The admiral signaled the communications officer to close the channel, but the noise of the crew's cheering could clearly be heard from about the ship. Illandra was able to completely drop her shield and swim in the confidence that the admiral had instilled into his men. She was even able to use some of the training that her mentor had instilled in her to amplify the emotion, making the crew's resolve that much sturdier.

The admiral swiveled over to the science officer to look at the readings. "How's it looking, Lieutenant?"

"I'm getting a good read on two of the ships, sir," she responded. "The third one seems to be keeping far enough back to keep hidden in the nebula."

"Ramirez," the admiral directed to the communications

officer, "can you open a channel to them?"

"One second, sir," replied the lieutenant as he hit a couple of buttons on the panel in front of him. "It appears they're receiving the signal, but I'm not getting anything back."

"Ambassador," the admiral said as he turned to the two guests, "I believe this is your area of expertise?"

"Let's hope so," Anthony said as he got up from his chair and stepped to the center of the bridge.

"Lieutenant, patch us through," commanded the ship's admiral.

The lieutenant hit a button on the panel and signaled the ambassador when his connection was complete.

"This is Ambassador Martin on behalf of the United Galactic Republic addressing the approaching fleet. You are about to trespass on Republic territory. In accordance with the Tri-Galactic Border Act, please identify the purpose of your presence here, or you will be met with the proper force."

There was a long moment of silence while the bridge waited for a response. The ship's admiral exchanged a couple of hand signals with the communications officer to verify the signal was being received.

"We suspect that you might be working under the terrorist group named the Cenari. It's currently unknown why you have such hostility against the United Republic, but your encroachment into our territory will not be tolerated. The Republic has done nothing to infringe upon your rights or the rights of the Consortium."

Suddenly, an image came on the screen, the image of a man sitting on the bridge of a ship. "You lie!" yelled the man.

"We know what secrets you hide, and we are here to expose them! We come for your allies, and nothing will stand in our way. The Cenari have returned."

Illandra was flooded with several contradictory emotions as she looked upon the Consortium ship's captain. It was hard to tell from the image, but she could tell that the man was much larger than average, his muscles almost disproportional in several areas, and she could see the faint hint of pieces of small metallic patches of what she could only describe as scales covering portions of his face.

"If you have proof that we've violated any law or treaty, this dispute can be handled peacefully in a Tri-Galactic court," pleaded Anthony, but the transmission was cut off before he could finish.

The room grew quiet as everyone accepted the fate of the unpreventable encounter. This ship's admiral stepped up and put his arm on the ambassador's shoulder. "You did your best, Anthony. They obviously didn't come here to talk."

"I know," sighed the elder man. "I just wish I knew what they were talking about."

"Sir," interrupted the science officer, "they're powering up their weapons."

"Activating defensive maneuvers," stated the tactical officer next to Race.

"My turn," stated the admiral as he took command of the bridge from his chair. "Have a couple Stingers break off and flank the first ship. Let's see what they're made of."

"I don't think that's such a good idea, sir," Race objected.

"Just do it," the admiral ordered, disregarding Race's objection.

"Yes, sir," the tactical officer said, cutting off Race before he could object again.

Illandra could feel Race's frustration as he returned to the console, trying not to be insubordinate to the admiral. The look in his eyes showed how his mind was already starting to redraw the battle plan he had drawn out.

Three of the ships broke away from the small fleet and attempted to approach the giant ships from the side. The crew watched as the weapons bombarded the side of the closest ship. When the dust had cleared, there was barely more than a scratch left on the intruding ship's hull. As the ships turned to set up another attack, a large beam shot forth from one of the aggressing ships, blowing right through a Republic Stinger. The Stinger shook as it started to lose control. Before it could do anything to stabilize itself, another shot from the second Consortium ship bore down on it, causing it to light up the sky with a giant explosion.

The remaining Republic ships tried to move in to give their fleeing comrades a chance to escape, firing everything they had at the massive intruders. Another shot from the Consortium ships ripped apart one of the covering ships, the explosion shaking the bridge of the *Puller* like a small earthquake.

With each ship's destruction, Illandra felt a large sting hit her mental shield. She could tell that even her mentor was feeling the emotional backlash of agony from the mass death caused by each ship's destruction.

"We just started this fight, and we're already down two

ships and haven't done anything to them!" yelled the admiral as he approached the tactical post. "I need options!"

"Sir, we need to concentrate all of our fire at one spot," exclaimed Race almost coldly. "We're not doing enough damage on our own."

"But where?" asked the tactical officer beside him.

"Here," stated Race as he pointed at the monitor in front of him. "Have everyone follow these commands. I'll keep relaying orders over the comms."

Illandra could sense the emotional struggle Race was fighting, trying to distract himself from the death of the fellow troops by focusing on the battle. He was doing too good of a job at it. It poked a memory of something Illandra had once heard her mentor say: *"Emotions are just a part of an equation for them."*

The admiral was silent as he contemplated leaving the entire defense of his fleet in the hands of an unproven sergeant.

"If you'd listened to him in the first place, you'd probably still have all of your ships," interrupted Anthony, pressing the admiral for a decision.

The admiral was visibly upset with the ambassador's comment, but knowing the sergeant's abilities, he had to concede the truth of Anthony's insult.

"Do it," he said, submitting. "Relay all tactics through Sergeant Allard," he commanded.

"Are you crazy?" yelled the ship's pilot. "There's no way this ship is capable of pulling that off!"

"If you can't, get out of the way so I can," Annette yelled

as she locked out the main pilot's navigation system.

"Are you mad!" the confused pilot screamed once again. "You'll tear the ship apart if you disable those!"

"I'm only going to do this once. Any more and we'd have a problem," assured Annette. "Ready when you are!"

"All the other ships are ready to perform the maneuver," stated the tactical officer.

"Do it!" yelled the admiral. "Just don't get us killed," he said almost threateningly to Race.

One of the Stingers led the attack, dodging the incoming fire as Race continued to feed them command after command through the shared channel. The lead Imperial ship started to change course to intercept the Stinger. The second Consortium ship fired at the three Republic ships as they broke formation to let the deadly beam fire harmlessly between them. Using the course of their momentum, they used their navigational thrusters to rotate, giving them a clear shot at the leading Consortium ship's underbelly. The Consortium ship attempted to fire one more time at the decoy ship, but the damage taken to its hull from the joint assault caused the blast to backfire and tear inward through the Consortium ship itself.

Several members of the crew cheered at the ship's self-caused explosion, renewing their faith that they still had a fighting chance.

"Why do I feel like I'm going to be sick?" the admiral demanded, holding on to his chair for dear life. "What's wrong with my dampeners?"

"What do you think? She disabled them," accused the

ship's pilot, still trying to regain access to the navigation console he'd been locked out of.

"I didn't disable them," corrected Annette, "I just had to reroute some of the power to some of the boosters for these maneuvers."

"Punch it!" yelled Race. "The other ship is about to fire!"

Annette pushed a lever toward the top of the panel and everyone was thrown back into their seats from the kick of the ship's engines thrusting the *Puller* forward as it narrowly avoided the incoming shot. Following Race's orders, still being systematically punched into the tactical panel as fast as his fingers could fly, the ships regrouped their formation behind the remaining attacker to avoid its deadly frontal weapons.

The Republic ships joined in on firing together at the back of the remaining communist ship, avoiding a few torpedoes that were thrown from its rather poor rear defenses. The crew was about to break into another round of applause when an energy beam fired from behind them. The blast almost completely disintegrated the rear of the Republic battleship, causing it to spin out of control.

"Where did that come from?" asked the admiral of the *Puller*, jumping over to his tactical officer's station.

"The last ship has just left the nebula, sir," answered the officer. "The Patton's engines are out, they're going to crash."

"Tell them to get out of there!" yelled the admiral.

"They can't, sir!"

"How did I not see that?" questioned Race, reviewing his screens.

"Now's not the time, Marine," the admiral said, shaking Race out of his shocked state. "We got one more ship to dispose of before they take the rest of this fleet out."

Race looked across the panel into the admiral's eyes before giving him a quick nod and returning to assigning orders. "Yes, sir."

The other ships completed their maneuvers as they fanned out from the disabled Consortium ship. The damaged battlecruiser used what little steering it had to ram itself directly into the back of the disabled Consortium ship, destroying both of them in a blinding explosion that sent several of the ships shaking.

Another wave of pain and suffering rippled throughout Illandra, who was barely keeping herself together as it was. She could feel the blood draining from her face as it turned pale. She tried to wipe the sweat off of her clammy hand and focus on her breathing.

"I hope you got something else planned for this last one, Sergeant Allard," commented the admiral, retaking the center of the bridge.

"The ship can't take much more of this," added Annette. "The extra power to the thrusters is going to burn 'em out, assuming we don't rip the ship apart."

"You think you can handle one more crazy maneuver?" asked Race, setting up another sequence in his terminal.

"I'll do what I can," replied Annette.

"There you go," Race said as he finished pushing the buttons on his panel.

"That's the craziest thing I've ever seen," stated the ship's pilot, still trying to regain control of his unit Annette had locked him out of.

"That's why they'll never expect it," Annette said, setting up the maneuvers. "If you think that's crazy, you should have seen what he came up with on Juniper 7."

The three ships turned about to face their last adversary. As they bore down on the ship, they executed Race's desperate maneuver, which had all the ships spinning around in a giant circle as if they were circling the drain toward the Consortium ship. The ships sometimes passed within meters of each other, triggering proximity alerts as they dodged incoming fire and approached their target. When their target was available, each ship focused its attack on the sector of the Consortium ship that Race assumed controlled the power to the ship's main cannon.

The Consortium ship tried to fire at the remaining fleet. However, the slow recharge of the weapon gave the advancing force a slight advantage.

One shot grazed the remaining Stinger just enough to cripple it and take it out of the battle.

Another shot just missed the *Puller* and nailed the other battlecruiser sending it spinning.

The *Puller*, operating well outside its means, continued its assault on the remaining cruiser. Illandra watched as Annette struggled to pull off the last of the crazy maneuver, the control sticks fighting her every step of the way. They dodged one last blast as it almost signed the hull on their final approach. Everyone watched breathlessly. The last attack had been cast, everyone knew it would be the last one. All they could do was wait, their stomachs turning with anticipation.

The weapons of the giant monster started to glow as it charged to prepared to attack. Illandra fought to keep her eyes open as she knew there was no dodging this attack at their current range, as did the rest of the bridge. The pressure mounted as they waited for the fiery blaze to engulf them.

Suddenly, small explosions started to boil up under the surface of the giant ship, blasting away other portions of the intruding ship's hull.

"I'm losing it!" yelled Annette.

"Pull out!" hollered the ship's pilot that had finally managed to gain access to his terminal.

"Do it!" yelled Race. "That should be enough."

Illandra watched as the energy faded from the ship's main weapon and dissipated into the emptiness of space. "Sir, their weapons are offline," stated one of the bridge officers.

"Have the remaining ships open fire on that thing, give them everything we got," commanded the admiral. "I want that thing turned to rubble as soon as possible."

"There's a lot of interference with communication right now, sir," stated the communications officer. "But I'll see if I can get them to respond."

"Sergeant Keegan, mind turning us around so we can finish this thing?" asked the ship's admiral.

"Working on it, sir," answered Annette. "The controls are really sluggish."

After some maneuvering, the Puller was able to join the

other ships where they could continue to fire upon the last of the intruders. The Consortium's ship took a large bombardment from the three remaining ships, as it too was experiencing maneuvering difficulties. Even with the combined firepower of the three ships, the Consortium ship still managed to take a sizable beating from its oppressors.

"Damn, that thing's got a tough shell," commented the communications officer as he watched the abuse.

"Sir, they're getting ready to activate their dimensional drive!" yelled the tactical officer.

"They can't be going back through the nebula," commented the admiral. "It'd kill them at that condition. What's their destination?"

"I'm trying to figure that out, sir," answered the tactical. The color suddenly drained from his face. "Oh, no!"

"Sir, they're heading for Taurus!" yelled Race.

"Hit them with everything we've got!" yelled the admiral. "Sergeant, can you move to intercept?"

"I'm sorry, sir," answered Annette. "I don't think she's got it in her."

"What about the other ships?" asked the admiral. "Can either one of them block her?"

"No, sir," commented the ship's communications officer. "They're reporting several systems offline on the Washington, and I can't even get a signal from the Jackson."

"Sir," alerted the science officer, "they're jumping."

The crew all turned to look at the holodisplay just in time to see the intruding ship slip away from the battlefield.

"Contact Taurus!" demanded the admiral as he charged

the communications station. "Warn them!"

"I'm trying, sir," said the communications officer, "but I can't get through. There's a large amount of interference; I don't know where it's coming from. I can't get a clear signal."

"Patch me through to engineering," directed the admiral. The communications officer flipped a few switches and signaled to the admiral that the connection had been made.

"This is Commander Trent," said the voice of a man over the intercom. "Go ahead, sir."

"Commander, I need this hunk of bolts to move as fast as you can. How long before the engines are back up?"

"Not long, sir," replied the man over the intercom. "The damage was quite minimal, it just blew out several circuits. We're replacing them now. We should be good to go in about twenty minutes. I never knew this ship could handle those turns; what the hell was Ericson doing?"

"It wasn't Ericson, Commander, we had a substitute pilot sitting in," stated the admiral. "You've got ten minutes. Millions of people are counting on us."

"We're on it, Admiral," answered the man from over the intercom.

The intercom cut off as the conversation was brought to a close. The admiral paced around for a bit trying to figure out his next move. After a couple of minutes, he went over to a science station to try and keep himself occupied while he waited for the repairs to finish.

"Commander," he said as he approached the main sensor station on the bridge. "What can you tell me about the radiation interfering with our communications? Can we alter our signal to get through?"

"I'm not sure, sir," answered the science officer. "I've never seen anything like this before. I think it's from whatever power source the Consortium were using."

"Are we in any danger?" asked the ship's admiral.

"The hull should protect us from most of the radiation," replied the science officer, "although I can't be completely sure. I don't think I'd want to stay here any longer than I have to."

"What about the remaining ships?"

"The radiation is interfering with most of our sensors, but from what I can tell both ships are in need of some repairs before they're operational again. I'm detecting several life signs on both ships, so I'm sure they are working on it."

"Good." The admiral sighed with relief. "Keep me posted." He then went back over to the communications station. "How long since we talked to Commander Trent?"

"About five minutes, sir," replied the communications officer.

"Put him on," directed the admiral. The communications officer hit a couple more buttons on his panel and signaled the admiral that his connection was active. "Commander Trent, your five minutes are up."

Under better circumstances, Illandra would have found the quick changes to the timetable amusing, but it was taking a lot of her energy just to keep her legs from falling out from under her.

"Yes, sir," replied the engineer's voice from over the intercom. "We've bypassed a couple of the circuits. We're replacing the last necessary one right now." He made a few grunting noises as a loud clunk came over the channel. "There you go, sir. She should be good to go."

"Lieutenant?" the admiral asked the ship's pilot.

The pilot played with the controls on the panel in front of him as the ship started to respond. "Still kind of sluggish but we're good enough to go, sir."

"Sir," interrupted the voice of the ship's engineer over the intercom, "I took the liberty of starting a diagnostic. I'm reading several micro-fractures in the ship's hull. We're going to have to block off some of the more severe areas. The ship is flyable, but I recommend getting her to a service station within the next couple of days."

"Noted, Commander," the admiral stated. "Get some men started on evacuating those sections and patching up what we can. I'm going to need you up here for a full assessment as soon as you can make it."

"Yes, sir," the engineer said as the connection was cut.

"Send out a message to Washington and Jackson, let them know that we're going to attempt to pursue the last ship before they reach the Taurus," directed the admiral to the communications officer. "Have them meet up with us as soon as they can. We'll send aid as soon as we're able."

"Acknowledged, sir," the comms officer said.

"Ericson," ordered the admiral as he headed back to his command chair, "get us on the tail of that ship as fast as you can."

"Yes, sir," acknowledged the pilot as he started to lay in the course.

"Commander, let us know when we're far enough away to put out a decent signal to warn the Taurus."

Soon, the ship was turned around and flying through subspace, desperately trying to reach its destination in time. After several minutes of dead silence on the bridge, the communications officer reported that he had finally gotten through to the Taurus. The admiral immediately had the communications officer open a channel.

"This is Admiral Montana of the United Republic Ship Puller with an emergency message for the Taurus space station."

An image of Admiral Casten of the Taurus appeared on the bridge's display. "Admiral, we were beginning to think the worst. We lost all sensor readings from the battle zone, and we're tracking a battlecruiser heading this way. We thought it might have gotten through all of you."

"We had some pretty spectacular help from the SORD unit you loaned us. We sustained some heavy losses; only the Washington and Jackson are left. They're both severely damaged. If you could relay a message to Command to get them some assistance, I'm sure they'd appreciate it."

"We've already got some on the way," replied the Taurus's admiral as he signaled one of his men to relay the message. "What can you tell me about this ship coming our way?"

"We were able to disable its weapon systems before they ran, but their hull is still pretty resistant. I have no idea what they're planning, but they have to be desperate. Be ready for anything."

"Thanks for the information, Admiral," Admiral Casten

said before he was interrupted by one of his crew. "What do you mean they're almost here? Admiral Montana, I'm going to have to let you go."

"Good luck, Admiral," Admiral Montana wished him as the signal was closed. "Lieutenant, are we within sensor range?"

"No, sir, but I should be able to link into the Taurus and display it onscreen," answered the science officer as she played with his controls to change the display to show the Taurus space station and the last of the communist ships closing the distance.

Even from the small image on the screen, it was easy to make out pieces of debris falling from the ship as its incredible speed took its toll on an already damaged ship.

As the ship approached the space stations, several of the crew's expressions changed to show their confusion. "Why aren't they slowing down?" asked the comms officer, expressing what everyone was thinking.

"They're going kamikaze!" cried Race from his station. He quickly used his terminal to open up a channel to the Taurus. "They're going to ram you; activate the emergency separation procedure."

The bridge watched helplessly as the Taurus fired every weapon it had trying to defend against the colossal. It appeared that Race's message had gotten through, as several sections of the ship flew off, attempting to avoid the large-scale disaster.

The main prize for the Consortium ship was lost, but it wasn't going to be completely defeated. The ship changed course to focus in on the largest piece of the border station, and within seconds, it collided forcefully with the section. The explosion cut the feed, preventing them from knowing how much damage really had been done by the explosion.

While the others could just stand and look on in total disbelief, the effect it had on Anthony and Illandra was a different matter. Anthony fell over as he grabbed onto a nearby rail to prevent him from completely hitting the floor.

Illandra was not as lucky. Her psychic wall meant to protect her was ripped to shreds as what seemed like thousands of tiny needles burrowed into every part of her brain at once, lighting it into an inferno of pain.

She grabbed her head and cried out with a blood-curdling scream before her whole body went limp and she fell to the floor as she faded from consciousness.

* * *

Race had known something was wrong with Illandra for a while, his senses fighting each other as they tried to alert him to both dangers at the same time. He had been forced to devote his attention to the battle, as it was the more prevalent threat at the time, but now that all the ships were destroyed his attention quickly turned to Illandra.

Illandra's scream had shaken most of the numbness from the crew as a couple of them rushed to her aid. Race was already in action, rushing to Illandra even before the banshee screams. Jumping over his terminal, he reached her just in time to catch her before her lifeless body hit the floor.

"What happened?" Race asked Anthony, somehow

knowing the issue was urgent and he would know where to turn.

"Something very bad," answered Anthony. "We need to get her to the infirmary, now." His eyes pleaded for the admiral's assistance.

"Sergeant Allard, Lieutenant Jefferies," commanded the admiral, "get them to the infirmary and report back here when you're done."

Race picked Illandra off the floor and carried her to the transport pod, the assigned crewman shortly behind him helping the ambassador to the lift.

"Alert the infirmary that they have two emergency patients coming their way," they heard the admiral order as the doors closed behind them.

The doors opened and the group found themselves in a crowded hallway. Race pushed his way past the line of people, letting them know he had a medical emergency. One of the medics was already attempting to have the crew clear a passage for Race and his patients. They entered the medical room to see several of the medical staff treating crewmen suffering from decompression sickness.

One of the medical personnel approached Race as he was walking in. "Is this the one from the bridge?"

"Yes," answered Race shortly, trying to find a place to put Illandra down.

"Lass, this girl needs your top neurological physician, preferably your chief of medicine if they're available," Anthony begged the nurse.

The nurse looked at the ambassador for a brief second,

realizing who stood before her. "I'll get her right away." She hurried off to pull her boss from one of the crewmen she was tending to. The chief medical officer was distinguished by a long medical jacket. She grabbed some supplies before approaching the group.

"What seems to be the problem?" she asked as she opened up her medical kit and took some of the devices out, setting them to Illandra's forehead.

"One minute, she was standing there," Race started to explain, "then she just started screaming and grabbing her head."

There was a pause as the medical officer waited for a reading from her gear. "She's got massive hemorrhaging in her frontal lobe. We have got to get her into surgery immediately."

The medical officer led them to a small room in the back, where she directed Race to set Illandra down on a medical table in the center of the room. The medical officer called the nearby nurses into the room to help with the procedure.

When they entered the room, the ambassador had his escort move him toward a communication panel on the wall while the medical officer used Race to help attach some monitors to her patient. After he pressed a few sections on the panel, an image of an elder man appeared on the screen. "Hello, Anthony, how are things going?"

"Not so good, I'm afraid," responded the ambassador. "I think we have a Spertanian class incident."

"Oh, no," said the man on the holograph, who was now suddenly hitting several buttons on his panel. "I'm patching into that medical station right now. Are you okay?"

"I can wait," answered the ambassador. "It's the other one that needs help right now. She's being prepped for surgery."

"Is that her behind you?" asked the image.

"Yes," answered the ambassador.

The image of the man suddenly disappeared as a full-figure hologram of the elder man appeared next to Race and the chief medical officer.

"You must be the chief medical officer," the hologram stated. "My name is…"

"Professor Simon McLain," the medical officer cut him off, trying to save him time. "Personal physician and medical advisor to the president, among others. If you'll excuse me, I'm about to perform surgery."

"Of course, I'm here to help you," the holographic professor stated. "I just need to fill you in on some important details regarding your patient. May I ask what clearance you have there, Commander?"

"Level 3," she answered, not letting the questions stop her from her preparations.

"Well, we'll have to change that," said the image as his hands started moving in front of him like he was hitting an imaginary panel. Suddenly the biosensor on the medical officer's forearm activated, displaying a message that the security level of the chief had been increased to level 1. "There you go. I'm guessing you were about to give her a neuro-stimulant to keep her brain activity functioning while you relieve the pressure?"

"Of course," answered the chief medical officer.

"Very good," congratulated the holographic man. "I'm going to send the formula for some added stimulants to one of your synthesizers. I need you to mix in about 20ccs of it for the girl. Give a dose for the ambassador, as well. While you're preparing that, I'll fill you in on the details. I'm going to need everyone else that doesn't have a level-1 security clearance to leave the room."

The biosensors on Race's and the lieutenant's arms started to flash, stating that they were in a restricted area and needed to leave. They finished doing what they could until they were forced to leave the room before their sensory units initiated countermeasures. The doors closed behind them, leaving Race to desperately wonder what would become of Illandra.

Race made a fist and pounded on the wall beside him in frustration, leaving a huge dent in the metallic structure when he pulled his hand back. The warning message on his biosensor was replaced by an image of Bella. "I know this probably isn't a good time, but I have some interesting information I gathered from the ship's computer."

Race stood back up and rubbed his face as he tried to regain focus, the strain from the lack of sleep almost too much to bear. "What do you have?"

"It seems that shortly before the cruiser crashed into Taurus, it sent out two signals. One was directed toward deep space, just outside the United Republic territory. It seems to be unencrypted, but I cannot find a language to compare it to for translations. The second was directed toward Consortium space. I believe I've discovered the encryption algorithm, but it's the same garbage as the other message."

"What languages have you tried?" Race questioned.

"All modern languages," answered Bella.

"Link up with the ship's library," Race commanded. "See if you can find some extinct languages; maybe they're trying to use one as a cipher."

"Also, the ship has discovered a power source emanating from deep within the nebula. It started shortly after the Consortium's data transmission. Early speculation suggests that it was triggered by the transmission, but any indication of its purpose is hard to determine at this time."

"It might be another ship waiting to attack," Race said.

"Any assessment is pure speculation at this point," Bella reported. "It seems to be coming from the thickest part of the nebula. All sensor readings are unable to read anything in that area."

"Except for the power source?" Race asked.

"Correct," the AI confirmed.

"We'd better get back to the bridge," suggested the lieutenant.

"Good idea," replied Race as the two headed back to the lift.

Chapter 7

THE SHΛDOWS

Record Date: 349.165 PGST

Race exited the lift with the lieutenant and the officer currently manning the bridge instantly redirected them to the conference area, where the rest of the senior staff were already discussing their status.

Admiral Montana, who had been leading the briefing, noticed the two joining them.

"Ah, Sergeant Allard, Lieutenant Jefferies, welcome back," the admiral interrupted the meeting. "To fill you in…"

"The sergeant was tapped into the ship's systems, sir," the lieutenant cut him off, attempting to save time. "We already know about the transmissions and the suspicious reading from the center of the nebula."

The admiral looked at Race with a questioning expression, trying to figure out how he'd compromised his ship's systems. "Experimental AI," Race answered, waving his arm with the attached sensor unit in the air.

"Very well," the admiral said, not entirely satisfied with Race's answer. "We are unsure what it is exactly in the nebula, but given the attempted incursion, we can only assume that whatever it is could be part of their backup plan."

"If this is a weapon, we can't just simply ignore it. Captain Jenson." The admiral turned to Race's CO. "I'm sending your team to investigate. We'll be loaning you some of our soldiers from the STF unit to help you out."

"I hear Staff Sergeant Amyas has been working with them," the captain said.

The admiral nodded his acknowledgment.

"I'd like him to pick out some of the more capable ones so we don't get bogged down."

"Very well," the admiral agreed. "The rest of us are going to make a stop by Taurus and help with whatever we can. After that, we're heading back to the battlefield to help with repairs until the reinforcements can get here."

"You've got about ten minutes before we reach your departure point. Any questions?"

One of the men in the back raised his hand.

"Go ahead, Ensign."

"How long before any reinforcements arrive, sir?" the junior officer asked.

"There were a number of ships deployed when the enemy ships were first detected. The ships that accompanied us were the only ones that could make it in time. You can expect the first of the reinforcements to be here within the next half hour."

Several people in the room let out a sigh of relief.

"Anyone else?" asked the admiral. There was a pause as the admiral gave the crew one last chance to speak up. "All right. Sergeant Allard, Sergeant Keegan, I need to have a word with you before you depart. The rest of you are dismissed."

Race sighed as he once again had to work his way through the flood of people trying to exit the room. Race's captain also stayed behind to ensure his Marines were being treated properly. When they were finally alone, the admiral addressed the two. "How are the ambassador and his assistant?"

"Illandra was taken into surgery; I believe the chief said something about brain hemorrhaging. I fear the same thing has happened to the ambassador, but he's insisting that they focus on her. He even called in a specialist to assist your chief medical officer."

"I'm sorry to hear that," commented the ship's admiral, possibly fearing the added stress to Race's circumstances might be more than he could handle. "Are you going to be okay to complete this mission?"

"Yes, sir," answered Race confidently.

"Good to hear, Marine," the admiral thanked him. "I have something to discuss with you two. I must admit that I am very unsatisfied with the damage the two of you have caused to my ship. It's going to take days for engineering to repair everything. I was actually considering having the both of you brought up on charges. There's no way you could have known what your actions would have done."

Race and Annette looked at each other, confused, as the admiral calmly rambled at them.

"Unfortunately, after reviewing the logs from the battle, both by myself and several others, those hairpin-turn maneuvers were about the only thing that kept us from ending up as rubble, like some of the other ships. You know what the joint chiefs are saying?"

"Uh," Annette mustered up the courage to answer, "no, sir."

"They say that we should give you some sort of medal for destroying the fleet and saving the lives of everyone on this ship. Hell, they're even talking about giving you both promotions. You know what I have to say about that?"

"No, sir." Race spoke up this time, attempting to take his share of the blame and not leave all the responsibility on Annette.

"I say…" What little anger he was playing with suddenly drained from his face and a sincere smile appeared. "Congratulations, Staff Sergeants. It should be official by the time you two get back. Without the two of you, none of us would probably be here now. Thank you." The admiral gave them both a pat on their shoulders as a show of his appreciation.

"Just promise me one thing, Staff Sergeant Keegan," the admiral asked, concluding their moment.

"What is that, sir?" Annette asked.

"You'll never jump behind the helm of this ship again," laughed the admiral. "I don't think I could take any more of your driving."

The laughter helped shake the last bit of nervousness from the room. Race wished they had time to enjoy it. The team was quickly dismissed and they had already wasted precious time before they needed to leave . Most of the senior crew was outside the office waiting to also thank Race and Annette for their efforts. Race and Annette split up as they returned to their temporary quarters. The battle had given the room a good shake, knocking over several of the decorations. Luckily, there hadn't been any time for them to unpack anything, so all of his belongings were still safely packed away, also making it pretty easy for him to quickly gather up all his things before heading to the shuttle-launching pad. He looked back longingly at the bed, realizing how long it had been since he had actually slept before the door closed upon him.

Race met back up with Annette at the lift as they headed to the launch bay. When they arrived, the rest of their squad was already hard at work, finalizing their preparations for takeoff.

"She's not much for weapons, Captain," the ship's admiral briefed Race's CO as he and Annette walked by, "but she's our heaviest armored transport, which will serve you better in the nebula. I've had our chief engineer attach a relay dispersing system. It's set to launch a probe every so often automatically; you shouldn't have to do anything. With all the interference around here and inside the nebula, it should allow us to stay in contact."

"Good thinking, sir," the captain replied. "We'd better be off; you have a mission of your own to get to and right now, every second counts."

The two officers saluted each other as they went on to complete their duties.

Race continued to follow Annette as she met up with Konway and the deck officer going over the shuttle's information before handing over to the unit.

"What do we have here?" Annette said, handing her bags off to Race as she took the datapad out of Konway's hands and began scrolling over the shuttle's history.

"Everything seems all right," Konway assured her.

"I'll be the judge of that," Annette dismissed him, continuing to read the information. "I see you replaced the port stabilizer recently. This model can be very picky about the compatibility."

"Yes, ma'am," answered the deck officer. "We actually had to wait a while for a decent part, but we got it in and the new one's been functioning fine for over a month now."

"Good," Annette said, still concentrating on the documents. "Been a while since its last service; we should check the core fuser before taking off."

"Jeffries," the deck officer yelled at one of the soldiers running around.

"Yes, sir?" the soldier said, approaching the officer.

"Pull the core fuser real quick and bring it here," the officer commanded.

"Yes, sir," the soldier responded, rushing off to complete the order.

"Everything else seems okay," Annette said, handing the datapad back to the deck officer.

"Who will be the main pilot?" the deck officer asked.

"I will," Annette said as Konway and Race pointed at her, knowing better than to argue with the team's vehicle specialist.

"Thumb here, please," the deck officer requested, turning the top of the pad toward her. Annette placed the thumb of her right hand in the red square designated for her to take control of the ship.

As they concluded the procedure, the soldier returned carrying a long device with a spotted glowing core. "It's not too bad, sir," the soldier reported, "but if they get stuck out there for too long, it might give them a problem."

"Why don't you issue us a new one just in case," Annette suggested. "If something happens, it's pretty likely that they're not going to send anyone for us, seeing as we're already in violation of the Treaty."

The deck officer paused for a second as he considered Annette's request. "I don't think the Treaty matters much right now, but it's probably better to be safe than sorry," the deck officer admitted. "Get 'em a new one, Jeffries. Double-time it."

"Yes, sir," the soldier acknowledged before darting off once again.

"I'll see you guys on the ship," Konway said as Annette took one last look around the hull of the ship.

"We'll be right there," Annette responded, climbing the ladder up onto the ship's nose to inspect the windows.

Race could hear someone coming up behind him. He turned to see the ship's main pilot approaching them, trying to keep his temper from getting the best of him.

Race signaled Annette to the pilot's approach. Annette rolled her eyes before coming down from the ship to stand next to him.

"You know what?" he steamed, approaching the two.

"You may have everyone else fooled, Sergeants, but you're not fooling me. You put the lives of everyone on this ship at risk with your crazy antics."

Annette looked up at Race, clearing seeking his input on how he wanted to handle the situation. Race could already tell that she was ready to punch the young officer in the face, and he wasn't sure how wise it was for him to get in her way. He lifted his arms and took a step back, giving her permission to handle the situation as she saw fit.

Annette's eyes glimmered as she got ready to tear into the naive pilot. "First off, if you would pull your head out of your ass, you'd realize that all of our lives were already in danger by being hit by one of those blasts, especially with your second-rate driving. Second, everything I changed I still kept within an acceptable tolerance. If you were a little more familiar with your ship, you probably would have noticed that. Don't get upset with me because I know how to operate your ship better than you do. Maybe you'd know better if you read through the Emergency Protocols, Subsection B2 of Operations Manual 773A. Now then, if you'll excuse me, I have a mysterious signal that's probably going to try and kill us all unless I go and stop it." Annette then turned and walked away, leaving the pilot dumbfounded.

"So how long do you think before he realizes there's no subsection B2?" Race asked as the two entered the back of the shuttle.

"Probably about the same time he realizes there's no Operations Manual 773A," Annette answered.

The two quickly made their way to the crew quarters

and put their belongings in the double-wide lockers, securing them with their thumbs on the biometric locks to claim them as their own. They then made their way to the front of the ship, where Annette kicked Zain out of the pilot seat.

"Just keeping it warm for you," Zain said, getting out of the way.

"Sure," Annette replied sarcastically.

"Hey, good job back there," Zain said, congratulating Race and giving him a quick pat on the bicep.

"Thanks," Race said, perching behind Annette as he watched her take control of the shuttle's systems. He always admired how at home she was behind any vehicle's steering wheel.

"Afternoon, Marines," the captain said as he walked between Zain and Race and took a seat in the co-pilot's chair.

"Afternoon, sir," the Marines said in unison, attempting their best to salute him in the tight quarters.

"Nothing crazy this time, Sergeant Keegan," the captain said, preparing his station.

"Not at all, sir," Annette acknowledged, trying to hide a faint smile. "We ready to go?"

The captain pressed a couple of buttons on the panel next to him. "All Marines present and accounted for," he confirmed. "Securing the hatch, initiating pre-flight checks."

"Command," Annette said after pressing a button on the console in front of her, "this is shuttle F476; we're completing our pre-flight checks. Please advise which launching panel is ours to use."

"F476," a voice came over the radio, "you've been cleared

for takeoff on runway four. Proceed when you are ready."

"Roger that, Command," Annette said, closing the channel. A yellow stripe overlaid itself on the window, advising them of the path they were to follow.

"Everything looks good," the captain told Annette. A noise came out of the console as one of the buttons lit up. The captain pressed it, which caused an image of the admiral to appear on the window screen. "Yes, sir?"

"Marines," Admiral Montana greeted the troops. "I'm sure you're all well aware of the risk, but I just wanted to wish you all the best of luck on your mission. Because of the unknown nature of this threat, I am clearing all of you for level-2 weapons use."

The biosensors wrapped around the arms of the Marines lit up as they acknowledged the admiral's command.

"We'll be doing our best to monitor you," the admiral continued. "The incoming reinforcements have been instructed to do the same in case we are unavailable. We're going to be deploying a couple more relay beacons along our path to hopefully boost our signals as well."

"Thank you, sir," the captain said.

"Good luck, Marines," the admiral wished them one last time before cutting the signal.

"I'm taking her out," Annette informed everyone as she grabbed a couple of the levers on the panel and the ship started to lift off of the ground. The shuttle followed the overlaid directions on the window across the bay until it reached the launch shoot.

"Command." Annette once again used the communications system. "This is shuttle Foxtrot Alpha 476. We're in position and ready for launch."

"Initiating gravity ramp accelerator," a voice said over the system. "You're good to go in five, four, three... Godspeed, Marines."

The ship launched forward, the long tube-like structure blurring past them as they accelerated out of the hatch at lightning-fast speed. Luckily, the shuttle's dampeners kept them from feeling the sudden change in speed.

The shuttle sped off, leaving the Puller in its trail. No sooner were they out of the ship than they saw it engage its transdimensional drive and abandon them to the emptiness of space.

"Setting course," Annette said, punching buttons on her console.

"Estimated time?" the captain asked.

"Hard to tell, sir," Annette answered. "The nebula is going to wreak havoc on our sensors; we'll have to slow it down to keep it safe. I'd say at least six hours, probably closer to seven or eight."

The very thought of having to stay awake for another six or seven hours made Race yawn. He tried to hide it by putting his head down behind the chair.

"The juice starting to wear off?" Zain asked, catching him.

"About an hour ago," Race said.

"What's the matter, Corporal?" the captain said. "My bad, it's Staff Sergeant Allard now, isn't it? Congratulations, Marine."

"Thank you, sir," Race answered. "I didn't sleep well last night. I was really anxious about my presentation today."

"Oh, that's right," the captain remembered. "It turned out to be an even bigger day for you than you expected, didn't it?"

"Yes, it did, sir," Race acknowledged.

"We shouldn't need you for any of this, Sergeant," the captain observed. "Why don't you make use of one of those bunks. We're going to need you in top shape for this when we get there. Staff Sergeant Amyas, why don't you get some of the other Marines and get a handle on our supply status just in case we're stuck out here longer than expected. See if you can whip up something for lunch, too."

"Yes, sir," Zain said as he and Race turned to leave the cockpit.

They went down the hall and each went their own direction. Race made his way back to the crew quarters, where he pulled out one of the bunks. He quickly took off his blouse and boots and lay down. Race didn't even remember his head hitting the pillow before he was asleep.

*　　*　　*

Race was unaware of how much time had passed when the door to the sleeping quarters opened and woke him up. He opened his eyes to see Annette standing there with a tray in her hand.

"We're almost there," she said, approaching him. "I brought you some food, I figured you'd be hungry."

"Thanks," Race said, sitting up. He took the tray and set

it down to the side of his feet.

"How was your nap?" Annette asked, taking a seat next to him on the bunk.

"Much needed," Race said, trying to find his boots under his rack. "Did I miss anything important?"

"Just me," Annette answered.

Confused, Race turned to face Annette, only to find that she had removed her shirt and was now sitting next to him in just her undergarments. Before he could object, she was upon him, kissing him with more passion than he had ever felt before. He fought to resist her, but the touch of her body was too much for him.

He knew he was asking for trouble to attempt to pursue this, but as she quickly took off his shirt and he felt her body come into contact with his, he couldn't help but not care for the moment. He grabbed her and pulled her close as he returned her passion, running his hands up her back and through her fiery red hair.

Race was still fighting himself to enjoy the moment when Annette suddenly ripped herself away and walked to the other side of the room, her back to Race.

"What's the matter?" Race said, almost relieved by the break from his own inner turmoil.

"It's all wrong," Annette cried, trying to cover herself from embarrassment.

"It's all right." Race got up to comfort her. "Maybe we're just not ready for this. Let's just forget this all happened."

As he reached out to grab her bare shoulder, she spun around to face him, but what he was looking at was no longer his fellow Marine. Instead, he found himself face to face with a dark-blue-skinned creature. Its face was long and flat with a couple of tentacles hanging from its chin like a beard.

Race jumped back as he let out a curse startled by the creature.

"You must find me," the creature said through a mouth that was barely visible when closed. It started to pursue Race with an outstretched four-fingered hand. The being was covered in a gold armor from head to toe. Race stumbled back farther, trying to get away from the outstretched hand.

He fell back into his cot and the monster followed him down to grab him by the shoulders. "Only together can we end the plague," the creature said, shaking Race, its hand burning Race's skin.

Race let out a yell as he fought off the creature to get out of his cot to make a run for it.

Everything disappeared as he fell out of his rack. He looked around the empty room as he tried to piece together what had just happened to him.

The tray of food that Annette had brought was nowhere to be found. He tugged at his army-green shirt that had magically found itself back upon his chest. A blanket was draped over him, most likely placed there by one of his friends.

"Oh, thank god," Race said to an empty room. "It was all just a dream."

He sat up on his rack and started to rub his face, trying to get off both the sleepiness and the fright at the same time. He could still feel the clammy palms of the creature from his dream on his shoulders.

The door to the room opened to reveal Zain on the other side. "Oh good, you're up," he observed. "We're about an hour out. Cap wanted you up so you could start shaking out the cobwebs. We left you some food in the preserver, help yourself."

"Thanks," Race said, his hands still a little shaky.

"You all right?" Zain questioned, seeing Race was clearly in a state of disarray.

"Yeah," Race answered. "Just a really"—he struggled to find the right word to describe his dream—"weird dream."

"Was she hot?" Zain asked, obviously missing the whole concept.

Race was reminded of how good the dream had started as he felt the blood start to rush to his cheeks a bit.

"She was!" Zain exclaimed, reading Race's embarrassment. "I want to hear all about it," he said, checking both directions of the hallway for any of the other occupants, "but later. Cap's got me supervising the loaners." He slapped the side of the wall before pointing and winking at Race and taking off.

If nothing else, the conversation had dulled the fright out of Race. He quickly gathered himself and put on the rest of his uniform before sliding his bunk back into place so the automatic cleaner could do its job.

He helped himself to the food that had been set aside for him. As he wandered the halls of the ship, he couldn't shake the feeling that the creature from his dream was still haunting him. His imagination tricked him by occasionally making him believe it was hovering just outside his peripheral vision.

He decided to head up to the cockpit to try and distract himself from his nightmare creature. The cockpit door opened to reveal Annette and the captain still sitting in their same spots. He could barely see anything outside the ship's windows, the foglike nebula hindering his vision. Behind the captain, Konway had activated a sensor station to go over some of the readings. Race took the chair behind Annette and activated another console that elevated out of the floor in front of him.

"Glad you could join us, Marine," the captain said, looking over his shoulder to spot him. "How was your nap?"

"Much needed," Race answered, starting to scroll over the logs and catch up on what he had missed. "Thank you, sir. How long was I out?"

"About a solid eight hours, I think," Annette answered. "We had to slow down a lot more than anticipated. This interference keeps getting worse the closer we get to this damn thing. I'm not even sure how we were able to pick up the signal; it must be on a frequency that's not affected by all this."

"What are you working on over there, Staff Sergeant Reece?" Race asked Konway, making sure to use his proper title in front of the captain.

"Actually, just that," Konway answered. "I'm trying to get a better grasp on that signal to figure out how it's cutting through all this fog. Maybe we might be able to do something similar with our own systems."

"Actually, now that you're here, Staff Sergeant," the captain interrupted, "we could use some of your programming skills. Let me send you this log file we've been collecting. It's a combination of all the sensor data and flight adjustments we've had to make. I want you to write a navigation program to get us out of here in a hurry in case something goes wrong."

"I'll get right on it, sir," Race acknowledged as he wiped the food off of his hands to take up the console.

When coming on board, Bella had already interfaced with the ship's systems and was already copying over his preferences and program libraries to the terminal he had just activated in front of him. She had even gone the extra step of writing several of the routines Race needed, possibly overhearing some of the bridge crew's discussions while he was sleeping. All that was left for him to do was fill in some of the blanks and finish some of the more complex procedures.

"All done, sir," Race said about fifteen minutes later. "I even enabled a live feed into the sensor array to take into account anything new we might pick up. I still wouldn't recommend going too fast, though."

"I told you he'd get it done faster than me," Konway said, continuing to examine several more readings.

"Well done, Staff Sergeant," the captain congratulated Race.

"I think we're getting close," signaled Annette as the computer sensors overlaid the image of its readings onto the ship's windows.

"I think so," Konway agreed as he looked at the reading on his terminal. "Looks like it's a pretty large mass, almost the size of a ship."

"Slow down and take it easy," the captain ordered. "When we get closer, deploy a sensor module and link it to the relay pods. Let me see if I can contact the Puller."

"I got it, sir," Race said as he configured the probe. He also hit a few buttons on the biosensor to attach Bella to both the pod and ship's computer. Within seconds, the display was showing several readings of the mass.

"Nah," Konway said as he started to draw his conclusion, "it can't be."

"I think it is," Race said, showing Konway the display on his forearm.

"What is it?" asked one of the loaner soldiers, coming in behind Race.

"I think it's a ship," Konway answered. "It's hollow and made almost completely out of dentorite. It's like it's just been sitting here collecting dust," explained Konway.

"You sure it's not some sort of camouflage?" asked the Marine.

"I don't think so," Konway answered. "I'm going to guess it's probably been damaged."

"I mean, how long would that take?" asked Annette, trying to see if there was a way to determine the object's age.

Race's terminal went crazy as Bella took control of it to measure the layer of dirt surrounding the vessel and pull the logs to calculate how long it had been there.

"I don't know," commented Konway. "Several thousand years, I'd suppose."

Bella displayed a much large number that Race decided

was best to keep to himself.

"So this signal we're chasing is this ship?" asked another one of the STF Marines as he joined the crowd.

"That'd be my guess," answered Konway.

"How does a ship that's been here for thousands of years have anything to do with a full-scale invasion that happened hours ago?" asked the first Marine that had been attached to their unit.

"I'm more concerned about how something so old still has the power to send the signal, and why we haven't heard it before," Konway said.

"All good questions," the captain acknowledged. "I don't think we're going to get a good answer until we get in there and find out. Any sign of an entrance point?"

"There appears to be a section missing here." Race used his terminal to highlight an area on the front display. "The rock layer there is kind of thin. With the help of some small explosives, we should be able to get access."

"Did you catch all of that, Admiral?" asked the captain.

"Yes I did, Captain," the admiral's static-filled voice came from over the shuttle's intercom system. "Go ahead and proceed, just keep in mind that this still might be some cleverly concealed trap."

"Yes, sir," replied the captain. "We'll keep the channel open for you." He then directed his attention to the men. "Staff Sergeant Reece, you'll stay here with me and help monitor things. The rest of you put on your space suits and get ready to go for a walk."

Konway gave himself a small victory cheer as he got to

remain in his chair. The rest of the Marines rolled their eyes as they made their way to the back of the ship where the airlock was. They donned their suits over their uniforms and locked their helmets into place. Much like the ship's digital windows, the glass shield for their face also contained a digital screen that allowed it to overlay imagery to enhance their vision. Each one ran through a quick configuration program to attune itself to the wearer and linked up with each user's biosensor.

Bella took advantage of this and added a small transparent image of her bust in the bottom corner of Race's field of view. They finished just in time for the captain to inform them that they were in position. The door to the ship closed, sealing itself off from the incoming void. The Marines rushed to secure anything left lying around to prevent it from floating off.

They all did one last check before signaling the captain they were ready. The Marines could feel the pressure from outside their suits weaken as the atmosphere was sucked out to be reused later.

The back hatch started to slowly creep open, exposing the suited Marines to the cold void of space. The ship had already been moved into position across from the strike point Race had pointed out earlier; only a couple of meters of empty space lay between them and the seemingly infinite wall of rock expanding in every direction that covered their target.

The Marines took out their sidearms, which had been strapped to the outside of their suits, and attached a device to the barrel that linked to a utility belt around their waists. Zain picked a spot on the rock a little bit away from their point of entry. Everyone fired their weapons at the area. A rod launched from their weapons and burrowed into the side of the asteroid, leaving long tethers leading back to the Marines. After a few tugs to make sure the anchors were secure, the Marines left the safety of their shuttle and glided through the void as they reeled themselves into the ghost ship. Once everyone was secure, Zain and the female Marine of the loaner unit started to unpack a small container.

"Ah, my favorite part of the job." Zain pretended to breathe in the scent of the freshly opened containers. "Demolitions."

"I like explosions, too." The woman smiled at Zain, making Race wonder if she wasn't perhaps suggesting something else as well.

Race realized that this was the first time he had met most of the Marines temporarily attached to them. Like his own unit, it consisted of three men and a woman. From the info being displaying on his helmet's display, their names were Simmons, Martinez, McKinsey, and Bennetts. It seemed while Zain was getting along well with the female member of the attachment, while the men were admiring the female member of his team.

They all appeared to be young, probably closer to Race's age than he was to his fellow teammates'. That also meant that they weren't as experienced as Race's unit. For some reason, Race was reminded of some of his unit's own objections when he had first shown up at the SORD facility. It had only taken a few assignments before Race had proven himself and was able to gain the team's trust.

"Okay," Zain started to explain, "the sensors showed about a couple meters worth of debris accumulated around the area. Underneath is complete dentorite, but we want to be careful not to destroy any possible access panels that might be down there."

"What if we pre-drilled a hole about a quarter of the way down and dropped in the explosives?" asked the female Marine that had been helping him.

"That's good thinking," Zain agreed.

"What are we looking at, about a four-ton explosion?" asked the woman.

"Oh, I love a woman that knows her explosives," said Zain, smiling. "Go ahead and mix it up; I'll start prepping a detonator."

Race started to wander around the area and examine what almost looked like a rocky desert terrain from his point of view.

"Staff Sergeant?" One of the Marines tore himself away from gawking at Annette to speak to him.

Race turned to look at the young Marine. Something seemed oddly familiar about him. "I know you, don't I?" he asked.

"Yes, Staff Sergeant," the young man said. "Lance Corporal McKinsey. I was the one you rescued from Sergeant A-hole, as we like to call him."

"Oh." Race's face brightened suddenly as he made the connection. "What can I do for you?"

"Nothing, Staff Sergeant," the Marine answered. "When I saw Staff Sergeant Amyas looking for volunteers, I insisted he let me come along. I just wanted to thank you for standing up for me and the others. We're glad someone was finally able to take him down a notch."

"That's the guy that beat up Sergeant Reynolds?" One of the other Marines suddenly snapped his attention away from Annette, who looked like she was about to hit her new admirers. He came over to shake Race's hand. "It's a real pleasure to meet you."

"Thank you," Race said, almost embarrassed by the attention.

"That should do it." Zain held up his masterpiece. "You might want to move the ship to a safe distance, Captain," he suggested as everyone took cover in a dip in the rocky surface.

"Roger that," the voice of the captain came over the radio as the ship already started to pull away from them.

Once they were sure everyone was safe, Zain used the detonator to trigger the explosion, sending pieces of rock flying everywhere. The group made their way back to the newly created hole and climbed inside the ship. As they got inside, magnets activated on the bottom of their boots to stick them to the floor.

"Look," one of the STF Marines said as they came to a door near the end of a hall, "this looks like some sort of access panel. You were right, Staff Sergeant."

"Of course I was right," said Zain with a smirk as he approached the panel. He took out his tool as the end transformed into something he could use to pry off the panel, exposing several wires. "Keegan, does this look like what I think it looks like?" Zain asked after a couple of minutes of examining the device.

Annette grabbed the panel and examined it for a moment. "I'm not sure, it looks kind of like Euro tech."

"That's about what I was thinking," Zain said as he took back the panel. "If that's so, then all I should have to do is pull this and plug it into here." As soon as he secured the cable, the door shot open, exposing a dark hallway behind it to the crew.

The Marines drew their rifles and turned on the mounted lights to give them some vision in the dark hallway.

"I'm reading a thin atmosphere in various areas of the ship," Konway announced over the radio. "Nothing breathable."

"All right," stated Zain, hitting a few buttons on his arm unit, "starting mapping procedures. The power source for this thing is a couple of levels beneath us; we should be able to access it from a shaft not too far from here."

Race was starting to develop that bad feeling in his stomach that he got when he knew something was wrong. He was also getting a familiar tug that requested his presence somewhere specific, much like the first time Illandra had shown up on the space station.

He looked behind him down the dark hallway. While his visor tried to fill in the blanks by overlaying borders on his display, there was one thing that it couldn't detect that Race could clearly tell was there. The faint outline of the

214

creature from his dream stared back at him from the end of the hall. He tried to make himself believe that it wasn't there, but the more he tried, the more it was obvious he was lying to himself.

The alien walked off around the corner, mentally beckoning Race to follow him.

"Captian," Race interrupted the discussion. "There's something I have to check out. Whatever you do, be careful. I don't think we're alone here."

"What makes you say that, Marine?" the captain asked over the radio.

"I just got that feeling, Captain," Race answered him, looking down the dark, looming passage. He jogged off down the corridor and turned the way he had seen his ghost move.

He was about halfway down the next hallway when he caught a glimpse of two space suits following him. He didn't need to look at his display to know who it was. He slowed down a bit to let them catch up, obviously ordered to accompany him. He wasn't sure what good they were going to be against what he was chasing.

"Captain told us to follow you," Annette said, catching up to him with McKinsey. "What are we looking for?"

Race answered with a sigh. She wouldn't believe him even if he told her. "We'll know it when we find it." He eyed the creature cloaked in the shadows of the ship before moving to follow it once again.

Race continued to follow the shadow down several of the tunnels. After they had been exploring for some time,

Race suddenly felt the alert of danger come from far off in the ship. He stopped to look behind him in the direction he felt the tug come from, but there were several layers of the ship between him and the threat.

"What is it?" asked McKinsey.

Race looked back at the ghost, which had also turned to observe the thing that had triggered Race's senses. The creature returned his gaze before nodding and vanishing once again.

"We don't have much time," Race answered, running off.

"Watch yourself, Marines," the captain's voice came over the Marines' radios. "I think we detected movement somewhere in the ship. We're going to continue to watch out for it."

"Did he know that?" McKinsey asked Annette as the two followed Race through the maze of darkness.

Annette answered, "You just learn to roll with it."

They went through a few more corridors before they finally came to a closed door. The shadow that Race had been chasing simply vanished through it as he approached. Race pointed to a control panel on the side of the door. "We're here."

Annette quickly took the panel off and reconfigured the wires as Zain had done so the door would open. The Marines slowly spread out into the room as they looked around. It appeared they had found the damaged bridge of the ship. Race couldn't tell if any of the equipment was still operational, as there were no lights on any of them and several panels appeared to have been stripped for parts.

"What is that?" Race heard McKinsey gasp from behind him.

The rest of the team turned to see what remained of a skeleton sitting in what had most likely been the captain's chair. The bones were a dark rusty color, a clear sign that time had taken its toll on the corpse. The team huddled around the remains as they attempted to get a closer look. While the others were shocked to see the creature for the first time, Race was already well acquainted with it as the one that had been calling him to this area.

"It isn't human," stated Race.

"Obviously," Annette stated. "Are you getting this, sir?"

"Just our luck," answered the captain. "We finally find intelligent life in the universe and it's dead."

The team let out a small chuckle.

"Can you take some DNA samples?" asked the captain.

"I'll try," answered Annette.

"Hold on," the captain responded. "Staff Sergeant Amy-as, that thing just showed up on the sensors again. It seems to be on the move, and appears to be heading toward your section of the ship."

"Thanks, sir," came Zain's response over their radio. "We're going to put up some proximity grenades just to be on the safe side."

"Good idea," stated the captain. "Staff Sergeant Allard, any chance of you being able to recover any of the information in the ship's databanks?"

Race was captured by the dark caverns of the alien's skull where its eyes should be; he didn't hear the captain's question. Annette jabbed Race in the side, snapping him out of his trance. "I'm not sure there's any power in here, sir, but I'll give it a look."

Race walked around the alien bridge looking for something he could tap into. There was one terminal with a faint glow that suggested it might still have enough power to open.

"Race." Annette stopped him. "That looks like a Euro data interface."

"Bella, do you think we can interface with it?" Race asked his biosensor's AI.

"I'll see what I can do," Belle replied as a small adapter came out of the side. Race took the adapter and plugged the end into the interface in front of him. "This is so archaic; what type of advanced race uses wired communication?"

Race chuckled a bit, his nerves still keeping him on edge from enjoying this miraculous find.

"It's a little tricky, but I think I've managed to gain access to the ship's computers. I don't yet understand the language, but the data seems to resemble the transitions for the Consortium battleship before it crashed into the Taurus."

"Do what you can. The most important thing is the ship's logs, if you can find them. Any schematics would be nice, too," requested Race.

"Sir," Zain's voice interrupted over the radio, "can you see this? It's amazing!"

Bella shot up a picture of the video feed from his camera on Race's visor so he could see the power source they had found. It consisted of a huge pillar of light in the middle of the room, several bracers extending up to seemingly hold the pillar in place.

"The power reading is off the chart," said one of the loaner Marines. "I can't even imagine what we could do with this if we could find a way to copy this technology."

"I think we're going to need a really good science-and-engineering team to come and take a look at this stuff, Admiral," the captain's voice commented.

"I think you're right, Captain," the admiral replied. "I'm relaying your feed to the joint chiefs. They've gotten several of their scientists looking over the information you guys are gathering. I wouldn't be surprised if they're already fighting over who gets to fly out here and look at it."

"Amyas, get what readings you can and fall back to the entrance. That thing just showed up again and it's getting closer to you guys," commanded the captain. "Staff Sergeant Keegan, why don't you and McKinsey start to head back, too. Allard, finish downloading what you can and regroup with the others, quickly."

"Yes, sir," the troops said in unison.

Race's escorts started to head back out the door they had entered the bridge from. Before leaving, Annette turned to look at Race, afraid to leave him by himself. "You going to be okay?"

"When am I not?" Race winked at his friend. "Don't worry about me, I'll be there shortly."

Race got back to work, trying to ignore the nagging feeling coming from the alien skeleton. It was calling to him, almost yelling for him to come for it. Race looked over his shoulder at the chair only to see the hollow eyes looking at him. He quickly looked down at his terminal.

"*Did it move?*" he thought to himself. He struggled to remember if the skeleton had been facing this way from the beginning. There was only one way to find out. He used his sensor unit to turn off the feed from his suit to the shuttle.

"Cutting off your live feed is against protocol," Bella questioned Race as he got up to confront the skeleton.

"I need to have a conversation with our friend here," Race answered. "And I don't want the others thinking that I've gone crazy."

The cable connecting Bella to the terminal continued to extend itself as Race slowly approached the remains. He swore the hollow eyes were following him even though he knew there was nothing there.

"You led me here, didn't you?" Race asked the inanimate corpse, slowly inching his way closer. "That was your ghost I saw in the halls. And that was you in my dream, too, wasn't it? What was it you said? 'Find me'?" Race continued to question the corpse as well as his own sanity. "Well, here I am. Now what? What's this plague you were talking about? What is it you want from me!" he yelled, finally reaching the chair.

He braced himself by placing his hands on the end of the armrest as he waited impatiently for a response. He continued to examine the skull from different angles, hoping to get a response.

"Maybe I am losing it." Race hung his head. He was about to give up when he felt a small vibration in the chair, as if its occupant had moved. He looked up to see the skull was now facing him directly in the eyes. Before he could pull back in fright, the corpse's hands shot up and grabbed the sides of Race's head.

Paralyzed in fear, Race was helpless to fight the creature. Several images started to flash before his eyes. He saw alien cities that sprawled over entire planets. A metallic kingdom at the center of the great empire. He witnessed battles take place across the stars. Race beheld lifetimes in mere seconds before the corpse collapsed into a pile of dust in its chair while Race fell to the floor, the helmet stopping his hands from grasping his head against the blistering pain.

He wasn't there long before he forced his eyes open. Bella's image on his visor was desperately trying to get his attention. "Are you okay?" she asked, sensing him finally becoming alert. "Your vitals were all over the place."

Race's hands were shaking as proof Bella's statement. "I'll be fine," he said, starting to sit up. "How much longer till you're done?"

"I've queued most of the important information," she answered. "I've found a wireless terminal and enabled a direct connection to the sensor pod. We can regroup with the others when you are ready."

"Then let's go," Race said as he picked himself up off the floor and stumbled out the door.

Race unhooked the cable from the console and exited the alien bridge. He walked down to the end of the hall, where he used the magnetic sole of his boot to step up onto the wall.

He squatted down as he took a second to implement some of his training he hadn't used for a while and clear his mind and heighten his senses. When he was done, he activated the recall method on his tether and launched himself down the hall as he pushed off like an Olympian swimmer.

*   *   *

Zain and his team had just finished what scans they could do. The science officers that had patched into his comm had been fascinated by the findings and had wanted the crew to look at all sorts of readings and panels. Eventually, they just figured that it was better for them to come out and check out the ship themselves.

The Marines packed up their stuff and prepared to head out.

"Staff Sergeant Amyas," the captain's voice came over his space suit's comm again. "You need to get going; that thing is really close."

"We're leaving right now, sir," Zain answered his commanding officer as he picked up the last of his gear and headed back the way he'd come.

As the crew reached the door, a loud bang echoed through the open chamber, grabbing everyone's attention. Zain turned to look in the direction of the source. Once again, a loud crash echoed through the chamber. This time, they could see the door bulge as if it had been hit with some sort of ramming device.

"I don't like the looks of this," commented one of the Marines.

222

"Me either," commented Zain, starting to rush toward the door. They could feel another crash vibrate through the area as Zain ordered the Marines to make a break for it.

They had made it to the shaft they'd used to enter the level when another bang sounded from the doors they had just closed behind them seconds earlier. The Marines scrambled into the shaft; Zain grabbed the control panel and crossed a few wires to close the door. He then pulled out his sidearm and fired into the panel to short it out.

Whatever was following them was soon banging on the access door. The Marines were in a dead sprint as they tried to reach their entrance into the elevator shaft. As the first Marine reached the door, the other door crashed open, flying into the elevator shaft. The Marines stopped to look back at their pursuer, but all they could see was the dark, empty hallway.

The Marines slowly stepped out of the shaft, one by one, weapons in hand as they scanned the darkness for the intruder. Zain, being the last one out of the shaft, grabbed the console he had used to hotwire the door open to close the door. The other Marines stood guard, aiming their rifles at the door, ready to fire at anything that dared to come through. Zain crossed a couple of wires to cause the door to start to close, but it failed to close completely.

"Why didn't it close all the way?" whispered one of the Marines.

"How would I know?" Zain whispered back through clenched teeth. "I'm going to try it again."

Zain took out the wire and put it back into the slot that

caused the door to slide open to about a quarter of the way. Before he could complete the jump back, the door bulged as a huge figure lunged from the shadows, swinging its large claws at the Marines through the tiny crack. The Marines screamed and cursed as they started firing energy rounds at the figure.

The gunfire lit up the hallway to the point that the Marines were almost able to see the face of the creature attacking them. The reptile-like torso of the alien protruded into the hall and was almost as tall as the Marines themselves. The giant club hand swung around the hall, trying to reach the Marines unloading on its scale-covered face. The Marines' fire appeared to do little more than annoy the creature as it harmlessly bounced off its exoskeleton.

Zain took one of his clips attached to his vest and set it to detonate. He dropped it at the base of the door and yelled at the Marines to make a break for it. A couple of seconds later, the clip exploded, thrusting the alien back out of the hallway.

"What the hell was that?" asked one of the Marines as he ran for his life.

"I don't know," Zain answered, continuing to push the Marines down the hall. "You're welcome to go back and ask it, though."

*   *   *

"You got anything on it?" asked the captain as he frantically pressed buttons on the console in front of him.

"Just the same thing you got, Captain," answered Konway, just as frantic.

"Keegan," the captain commanded over the comm systems, "head to intercept the other team; they're about three corridors down. Lay some proximity detonators and give them some cover fire."

"Yes, sir," Annette's voice came back over the intercom system.

"Allard, you'd better start heading back here," the captain continued. "I don't want you stuck on that ship alone with that thing."

"Already heading back, sir," Race replied. "I should be there pretty quick."

"Holy crap," gasped Konway, looking at the map of the area. "He isn't kidding, sir."

The two watched the screen as they saw the dot that represented Race clearing corridors along the ship's passageway in a matter of seconds.

"What the hell?" the captain asked himself. "Did he grow wings? Bring up his display."

"It's still offline," Konway responded, earning him a scowl from his officer.

*   *   *

From what he could hear over the radio, Race knew he didn't have that much time before something bad happened to one of his friends.

He zipped down the hall, bouncing from wall to wall, each time pushing off to increase his speed with each thrust. He had configured Bella to activate the magnets in his boots for only a quick moment when they made contact with the floor so as not to slow him down. With the assistance of the emergency recall from his tethering system, he was practically flying through the ship's corridors. He only slowed his speed just enough to keep him from slamming into the walls as he navigated the corners.

It didn't take any time at all before Race was zooming by their entry point into the alien spaceship. Race continued along the corridors, following the other Marines' tethers, seeing every nook and turn even before they were upon him.

As in many of his exercises in boot camp, Race's awareness had spread to everything around him. Every movement had a purpose, even though that purpose wasn't completely known to him at that very second.

Race reached the corridor where Annette's team had set up their barrier to provide assistance to their friend. Using their zero-gravity combat training, they had used the magnets on their boots to climb to the ceiling of the corridor in hopes that it would give them a better angle over their teammates' heads. Race zoomed down the hallway and made the corner just inches away from Annette, once again thrusting off various walls to pick up speed as he rushed to help Zain and his team.

A few more kickoffs and Zain was in his sights. He could see him dragging one of his team member's unconscious body by one hand as he fired behind him with the other, a trail of blood floating behind them as it leaked out of a hole in the unconscious man's suit.

Race continued past the retreating team as he homed in

on their pursuer. The creature was charging down the hall on four legs. The two locked eyes as they headed for an unavoidable collision. The creature stood up on its hind legs and yelled a challenging roar at Race, hungry for a worthy opponent. Race took another lunge off the floor to increase his speed and help spin himself around. He stuck his feet out so they would impact with the creature first.

Race's feet collided with the monster's chest with enough force to crush a normal person's rib cage. The alien reared back as the collision sent him staggering, landing on his back several meters down the hall. Using the force of the collision, Race once again launched himself down the hall away from the wounded alien.

"Zain," Race said as he lunged toward his friends, "disengage your magnetic locks and hold on tight to each other."

Zain and his teammates quickly used their biosensors to follow Race's instructions. Race reached out and grabbed the floating Marines, jerking them along with him as he flew down the corridor to the safety of their remaining teammates.

"Annette," Race said as he flew back down the hall, "Simmons's suit is leaking and he's bleeding. Get some patches ready."

"On it," her voice responded over the receiver in Race's suit.

Within seconds, Race was back with Annette's group, still dragging the rest of Zain's team behind him. He activated his boots once again to stick to the floor, using the drag to slow them down. Zain had already grabbed the edges of the hole in the wounded soldier's space suit and held it out to Annette, who quickly stuffed a large bandage over the Marine's wound. She then ran a device over the hole in his suit, melting the two sides together to recreate an airtight seal. The two quickly worked to wrap a belt around the Marine in hopes that it would help the bandage inside stop the bleeding.

"Activate your emergency-recall procedures," Race yelled to the Marines. "I'll cover you."

Everyone tapped their screen as the reels started pulling them back to the shuttle, almost as fast as Race had been able to navigate to them.

Annette remained behind to help activate the wounded Marine's recall and make sure that everyone else was safely away. When everyone else was clear, she stood up and started to activate her own recall. Her finger stopped just short of hitting the button as she gazed up at her fellow teammate preparing to do battle once again with the creature. She couldn't let herself abandon him to face the demon alone. She redrew her rifle from her shoulder and prepared to join Race in his battle with the monster.

As she took a step forward to join Race, the huge creature leaped from the shadows, screaming as it lunged to shred the remaining stragglers. Race spun around to meet the foe, raising both arms to the alien attacker. The creature's attack fell short as its fists encountered a wall of electricity blocking them. Annette watched, mystified, as trails of electricity sparkled out from the impact with the alien.

Shocked and confused by the force field's appearance,

it started to assault the barrier with all its might. Each time it collided with the barrier, another wave of electric arcs sprawled out from the impact.

Race took a step toward the creature, bracing himself. Pushing his hand forward, he threw the beast back into the darkness from which he had come. Race looked back at Annette, who was completely awestruck by what she had just seen. As shocking as the display of power was, it was nowhere near as terrifying as the change in Race's appearance. She tried to look into the eyes of the man she had called a friend for the past year, but where his eyes were, a cold blue flame burned with a chill that went down her entire spine.

"Go," Race ordered Annette in a tone she was unfamiliar with. Before she could object, the emergency-recall program activated itself and whisked her away from the battle.

Race walked down the hall looking for the alien he had thrown. The light from his helmet revealed the creature getting back up from his previous blow. Several of the creature's bones snapped out and back into place as it assumed a new standing posture, still slightly hunched over to fit into the small hallway.

Their eyes locked in an immortal staring contest as Race came face to face with the creature. The creature had experienced some damage from its encounter with his fellow Marines, but he could tell from his dream and the skeleton that this creature was somehow related to them.

"*Who are you?*" the alien questioned through razor-sharp teeth in a language Race somehow understood as fluently as his own.

"I am the one you've feared would come," answered Race in the same language, causing the alien's lidless eyes to bulge. "I am the cure to your plague."

"The Cenari are not the plague; we are the cure," snarled the alien creature, sizing up Race. *"And we know no fear."*

"You fear one," corrected Race, not entirely sure if he understood what he was talking about. *"The destroyer of your kind, foretold in your story before you were even born. In this form, I am that one. I am the Run'hura."*

Angered by Race's comment, the alien lunged at Race, intent on killing him. Race lifted a hand to meet its blow as it collided once again with a field that caused electricity to dance around the impact. Frustrated, the alien continued to flail its clawed arms at Race, each meeting another shield as Race put his hand up to defend against it.

Race took the offensive by letting an overhand swing brush by and hit the floor, leaving a big dent by his feet. Somehow, instinctively, he wrapped his fist with one of the fields and uppercut the beast, sending it flying up into the ceiling before being able to grab back onto what they were using as the floor.

The creature sprang back to its feet and attempted to decapitate Race with a giant swing of his arm. Race ducked under the creature's swing and grabbed its returning backhand to pull it to the ground. Using another fielded fist, he started to strike the creature with all his might, each time dazing the creature more and more.

The creature took several blows before it had built up enough anger to push Race's force-fielded armbar off of him, throwing him down the hall.

Race caught himself flying down the hall, sliding across the floor as his boots once again tried to stick to the surface. He was vaguely aware of the fact that he was mentally controlling the magnetic soles without the need of Bella or his interface.

Race and the creature once again locked eyes as they considered the next stage of their battle. The creature charged at Race again, running on all fours, bloodlust in its eyes. Race watched intently, all emotion removed from his face as the cold fire still burned in his eyes.

When it was close, the beast lunged at Race, its razor-filled mouth open as it hoped to tear into its target's flesh. Race waited until it was close enough and dodged between its outstretched claws and around the creature's gaping mouth.

He reached around the creature's giant head and wrapped his arms around its massive neck. Using his new telekinetic strength, he forced the creature's head down, using the momentum of its own back half to twist awkwardly in midair.

As the creature's body contorted past him, Race quickly shifted his stance to the other side, forcing the skull in his arm to rapidly change direction. He felt the neck snap in his arms as the different forces took place on the creature's body. He let go of the carcass and let it float lifelessly away.

Race knew the fight wasn't over. He walked over to the carcass to see what he guessed was the creature trying to repair itself on the floor. Using his foot to brace the creature on the floor, Race reached high above him. Another telekinetic field materialized, stretching between his hands. With one giant swing, Race brought the kinetic field down like a large guillotine blade, decapitating the beast with such force that his field cut deep into the floor beneath it.

Race turned to leave the fallen creature, intentionally kicking its skull off into the shadows. With each step, he felt the release of the power that had flowed within him. The farther Race got from the creature, the closer he felt like himself. Soon, there was so little energy in him that he was forced to fall down to his knees.

During the encounter, he hadn't taken a second to even question what was going on; it was like he was working on instinct. That cloud was now beginning to disperse. It allowed his reasoning to start to come in, and it was full of questions.

He had been so full of anger at the creature during their encounter, yet he had no idea what it was. How could he hate something he knew nothing about? And the alien language that he understood so well? He'd even managed to speak some of it to the creature. But it was all so cryptic, he didn't even know what it meant. Could it have had something to do with the alien on the bridge? The more he searched inside his head for answers, the more questions raced through him.

He looked around the room, the fire in his eyes that had coated everything in a blue haze beginning to fade. He saw a figure running toward him, one of his fellow Marines in their white space suit. He didn't have to think twice about who it was.

"Annette," he whispered as the last of the flame extinguished from his eyes, allowing him to look at the one person who always seemed to be there for him since they had first met.

When she reached him, she quickly looked him over for any damage. "I've got you," she said, helping to pick him up off the floor. Even in the weightless environment, his muscles ached as if he were walking in gravity a hundred times more than he was used to. Every joint in his body was filled with pain every time he tried to move.

As she dragged him back to the shuttle, he looked down to see the damaged reel that attached to her tether. She had obviously destroyed it after he'd activated her recall procedure to return to his aid.

"How much did you see?" Race asked, barely able to speak.

"Enough," Annette responded, not wanting or caring about the details at that moment.

"The others?" Race asked, afraid of what they might think of him.

"Not much," Annette answered shortly. "I cut off my feed, too."

"Thanks," Race whispered, some of his normal strength starting to return to him with his friend's assistance.

Annette hit a button on her arm unit to activate her communications once again. "Captain, the creature is dead. I've got Allard. We're heading back to you now."

"What kind of condition is he in?" asked their commanding officer. They could hear both the concern and anger in his voice.

Annette twisted Race's arm to look at his biosensor. "No major injuries, sir," she reported. "He just seems a little out of it. We should be there soon."

"Roger that," the captain said, closing the connection.

The two continued their return trek to the ship. About halfway, Race was finally able to move by himself without the need of his friend's assistance. After they boarded the ship and went through the re-compression chamber, he was greeted by several awkward stares from the ship's crew.

"How's Simmons?" Race broke the silence, trying to change the subject before it could be broached.

"I think he'll be okay," answered Zain. "Still needs medical attention, though."

"Admiral," the captain interrupted, "I think we're heading back your way."

"Good," the admiral of the Puller responded over the system. "We just finished repairing the other ships. We'll rendezvous outside the nebula where we dropped you off."

"We'll see you when you get there, sir," the captain said as he signed off.

Chapter 8
RECOVERING

Record Dates: 349.166 – 349.193 PGST

THE PAIN IN ILLANDRA'S HEAD made her think someone had buried a hatchet deep in her skull. She even tried to feel around for the mystery object, but all her fingers came across was a sanitary bandage near the top of her head. She looked around to find herself in a small bed with a dull-colored blanket draped over her. Her clothes had been removed, and she now found herself dressed in the worst of medical gowns. There were several digital panels in the wall next to her displaying what she guessed were her vitals. There were a couple of walls in place to grant her some privacy, but they were thin enough that she could hear several people moving around just outside its barriers.

She tried to sit up, but the entire room spun. Her head quickly landed back on her pillow. She called out to see if anyone could hear her, catching the attention of a medic in the area. The medic tried to calm Illandra, not that she had the strength to do anything to fight her. Once the nurse was sure Illandra wasn't going to try and run off on her own, she went to retrieve the medical chief.

Minutes later, the officer entered Illandra's private area. "How are you feeling?" asked the blond lady draped in a doctor's uniform as she entered the room.

"I feel like I was hit by a cruiser," Illandra said, still holding her head, hoping it would somehow stop it from spinning. "What happened?"

"Why don't you tell me what you remember?" the officer said, reviewing some of the readings on display in the wall. "That way we can tell if there's any further damage we need to look into."

Illandra tried desperately to remember what had happened. "I...I remember being on a ship. I was on the bridge. There was a battle..." Illandra continued to struggle as the memories slowly started to come back to her.

"Is that all?" asked the doctor.

"No," Illandra said, "but the rest is still kind of fuzzy."

"That's not bad," the doctor said as she examined Illandra's eyes. "A little fuzziness is to be expected. You remember some decent details before the accident. Enough not to be too concerned, anyways. You and the congressman were assigned to attempt diplomatic relations with an invading force of ships. You're on the..."

"The Puller," Illandra said as the doctor's description helped bring several of the images into focus.

"Yes," the doctor smiled, pleased at Illandra's progress. "We met the Imperials and barely survived the encounter. One of the ships survived, as well, and before we could deal with them, they fled and made a suicide run for..."

"Taurus." A cold wave went up Illandra's arm and down

her spine. It was coming back to her now. She remembered the moment the ship had collided with the space station, her head filled with the stings of a thousand hot needles igniting in her mind. "All those people." Illandra shuddered.

"I'm sorry," replied the doctor, taking a moment to sympathize with her. "You and the congressman, you both seemed to have had a brain hemorrhage that correlated with it. I'm sure you're aware of the special circumstances involved with your situation that might explain it."

Illandra nodded her acknowledgment of the doctor's implication.

"We were forced to perform surgery to bring down the swelling," the doctor continued. "You obviously have some powerful friends; Congressman Martin called in the president's personal physician to consult on the surgery."

"So...am I going to be brain-damaged?" Illandra asked, her body cringed at the possibility.

"This isn't the 20th century," said the doctor, smiling. "The chances of that are really small. Not to mention you had some of the best doctors in the galaxy working on you. I wouldn't be surprised if your brain's in better shape than it was before the whole incident."

Illandra let out a sigh of relief before her thoughts quickly turned to her mentor. "You said the congressman experienced it, too? Is he okay?"

"His wasn't as severe. We were able to treat it with medicine alone. He's already up and walking around...against doctor's orders," the doctor said, rolling her eyes. "Stubborn old man."

"He can be," laughed Illandra. "Is there any chance I can talk to him?"

"I believe he's resting now, but maybe I can have someone bring him in if he wakes up," replied the doctor.

"I can rest when I'm dead," said Anthony as he appeared the doorway, bracing himself against the frame to keep from falling over.

"Congressman," scolded the doctor, "you need to be resting."

"I promise I'll go back to bed as soon as I'm done," replied Anthony. "I just want to make sure she's okay."

"I'm fine, Anthony," Illandra said, trying to get her mentor to follow the doctor's orders. "You shouldn't be up."

"I just need five minutes," protested Anthony. "Give me five minutes, and I'll do whatever you tell me to."

The doctor threw her hands in the air and stormed out of the recovery room, leaving the two alone.

"So how are you feeling, lass? Really?" asked Anthony as he entered the room, his legs barely able to support his weight.

"I have a horrible headache," Illandra admitted.

"I'm sorry you had to go through that," Anthony apologized as he eased himself into a seat that came out of the wall. "I would rather it had been me alone."

"Then I'd be dead like everyone else on that station," Illandra said grimly. "What really happened to us?"

"Sensory overload, very hard to defend against," he explained, trying to find a way to get comfortable in the solid chair. "There have only been a couple of major catastrophes where a pathic was near. From what we understand, the brain overloads with all the pain from the victims. Violent death is never a pleasant emotion. Projected from several thousand people at once, our receptors simply can't handle it. It's almost like it's us in that burning inferno a hundred times over."

"It sure felt like it," Illandra said, fighting to keep the memory of the feeling from surfacing once again. "How come it affected me so much more than you?"

"Oh, lass, you have the potential to be so much stronger than I ever could hope to be. You were naturally going to have a stronger flux. You also have a knack for creating mental links to people, several of whom were still on the station. And of course, you never like to keep up your mental blocks like I try and teach you."

Illandra moaned at receiving yet another lecture from her mentor. "Has anyone ever died from it?"

"Yes," said Anthony as his face took on a grim look. "About six years ago, there was a young lad who was on a mission of peace to a mining station, the Spertanian. After a couple of days, negotiations took a bad turn. Fearing things were going to get violent, he was recalled. He hadn't even made it out of the solar system when a riot broke out. Someone blew up the station. The lad died before they could get him to a qualified doctor. But that's also what led to the discovery of most of the procedures that saved our lives."

"Your son," Illandra said, putting the longtime puzzle together.

"How..." Anthony said, flabbergasted at how accurate

her assessment was.

"My parents told me," Illandra answered, embarrassed by her lack of tactfulness. "I'm sorry, I didn't mean to bring up the memory."

Anthony let out a big sigh as several memories seemed to dance over his face. "It's not your fault, lass. The two of you actually had a lot in common. You would have liked him."

"Only if he wasn't like his father," Illandra teased her mentor, hoping to lighten his mood. There was a short pause before Illandra spoke up again. "Have you talked to her?"

"Hmm?" Anthony asked, coming out of his daydream.

"Your wife," Illandra answered. "You should call her."

"Oh, she's not worried about me," Anthony fussed.

"We almost died," Illandra scolded her mentor. "Is this really how you want things to end? It was obvious when I met her that she's still madly in love with you. How long are you going to keep her waiting?"

Anthony went quiet as he mentally fought with Illandra's declaration. "You're right, lass," he said, submitting. "And I thought I was the teacher here."

"You know us kids, always think we know everything," Illandra said, smiling.

Just then, the door burst open as the doctor stormed in with two assistants following closely on her heels. "Five minutes are up."

Anthony struggled to get out of his chair and staggered over to the doctor. "Did you have to bring the muscle?" Anthony said grumpily. "I told you I'd do whatever you wanted."

"I know, but you're too heavy for me to carry on my own," said the doctor as she pulled out a device she used to inject some medication into Anthony's arm.

Anthony quickly lost his footing and stumbled over. The men accompanying the doctor were barely fast enough to catch him before he completely lost his balance and tumbled to the floor. The two men worked together to drag the ambassador back to his room.

"I like your style," complimented Illandra as the doctor was leaving. The doctor just smiled devilishly as she prepared to leave. "Can I get you to do me a favor?"

"What's that, dear?" The doctor eyed her suspiciously, afraid Illandra might try something like her mentor.

"Can you notify the congressman's wife of what happened? Maybe have her available to talk to him next time he comes through?"

"I think I can do that," the doctor said, relieved it wasn't anything that would jeopardize her patient. "Now you need to get some rest, too, or I'm going to get another one of these," threatened the doctor, waving the device she had used to sedate Anthony.

"Yes, ma'am," Illandra laughed as she saluted the doctor before she exited her personal recovery room.

*   *   *

The trip out of the nebula seemed to take forever to Race. It most likely had something to do with the fact that he had been asleep for most of the trip coming in. The captain had given both him and Annette a stern yelling for cutting

241

off their feeds during the mission. Race was glad to accept it in place of the criticism he would have received had they witnessed the full encounter between him and the aliens, both the dead one and the one he'd killed. He did feel bad for Annette, who was also being disciplined for his actions. She had done it to protect him—for what reasons, though, Race was too distracted to even start thinking about.

After they had received their punishment, the captain put Race in charge of the return trip while the rest of the unit was allowed to sleep. It didn't really matter to him; even though the whole experience had physically drained him, he doubted he could sleep any. His mind was still continuously replaying the encounter from start to finish, searching for answers. Luckily, the program that Race had written earlier was able to do most of the piloting while he was busy with his distractions.

They were about a quarter of the way out of the nebula when Race heard the footsteps coming down the corridor that led to the cockpit. Without even looking, he got out of the main pilot seat and moved over to the co-pilot's chair.

Annette silently sat down in her proclaimed spot and checked the ship's status. There was a long, awkward silence as the two went about trying to appear busy on an auto-driven machine.

"I'm sorry you got reprimanded because of me," Race said, breaking the silence. He felt he at least owed her that.

"It's okay," she said quietly, trying not to make eye contact.

"Not really," Race said, thinking of all the things that

were wrong with the situation.

"You want to talk about it?" Annette offered, obviously still nervous about the events she had witnessed.

"I don't even know where to start." Race laughed nervously.

"Why don't you start with what caused you to run off by yourself on the ship?" Annette suggested.

Race grew nervous as he quietly recalled the frightful sight of the alien that wore the shadows like a cloak. He somehow knew he was the key to all of this.

"If you don't want to talk about it, we don't have to," Annette said, cutting into the silence and snapping Race out of his dream state. Race could see that she was trying to force herself to look at him, but she still lacked the nerve to look at him directly.

"No," Race objected, "I need to. I'm just not sure I believe much of it myself. I doubt you will either."

"I can try," Annette said, still trying to be supportive, finally gaining the courage to look Race in the eyes.

"Okay," Race said, taking a deep breath. Race went on to recap how the alien had invaded his dreams, leaving out the details of Annette's involvement in it. Then how that presence had again appeared in the ship and led him to the bridge where they'd met the alien corpse. He could see the skepticism in her eyes as he continued to explain the lifetime of images he had experienced when the alien touched him, and how that had led him to the battle with the other alien.

"You think this dead alien somehow summoned you? Then possessed you and gave you the powers you used to kill the other one?" Annette asked once Race had concluded his story.

"I told you that you wouldn't believe me," Race said, trying to drop the discussion and return to his console.

"It's not that I don't believe you," Annette lied. "We've all been through so much stress in the past twenty-four hours, I don't even know if I believe what I saw."

Race had been so worried about what the others would have thought had they seen him, he hadn't even thought about how her perception of him had already been changed by what she had seen. "What did you see?" Race could see the fear on Annette's face as she recalled the horrifying event from her perspective. "Please, I want to know."

She looked down, almost ashamed of her feelings. "When the creature first attacked, you just lifted your hands and stopped it," she said, mimicking Race's movements, "almost like you had willed it. And when you turned to look at me…" Her already quiet voice dropped off.

"What?" Race begged her to continue.

"Even though your eyes were glowing with that blue fire, I could still see them," Annette said. "It was passion, your passion. But there was something else." She almost hesitated again. "Rage. Enough hate to last a lifetime. When you spoke, it didn't even sound like your voice. A part of me didn't even want to go back," she admitted, "but I couldn't let you face that thing alone. By the time I cut the rope to my tether and made it back, I saw you squaring off with that thing again."

She took a moment to replay the scene in her mind once

more. "You manhandled that thing like it was nothing," she continued. "Three times your size and you handled it like a puppy. And when you were done, when you had..." She once again used her hands to signify how Race had decapitated the creature. "It just seemed like you were so satisfied. Like you enjoyed it."

While Race was well aware of the anger he'd felt for the creature, he'd never thought the creature's death gave him any pleasure. Race's job often put him in the position of having to kill people, but he never enjoyed taking another life. He often tried his best to prevent it, trying to wound his opponent instead. All life was to be cherished. The thought of him getting any type of satisfaction in killing something stirred something troublesome inside him, and he suddenly understood what had troubled Annette so much.

"Thank you," Race said, breaking a long silence.

"For?" Annette asked, confused.

"Everything," Race smiled. "Being such a good friend. Telling me your side, not abandoning me on the ship, turning off your feed. Why did you turn off your feed, anyway?"

"I overheard the captain yelling at you over the comm for shutting yours off. After seeing your face, I kind of figured you didn't want anyone to see it, so I shut mine down as well."

"I don't know what I did to earn a friend like you, but I'm glad I did it," Race complimented her with a smile.

"You'd better be." Annette winked back, getting up from her seat. "I'm gonna go get some rest. We're through the worst part of the cloud. Your routine seems to be doing a pretty good job navigating by itself."

"Duh," Race mocked her, "galaxy's greatest programmer here."

Annette teasingly gave him a tiny smack on the back of the head before leaving Race in the cockpit alone.

"Bella," Race said, activating his arm unit when he was sure he was alone.

"Yes?" The image of his AI appeared on the front window.

"I turned off my feed, but I didn't break your connection with the suit's camera, did I?" Race asked.

"That is correct," the overlay answered.

"How much of it did you record?" Race asked.

"All of it," she informed him, "including the stuff from Sergeant Keegan's unit as well."

Race was tempted to have her delete the recordings before anyone could attempt to recall them, but seeing it again might help him to understand what had happened.

"Play it," Race ordered.

*   *   *

Illandra woke up with another throbbing headache. The pain medicine the doctor had given her earlier was clearly wearing off. Then again, the small tug on her still-recovering senses might be causing some of the distress as well.

She knew she was tempting fate by attempting to use her abilities so soon after the incident, but she couldn't help but see what was going on. She reached out with her mind and tried to find the source of the turmoil. She found her powers very difficult to control at first, mentally brushing past several people as she tried to focus in on the source.

It wasn't long before she discovered Race back aboard the fleet flagship. The doctor had informed her that Race had been sent off on a mission and was unavailable. From what she was reading off him, she could tell that something disturbing had happened.

Illandra could tell that something was different, and not just with Race, but with herself as well. While it still pained her to use her abilities, she found it was much easier for her to probe Race's mind, even from such a great distance. She was even able to see some of Race's memories, and what she saw disturbed her.

There were still a couple of other sources tugging at her senses for her to investigate. A quick scan of Annette verified some of the things she had seen from Race. But that wasn't what was disturbing her. She moved on to the next person, Race's captain, and found what she was looking for. A discussion between the captain and the fleet admiral about what had happened.

There was another person involved, one whom she was already familiar with but who was too far out to read. She didn't need to, though. She was able to get all the information she needed from the other two. She got the last of the details she could before the pain in her head forced her to stop.

"Wake up, old man," Illandra said, pounding on the flimsy wall that separated her from her mentor. "We have work to do."

*   *   *

The shuttle's crew was given little time to recuperate after docking with the U.R.S. Puller. They had checked in and were given enough time to unload their stuff before being sent back to the bridge to wait in the conference room to see the admiral. Race was unsure how he was going to explain the whole thing to everyone. He knew he owed them all an explanation, but he was still trying to figure out exactly what had happened himself.

Konway's arm unit lit up as it received a message. "Staff Sergeant Reece, report to my office," said the admiral's image before disappearing.

The group exchanged several questioning looks with each other. The Marines were accustomed to debriefing as a group.

"He's going to debrief us all separately?" asked Zain, saying what they were all thinking.

"I guess so," Konway answered, getting up and leaving the room so as not to keep the admiral waiting.

"I don't like it," Zain said after the door had closed.

"What?" Race asked.

"This." Zain stood up to start pacing around the room. "Something's not right here. Calling us out one by one."

"Maybe the admiral just does things differently here," Annette said, trying to calm him down.

"You think a fleet admiral coordinating all these ships on the edge of war has so much time on his hands that he'd just decide to brief us all individually instead of as a quick group and get it over with?" Zain argued.

Annette and Race looked at each other speechless. They couldn't find any flaw in his argument. Race started to panic. Was it possible they had recaptured some of the footage from his encounter? He knew he should have deleted it, but there was so much information that he couldn't bear to let it go.

They waited nervously for Konway to return. When he came through the door, Race could tell by the bleak expression on his face that Zain had been right.

Zain rushed up to meet him as he came through the door. "What happened?"

"It's not a debriefing," Konway said, obviously upset by the whole ordeal.

"What is it?" Zain asked anxiously.

"It's an investigation," Konway answered shortly.

"What?" Annette and Zain asked almost in unison.

"What are they investigating?" Zain asked, barely able to contain his temper.

Konway answered by gazing over at Race, causing him to sit up straight in his chair.

"That's bull crap," Zain exclaimed, finally unable to control himself. "He saved all of our lives out there. I wouldn't even be here if it wasn't for him."

"It's more than that," Konway responded. "Your whole history is in that room," Konway said, looking across the room at Race.

"What?" Zain asked, the confusion replacing the anger he had just felt.

"You'll see," Konway informed Zain. "You're next."

Zain shot up straight, attempting to regain his composure. "What did you tell them?"

"Nothing they didn't already know," Konway said, taking a seat.

"Let's keep it that way," Zain said, pointing at Annette and Race, making sure they understood that it was an order. "At least until we figure out what it is they want."

Annette nodded her agreement before Zain left the room for his turn in the interrogation room.

Race couldn't help but feel touched by his teammates' commitment to him, even though he had a hard time understanding why they did so. He'd known them just over a year, and already they were willing to face a possible court-martial for him, risking their lifelong careers. He couldn't help but think they were making a mistake. While he'd probably do the same for any of them, he didn't feel he had done anything to deserve it. Did he have the right to ask them to make such a risk for him?

"I'm going to tell them everything," Race interrupted the silent room.

"What?" Konway said, snapping out of his trance.

"You can't," Annette said, just as shocked.

"I have to," Race said. "I can't let you guys risk your careers for me."

"We don't even know what this is about," Konway responded, a little confused as to how Race had drawn his conclusion. "I doubt they're going to threaten us with a court-martial or anything. Let's just take this one step at a time. Find out what they want and then we'll take it from there."

"Sorry," Race said, ducking his head, slightly embarrassed. "I just don't want you guys getting into any more trouble because of me."

Annette reached out and put her arm on Race's shoulder to comfort him. "It's like I always tell you. We're a team," she said. "We've always got your back."

Konway didn't say anything, but Race could tell from the stern look on his face that he agreed.

"Thanks," Race said once again. He seemed to find himself doing a lot of that lately.

The door to the conference room swooshed open as Zain walked in, looking relieved that his part was completed.

"Well, good news and bad news," he said, coming in and taking a seat across the room. The rest of the group waited anxiously for Zain to fill them in on his experience. "Good news is that Captain seems to be on our side; he isn't happy with this whole thing, either."

"I got that impression, too," Konway agreed.

"And the bad news?" Race asked.

"I don't think it matters much," Zain said. "That general's after something very specific, but I can't tell what it is."

"General?" Annette asked.

"Yeah," Zain answered, "he's holoed in. A General Vyson, I believe."

That name struck a memory in Race, but he couldn't place it. He anxiously bit on his nail as he tried to recall where he had heard that name before.

"You know him?" Konway asked, reading Race's expression.

"It sounds familiar," Race acknowledged. "I just can't remember where." Race slapped the table as it dawned on him. "Boot camp. All that extra training Straum and I got. He oversaw most of it."

"You sure?" Zain asked.

"Yes," Race exclaimed. "I never got to meet him, but I overheard several others talking with. He was always in the back, just watching."

"What do you think it has to do with this?" Konway asked, trying to help put the puzzle together.

"I don't know," Race admitted, "but I bet it has something to do with all of this. Me, being here on this ship. Leading tactics on the assault. Maybe even my assignment to SORD."

"You think one man has that much power to direct your life?" Konway asked, somewhat skeptical of Race's conclusion.

"I don't know," Race answered, his confidence on the rise as he started to put things together, "but I'm going to go find out."

"Well, you're going to have to wait," Zain stopped him. "You next," he said, pointing at Annette and motioning her to the door. "Just remember, anything that isn't in a file or on a recording, you don't know. You barely know the guy outside of work."

Annette nodded her agreement as she got up and left the

room. Race noticed that she had been quiet for most of the discussion since Zain had returned. He wasn't able to dwell on it long before he was up and pacing around, his mind now distracted by the large puzzle of events he was trying to put together.

*   *   *

Annette wasn't looking forward to her questioning. She had seen more than the others, which was probably why she was next to last. She took a deep breath before signaling the door that she was ready to enter. The door opened as she approached the admiral's office.

The admiral and her captain were standing off to the side. Neither one looked like they were too pleased with the current situation.

"Staff Sergeant," said a hologram of a man that had taken over the admiral's work area, "please sit down." Annette did as she was instructed, taking a seat in the chair across from the semi-transparent man. "Please state your rank, name, and ID for the record."

"Staff Sergeant Annette Keegan," Annette said, trying to get a read on the man questioning her. "773A9-TC1."

"Wait," the man said, suddenly caught off guard by Annette's answer, "what was that?"

"Staff Sergeant Annette Keegan, ID number 773A9-TC1, sir," Annette repeated. She could tell that even the two officers that had been shoved off to the side were a little confused by the general's reaction to her personal information.

"I had forgotten all about that," the man responded, his

hands moving around in the air as he attempted to look up information using a terminal on his side of the connection. "Well, that complicates things a little."

"I'm sorry, sir," Annette faked an apology.

The hologram stopped playing with his devices and returned his attention to Annette. "My name is General Vyson," the hologram stated. "I'm in charge of some of the military's most secretive operations."

"Like an alien ghost ship," Annette said, playing dumb. Like her fellow teammates, she had been trained in counter-interrogation techniques, which she planned to make full use of in her current situation.

"Like an alien ghost ship," the general acknowledged, thinking he had the upper hand. "Can you tell us what happened after you and your team boarded the alien vessel?"

"As the mapping system was getting a layout of the ship," Annette started to tell her story, trying to be as short as possible, "Staff Sergeant Allard decided to investigate one of the sections of the ship. McKinsey and I went along."

"Does Staff Sergeant Allard usually take off on his own like that?" the general interrupted.

"Yes, sir," Annette answered shortly.

"And you don't think it's odd?" the general asked.

"Not anymore, sir. It was the first couple of times after we first met him," Annette explained, "but after he saves your life a couple times, you just put your faith in him."

"Fair enough." The general nodded, making a note. "Please continue."

"We discovered the bridge with the alien corpse on it.

As we were looking around to see if we could gain access to one of the terminals, the captain ordered us to fall back and assist Staff Sergeant Amyas's team. He was getting some readings of movement on some of his sensors."

"Did you notice anything unusual about Staff Sergeant Allard's behavior before you left the bridge?" the general interrupted once again.

"No, sir," Annette lied. "He was focused, trying to get his mission done so he could assist the rest of the team."

She could see the general's jaw tense up as he was upset with her answer but trying not to show it. He waved her on to continue her story.

"We returned to the entrance point and followed Staff Sergeant Amyas's tether until we found a nice place to fortify. We were preparing to make a stand when Staff Sergeant Allard flew by us."

"He got there pretty quick then," the general questioned.

"I suppose so, sir. I hadn't really thought of it," Annette admitted.

"And then?" The general anxiously grabbed a datapad, ready to take some notes on the next section of the encounter.

"Staff Sergeant Allard disappeared down the corridor and returned a couple of seconds later carrying the rest of the team. One of them was injured, so I had to patch his wounds. Staff Sergeant Allard instructed us to activate our emergency-recall programs while he covered for us."

"At what point did you activate your recall, Staff Sergeant?" the general asked, sitting up in his chair, waiting intently for her answer.

Annette had to consider what information she could get away with here. She knew she could lie, but she knew her system was still recording at that time. "I didn't," Annette said, determining it was better to be honest at that point. "I wasn't about to abandon one of my teammates to that creature. I grabbed my rifle to join him, but as the creature attacked, my unit must have malfunctioned or been remotely activated."

"Are you sure that's what happened?" asked the general, staring at her through intimidating eyes.

"What else could it have been, sir?" Annette asked, picking up on some of the general's motives.

"What about Staff Sergeant Allard at that point?" the general asked, frustrated that she was dancing around his questions.

Annette could tell by her captain's smile that he was enjoying the general's frustrations. "I didn't get a good look, sir," Annette lied again. "The recall procedure activated before I had a chance to see what was going on with him."

"At what point did you break your tether?" the general asked, trying to keep his calm.

"I couldn't tell you, sir," Annette said. "I think it had pulled me back a couple of corners before I was able to cut the line."

"And when did you stop your live feedback to the shuttle?" the general asked.

"I cut my feed?" Annette asked, trying to appear innocent.

"If you're attempting to play dumb with me, Sergeant, I highly recommend against it," the general warned her.

"Not at all, sir," Annette defended herself. "I wasn't aware that my feed had stopped. I must have turned it off by accident when I was trying to disable my recall. Or perhaps it got damaged while I was being dragged back to the shuttle. I did take one of those corners pretty hard."

The general's face was starting to turn red in frustration as with each answer Annette attempted to skirt around what he really wanted to know. "And when you made it back to Staff Sergeant Allard?"

"By the time I got back to him, he was almost passed out on the floor. He had somehow managed to kill the alien, but it seemed to have taken everything out of him," Annette concluded her story.

"You didn't see anything?" the general said, clearly not buying Annette's story.

"No, sir," Annette answered sternly, hoping to get him to back off.

"Staff Sergeant Keegan, if you plan to continue your career in the Marines, I suggest you start being honest with me," the general demanded.

"I am, sir," Annette assured him.

"May I remind you that you're under oath," the general argued.

"You never swore me in, sir," Annette argued. If she could have punched the general in the face, there wasn't much that could stop her right now. "And if you did, I still would have told you the same story I just told you."

257

The door to the office opened up to reveal Congressman Martin being pushed in a wheelchair by one of the medics. "I think that's enough," the congressman ordered.

"Anthony," the admiral said, excited at the intrusion, "good to see you up and about."

"I'm doing my job here, Martin," the general said intently.

"Well, you're doing it wrong," the congressman argued as he floated his chair toward the desk. "You're giving these people the impression you're on a witch hunt, and they're responding to it like one."

The general looked at Annette, finally realizing why she had been fighting him so hard for the answers he wanted.

"If you want your answers, you're going to have to come clean," the congressman urged him.

"I was going to," the general admitted. "But there's been a complication."

"What?" the congressman almost demanded.

The general answered by looking over at Annette out of the corner of his eye.

"Return to your friends," the congressman ordered Annette. "We'll call you back in a minute."

Annette quickly saluted and removed herself from the room. She jumped the couple of steps to the door to the conference room and went back to her team.

"That was quick," Zain observed.

"I guess that means it's my turn," Race said, preparing to walk out the door.

"Not yet," Annette said, stopping him. "Congressman

Martin put a stop to the hearing."

"Oh, thank goodness." Race nearly collapsed in relief.

"They know about your abilities," Annette warned Race.

"What?" Race tensed up, his relief short-lived.

"I don't know," Annette answered. "It sounds like it's not going to be too long before we find out."

Before any of them could respond to Annette's statement, all of their arm units lit up, summoning them to the admiral's office.

They made their way into the small office, the lot of them having to stand at the back, as there was little room for all of them together.

"Let me first apologize if I made any of you feel uncomfortable," the general started to explain. "I see now that I approached this all wrong. By doing so, I put you all in a defensive position. What I'm about to tell you is of the highest security, equivalent to your discovery in the nebula. Because you're all already involved and aware of it, I'm enacting special security permissions so that I can discuss this with you."

The hologram started pacing the room. "As you all know, my name is General Vyson. It's my duty to track and monitor enhanced humans. For some time, the human race has been on the cusp of the next stage of evolution. Every day we're using more and more of our brains, and every so often someone comes along that's able to access a part of the brain that gives them enhanced abilities. Staff Sergeant Allard, you are one of those individuals." He stopped in front of Race to look at him face to face.

The general paused long enough to let the information

sink in to the four soldiers lined up in the room. They tried their best not to lose their composure.

"You're one of the strongest to date, Staff Sergeant," the hologram continued. "You have an innate sixth sense that allows you to accurately predict things before they're going to happen."

The general turned back around and walked to the desk, using it to prop himself up. "Most of your additional training was developed to hone that ability. It was meant to give you an edge, thus giving us an edge, like the fending off of the invasion you were so instrumental to. We don't normally tell people about their abilities until they're much older; however, not only are you one of the strongest precogs, you're also the first enhanced human with dual gifts, which surfaced yesterday. You have the ability to create some sort of telekinetic force field. We've seen you use the ability a couple of times before, but usually on a very minute level. Barely noticeable, even to you. Now that you're using them on such a large scale, it seems we can no longer hide it.

"Part of my job is to discover enhanced individuals and develop their abilities with training, just like we did with you," the general just about finished up his explanation. "I was questioning all of you because I was trying to determine how Staff Sergeant Allard was able to activate his telekinesis. Understanding that might let us know what to look for in others. So, if you all don't mind, I'd like to start this briefing over again, and this time I expect you all to cooperate a little more," the general scolded the crew.

Annette looked to Race for guidance on how he wanted

to proceed. She could tell that he was having a hard time taking in all the information, but several of the pieces were starting to fit together for all of them.

"Everything that happened over there, that was all me?" Race asked, not sure how much he believed.

"Unless you know something we don't, Staff Sergeant," the general stated.

"No, sir," Race said, obviously not ready to discuss his full encounter yet. "I just thought that maybe something on the ship might have caused it."

"Possible," the general stated. "I've had some people going over the readings, but haven't found anything unusual on the ship yet, other than two dead aliens."

"Let's just get to the point," Congressman Martin said. The congressman was slouching in his chair, about ready to fall out of it. "Do you have any idea of what activated your abilities?"

Race took a minute to think about it. "Honestly, sir, I don't have any clue. I didn't even really feel like I was in charge of myself. It felt like I was just working on autopilot. When the creature attacked, I just put out my hand and willed it into existence. I knew it would appear."

"This 'autopilot,' was it like your heightened senses from other instances?" the general asked.

"Partially, sir. Like when we were taught to meditate before a big fight," Race explained.

"Not surprising," the general said, starting to ponder the situation. "You once took down a whole fleet of special forces in that state."

"Exactly like that, sir," Race exclaimed, recalling the instance.

"That's what I was afraid of." The general sighed disappointedly. "Most likely your telekinesis was triggered by your primary ability."

"May I offer a suggestion?" The team's captain spoke up from the back of the room. "Now that we're all in the loop about it, maybe we could do some experiments to further explore Allard's abilities, get a better understanding of them and what he's capable of."

"I'd be willing to permit that," the general agreed, almost enthused by the prospect, "as long as it's done in a secure environment."

"SORD HQ has all that, sir," the captain answered, "assuming it's still in one piece."

"Very well," the general agreed. "No one else is allowed to see any of your test results except for me."

"Understood, sir." The captain nodded.

"I guess we're done here?" the congressman asked warily.

"I believe so," the general responded. "Dismissed." The general hit a piece of space in front of him that caused his image to disappear.

"Since we had to send my nurse away, would you be so kind as to wheel me back to medical, Staff Sergeant Allard?" the congressman requested.

Race looked over to the two officers finally coming out of their confinement in the corner of the room now that the general was gone. They both nodded their permission, causing him to rush to the congressman's side and push his chair.

"I'm sorry about that," the admiral said, taking his seat back. "That's not how I would have liked that situation to go. You've all done a remarkable job here, and I want to thank you all for your help. As for your next assignment, you'll be returning back to the nebula. We'll give you a few days to get properly geared up for the task before sending you out. You need to secure the ship, do a full sweep for any more hostiles, and see what you can find out about it before the science team gets here. We'll be reissuing you the same shuttle for you to go back and forth, but you might as well just consider it your home for a while, as you're only going to be coming back to resupply and debrief every couple of days."

"Understood, sir," the captain acknowledged. "Will we have any support?"

"I'll still make the Marines you took with you available," the admiral offered, "but we don't want anyone else to find out about this. The fewer people that know, the better. I'll see if I can swing some power armor for you, too."

"Sweet," Annette heard Zain whisper next to her.

"Very well," the captain said. "Anything else, sir?"

"I think that will cover it," the admiral stated. The two officers exchanged a salute, causing the rest of the team to salute in turn. "Dismissed."

*　　*　　*

Illandra was excited. She could feel Race approaching the medical center. She did her best to relax, but it was hard to not reach out and touch him with her mind. She was still experiencing somewhat of a headache from her last attempt. The doctor wanted to give her some medicine to relieve the pain, but she had managed to talk her into holding off for a little while, at least until Anthony returned and informed her of what had happened.

She hadn't expected him to bring Race back with him, but she was glad that he was. She quickly checked herself over using one of the wall monitors as a poor mirror. "Eh," she said, disappointed with the appearance the medical center had left her in, "he's seen me worse."

She heard a door open in the outer hall as it filled with Anthony's voice. She could barely contain herself; it took everything she had to act natural and not jump up out of bed to go see them. Not that she would have made it very far in her current condition.

Illandra could hear them on the other side of the dull gray wall next to her as Race helped the congressman into his bed.

"Thanks for your help, lad," she heard Anthony say. "You'd better go check on Illandra while you're here. I can tell she's anxious to see you."

"Way to be subtle, old man," Illandra cursed to herself.

"She's okay?" Race asked, almost as excited as Illandra was.

"Who do you think sent me to go rescue you from your trial?" Anthony answered. "She would have gone herself, but the doctor wouldn't let her get out of bed. She's in the room right next door."

"Do you think she's awake?" Race asked. "I don't want to

disturb her if she's resting."

"I'm awake," Illandra answered over the wall.

She could hear the opening and closing of Anthony's door as Race hurried to make his way over to her room. The door to her little room opened a second later as Race came bursting through.

"Oh my goodness," Race said, almost on the edge of tears, "I'm so glad you're okay." He ran over to her and wrapped his arms around her, practically lifting her off the bed. Even though they hadn't been that physical since their reunion, it really made her feel happy to be back in his arms again.

"I heard you were pretty busy," she said, taking one last moment to enjoy it before pushing him back enough for her to breath.

"I wanted to stay, but…" Race jumped to defend himself.

"I wasn't blaming you," Illandra said, cutting him off. "I just heard you had a lot going on."

"You wouldn't believe it," Race said, relaxing a bit. "I'm not even sure I believe it. I was there."

"Oh, you'd be surprised." Illandra smirked, trying not to give too much away.

"Have they told you how long they're going to keep you here?" Race asked.

"A couple of days for observation," she answered. "I've still got this mega-huge headache. They said I was lucky you got me here so quick. Otherwise things could have been much worse. Any idea what's going to happen to you next?"

"I think we're going back out to the nebula for a couple

of days," Race said. "I'll try and stick around as much as I can, though."

"Don't worry about it too much," Illandra said. "I need to catch up on my beauty sleep as it is. Speaking of which, I think it's almost time for some."

"Oh, I'll let you rest then," Race said, getting up off of her bed. "I need to catch up with my crew, anyways. If you need anything, just let me know."

"Could you tell the doctor that I'm ready for that medicine she wanted to give me?"

"You got it," he said, giving her one last hug before heading out the door. "I'm really glad you're okay."

"Why didn't you talk to the boy about what happened?" Anthony asked over the wall once Race was clearly outside of the room.

"He wasn't ready," Illandra answered, annoyed with her mentor's eavesdropping. "Plus, this isn't quite the best environment to do it in."

"I guess you're right," Anthony yawned. Illandra could feel the toll his little trip had taken on him. "I wouldn't wait too long, though. We'll probably be shipping off here soon after we're cleared."

"What?" Illandra said, already pulling the answer from his mind.

"Peace has obviously failed on this front; it's now the military's job here," Anthony explained. "It's only a matter of time before they reassign us somewhere else."

The joy Illandra had felt from seeing Race again quickly faded as she realized he was once again going to be ripped away from her.

"Don't worry, lass," her mentor said, trying to comfort her, "I don't think the universe could keep you two apart, even if it wanted to."

*   *   *

Illandra regretted telling Race not to check on her. He only stopped by once to see her before leaving. There were several lonely days in the medical center after that while they waited to be cleared. Anthony had been able to work from his little room when the doctor allowed him to. With each discussion, Illandra could hear his prediction of them leaving coming closer to fulfillment.

The calls that she enjoyed most were the ones that he received from his wife. The discussions made Illandra feel nostalgic and miss some of her own family. Enough to call her own parents and inform them of what had happened. She'd barely even finished her story before she had to talk the both of them out of jumping on the next transport to see her.

By the end of the week, the medical chief had lifted the restrictions on Illandra and Anthony. They returned to assist the ship's staff. Anthony had requested that they be allowed to sit in on the staff briefings so he could at least be informed on the matter at hand. The meetings were terribly boring, but it did allow Illandra to see Race when they were back resupplying.

The meetings took place in the admiral's conference room. The long crescent table was usually packed by the senior staff, with twice as many people packed into the staging area directly next to it. Anthony was oddly out of place in his official suit. Illandra's white uniform looked very similar to the United Forces uniform; the black accents in the shoulders were the only thing that made her stand out. The Marines' uniforms stood out almost as much as her mentor's. The blue jackets covered white dress shirts. They looked like stiff boards. When she caught Race in his uniform it made her heart beat a little faster, no matter how many times he clawed at the neck.

Then the morning came that Anthony had warned her about. The president had finally ordered Anthony's presence in a series of conferences to attempt a peaceful resolution to the conflict on the Consortium capital planet. There were also a couple of meetings scheduled with representatives from the Euro-Alliance in the hope of gaining their support. Illandra knew from her political education that the Euro-Alliance would attempt to retain neutrality in the conflict, but considering the situation, she knew the president felt it was at least worth trying.

Illandra and Anthony were in one of their last meetings aboard the Puller when Illandra felt a weird feeling coming from within the room. It was one of the few occasions when Race and his team were aboard; she had just seen him the night before.

Illandra attempted to scan the room, looking for the source, which she tracked down to a man that had accompanied Race and his team on their special assignment. Illandra recognized the Marine as Corporal Simmons from the infirmary; he had sustained some sort of injury on their first mission in the nebula. He had only been there for a short time, having been released early as his wounds healed miraculously overnight. Illandra recalled the chief's concern over the expedited healing she had observed.

"Why can't anyone hear me?" a ghostly voice suddenly echoed through the room.

Illandra looked for the voice but couldn't see anyone talking to match it to.

"You're all in danger!" the voice came once again, shouting this time.

Illandra saw a faint image of the corporal's face superimposed over itself as it tried to talk without moving its own mouth. She had tried not to use her abilities that much since the accident per Anthony's recommendations, but she was starting to get the feeling that she didn't have much of a choice.

Illandra looked around the room to see if anyone else had noticed the disruption. She could tell that both Anthony and Race were scanning the room for something as well, but they obviously hadn't heard the same thing she had. For the first time, she was able to sense Race's abilities kicking in to address a danger. She wanted to continue to explore the unusual experience as the distractions started to peel away and details sharpened, but the danger at hand didn't give her that opportunity.

Illandra reached out with her mind, hoping to find the source, hoping she could talk back to whatever it was. *"Who are you?"*

"Oh my god! You can hear me!" the ghostly image shar-

ing Corporal Simmons's body said, a little more clearly now that she was making a connection.

"*Yes. Now, who are you?*" Illandra demanded.

"*I'm Corporal Simmons,*" the ghost said. "*This...this thing's taken over my body. I'm no longer in control. It's been doing something on the alien ship. You have to warn them!*"

"*What do I tell them?*" Illandra asked. "*How do I explain this?*"

"*I don't know. You have to find a way,*" the ghost said. "*He's been doing something in one of the deserted corridors. If he's not stopped soon, something bad is going to...*" The voice drifted off. She could see Race reaching under the table to put his hand on his sidearm. "*Oh no... It knows. The chest! The proof is on his chest!*"

Before Illandra could respond, the overlying ghost was enveloped by shadows as Illandra felt it ripped from existence. Fear trembled down to Illandra's core as she jumped back, almost falling out of her chair.

Race had also jumped up from his chair, pulling his sidearm and pointing it at Corporal Simmons.

The conversation suddenly stopped as everyone in the room looked at the standing duo.

"You monster!" yelled Illandra. "What did you do to him?"

"What are you talking about, ma'am?" said the impersonator.

"Captain. Admiral." Race came to Illandra's aid. "You know that thing I'm not supposed to talk about? Well, it's on fire right now, and it's all pointing to Corporal Simmons right now."

"Admiral," Illandra pleaded, trying to put the nearest guard between her and the imposter, "something has taken over Corporal Simmons's body. He's been doing something on that ship. We're all in danger."

"I don't know what you're talking about, ma'am," the doppelganger objected, cool as ice.

"How do you know this?" Admiral Montana asked, trying to get the situation under control.

"Corporal Simmons told me," answered Illandra. "The real Corporal Simmons! He said the proof would be on his chest. Take off his shirt!"

"What?" protested the creature. "I'm not taking off my..."

"Do it," threatened Race with a tone dark enough to send chills down Illandra's back.

"Corporal Simmons," interrupted the admiral, "if something as simple as taking off your shirt will resolve this, let's just get it over with."

"But, sir..." objected the creature.

"That's not a request, Corporal," the admiral interrupted. "Take your shirt off, or I will have these two Marines hold you down and take it off for you."

Two of the Marines approached the imposter, taking up positions on either side of him. The impersonator let out a sigh as it stood up and started to unbutton its outer blouse. The room was silent with anticipation as they waited for the results.

The creature placed the top of his uniform on the chair

271

in front of him. A kick from the monster caught everyone off guard as it ripped the large conference table from the ground, sending it flying toward the staff on the opposite side. Race caught the massive table with a single hand and nudged it back safely to the ground, preventing any injury to those near him.

The creature used its empowered fists to send its guards flying with one massive blow each. Race jumped the table and planted both of his feet in the creature's chest, sending the beast flying back to join the two soldiers. Race charged the creature, making sure that it focused on him as the major threat.

As the creature got to its feet, it was already attempting to dodge Race's punches. It tried to fight back, but Race was always one step ahead of it, each time blocking the blow or dodging it to quickly hit him somewhere else.

Several soldier in the room were in awe of the display of physical prowess between the two, but none so much as Illandra. Inside Race's head, she could see his abilities in full awe-inspiring motion. She could see how Race knew every move the creature was going to make ten moves before he even did it. Her mind literally had to slow everything down just for her to experience the full effect of it, the fight almost moving at a snail's pace as every detail became hyper-focused for her.

There was a break in the battle as Race caught one of the creature's arms and forced it to bend over. The arm snapped under the force of Race's pressure, almost startling everyone in the room. "Sir," Race addressed the admiral, "I'm sure these soldiers would feel better if they could use their weapons."

The broken arm miraculously repaired itself as the creature made a dash for Admiral Montana to stop him from activating the defenses against him. Race hooked the creature's foot with his and brought him back to the floor, twisting its leg around his knee to break it like a twig.

The admiral quickly shouted the command to activate the Marines' weapons and designate Corporal Simmons as hostile; they were now about to direct their fire at him. The Marines pulled out their weapons and aimed in as Race kicked the impostor in the chest to create some distance between them. The wave of ammunition started to sting the creature, causing it to try and take cover. The attack didn't seem to be doing any real damage. The creature ran toward the door and hit it with its fist, a huge dent appearing in the reinforced metal where its hand had struck.

The remaining members of Race's team had taken a position in front of Illandra to protect her from the creature should it escape Race. The creature continued to beat away at the door, another dent forming from each massive blow.

The Marines' fire was tearing away at the creature's clothes. Illandra could see the wounds instantly healing themselves even as the projectiles were coming out the other side of the corporal's body. She also saw what the real corporal had tried to warn her about. A good portion of the creature's chest was now covered with patches of metal scales, strong enough that the Marines' onslaught bounced off of it in some places.

Race had been standing off to the side fiddling with his weapon but had yet to pull the trigger. "Set your weapons for high-powered energy output and prepare to fire," Race yelled to the Marines.

The creature turned to look at Race, its eyes bulging as it heard Race's plans. It started to charge Race just as something went wrong with its arm. The creature staggered to its knees, its face turning red in agony as it desperately clawed at the device around its forearm.

"Now," Race yelled.

Several bolts of lightning coursed through the room, attacking the corporal's body. After a couple of seconds, the batteries in the Marines' weapons started to drain, the number of beams fading.

Illandra could feel Corporal Simmons's presence start to come back to him. He looked around the room somewhat dazed, the attack finally starting to die out. When he saw Illandra hiding in the back, he smiled at her. "Thank you," he said before falling lifelessly to the floor.

Illandra tried to hide her face as a tear rolled down her cheek in mourning of the Marine.

Chapter 9

REVELATION

Record Date: 349.193 PGST

"STAY BACK," RACE SAID, BLOCKING a Marine who was about to go check on the fallen corporal.

"You think he's infectious?" asked his captain.

"Maybe. Something's still wrong." The sense of danger was still coursing through most of Race's body.

The ship's admiral punched a command into his comm unit. "Chief Medical Officer Tenaway," he ordered.

"Yes, sir," the image of the ship's head doctor said as it appeared upon the admiral's unit.

"We have a situation. I need you up here with a quarantine team right away," commanded the admiral. "Bring a body bag with you."

"On my way, sir," the medical officer replied before the admiral's sensor unit went blank.

Some of the other soldiers were checking on the two that had taken the possessed corporal's initial attack. The mighty blows had done a number on the two soldiers; one was suffering from several cracked ribs while the other was having difficulty breathing.

"I think his lung is collapsing," Annette stated intently, causing some of the crew to rush in response. "Someone get me an emergency kit!"

One of the officers hit a panel in a wall to release a small case that he rushed over to Annette. She opened the container and started fishing around for supplies. She pulled out a couple of devices that she quickly pieced together and was about to slam it into the wounded man's chest when the doors opened up. The medical staff and her team entered the room. One of the medics immediately caught sight of Annette with the device in her hand and rushed over to stop her.

"What's the matter?" he asked, his voice slightly distorted by the quarantine suit he was wearing. "Collapsed lung?"

"Yup," Annette said, lifting her hands high above her head in preparation, "and he's fading fast."

"Hold on," the medic said, stopping Annette in her tracks while he reached into his medical kit. "I've got something a little better than that. Show me the medical readout from his sensor."

Annette quickly dropped the device she was about to plunge into the soldier's chest and picked up his arm so the medic could see the panel on the soldier's arm. The medic took a quick look at it and punched in a couple of settings on the device he had pulled from his kit. He pinched a pair of clamps on the outer edge of the device and attached it to the soldier's bare chest. Within seconds, the soldier was breathing normally.

"This does that," the medic explained, pointing at the

two devices, "but it also injects medicine and can help repair any damage to the lung. Nice diagnosis, though. Don't meet too many grunts that can diagnose that."

"We've had a lot of special training," Annette answered modestly.

"Keep an eye on him; I'm going to go check on the others." The medic moved on to the other injured soldier. "Come get me if his status changes."

The rest of the medical team had started handing out containment suits to the individuals stuck in the room. The suits were a classic bright orange that was painful on the eyes. Race took his suit to the back of the room, making use of a bench that had been pulled out of the wall to support him. The power that had coursed through his body while fighting was starting to fade, leaving him weak and drained. He quickly removed his loose outer garments and put them in a quarantine bag before donning the suit over the rest of his clothes. Using the strap, he slung the bag containing his belongings over his shoulders. He activated the suit's systems, which vacuumed out all of the air, making the suit almost skintight, while he took a seat on the bench to regain his strength. He was almost happy to have the suit on; he hadn't even been aware of the smell from the charred soldier until the quarantine suit had filtered it out.

Race started replaying everything that had just happened in his head. He had tried not to use the full strength, as he had before when fighting the alien, but it still took a toll on him. Now that everything had an explanation, there wasn't much for him to question. He still felt that he was missing something, though. "Are you okay?" a stranger's voice came from behind him.

Race turned to see one of the younger nurses standing near him in an identical orange hazmat suit. He had seen her a couple of times before when visiting the medical center on the ship, catching her looking at him for some strange reason. He hoped it wasn't news of his feats making the rounds. "I'm fine," Race answered, turning back to his mental replay.

"I heard you were in a scrap with the madman over there," she explained. "I should do a quick scan just to make sure."

"It's really not necessary," Race tried to object.

"It will only take a second," the nurse protested, taking out a long cylindrical device and pulling on a handle to have a large screen come out of it.

"Don't be stubborn," he heard Illandra scold him from off to the side.

Race sighed and nodded for the nurse to do her job. She held out her hands and traced Race's body using the device. The device overlaid Race's skeletal and muscular structure on top of him for the nurse to get a good reading.

"Have you been working out lately?" the nurse asked.

"Not since this morning," Race answered. "Why?"

"It's just that you have a lot of scarring throughout your muscle tissue. I wouldn't expect to see something like this unless you were a massive bodybuilder just finishing a strenuous workout. Even then…"

Race could sense Illandra raising a concerned eyebrow at him as she stopped her nervous pacing for a second before resuming.

"It was a pretty strenuous fight," Race explained, pointing to the now-closed body bag. "I had to push myself pretty hard."

"Well, it doesn't look too serious," the nurse concluded. "I'll give you a little something for the soreness; it should help rebuild the tissue as well."

"Thanks, doc," Race said as the nurse injected him in the back of the arm using one of the suit's built-in medicine compartments.

"If you like, stop by medical some time. I'll give you the recipe I use for my post-workout drink." She smiled before taking off.

"She likes you," Illandra blurted out nervously, biting one of her nails.

"What makes you think that?" Race chuckled in disbelief.

"It's pretty obvious," Illandra said, crossing her arms. "Why else would she try and get you to come to see her later?"

"She was just being nice," Race said, defending the stranger.

"Clueless as ever, I see." Illandra amused herself. "I just spent two years in the university learning how to read people."

"Is that how you knew what was wrong with him?" Race asked, motioning her to take a seat next to him on the bench.

"Kind of." She nervously dodged the question while sitting down. "I never had someone try and kill me before; it's pretty nerve-racking."

"You get used to it," Race assured her.

"Really?" Illandra asked, shocked at the possibility.

"Nope." Race smiled.

Illandra let out a barely audible moan to show her disappointment with Race's untimely humor.

"Staff Sergeant Allard, Miss Page," the admiral called for them to join his conversation with Race's captain. "A moment, please."

The two got up from the bench and made their way to the admiral along with Congressman Martin, who felt he should also be a part of the conversation. Race could feel the soreness throughout his body as he got up. "Yes, sir," Race reported once they had reached him.

"Quite a show you two caused. Care to explain what just happened?" the admiral asked.

"I can already tell you that this involves some of those highly classified topics such as those we discussed the day this lad came back from the nebula out there," Anthony cut in before either of them could answer.

"I'm not going to be hearing from your friend the general, am I?" Race's captain asked, already upset at the notion.

"I doubt it," Anthony assured him. "He'll probably pull most of what he needs off the ship's video systems. He might call if he has a few follow-up questions."

The admiral snarled at the suggestion. "All right. We'll meet later to clarify all this. The two of you should change into your quarantine suits," he suggested to Illandra and Anthony, who were still wearing their normal attire.

"I was just waiting for a booth to open up," Illandra responded, pointing to the corner of the room where the medical staff had set up some dividers to give privacy to some of the shyer members of the room. "This dress isn't the easiest to get in and out of."

"Understood." The admiral smiled.

"Looks like one is opening up now," she said, noticing someone stepping out of one. "If you'll excuse me."

As Illandra walked off, the chief medical officer approached the commanding team. "What happened here?" she asked.

"The corporal there went crazy," the admiral stated, once again pointing to the black bag that held the burnt body in it. "Started throwing people around. The staff sergeant here engaged him in combat, broke some bones that we all watched repair themselves. So we fried him."

"What's that all over his chest?" the chief said in disbelief.

"We're working under the assumption that he was exposed to something in the nebula," the admiral clarified. "Maybe his encounter with the thing that attacked him."

"I'll have to do an autopsy," the chief sighed. "It's going to be rough with so little to go on."

"If I may," interrupted one of the few men not wearing a uniform. What hair the man had was restricted to the sides and back, and mostly gray. "I'm Doctor Filmond; I'm a biologist on the advanced teams sent here to examine the life forms. May I be of any assistance?"

"Doctor Filmond," the chief medic gasped, "I had no

idea you were on board!"

"Sorry, Doctor…"

"Tenaway," the medical officer supplied.

"A pleasure." He nodded respectfully to the medical officer. "Anyways, I'm still waiting for members of my team to get here. I've done enough preliminary research that if there is a tie between this man and the alien, I should be able to help you discover it."

"Chief?" The admiral asked for her blessing.

"Why, yes!" the chief said ecstatically. "I'd never turn down the opportunity to work with such a great biologist. However, I think your skills would be underutilized performing a simple autopsy."

"Whatever gets us out of these suits," commented the admiral.

"I think I should go, too," Race interrupted.

"You still think there's a threat, Allard?" the captain asked him.

"Yes, sir," Race confirmed.

"I'd like to go, too," Illandra said, rejoining the group in her orange quarantine suit that managed to be tighter than her uniform.

"Admiral…" the doctor started to object.

"Trust me, Chief," the admiral cut her off. "It's for your own good. These two exposed the corporal; they could be the key to helping you solve this mystery."

"Staff Sergeant Allard has a knack for doing his own thing when the time calls for it," the captain said quietly, conferring with the admiral. "I'd like another one of my men to go with them to protect the congressman's assistant and back up Allard if there is any danger."

The admiral pursed his lips as he considered the captain's request against his chief medic's concerns. "Very well," he agreed.

"Staff Sergeant Keegan," the captain hollered across the room to Race's teammate, who seemed to be on the verge of losing her temper at some unwanted attention from some of the room's male audience.

Annette quickly rushed over to join the small group. "Yes, sir?" she reported upon arriving.

"They're taking the body back to the medical center for investigation. I want you to go and back up Allard if he needs it, but your priority is Miss Page's safety," the captain briefed her.

"And stay out of the chief's way," the admiral added. "All of you."

"Yes, sir," the three acknowledged as the medical officer's concerns were addressed.

Race moved to help the medical staff pick up the equipment they needed to take back with him. They ended up putting it on the gurney with the corpse, which Race and Annette carried out. The gurney had some gravity reducers to lighten the load, but Race still struggled to lift it in his weekend state. At least the medicine the nurse had given him was starting to help his condition.

Upon reaching the medical bay, Race and Annette took the corpse to a private room in the back. They placed the black bag on the table in the center and removed the auxiliary equipment so the doctor could do her job. Once they were done, they retreated from the operating area into a small observation room off to the side.

Race had barely entered the room before he was hacking into the medical bay's computer system, using the window's built-in display to start streaming loads of data. It didn't take him long before he ran out of space. He started switching streams, focusing in on a couple at a time, trying to figure out if he could determine the source of the danger he was still feeling.

"I hate it when he gets like this," Illandra said, taking a seat in one of the chairs in the small room.

"Like what?" Annette asked, taking a sentry position as far away from Illandra as possible.

"All data-comatose," Illandra explained, kicking her feet like a bored child.

"I think it's kind of fascinating," Annette admitted.

"It is," Illandra agreed, "but you can't get him to say two words to you when he's like that. We could be making out right now, and he wouldn't even notice."

"What?" Race said, his attention suddenly pulled away from his data.

"Okay, maybe not." Illandra smiled amusedly. "But it's not going to happen. Get back to work."

Race shook his head before returning to the window chaining through the different streams.

"I hear you're quite the pilot," Illandra said to Annette after the boredom began to wear away at her again. "Well, I say heard, but I did experience it firsthand during the invasion. Very impressive."

"Thank you. I like to think so, ma'am," Annette answered, retaining her guardlike façade.

"Please, call me Illandra," Illandra insisted. "You and Race are practically family, no need to be so formal."

"Yes, Illandra." Annette choked on the name.

"So what got you so interested in piloting?" Illandra asked, motioning Annette to sit next to her.

Race took a second from shifting through his data to note to himself that this was the most time the two women had ever spent together, and it was making him very nervous.

Annette waved with her hand to say she was fine where she was. "My dad likes to think it's genetics," she answered. "He would even tell you that I started piloting before I could walk. The last three generations of Keegan's designed and built about three quarters of all the ships in the UGR, even consulted on some for the other governments as well. I was raised on shipbuilding platforms. I spent most of my time helping him with testing and repairs."

"What was wrong with all the other kids?" Illandra asked. "Why weren't you hanging out with them?"

"I did. Some." A reminiscent smile appeared on Annette's face. "I think my dad got tired of all the calls from parents complaining when I beat up their kids."

"I'm not surprised," Race mumbled, enjoying hearing Annette's story. It hadn't occurred to him that he barely knew anything about Annette's life story before joining the Marines. It had taken Illandra to even bring it out of her.

"Shush, you," Illandra said, trying to kick him from across the room, her short legs not even getting close. "This is girl talk. What about your mother?" Illandra said, turning her attention back to Annette.

"She died when I was young," Annette said softly. "An accident on one of the construction jobs."

"I'm sorry to hear that." Illandra felt awkward that she had brought it up.

Even Race was upset by the news. They constantly talked about Zain's huge family and Konway's wife and kids, but he barely knew anything about Annette's family.

"Maybe that's why you two are so comfortable around each other." Illandra waved her finger between the other two individuals in the observation room, stating Race's unspoken thought. "Did you know Race has never met his father?" she asked in response to Annette's questioning expression.

"He hasn't?" Annette said, somewhat surprised.

"That's not something I like to talk about," Race said, revealing that he was paying more attention to their conversation than they probably liked.

"I know," Illandra acknowledged, brushing off his concerns. "We actually had a whole module dedicated to the subject back at the university. Abandonment issues and such. One of the more contradictory subjects we covered. You'd probably benefit from a couple of sessions with a professional counselor."

"You're not helping," Race said, still rolling through the streaming data.

"Sorry, you know I get chatty when I'm nervous," Illandra defended herself. "I get chatty when I'm nervous," she repeated to Annette.

"It's fine," Annette said, almost amused by Illandra's behavior. "What are you nervous about?" she asked, trying to give Illandra something else to talk about.

"Well, I did just have a conversation with a dead soldier who then turned around and tried to kill us. I also just found out we're being reassigned, so I only have a couple more days on the ship here. Not to mention I'm wearing way less than I care to admit under this godforsaken outfit."

"How do you mean you talked to a dead soldier?" Annette asked, trying to process the load of information that had just come rambling out of Illandra.

"It's kind of hard to explain," she said, sitting up straight in her seat, realizing something might have slipped past her lips that shouldn't have. "Probably not even the right way to put it."

"What do you mean you're being reassigned?" Race interrupted their conversation.

"Well, this is a military matter now," Illandra said, a little bit more comfortable with this subject. "We're going to try some more direct routes, negotiating with the IGC and others directly."

"When are you…" Race's attention was suddenly drawn back to his data as the two doctors seemed to have found something that alerted his senses.

He quickly brought up the interfaces on his display to see what it was they were looking at.

"What is that?" Race called into the intercom adjoining

the two areas.

"I almost don't believe it," Doctor Filmond said, turning to look over his shoulder at the observation room. "I think they're nanites. But they're some of the smallest I've ever seen. The thing is, I recognize them."

"From where?" Chief Tenaway asked, surprised.

"Our headless specimen from the nebula," the doctor answered. "Did they have any contact on the ship?"

"Yes," Race answered. "He gave him a deep cut on his chest."

"That wound healed remarkably fast," the chief noted, recalling the incident. "I just thought he was one of those rare people that reacted exceptionally well to the medication."

"It's possible that it infected him in the process," the doctor thought out loud. "Most nanites are symbiotic and serve a medical purpose; the first thing they'd want to do is repair any fatal damage. That could explain the wound, and the quick repairs from the fight with you, Staff Sergeant."

"And then what?" Race asked. "It just took over him?"

"It's possible," the doctor said, rolling the idea over in his head, not completely able to accept it himself. "Stop the flow of information from the brain and replace it with its own transmission. There does seem to be a high concentration of them near the top of the spinal column. That would mean that the person would almost be a prisoner in his own body."

"Or worse," Illandra whispered coldly.

"Do you have a specialist on nanotechnology on board, Chief Tenaway?" the doctor asked. "I'd love to get a better look at them."

"Our engineer is a specialist in the field," the chief informed him. "I'll call him right up."

"Let me see if I can find some that are still active while we're waiting," the doctor said, returning to the body.

"Commander Trent." Illandra resumed chatting after Race disabled the intercom. "They're dating. They'd like to take the next step in their relationship, but she's not too sure about it. He doesn't take a lot of things seriously, and she's afraid their relationship might be one of them. But she really enjoys her time with him, so she's thinking about giving it a chance."

"And they told you this?" Race asked, attempting to refocus on the task at hand.

"Most of it," Illandra answered, returning to scanning the room for something to entertain her. "I'm a people person, it's what I'm trained to do."

"I'm beginning to think there's something else going on," Race objected, causing Illandra to flinch in surprise. "As long as I've known you, you've been able to make people just open up to you. I've known Annette for a year and a half now. I doubt I ever would have learned all that stuff about her had you not just gotten her to casually open up about it like you were best friends. How do you do it? What's your secret?" The more Race questioned her, the more Illandra started to tense up, hinting that he was onto something. "What are you hiding?"

Before Illandra could answer, the door to the lab opened up as they were joined by the ship's engineer. The whisper of danger in Race's ears was starting to crescendo as he focused in on the device the commander was carrying. "We're not done." He abandoned his interrogation and returned to his wall of data streams.

He could feel his senses starting to kick in. Now that he understood them more, it was easier for him to relax and let them do their thing instead of questioning them and complicating the process. By the time the commander had set up his station, Race had already cracked most of its systems and added several new streams to his wall of data. Bella had also taken over his display, converting some of the raw data feeds into a streaming graph to make it easier for Race to see.

Doctor Filmond handed the commander a sample of the nanites he had obtained. "They're starting to die out. Can you supply them with an electric charge for them to feed off of?"

"Sure," the commander answered, placing the sample in his device. "How much would you like?"

"A hundred watts should do," the doctor answered. "That's about what they would get from inside a human host."

"Done," Commander Trent responded after hitting a couple of buttons on his device. "Now let's see what we've got here."

Illandra had come up behind Race to peek over his shoulder, resting her arm on his shoulder. He could feel something strange come over him as she joined him, almost like he was sharing everything he saw with her.

"You may think what I do is intriguing," Illandra gasped

in astonishment, "but when I see what you do, it's just as fascinating."

"What are you talking about?" Race said, not really paying attention to her anymore.

"Come here." Illandra beckoned Annette to join them. "You've got to see this."

Annette took a second to debate whether she really wanted to take Illandra up on the proposition, but she caved in to her curiosity. She joined the two at the display. Illandra took her hand when she came near and pulled her close, a little closer than Race or Annette really felt comfortable with.

Annette just looked at the screen as she watched Race continue to figure out what was going on.

"I don't…" Annette stuttered. "I don't even know what to say. What's happening?"

"This is what it's like seeing things through Race's eyes. It's like someone took a bunch of puzzles and threw them all together and you're going through all the pieces you need at lightning speed," Illandra told her, enjoying the experience.

Race's attention suddenly snapped on the commander's device, the two girls mirroring his movement almost in unison. The holoscreen on the device that the commander was using had started to flash as something seemed to be interfering with the signal. Annette reached out and hit the intercom button almost in response to Race's impulse to do so.

"…broken again," they heard the commander's voice say as the channel activated.

"I don't think that's the case," Race said, causing the three working on the nanites to glance over at him momentarily.

"Nah," the commander said, "it's been acting up lately. I've just been putting off replacing it until I could get the credits."

The holo-image cleared as a strange face suddenly came into view.

"Or maybe not?" Commander Trent declared, stepping back from the hologram. "I definitely didn't program them for that."

"Did the nanites take over your device?" the doctor asked, almost as terrified as he was excited.

"I…I think so," the commander answered, just as excited. "But that's… I don't believe it."

"First attempt of incursion failed," the holographic image crackled. "Threats to incursion must be dealt with before next wave. Identifying…"

"Commander," Race addressed the engineer, "does your device have anything potentially dangerous?"

"Not really. It's mostly just tools and sensors," the commander explained.

The window that Race was using to stream his data suddenly shifted as the data suddenly became scrambled. Race knew that the nanites had taken over the lab.

"Get down," he yelled in unison with Illandra and Annette.

A surgical laser shot out from some of the operating equipment, hitting Commander Trent. Luckily, the commander had moved enough for it to only tag him in the arm before he got to the ground and took cover behind one of the tables. The medical chief wasted no time pushing Doctor Filmond into an adjoining office.

Even as the lasers were turning to target the trio in the observation room, Annette was pushing Illandra to the ground. Race turned to catch the two, using his body to shield the two women from the broken glass as the window shattered from several laser blasts breaking through it. As the trio fell to the floor in unison, Race knew that it was only a matter of time before the lasers burrowed their way through the wall between them or found another way to kill them. Making sure to keep low, Race sat up and reached for the door. He tried to open the door to no avail; the program had confined them so they'd be an easier target. There was only one thing for him to do, as much as he loathed the idea.

He took a quick look at the two women cowering on the floor. Annette was still holding Illandra, covering her with her body. "I'm sorry," he said as he met her eyes, almost regretting the fury he was about to release.

Race closed his eyes and took a deep breath through his nose. As he released his breath, he felt the transformation. He opened his eyes; the haze from the blue fire coated his sight. Race stood and turned to the door, his palm stretched toward it. The door exploded in front of him under his will. He entered the examination room, blocking a laser blast destined for his head with one of his telekinetic shields. With his other hand, he created another razor-like force field that he used to cut the laser from its control arm. Two more lasers attempted to cut him down, both meeting another charged field pulled out of thin air. Grabbing one with his powers, Race turned its fire onto the other before crushing it into rubble.

Race just ripped the last laser out of the ceiling before it could start to fire upon him as he continued his steady pace across the room to the device the nanites had taken over. The crude holographic face was looking at him intently. "You have no place here," he said to the machine, using the alien language he had used before.

Before the machine could respond, Race slammed his outstretched hands together, his power crushing the device as it mimicked his motion.

The danger was gone, but there was still one thing he needed to do. He walked over to the nearest console in the room and reached out with his hand. Taking control of the device with his mind, he started to complete one last task.

*　　*　　*

Even though she had seen it all from her connection inside Race's head, Illandra was still shaken from the whole experience of getting shot at. Race had left the observation room, leaving her pinned to the floor by Annette. She had seen Race's transformation as he tapped into his new power, but more importantly, she had felt the fear that it had struck into Annette. Probably because it only amplified her own fear of what emerged from Race's trance.

The noise from the attack had died down, but she wasn't sure it was safe. She had heard Race mumble something intangible just before the final crash that silenced the room. She had reached out to try and touch his mind, but something was interfering with her ability to do so.

"You know if he sees us like this, we'll probably never live it down," Illandra commented to her protector, hoping to persuade Annette to get off of her.

"I think your safety is a little more important," Annette replied sternly.

"I'm pretty sure the danger has passed," Illandra argued. "The noise seems to have died out. I think it's safe for us to get up."

"Let me check," Annette said, sitting up to peek over the ledge that had been blown away, using one hand to keep Illandra pinned on the ground.

Illandra used their physical connection to see through Annette's eyes and investigate the room. The danger was gone, but for some reason, Race was still in his state of blue-eyed fury.

Illandra sat up on the floor and tugged at her suit, wishing it would somehow loosen on her, to no avail. She started to stand up and head for the door.

"I don't think you want to go out there," Annette warned her.

"Me, either," Illandra replied before leaving the safety of the observation room.

The medical area looked like it had been torn apart by a miniature tornado. Several pieces of equipment were ripped to shreds and scattered about. Most of the damage was around a section of the ceiling that had been ripped down, some small support beams even managing to peek out. Illandra made her way carefully through the war zone as she tried to reach Race on the other side of the room.

She could hear Annette attempting to follow her through the rubble. Whether she was following her mandate to protect her or just afraid to be alone, Illandra couldn't tell, but she guessed it was probably a combination of both.

Illandra could see the blue blaze reflecting off the terminal Race was manipulating, and she could feel the uneasiness it was causing in Annette.

"Race?" she called out while simultaneously trying to reach him with her mind. "Are you okay?"

He didn't respond to either of her probes. She inched herself closer, reaching out with her hand to touch him. As she tried to clasp it around the back of his arm, a weird sensation coursed through her body. She could feel the rippling of power infusing Race's body, as terrifying as it was exhilarating. She pushed through the resistance as she tried to grasp for him.

After enough struggle, she was finally able to reach her goal. The physical connection made, she was now able to try and connect with him mentally. What she found was as foreign to her as it was familiar. There were definitely parts of Race there, but there was also something else that she couldn't comprehend. Was it part of him, something she hadn't noticed before? Was it a mental side effect of his powers? She had no way of knowing for sure, but she was convinced it wasn't her Race.

Death-gripping his arm in fear that the strength of his power would fling her away if she got careless, she slowly moved past Race's side to look him in the face. His face reflected what she connected with in his head, both the man she cared deeply for and a stranger she had never met.

"Who are you?" she asked, hoping that he could hear her.

He just ignored her, continuing upon his task on the terminal in front of him. She looked at the information he had pulled up on the screen. He had accessed some information from the incursion; it looked like something to do with the messages the ship had sent out shortly before ramming into a section of the Taurus space station. In another window, commands were magically building some large program. Amazingly, he was doing it all using the power of his mind, willing the code into existence.

Without warning, Race went almost lifeless as his task completed. Annette's previous encounter prepared her to leap to Race's other side and help keep Illandra from crashing to the floor. They helped him over to a nearby chair to set him down so he could rest. Both his mind and face appeared to have reverted back to his normal self.

"Are you okay?" Illandra asked, sure he would answer her this time.

"I'm fine," Race said, dazed from his experience.

"What were you doing with the terminal?" Annette asked him.

"I was making a translation program," Race answered, still trying to get his bearings. "We should be able to use it to go through the records on the alien ship. It also works for the messages we intercepted from the Consortium carrier. I had to know what they were saying."

"They're the same language?" Annette said, everything almost making sense now.

Race struggled to nod. "Whatever happened to Corporal Simmons must be happening in the Imperial Consortium, but on a much larger scale."

"How can that even be possible?" Illandra asked in disbelief. "Are you sure?"

"Maybe." Race's head bobbed around on the edge of unconsciousness.

"You don't like making things easy, do you?" Illandra scolded him.

"Easy's boring?" Race struggled to smile, looking up at her.

"Is it safe?" the chief asked, peeking out from the adjoining office.

"Yeah," Race answered with a wave for her to come out of hiding.

"Where's the commander?" she asked as she carefully entered the room.

"Over here," the voice of Commander Trent came from behind some equipment he had chosen for his cover.

The chief medical officer quickly went to check on him. She looked over the wound that he had received from the attack. "You're lucky," she stated. "The laser cauterized the wound. We'll have to rebuild some of it, but you should be okay in no time."

"I don't see how getting shot makes me lucky," he said, grunting in pain.

"How about you're lucky it didn't dissect you as intended?" Chief Tenaway said as she went to grab some of her supplies to treat the wound.

"Fair enough," the commander said, trying to use his good arm to sit in a better position.

"What happened here?" Doctor Filmond asked, finally joining the rest of the group. "It looks like a war zone."

"The nanites used Commander Trent's device to hack into the medical bay," Race explained, trying to push the two girls away from him as his strength started to return. "They tried to turn the surgical lasers against us."

"Why us?" the commander asked.

"We exposed it," Illandra said, picking up on Race's thoughts. "It even said we were a threat, it had to deal with us before it could try again."

"Is there any way to see if anyone else is infected?" Annette contributed.

"Now that we know what we're looking for, we should be able to tune the sensors to look for it," the doctor explained. "Let me see if I can get started." He carefully made his way around some of the rubble to access another terminal that hadn't been destroyed in the battle.

Race tried to stand up, not making it that far before having to sit back down.

"Are you okay?" Chief Tenaway asked, noticing Race's struggle as she treated the commander's arm.

"I'm fine, ma'am," Race assured her. "The whole experience is just a little draining."

"I'd better take a look at you," she said. "Just let me finish up here."

"No rush, Chief," Race said, deciding it was better to relax in his chair.

The three waited for the chief to finish treating the wounded while the doctor finished testing everyone and cleared the quarantine. Given Race's condition, the chief insisted that Race stay for a couple of hours for observation. It was clear to Illandra that using his powers took a great deal out of him. Using them twice in so close a period left him barely able to stand.

She was still a little timid about what she had mentally touched while he was coursing with power, so she didn't think a little distance was bad. If nothing else, it would give her some time to process what had happened.

She had been called back to help Anthony explain what had happened during Corporal Simmons's ghost-like encounter and the follow-up in the medical section. Afterward, she had a private discussion with her mentor where she disclosed some of the finer details and her concern for Race's mental state. When she exited the room, she found Annette still waiting for her, given one last task before being relieved.

The day almost over, Illandra decided to head back to her room so she could change out of the disgusting orange suit she was wearing.

"What a day," Illandra said as she walked down the hall, her escort next to her. "Two attempts on my life."

"You get used to it," Annette said casually.

"Race told me the same lie." Illandra chuckled.

"Kind of a joke of ours," Annette clarified. "It does get a

little easier. Never completely get over it, though."

"Are you guys in danger a lot?" Illandra asked.

"Every couple of weeks or so," Annette smiled, checking the hallway for possible threats. "Just kind of the nature of the job."

"If today is any indication, I couldn't handle it," Illandra decided. "I can't even imagine what my parents are going to say. It was hard enough to keep them from flying out here after my surgery."

"They must care about you very much," Annette said, keeping her stone-like attitude.

"Yeah." Illandra smiled. "You might say I'm following in their footsteps. My father was a senator at one time. It involved a lot of traveling for us when I was younger. Thank goodness he retired before I got too old. But of course, just as I was getting accustomed to being stationary, here I am, off doing it on my own."

"Have you decided when you're going to run for an office?" Annette asked, trying to keep the small talk going.

"It's still a ways off," Illandra answered as they reached the entrance to her room. "I won't even be eligible for a couple more years. I guess however long it takes for Congressman Martin to say I'm ready."

"I'm sure you'll make a great senator when the time comes, maybe even president," Annette said supportively. "Now that I've seen you safely to your room, I think I'm going to go change out of this horrible thing."

"Have a good night." Illandra smiled as she said goodbye to her escort.

Illandra opened the door to her dark, empty room aboard the Puller. She knew what was going to happen if she entered the room. She'd spend the rest of the night pacing around nervously, thinking about all the events from the day until it drove her crazy. The imprisoned soldier in his own body, the stranger in Race, and the not one, but two attempts on her life. Could a day get any more stressful?

"Annette?" Illandra called to the soldier before she had walked off too far.

"Yes, ma'am," Annette said, turning to address her.

"I don't think I'm ready to turn in," Illandra explained. "Would you like to go do something?"

"I was going to go check on Race," Annette started to explain.

"He's fine," Illandra dismissed her concern, hoping to give Race the much-needed breather she felt he needed. "He just needs to rest. Why don't we go check out some of the stores on board? For some reason, picking out new clothes always help me de-stress."

"I'm sorry, I doubt I'd be much help." Annette smiled. "I've never been much into fashion. I think I've only owned one dress and it had a little bit of an accident."

"Really?" Illandra asked, not too surprised.

"I'm afraid so," Annette said, reliving the incident in her mind for Illandra to see.

"Well, let me help you pick something out?" Illandra offered. "You know what? I'll even buy you an outfit. It's the least I can do for saving my life earlier today."

"I was just doing my job," Annette objected modestly.

"I know," Illandra said, reaching out to grab Annette's forearm, "but that doesn't mean I still can't thank you properly for it. Come on, it will be fun."

Illandra could tell that Annette was fighting to come up with an excuse to reject Illandra's proposal. The two were complete opposites; the only thing they really had in common was Race. Their feelings might have been more similar than Illandra cared to admit. But the endless hours of self-torment staring at her from her empty room made Illandra desperate for company.

"Please," Illandra pleaded one last time. "It's been a really long day, and I really don't feel like being alone."

Annette took a deep breath that exited in a sympathetic sigh. "Fine," she submitted, "but can we at least get out of these containment suits?"

Chapter 10

TRANAGRA

Record Date: 349.206 PGST

RACE HAD BEEN WANDERING AROUND the halls of their little freight shuttling them back to the nebula, not even certain what he was looking for. Maybe he was lost; he wasn't sure. Really, he just wanted to find a place to be alone. He finally settled on the cargo area where they kept most of their spare supplies. Zain had cleared a small area to add some exercise equipment. It wasn't much, but it gave the Marines something to do while traversing the nebula. It was usually better to find something to keep yourself busy rather than having the captain find it.

Race took the blouse of his uniform off and laid it nicely on one of the containers. He used another container to step up to the pull-up bar and tried to do a couple reps. He barely made it up halfway on his first set before his arms started screaming at him and he had to drop down from the bar. It had been a couple days since the fight with the infected soldier, yet his body was still recovering from it. "Maybe they're not really powers at all," he whispered to himself, massaging the pain in his bicep. "Maybe it's just a well-disguised poison

304

killing me slowly."

"You okay?" came the soft voice of his teammate from the entrance behind him.

He looked over his shoulder to see the door closing behind the fiery-spirited Annette. She always seemed to find him, not that he minded that much. With any luck, she hadn't heard him.

"Yeah," Race answered. "Still a little weak, that's all."

"It really takes it out of you, doesn't it?" Annette asked.

"I guess," Race said, eying the cursed bar once again, wondering how much he wanted to try a second attempt.

"I remember the first time you used them." Annette brought up a memory Race had tried hard to forget. "You were so weak, you couldn't even stand in zero gravity."

It was an interesting point. The ship's gravity generators simulated normal conditions, unlike the first time. Maybe it was just something his body needed to get used to. He remembered something the medic had said after examining him, about his muscles being more torn than a bodybuilder's. Maybe he should look her up next time he was on the ship for a copy of that formula she had offered. Zain might have a couple suggestions on that matter, too. Unless his powers really were poison; then it would just be finding a way to kill him faster.

He stepped up to the bar again and pushed himself to do a couple more pull-ups.

"You really shouldn't push yourself too much," Annette scolded him.

"We're Marines," Race reminded her as he strained to

reach the top of the bar. "It's how we get better."

"A broken Marine is no use to anyone," Annette reminded him, now moving around in front of him so he couldn't as easily ignore her.

He knew she was right, but it didn't stop him from trying to pull himself up one more time. He dropped down after barely succeeding, Annette only a couple feet from him, wearing a look similar to the one that Illandra would have given him when he was being stubborn.

"You're right," Race apologized, more to himself for the pain he had now put himself in. "I'm sorry."

"Give me an assist," Annette said forgivingly, taking her turn to step up to the bar. Race put his hands on her back just above her hips and waited for her to pump out a full set before he needed to put some strength into his arms to help her complete the last couple.

He was a little jealous of how easy it was for her. He probably would have been able to push out as many if he was half his weight, too.

The two took a short break and sat on a couple containers not too far apart from each other.

"I never knew about your mother," Race said, his mind returning to that day in the lab.

"I never knew about your father," she threw back, trying to shield herself.

"It's funny," Race apologized, "we spend so much time together, talk about so many things, but when it gets down to it, we really don't know a whole lot about each other."

"We know enough," she replied, almost more hurt by

that than by his previous comment.

"Like what?" Race asked, hoping his smile would lighten the mood.

"Our loyalties to each other and that we'll always have each other's back," she said.

"True." Race half shrugged, half nodded. He tried his best not to say anything further; it would probably be easier to keep his foot from going in his mouth that way.

"I'd been thinking about her a lot lately," she said, her eyes drifting off to some faraway memory.

"What was she like?" Race failed to keep silent. He jumped to add, "If you don't mind me asking."

"Wonderful." Annette smiled at the memory. "I got her hair color, but not her ability to command a room with it. She had a way with people. Whenever she talked, everyone listened. My dad loved that about her; he let her do all the presentations. She had a passion for everything she did, putting her heart and a little bit of herself into it."

"She must have put some of that passion into you," Race said admiringly. "You seem to put a lot of it in whatever you do, too."

A tear started to gather in the corner of Annette's eye that she quickly pulled back. "I wasn't that old when the accident happened. I think I was about eight or nine. Sometimes I struggle to remember what she looked like, but then I remember what my dad always said. 'Just look in the mirror; everything that was great about her is in you.' It couldn't have been easy for him, looking at me and seeing memories of her all the time. Sometimes I'd catch him looking at me, fighting to keep the tears back. That's one of the reasons I was so anxious to join the Marines, to give him some distance to let the wounds finally heal some."

Race could feel his whole body tensing up just thinking of that kind of torture, and a certain sympathy went out to the poor man. "I wish I could have met her."

"Me, too." She looked at him for a second before looking down to hide her face, the tears fighting harder than ever to break through.

Race wasn't sure what to do. Anything he could do would most likely cause her to lose her composure and let the tears break through, so he did his best not to do anything.

"So you never knew your father?" Annette said after she had calmed down a bit and the silence was deafening.

"No," Race answered. He really didn't want to go into it, but he didn't know if he had the right to deny her after prodding into her past. "I didn't even know what a dad was for the longest time. I remember sitting at a table during lunch and everyone was talking about how awesome their fathers were. I felt so awkward not having one, I just zipped my head up in my jacket and pretended like I was taking a nap or something.

"I felt like such a freak, you know?" Although she probably didn't. "How could all these people have dads and I didn't? When we're kids, our whole worlds revolve around us, so I thought there must be something wrong with me. I was so afraid that they'd find out I was somehow flawed, I was too embarrassed to make friends." Race was beginning to understand how it felt for Annette to tell her story as he did his best to keep his emotions from coming to the surface.

"You mom never told you anything about him?" Annette asked unwillingly. She didn't want to push him on, but she was too curious not to.

"Not really," he struggled to answer. "Whenever I'd get brave enough to ask her, it seemed she just made up some random story. I had several of my own. Maybe he was a spy or a pirate or something, which was why she couldn't tell me. She had to keep me hidden until it was safe for him to come back and get me. You know, whatever it took for things to make sense.

"For a while, I wondered if I even had a father or if I had been made in some sort of lab or something until I forced her to show me a picture of him one day." Race tried to pretend that the tears the memories were pulling out of the corners of his eyes didn't exist, but that didn't seem to make them any less real as he did his best to wipe them away without it seeming like he was doing so.

It was Annette's turn to do nothing.

Race took a deep breath; it seemed to help a little. "As I got older and I realized it wasn't really me that was the problem, it was him, I was so angry. All I could think was 'How could he do this to me?' No matter how hard I tried to deal with it, it just grew inside me. I was angry all the time. At everything. All I could do was…" His voice trailed off, not wanting to say the word.

"Hate," Annette finished for him, and she was right. It was something one picked up from experience; she must have faced similar demons of her own when dealing with the loss of her mother. Amongst all the turmoil, it was nice to have someone that could understand his pain. As close as he was to Illandra, she never could have understood how it felt. She had a loving family, two wonderful parents that loved her immensely. She would never understand the way he felt.

"Yeah," Race agreed. For some reason, Race didn't feel quite so alone anymore. Getting it out had somehow made him feel a little better.

Race had been so busy keeping his emotions under control, he hadn't even noticed that Annette had moved over to his container and had placed her hand on his. He fought the automatic reaction to pull his hand back; a part of him found it rather comforting.

"I think we could both use a drink," Annette suggested after a brief silence.

Race felt a drink would do him some good right now. "That sounds good, but there's one problem."

"What's that?" she asked. Race hadn't thought she had forgotten.

"There's no alcohol here on the shuttle, and I'm not old enough," Race reminded her. He was the youngest of the group. Sometimes they forgot he couldn't participate in all their activities. It wouldn't be for a couple more months that he could legally join them. Most of the places they went would allow him entrance, but not the pleasure of drinking with his friends.

"You honestly think Zain and Konway didn't sneak on a

310

couple packs before we left?" Annette laughed almost magically. "Besides, there are no bouncers here."

The idea sounded nice, but he wasn't sure how good. "Still not sure if it's a good idea. They just released me from the clinic."

"Did they give you any drugs?" she asked curiously. "Did they tell you anything about not drinking?"

"Well, no," he started to argue.

"Screw it, then." She motioned him to join her. "After all we've been through, we deserve a little kickback."

Race thought it over a little bit more. The longer he considered her proposition, the more tempted he was by the offer. "All right," he finally gave in.

"Great." She smiled excitedly. "Let's see if we can track down the twiddles."

*   *   *

It had been a couple of days since Illandra had seen Race. She had tried to keep her distance, giving him time to cope with his last experience. It had taken all the effort she had. His team had left back into the nebula shortly after he was released from the medical bay. His crew had just recently returned from another trip to the nebula. She had felt him back on the *Puller* several hours before he even contacted her. It was obvious he had wanted to talk with her about the incident; she figured at least she could use the opportunity to see him dressed up.

Illandra enjoyed Race's company once again as they strolled back from their dinner. They'd all been so busy lately. She couldn't even remember the last time they'd had any time to themselves. The halls were as vacant as a ghost town; the two only ran into a rare crew member as they wandered aimlessly through the hallways.

"Illy," Race said after they had enjoyed some of the scenery on the ship's observation deck, "I wanted to apologize for the other day. I know things were kind of crazy in the medical bay. I'm sorry you had to see me like that."

"You only did it to save our lives," she explained. "It's nothing to be sorry for."

"Still…" Race's voice trailed off as he remembered the incident in the medical lab.

"I know you're scared." Illandra confronted Race as they started to make their way to her quarters. "Well, maybe confused is a better word for it."

"Probably a little of each," Race responded with a nervous laugh. "Full of questions and not sure how much I'm going to like the answers."

"What's the biggest question you're scared of?" Illandra asked, hoping she could help.

"I don't know," he lied casually. He was getting better at it.

"You're afraid you're going to hurt someone?" Illandra said, picking up on some of Race's thoughts.

"Yeah," Race conceded, looking down at the ground. "I already decapitated an alien. I'm pretty sure he deserved it, but how do I make sure that it isn't someone I care about in the future? How much control do I really have over this thing?"

"Whatever you might think, you're still in control," Illandra assured him, not sure how much she believed it herself. "You're not going to do something you don't want to do."

"You can't possibly know that," Race objected as they came to a stop at her door.

"I can," Illandra argued, "and I do."

"How?" Race laughed. "It's not like you're some sort of mind-reader?"

"I am," Illandra said, relieved to finally have the truth she had held from him for so long in the open.

"Well, if you're not going to be serious, I think I'm going to call it a night. It's late, and I have another early day tomorrow." Race gave her a small kiss on the cheek before turning to walk away. "I'll try and call you before I leave."

Illandra pursed her lips in frustration. Not able to contain herself, she reached out to Race with her mind. "You're not the only one with special powers, you know," she projected to him.

Race stopped in mid-step as he received her mental message. He turned slowly to look at her, still in disbelief of what he had just experienced. "Was that…?" He hesitated.

Illandra nodded her confirmation as she smiled slyly.

"And you can just read my thoughts?" Race thought to test if she really could do what she was implying.

"Yes," Illandra projected back.

"Is that why I can never get away with anything with you?" Race mentally asked, realizing just how much the cards had been stacked against him their entire relationship.

Illandra covered her smile as Race finally caught on to her longtime secret. Overwhelmed with excitement, he quickly made his way back to Illandra. "I can't believe it," Race said, dropping the mental part of the conversation. "All this time I thought I was different."

"Everyone is different," Illandra corrected him. "We're just a little more different than everyone else."

"I guess," Race said, not really believing her.

"It's true," Illandra confirmed. "Here, I'll show you." She held up her hand for him to grab.

"What are you going to do?" Race asked, not sure if he was ready for what she was going to show him.

"Just a glimpse," Illandra assured him. "It's only fair; I've been poking around in your head for some time now. I even gave Annette a little peek that day in the lab."

"You let her into my head?" Race said, feeling somewhat violated.

"Relax. I just showed her how your abilities work," Illandra assured him. "How the world looks through your eyes when you're doing your thing. Now you can do the same thing with me," she said, motioning toward her waiting hand still in front of them.

Still uncertain, Race reached up and placed his palm to Illandra's, their fingers interlacing as their hands embraced each other.

"You think you're all alone, that no one understands how it feels to be you," Illandra explained as she opened herself up to him and activated her abilities. She started to probe the nearby floors for crew members to pick up on some of their emotions. "What you don't understand is we all have our doubts, our fears, our joys. Our pleasures and our pains. We're all the same, just as we're all different. That's what it means to be human. Even feeling like you don't belong sometimes proves that you do, because that's what it means."

Race's eyes started to tear up as the sheer mass of emotions started to overwhelm him. "I'm sorry," Illandra apologized while breaking the connection and releasing Race from the emotions. "Was it too much?"

"Yes?" Race said, trying to pull himself back together. "No? Maybe?"

"I'm sorry," Illandra apologized again. "You keep all your emotions so buried, I should have known not to kick it in so high. I just wanted you to know you weren't alone. Just be glad I didn't go full blast."

"You experience more?" Race said in disbelief.

"Oh yeah," Illandra was happy to brag. "I mean, I could do the whole ship if I wanted. If I let my guard down, I just start to receive it all, anyways. Unlike you, I have to focus just to keep it all out."

"But it's so wonderful," Race said, astonished, his emotions finally coming under control now that it was just his alone.

"Well, I'm not sure if that's the word I would use," Illandra said, caught off guard by Race's description of it.

"But it is," Race defended, "to be a part of something so...grand. To be a part of anything."

"You are a part of it," Illandra tried to convince him, taking his hands. "That's what I'm trying to tell you. Your teammates think of you just as highly as you do of them. You almost hate to admit it, but you do have friends and family that care about you. They're here for you, just like I am."

Illandra could almost feel the shift in Race's perception as he realized the universe might actually be a little less lonely than he had originally thought.

"Thank you," he said, a little happier than she had seen him in a while.

"I can show you something else if you're interested," Illandra said, using the side panel to open the door to her quarters. "Something I know you really wanted to see."

"What's that?" Race smiled curiously.

Illandra walked a few steps into her room before turning to look at Race. "Exactly how little I'm wearing under this outfit," she said, unzipping the front of her dress to expose some of her bare flesh underneath.

Race took a deep breath as he viewed the tantalizing portion Illandra had exposed, almost scared to move in fear that it might somehow disappear.

"Well, are you coming?" she asked him, surprised he was still standing there. "Offer's about to expire in three."

"I hate it when you don't play fair." Race fought the urge to jump through the door and take Illandra up on her offer.

"I thought you'd learned by now, I never play fair," she teased, pulling at the shoulders to reveal a little more skin.

"Exactly," Race said, closing the door behind him.

*　　*　　*

Illandra awoke early the next morning with Race's arms

wrapped warmly around her. They hadn't been intimate for a long time, and never quite as intimate as last night. What had possessed her to choose now was beyond her reasoning. Most likely, the compounded stress from over the past month had come to a head with the past days' events. Maybe it was something about the brief connection they'd shared in the hallway prior. Regardless of the reason, she was quite happy with her decision.

It felt good to be in Race's embrace again. His body had changed drastically since the last time she had occupied the space between his arms. Where once was a scrawny boy, she could now feel the solid muscles that made up the man beside her.

Race was still in a deep sleep, practically dead to the outside world. She had considered seeing if she could use her powers to enter his dreams, but considering how violated he had felt when she told him how regularly she had entered his mind, she decided it was best to give him at least a little privacy.

Instead, she attempted to snuggle in and see about getting another hour of sleep before the alarm went off.

"You're still an ugly species," echoed a thought from inside her room. "Getting rid of the hair was an improvement."

In fright, Illandra opened her eyes to investigate. Her mind plainly told her there was something there, even though her eyes clearly showed her there wasn't. Not knowing what else to do, she decided to let her eyes believe what her mind perceived. The more she let her power decide what was real, the more she was able to believe something actually was there.

Clearing the last of her doubt, she was finally able to see the being before her. She recognized it almost immediately; she had seen the memory where Race had chased it through the shadows of the alien vessel. Illandra's size made her used to her peers towering over her, but the creature's massive size was well outside her comfort. The alien's face was smooth, from its oversized forehead down to its lower jaw. The only breaks in the form were the insets for the black eyes and the two triangle slots that almost made a diamond where the nose should be. Even the lipless mouth was barely detectable in the flat canvas.

Not only did she recognize the image of the creature, but she also recognized a part of its mind.

"*You,*" she said, sitting up in her bed, trying her best to cover her naked body with the sheets.

Race moaned before grabbing the top blanket and rolling himself up on the opposite side of the bed. Illandra was about to hit Race when she noticed the alien's image flicker in response to Race's stirring.

"*Shhhhh,*" the alien hushed her. "*I can only regain my consciousness when the Run'hura slumbers. I'm speaking the language of thought. You must speak it as well for me to understand you.*"

Illandra wasn't sure exactly what it meant, but she was pretty sure he wanted to have a mental conversation with her. She pushed her thoughts out to the alien much like she had with Race the day before.

"*Who are you?*" Illandra asked the creature mentally.

"*No,*" the creature responded sourly, waving its ghostly hand at her, "*you're thinking in tongue. You are a weird species. How can I explain this? Before you say the words, you think them into the structure; before you think them, you have the thought. Send the thought.*"

Illandra was unsure why she was listening to the alien, but she felt a weird sense of trust in the creature. She wasn't quite sure what the stranger meant, but she decided to try and follow his instructions. She tried to backtrack the process and send the thought to the creature.

"*Better.*" The creature was happy with her progress. "*My name is Tranagra. My people inhabited this area of space long before your race existed.*"

"*What do you want?*" Illandra awkwardly transmitted the thought, finding the process like hitting send on a message before she even had a chance to type it in.

"*To help,*" the creature answered. "*To finish the task I started several millennia ago. The destruction of the Cenari.*"

"What are they?" Illandra asked, starting to get a little more familiar with the process.

"*They were our greatest invention. They were originally meant to heal us, to extend our lives. We thought we had found the key to immortality. But somewhere along the line, their programming became corrupted. They turned on us. At first, we thought it was a civil war; it wasn't until some time later that we realized that it was our own invention that had turned against us.*

"*On the edge of defeat, I took our final weapon against them and flew my ship to the center of the conflict and*

319

launched our last weapon against them. The weapon destroyed all technology the Cenari were dependent upon throughout this quadrant, and much more."

"But they survived." Illandra drew her own conclusion to the creature's story.

"It appears so," the alien answered, "although I do not know how. A transmission awoke one that had snuck upon my ship during the final battle. Your species must have stumbled across a batch that had found a way to survive the destruction and released the plague anew."

"How can we stop them?" Illandra asked, trying to don a robe while she listened to the creature's story. It was hard to explain the transmission of thoughts from the creature. Not only did she get words, but she also got images and memories all at once.

"He is the key," Tranagra's projection answered, pointing at Race's slumbering body. "In my race, the people with the future sight like him formed the religious order. They helped guide us, but even they were not strong enough to defeat the Cenari. But they foresaw the one that would. The Run'hura. Vengeance incarnate, the one that would burn the plague from all existence and avenge my people."

Illandra looked down at the Race sleeping peacefully behind her on the bed. "That doesn't sound like Race. Race is many things, but he's not vengeance. He may be a soldier, but he's a very peaceful person."

"He will be," the alien responded. "Just as the prophets foresaw his existence, they also knew that I would be the one to find him, and I have."

It didn't seem possible that everything that was happening had somehow been predestined millions of years ago. *"How do you plan to do that?"* Illandra asked.

"I must regain my being," Tranagra stated. *"Enough to where I can converse with the Vengeful One so we can begin his training. My extended time in Tu'rakmur allowed me to wither to near nonexistence. You are one of the mind's eye; you can help me regain my strength. In return, I will train you to use your abilities as well. You are strong for your people, but you have the potential to be much more. Using the knowledge of my people, you could rival the Run'hura himself."*

Illandra knew the alien was speaking the truth. It was much harder to tell a lie with your thoughts, as the deception would have been woven into them. The level of power the alien was thinking was tremendous. Her mentor already regarded her as one of the strongest psychics in existence, but that paled in comparison to what the alien promised her. But what was the cost? This being had become a part of Race. Would she be helping him take over the man she held so dear to her heart?

"And what about your connection to Race?" Illandra thought to the creature.

"It cannot be reversed," the alien said almost regretfully. *"But I can promise not to interfere with his life once our task is complete. My time, like that of my people, is long over. I have no right to this world. I only wish for you all not to burn for our mistakes."*

The ghost waited while all the different questions raced through her mind as she tried to decide which one to ask.

"Our time grows short," the alien said right as Illandra made up her mind. *"The Run'hura is starting to awaken from his slumber. You have many questions, I know. I will answer all that I can next time we speak. You have done much to ease his spirit, and for that, I thank you. I fear I must ask you not to tell him about me, not until I am stronger. If he is aware of me, he might attempt to resist and complicate the process. You will need to be close for us to talk again, which is why I must apologize for planting the suggestion for you taking him to your bed during your shared experience last night. We shall talk again."*

The ghost vanished as her eyes bulged in response to his last statement. Had he really just admitted that he had persuaded her to seduce Race into her room? She suddenly had a creepy feeling much akin to Race's when she'd discussed the matter with him last night. It was enough to make her rethink her whole morality on how freely she entered other people's minds.

"You're up early," Race said, stretching out in her bed as he opened his eyes to look around.

"Oh," Illandra said, turning around to face him, "I forgot I had an early morning, too. I need to go speak with Tony before the morning meeting."

"I guess I should be getting ready for it myself," Race responded, not really wanting to get out of the bed. "What time is it?" he asked, looking down at his forearm where his sensor resided before moaning in response.

"Still not much of a morning person?" Illandra asked, trying not to act as preoccupied with her thoughts as she really was. "You'd think two years in the military would have changed that."

"You mean two years of waking up whenever there's an emergency?" Race said, sitting up in the bed and looking for his clothes. "It doesn't do much for one's sleeping schedule."

"I can image," Illandra tried to sympathize, still feeling awkward about all that had just been revealed to her.

Illandra tried to act naturally as she started getting ready. She even felt repulsed when Race went to give her a goodbye hug and kiss. Once he was gone, she quickly raced to get ready and ran for her mentor's room.

"Ah, Illandra," Anthony said, answering the door. "I was just thinking about calling you, but now that you're here, I'm beginning to think maybe I was picking up on something."

"Probably," Illandra answered shortly. "Can I come in?"

"Of course," her mentor said, inviting her into his quarters. "Would you like something to drink?"

"Please," Illandra begged, quickly ducking into his quarters.

"What has you all shaken up, lass?" the congressman said as he tried to make her comfortable.

"Well, last night after Race's and my date, I invited him back to my room," Illandra started to explain.

"I wasn't aware you were thinking about taking your relationship that far with him, especially with us leaving soon," Anthony said, surprised. "Not that it's any of my business."

"I wasn't," Illandra agreed.

Illandra went on to explain her encounter with the alien that had taken up residence in Race's subconscious. She also explained how she had touched a part of him when Race was in his blue-eyed power state, and how it had apologized for compelling her to take Race into her room that night.

"Ah," Anthony said when she had finished her story, "now I see why you're upset."

"I feel violated," Illandra said, trying to wipe off the icky feeling she had all over her.

"Have you and Race been intimate before this?" Anthony asked.

"Not that intimate," Illandra replied.

"Had you thought about it before?" Anthony continued his querying.

"Well…maybe," Illandra said, not quite wanting to admit to it. "What does that have to do with anything?"

"When we compel someone to make a certain choice, it's usually because they're on the fence about it in the first place," Anthony started to explain. "We can't outright force someone to do something they are completely against, like jumping off a building. We just give them a little nudge by making them focus on the issue that we want them to. I would expect that last night, while you may have done something you may not have been ready for, I doubt you did anything at least a part of you didn't want to."

"That doesn't make it any easier," Illandra said, playing back the past several weeks in her head, realizing that his statement was in part true.

"I didn't think it would," Anthony said, taking a sip of his beverage.

"This whole thing still seems all wrong," Illandra sighed.

"He didn't have any right to make me decide that. How do we know when we've crossed a line? When we've gone too far?"

"Kind of hard to cross a line that no one knew existed," Anthony reminded her.

"We know," Illandra said sorely.

"Did you enjoy it?" Anthony asked.

A smile crept onto Illandra's face as she remembered the night she had shared with Race.

"Then try not to dwell on it too much," Anthony replied to her unspoken answer. "What's done is done; you can't take it back now. Besides, you may have discovered the greatest ally we have during this war."

Illandra gave her mentor a puzzled look in response to his question.

"If your boyfriend and this alien are correct and this really is a rebirth of the nanite plague, you may have just provided us with the one person that knows them better than anyone and has defeated them in the past. On top of that, if he can elevate your and Race's powers to the levels you hinted at, there's no telling what we might be looking at."

"You think I should take him up on his offer?" Illandra asked.

"I'm saying you should definitely consider it," her mentor answered. "You'll just have to give me some pointers when he's done training you. I was one of the strongest pathics until you showed up."

"I'll think about it," Illandra pouted.

"Don't think too long, lass," the congressman answered.

"We're only here for a couple more weeks. You're lucky they extended our stay here for us to check out the alien ship to better determine if there actually is a connection to this alien and the invasion."

"That shouldn't make things awkward at all," Illandra snarled sarcastically.

"I'm sure you'll find a way to deal with it," Anthony said, giving her a one-armed hug to ease her tension. "We'd better be going, though. It's almost time for the meeting."

Chapter 11

DREAMS

Record Date: 349.247 PGST

THE WEEKS FOLLOWING HIS NIGHT with Illandra had gone by pretty fast. The problem was that they had barely had any time together since then. There had been a couple of late nights where Illandra had once again let him sleep over, but they had not been anywhere as intimate as that night. Every time that Race had attempted to confront her about it, she always seemed to have something important going on or someone around to prevent him from going into it. Illandra and Anthony even went with them into the nebula to visit the alien ship, at which point Race thought he would have had plenty of time to discuss things with her, but she still ended up finding ways to avoid him, and usually with his female co-worker Annette. Given Race's newfound knowledge of her powers, he was beginning to wonder if Illandra was intentionally avoiding him, but what really had his mind working overtime was the "why."

"Get your head in the game, Marine," Konway said, tapping Race on the back of his helmet. They had been clearing out another section of the alien ship.

"Give the kid a break," Zain defended him. "Can't you see he's got girl problems?"

"Those are the worst." Konway rolled his eyes sympathetically.

"Sorry, guys," Race apologized, lifting his rifle to properly examine the area. "Clear."

"Don't sweat it," Zain brushed him off. "We've been here for almost a month now and haven't seen any sign of life since the one you *grrrlck*." Zain tugged at an imaginary noose to symbolize the one that Race had decapitated.

"That's no excuse to get lazy," Konway said, checking the next room.

"If there was something of any danger here, don't you think his doohickey would be going off?" Zain waved his gloved hand toward Race's side of the hallway.

Race's abilities had become a point of discussion amongst his team, more than he cared for. Since Race's power really only activated when he was in danger, this had caused them to get rather creative with some of their tests, a few of which had given him a fresh scar to bandage. It was bad enough that the two women he cared about most were avoiding him, but now the two guys who were like brothers to him were treating him more like an experiment than a friend.

Konway didn't respond, knowing it was true but probably feeling it wasn't enough of an excuse.

"Want to talk about it?" Zain asked after a few minutes of silence.

"Eh," Race said, not feeling like being the source of Zain's distraction from the somewhat daunting task at hand.

"It can't be that bad," Konway said, clearing another corner.

"Illandra and Annette have been spending time together," Zain explained. "Lots of time."

Konway made a face like he had just swallowed the sourest of lemons all at once. "Sorry, dude."

"That's not it," Race said, trying not to lose his focus. "Wait, why is that a big deal?"

"The last thing you ever want is two girls you're romantically interested in to become friends," Zain said, giving Race a quick pat on the shoulder as he passed him in the hallway. "What if they start comparing notes about you?"

"I'm not interested in both of them," Race objected, his progress down the hall coming to a stop.

"That's not what you were telling us a couple months ago," Konway replied, continuing down the hall.

Race took a moment to think back to before the first invasion. So much had changed since then; everything seemed so right side up, regardless of the turmoil of the time. The whole thing had actually ended up strengthening his bond with both women, but more so with Illandra after finding out that she had powers like him. But Illandra would be leaving soon. What did that mean for their relationship? Not that they had much of one right now. Would that open things back up for Annette? While he still cared deeply about Annette, he wasn't quite sure where he stood with her. She had been there the first time his powers had manifested, and things had been awkward between them ever since. There was no telling how her new friendship with Illandra might make things even more awkward.

"Keep up, Marine," Konway's voice came over the radio in Race's space suit.

Race cursed his teammates for bringing up the thoughts now coursing through his head as he started to sprint to catch up with them.

"If it's not that they're together, then what is it?" Zain asked after Race had caught back up to them.

"Nothing," Race said, trying to divert Zain's attention. "Illandra's just been acting weird lately."

"How so?" Konway asked, now almost interested in the conversation.

"Well, things were going all good, and now all of a sudden she can't stand to be near me," Race said, taking his turn to clear the next corner.

"How good?" Zain asked.

Race's space suit sudden became very hot as he remembered the night they had shared.

"Everything all right, Sergeant?" the captain's voice broke in over their radios.

"Yes, sir," Race responded quickly. "It's…nothing, sir. It's nothing…sir."

"Are you sure, Sergeant? Your vitals were starting to spike a little," the captain asked, concerned. Race's two teammates were trying their hardest not to burst into laughter.

"Yes, sir," Race awkwardly responded again. "Nothing to be concerned about, sir."

"All right. Finish up that corridor and report back to the shuttle. I have a surprise for you all," the captain commanded.

"Yes, sir," the group responded in unison.

Zain and Konway waited a couple seconds for the connection to close before letting their laughter burst out of them. "It must have been some night," Zain teased. "I didn't know you could turn that shade of red."

"Shut up," said Race, slapping Zain's shoulder with the back of his hand.

"So she went from being super-hot for you to icy cold?" Konway summarized Race's predicament.

"I guess," Race said, still mad at his friends for making him the target for their distraction.

"Was this before or after their departure got delayed?" Zain asked as they neared the end of the corridor.

"Before, I think," Race answered, checking the last corner.

"Well, that's it," Konway said, thinking he had figured it out. "It was breakup sex."

"What?" Race gasped, shocked at the suggestion.

"You might be right," Zain said, catching on to Konway's logic.

"You see, the natural process is supposed to be 'great sex,' 'nice morning,' and 'I'm leaving, let's be friends,'" Konway educated Race as he pointed out each one on his fingers. "Your 'nice day' got complicated by her extension, which means if she broke up with you, then you'd both have to awkwardly be getting along."

"We're already doing that," Race scorned.

"But it's not a completely awkward awkwardness that

affects everyone, ya know? It's just you're kind of moping around going, 'what'd I do wrong?' awkwardness." Zain did a lousy impression of Race dragging his arms behind him that made him look more like a gorilla than Race.

Race wasn't even sure what that meant, nor was he too amused with the impersonation.

"Basically, yeah," Konway tried to agree with him. "I think."

"It doesn't work that way," Race protested. He looked at Zain for confirmation before dismissing him, realizing he wouldn't get any.

"If you say so," Konway replied.

"I hate you guys," Race pouted, as another set of worrisome ideas had been added to his thoughts.

"We should probably head back," Zain changed the subject. "I'm interested to see what the captain's surprise is."

Race trailed behind the others as he continued to dwell on the ideas they had suggested. He was pretty sure they were wrong, but he couldn't help but wonder about the possibility of them being right. It had taken them a while to return to the breach point they'd used to enter the alien ship.

"I don't believe it," he heard Konway gasp. He had been so busy looking at the ground that he hadn't noticed they had nearly reached the exit.

Konway started reciting some poem that rolled almost magically off the tongue. Race attempted to see what it was that had provoked such a response from his fellow team members, but their massive size and the narrow passage made it difficult to see.

"What is it?" Race said, trying to restrain himself from jumping like a child to see over Zain's massive shoulder.

"Look for yourself," Zain said, turning to the side so that Race could get a better view.

Race stared, awestruck, at the space in front of him. The unforgiving clouds that normally greeted them had been pushed aside, almost as if they were making way for the colossal structure coming toward them. All three men knew the domed structure burrowing its way through the nebula to them. A smile pushed its way onto Race's face as a burden he hadn't even known was there lifted. A light cut away the darkness before them as the bottom section of the Taurus space station approached them. It was the section dedicated to SORD development and training. The place where he had worked and lived for almost the past two years.

They could almost make out Annette piloting the section from a small area toward the front of the structure. "Welcome home, boys," she said, putting it best.

*   *   *

Race was lying in the bed of his new quarters. It felt so good to not be cramped in the small room on the shuttle he had been forced to share with his fellow Marines. It felt good to be back on the Taurus, at least the small section of it Annette had piloted through the nebula. They had anchored it right to the side of the meteor-like spaceship, the bowl-like structure almost half the size of the lonely giant that had been inside the nebula for so long.

The capacity of the research center of the station made a

perfect base of operations for the research teams starting to show up to help the excavation of the sleeping giant. It would also mean fewer trips in and out of the nebula for supplies, as the subsection of the station was a little more self-sustainable. Race's navigation program had cut off a couple hours of the flight time, but he still dreaded the painful trip.

Once Annette had positioned the section into place, they had made a quick scan of the area to make sure nothing had shifted in transit before taking to fighting over rooms. The station's appearance had changed the mood of the entire team. Race had been unaware of the amount of stress the whole ordeal had put on the team, but the moment they had set foot back on the section of the space station, most of it had seemed to vanish. Race equated it to returning home, as it was the only place he had called home since leaving for the Corps.

The captain had been nice enough to dismiss them early. They tried to make themselves at home in their new room. Race had finished quickly and lain down on the soft bed to relax. It didn't take long before his thoughts turned back to the ideas his friends had so graciously placed in his head earlier that day.

He didn't know how long he'd been staring at the ceiling when the door alerted him to someone requesting permission to enter. He got up and quickly pulled the wrinkles out of his bed before answering. He checked the door to see an image of Illandra on the other side.

He hit the button on the door to let her in. She was wearing some tight workout clothes and looked like she had just come back from a really intense workout.

"My god, you're an emotional roller coaster today," she said, barging past him, not even waiting for him to invite her in.

"Sorry," Race said, even though he really didn't feel like he had any reason to apologize for what went on inside his own head.

"No, you're not," she said, ducking into Race's bathroom to grab a towel to start patting the sweat off her upper body. "And you're right, you have no reason to be."

Race sighed. These types of conversations made a lot more sense now that he had been let in on her secret, but it didn't mean he liked them any better.

"I'm sorry," she said, once again picking up on his thoughts as she pulled out the chair from his little desk to sit in. "They're getting stronger, and harder to control," she explained.

"Your powers?" Race asked curiously.

"Yes," she confirmed. "And the headaches, too. It's hard as it is with just the small amount of people here; I'm dreading heading back to the ship. Really not looking forward to next month when I'm back on a planet."

Race could almost feel the dread coming off of her. "Anything I can do?" Race asked, hoping he could somehow get back in good favor with her.

"Stop thinking?" She looked up at him hopefully with a bit of playfulness in her expression.

"If only I could." Race returned a playful smile.

"I know." She smiled. "Anyway, I came to apologize. It's

obvious I've been avoiding you lately. I just wanted you to know that it wasn't anything you did, and I'm really sorry if I gave you the wrong impression."

The questions Race had been saving up suddenly started lining up in his head.

Illandra sighed. "No, it wasn't breakup sex. Yes, it was amazing. Maybe it has a little something to do with me leaving soon," she said, rattling off the answers to the list forming in his head.

"Then what's really the matter?" he said, hoping he could get it out of his mouth before she could pick up on it.

"It's hard to explain," she said, a little nervous. "Part of me really wanted to be with you that night, but I just don't think I was completely ready for it."

"Would you take it back if you could?" Race asked, not sure if he really wanted to know.

There was an awkward silence as she thought about it, replaying the night in her head. "I guess not," she finally answered, with the slightest hint of a blush.

"I can respect that you may have overstepped your intentions that night. I may not like it, but I can respect it." Race waved his hands, helping his opinion out. "I really wish you would have at least talked to me about it. You're leaving in what, a couple days?"

Illandra nodded her acknowledgment.

"And you've wasted the last two weeks, possibly the last two weeks we might ever have together. Even without the sex, you're still really important to me. You know I…can't believe I'm still talking when you've probably heard it all in my head already?" Race concluded.

"I wanted to hear you say it." Illandra smiled at him.

"No," Race said, folding his arms and turning away from her.

"Fine," she said, getting up from her chair. "I'll just have to settle for the thought." She grabbed him by the arm to pull him down enough for her to kiss him on the cheek.

"I hate when you don't play fair," Race said, trying to hide the smile creeping onto his lips as he watched her head for the door.

"I never play fair." She smiled, hitting the panel to open the door.

"Exactly," he replied.

"I'm going to go take a shower," Illandra informed him. "Try not to picture me naked."

It was almost like she had said it just to plant the image in his head.

"That's just him, right?" Zain said, peeking around the corner.

Somehow, in her desire to tease Race, Illandra hadn't picked up on his friend's approach. All Illandra could do was blush and walk off.

"Hot again?" Zain smiled as she walked away.

"I guess." Race shrugged.

"Well, grab your gear. Now that she and Annette are done with the training bay, it's our turn," Zain ordered. "It's been a while since I've been able to shoot anything."

"Fine," Race sighed as he went toward his locker.

*   *   *

Race had slept well that night. No sooner had his head hit the pillow than he was deep in sleep. Instead of his nice cozy bed back at the SORD headquarters, he was dreaming he was back in the shuttle's small sleeping quarters where a half-naked Annette was once again jumping on him.

Of course, that only meant one thing. This dream always preceded a visitation of his new friend. He pushed Annette away and got up, only to turn and see her still kissing a phantom image of himself.

"All right," Race said as he looked around. *"Where are you?"*

"Wherever you put me," the dark, hoarse voice said.

Race turned to find the creature sitting in the common area of the shuttle. The scenery changed quite regularly in his dreams. As with most dreams, he'd struggle to remember it when he awoke, just like the creature now stationed inside his head. He only seemed to be aware of them here in this place.

"You know, this dream wouldn't be so bad if you wouldn't always come along and ruin it," Race said, picking up a cup to take a drink. For some reason, some warm milk always made him a little more comfortable in his dreams.

"Interesting." The alien played with a tentacle hanging from his lower jaw. *"I thought you would have figured out that this wasn't a dream by now."*

"What?" Race panicked.

"Most of my consciousness is tied to your abilities," Tra-

nagra explained. *"This isn't a dream; it's a premonition."*

Dream images of Zain and another doppelganger of himself walked by, talking some weapon schematics.

"You mean all this is going to happen?" Race said in disbelief.

"Not exactly. They're all possibilities of events that can happen," the creature said, getting up from the table. He joined Race for a stroll and soon they were in a deserted room Race had never seen before. *"Your powers are strong and are most easily accessed by your subconscious. Dreaming is the domain of the subconscious, so it makes sense that your powers would be more active here. It may be that your subconscious is looking for threats to prepare for."*

Race found the very thought of scanning the future interesting. *"I wish I could do this when I'm awake."*

"In time," the alien said. *"Once we've focused your powers and accepted them as a part of you."* They stopped walking as the alien turned to him. *"I need something from you."*

"What is it?" Race asked, not really sure how far he wanted to go for the creature inside his head.

"Your friend, the short dark-topped one," he said.

"Illandra?" Race asked, a sudden alarm coming over him.

"Yes," the creature said. *"She is not well."*

"What's wrong with her?" Race panicked, now ready to do whatever the creature asked of him.

"Her powers have grown strong, but there is a problem with her," Tranagra explained. *"She cannot turn her powers off. They are starting to take their toll on her. Your powers*

are like muscles; they can be developed and trained, but they require rest to allow for recovery."

"*Like when I go limp after using my powers to enhance my strength,*" Race guessed.

"*No.*" The creature shook his head. "*But suitable. With her abilities always on, she is constantly exerting herself, and well over her limit. It would be like holding a large weight until your body gave out. If we don't act fast, you might lose her forever.*"

"*What do you need me to do?*" Race was ready to wake up so he could get started.

"*The ship you explored was experimental, and not completely finished,*" Tranagra explained as Race listened intently. "*With any luck, the builders finished the prison. My people all have some telepathic abilities, and the greatest punishment for any of my people is to be removed from the collective consciousness.*" The four-fingered hand reached out; a small circular ringlet hovered in his palm. It looked like a bluish-gold crown, complete with a couple of gems socketed into it. "*If you can find one of these, you should be able to modify it to your people so that when she uses it, it will force her powers off. You must guard it carefully, though. It can also be used to limit your own abilities if it falls into the wrong hands.*" An obelisk sticking out of the ground suddenly caught the alien's attention. "*It can't be.*"

A dust storm suddenly kicked up, causing Race to lift his hands to protect his face. "*What is it?*" he attempted to scream over the storm. He tried to read the images, but they were too blurry to make out.

"It's a marker of my people," the alien said, rubbing his hands over it. *"Your powers aren't strong enough to get all the details off of it I need. You must find it. I have to know if my people survived. If they have, they can help you finish this fight."*

"I'm sure I will," Race said, pointing to the side, where another copy of himself made his way through the storm with the rest of his team. *"It's just a matter of time."*

The scenery suddenly changed again, this time leaving them on the hull of a strange ship. Race watched as another copy of himself worked on trying to get through the exterior of the ship with Annette close beside him. Race could feel his heart starting to pound in his chest as if he knew what was going to happen next. It dawned on him that he probably had watched this a couple of times if this had been a reccurring dream of his.

His copy stopped, sensing trouble kicking in. The clone quickly turned around, pushing Annette out of harm's way as a beam of light attacked him. Race could see the ship in the distance as it fired its weapons on him. The blinding light made it difficult for him to see what was going on inside the beam. A shadow of himself attempted to use a force field to try and push the giant beam back. Race watched, horrified, as cracks started to appear in his copy's shield.

The light got brighter as the intensity of the weapon continued to rise. The copy cried out, almost in unison with the dream version of Annette as the blast shook the ship beneath his feet. When the beam vanished, there was nothing left where his copy had stood but the blackness of the damaged hull.

He stared, almost hopeless, at that black scars that re-mained, Annette's hollow cries sounding in the distance.

"Did I just witness my own death?" Race asked the alien, trying to keep from falling to his knees.

"This future is not certain," the creature said, trying to comfort him. *"Even now your abilities work to prevent this."*

"Then why aren't we switching to another scene?" Race demanded.

The alien stood there speechless, not able to supply him with the answers he wanted. Annette's tears stopped as she faded away from the scenery.

"You'd better go," Race finally advised the creature.

The alien nodded sadly and faded away, leaving Race to contemplate his fate on the hull of the damaged ship.

Chapter 12

THE PLEA

Record Dates: 349.248 – 349.252 PGST

ILLANDRA WAS IN HER NEW chambers getting ready for her pre-sleep procedures. Tranagra had been instructing her the past couple of weeks on how to better control her powers if she took the time to prepare herself before sleep. She lay down on her bed and got as comfortable as she could, which was a lot easier now that she was in her new chambers. She cleared her mind and started the process of disconnecting her consciousness from her body. After a couple of minutes, she looked down and opened her eyes to peer down upon her resting body. Her consciousness was bodiless for a moment. She could perceive things in all directions, her powers not restricted like her eyes.

Illandra concentrated on giving her mind a body. The details didn't matter much, but she still took the time to ensure her astral body was as accurate as possible. If it were possible, Illandra would have liked to check herself in the mirror, but astral bodies didn't have reflections. When she was content with her form, she hovered out past her room and started toward her destination. She enjoyed roaming the halls like a phantom in the night, the ability to go anywhere without anyone being able to stop her.

Upon reaching her destination, she ghosted through the door and entered the quarters. Race was knocked out on the bed, snoring so loud even the soundproof walls had a hard time concealing it. She reached out an invisible hand and touched Race on the forehead, looking for her new mentor. He was in a deeper sleep than usual; she guessed it was due to the strenuous workout he had done earlier. It made it easier to find Tranagra; he was already well-formed. She latched onto him and pulled him out of Race's mind, allowing the massive alien to take shape next to her.

The alien let out a roar as the last of his body formed in around him, the golden armor attaching to his dark-blue skin. *"Greetings, mindful one,"* he said after he was sure all was in place. *"The Run'hura sleeps well tonight. I had hoped to be fully formed by the time of your arrival."*

"What does he dream of?" she asked, curious to see if she had any effect on his dreams. She had checked in on him regularly. The mental projection had meant that she no longer had to be so close to him, which meant no more awkward excuses to be around Race. She still hadn't quite gotten over her feelings about being tricked into taking Race into her room that night; she had spent almost the entire first night with Tranagra lecturing him on the ethics of it. Enough to where he'd promised never to do it again, probably just to get her to shut up.

"Tonight, he does not dream," Tranagra informed her. *"His future sight is active. He now deals with what might be,*

344

and the possibilities are not so pleasant."

"*Is his power so strong he can predict the future?*" Illandra gasped.

"*The future is a chain of events, most determined by their predecessor. Some things must always be, some things can be without,*" he explained. "*What he does now is see the possible futures in hopes of changing something that must not be.*"

"*What is he trying to stop?*" Illandra asked curiously, once again surprised by just how amazing Race's powers were.

"*His destruction,*" Tranagra said regretfully.

Illandra was suddenly terrified of losing Race from her life. She remembered his comment earlier about her wasting what little time they had left together and cursed herself for not taking it to heart.

"*Is there anything we can do to help?*" she asked, not willing to take no for an answer.

"*This is a burden he must carry,*" the alien said. "Come, we must make use of what time we have."

"*One second.*" Illandra stopped him. "*I want to see it for myself.*"

"*You may not like some of the things you might witness,*" Tranagra warned.

"*I know,*" she agreed with him, knowing it couldn't stop her. Illandra reached out with her mind to see what was happening inside Race's dream. The subconscious was a lot different than the awake mind. The lack of focus was somewhat disturbing and made her a little dizzy, even in her bodiless form.

Finally, she made it to the place where Race dwelled on the hull of a strange ship. Several scenes raced back and forth in his mind, as if he were examining each as if they were part of a movie. Regardless of the sequence, it all ended in the same manner. She was forced to watch the brutal scene over and over in his mind before she could no longer stand it and was forced to leave Race's mind on the edge of tears.

"*I'm sorry,*" the alien apologized once Illandra had returned to her corporeal form.

"*Let's just get started,*" she said, trying to forget what she had seen.

"*Very well.*" Tranagra nodded.

They continued their training, like most of the nights before. Illandra grabbed Tranagra and pulled him into a void of space where they could work. The area was one where only the mind existed. The area took on different places depending on her mood; sometimes it was a tropical island, or a spa to help her relax if she'd had a stressful day. After what she had seen, she wanted someplace safe. Her pocket world gave her just that, by forming her private area into the safest place she knew.

"*You tend to favor this place,*" Tranagra said as he made himself comfortable.

"*No place like home,*" she said, wondering if the alien would get the idiom. She sat down on the grayish couch of her parents' living room. The smells of her home were all there, and if she listened carefully, she could almost hear the boards creaking from her mother's and father's footsteps in the rooms above.

"My people have a similar saying," he acknowledged. *"Shall we begin?"*

She nodded. They began running the same routine they had done since she had learned how to create her own private mental place. She had learned various techniques on how to expand her awareness. In return, she spent some time each night sorting through Race's consciousness, trying to piece the alien into its own corner. They usually only did this process for a couple of hours, as Illandra still needed to let her mind rest. Before she left for the night, Tranagra mentioned that Race was going to bring her an item to help her with her abilities. Its true purpose made her stomach curl, but its necessity was clear. The headaches were getting worse. She would do almost anything to rid herself of them.

"I feel we should move on to some more advanced techniques next time," Illandra suggested as they were preparing to say their goodnights.

"The mind's eye is not something to be taken lightly," Tranagra scolded her.

"It's not that I don't respect the training," Illandra explained. *"It's just that I'll be leaving soon. In a couple of days. We should make the best of the time we have. This time next week, I'll be half a galaxy away."*

The alien's lipless mouth frowned as it pondered the situation. *"As strong as you are, even you could not mentally breach that distance. Not without an anchor at least."*

"An anchor?" Illandra questioned. The term wasn't correct, but it was the closest her mind could interpret the word he had attempted to use.

"*Yes,*" the alien said. "*Someone you can mentally link to. Someone to manifest yourself through.*"

"*Race and I have a pretty strong link,*" Illandra thought hopefully. "*Could I not just travel through him?*"

"*He is already too crowded with my presence.*" The alien shook his head. "*Adding yours would just make things far too complicated. It must be someone else. Someone close to him, who will remain close to him for a long time to come.*"

She could already tell who he had in mind, and she wasn't happy with it.

"*I don't think that's such a good idea.*" Illandra tried to head off the conversation.

"*She's the best choice,*" he argued. "*You've already started building a bond with the hair of fire. You know she'll never leave his side.*"

"*That's because she cares for Race as much as I do,*" she objected.

"*Then you already have something in common to start the bond with,*" he concluded. "*The fiery one is the best candidate.*"

"*I'm not going to ask her,*" Illandra exclaimed, folding her arms.

"*Then there is nothing more I can do for you,*" Tranagra said as he started to fade away, a sign that Race was about to wake from his sleep.

Illandra let a few curses echo inside her mind. "Fine," she said before he was completely gone.

"*She must agree to it on her own,*" Tranagra said, his voice no louder than a whisper. "*You cannot use your powers to persuade her. If you do, she will find out that you have tricked her and the link will be corrupted."*

*　　*　　*

Illandra hadn't really been paying much attention to the exercise when she was knocked off her feet by the simulation. She was having a hard time understanding what possessed her to agree to it in the first place.

"That's the last time I ever complain about being bored," Illandra said, rolling over on her back.

"I'm sorry," the red-haired Marine said, stopping the simulation before her partner received any more damage. "There's actually not a lot to do on this small section of the station. It's mostly dedicated to training and research."

"That's okay," Illandra said, taking Annette's outstretched hand to get back to her feet. "It seems like it would've been fun if maybe I had some of your training. I probably need it where I'm going; my head just isn't in it today."

"Have a lot on your mind?" Annette asked, grabbing a pair of water bottles she had gotten before the workout and tossing one to Illandra.

"I wouldn't want to bore you," Illandra said, still trying to figure out the best way to broach the subject with her. "I'm not looking forward to leaving soon."

"You not ready to say goodbye to Race?" Annette asked as her eyes wandered from contact, embarrassed by the feelings she tried so hard to hide.

"A little," Illandra responded as they started to make their way out of the training chamber. "There're a lot of other stresses that I'm really not looking forward to, though."

"Anything I can do to help?" Annette asked as she opened the door for them.

Loan me your brain, Illandra thought to herself. "Not really."

"Well, since you are leaving soon, I feel I owe you an apology," Annette said, almost to Illandra's surprise.

"Why is that?" Illandra queried out of kindness.

"When you first arrived at the station, I didn't give you a fair chance," Annette explained. "Now that we've had some time to get to know each other, I really enjoy having you as a friend. I've spent so much time with guys, I didn't even know how much I would enjoy actually having a girl as a friend. I actually find myself wishing it didn't have to end."

Illandra wondered if she was ever going to get a better chance, but she didn't think so. "Well, funny you should mention that," Illandra said, trying not to choke on the words. "There actually is a way…sort of."

"How?" Annette said as her brow scrunched up to show her confusion.

"It's hard to explain," Illandra replied. "Come by my room in a bit and I'll try and explain."

"Okay," Annette said, still baffled.

The two said their temporary goodbyes and headed to their rooms to refresh themselves. Illandra took a quick shower to get ready for the night. Illandra was pacing nervously around her room when Annette finally showed up. She opened the door and let her in. They sat down at the small round table inside her room while Illandra continued to struggle with how to talk about it.

"How much do you remember from the day in the lab when we were attacked by the nanites?" Illandra finally decided that was the best place to start.

"I don't know." Annette tensed up. They hadn't talked about any of that since that day. "It all happened so fast."

"Do you remember seeing Race's abilities when he was data-mining all the stuff?" Illandra asked.

"Yeah," Annette said, glad to not be talking about the stuff near the conclusion of the encounter.

"How do you think that happened?" Illandra asked.

"I don't know," Annette said, "I just thought he wanted to… Wait. You mean you?"

Illandra smiled her acknowledgment. "Race isn't the only one with special abilities. I have powers, just like Race. But my powers are telepathy. That day, I used my powers to plug both of us into Race's mind."

"That means you…" Annette said, feeling more uncomfortable now than at the start of the conversation.

"Yes." Illandra nodded. "I try not to do it without permission, but sometimes I just pick up on things without trying."

"How much?" Annette asked nervously.

"Enough to know how much you like Race." It was better to not have any secrets, as they would all be exposed if she agreed to the link. "And I don't blame you. I actually think you guys would make a great couple."

"What does this have to do with what you were suggesting?" Annette said, trying to regain her composure and guard her thoughts.

"Well, that's the part that's hard to explain," Illandra said, now taking her turn to be the nervous one. "There's still a lot going on here, and I need someone here that I can create a permanent mental link to, so I can help out."

"You want to create a link to me?" Annette raised her voice, almost angered, as she stood up so fast that her chair nearly fell over from the force.

"I really don't want to create a link with anyone," Illandra admitted. "But I kind of have to."

"Why?" Annette's rage subsided slightly.

Illandra went on to explain the whole encounter with the alien that was now inside Race's head, and how he had been the one to help Race activate his powers. She continued to explain how it was helping her with her powers in return for her helping him to regain his consciousness. They were at it for several hours, discussing the ancient war and everything she had learned from Tranagra during their late-night sessions.

Illandra thought Annette handled the whole thing rather well. She just sat there and listened most of the time, only interrupting Illandra's lengthy explanations every so often to ask a question for clarification. When Illandra was done, she knew it still wasn't enough.

"It's a fascinating story," Annette said, preparing to leave. "But I just don't know how much of it I can believe."

"I can introduce you to Tranagra if you like," Illandra offered, secretly hoping Annette would continue to think she was crazy and just walk out the door.

"I don't know if that would do any good," Annette said, flashing a mental picture of her choking the alien to get it out of Race. "I just don't think I'd be comfortable with another person inside my head."

"I totally understand," Illandra agreed. "I'm not too keen on the idea myself. But before you say no, there's just one last thing I need you to see."

She just hoped Race was still having the same dream.

Chapter 13

SECOND INCURSION

Record Date: 349.342 PGST

IT HAD BEEN ALMOST A month since Illandra had departed for the Imperial territory. Race had buried himself in his research, trying to pretend that he hadn't lost her once again. Some nights he could almost feel her presence as if she were still around, like the last night they had spent together before she had left. He knew he had to move on with things, but he couldn't help feeling like he was stuck.

He was poring over some readings he had taken from the alien ship's computers when Konway interrupted him.

"How're things?" he asked.

"All right," Race said. "Just running some logs through this translator program."

"Find out anything new?" Konway asked.

"Not really," Race replied disappointedly. It had been a while since they'd had any level of breakthrough. Most of the ship's records were blank; if he was forced to make a guess, he would have said it hadn't even been officially manned yet.

"Bummer." Konway didn't sound too surprised. "You got a minute to help me with something?"

"Sure," Race said, trying to let his eyes focus off of the screen he had been reading. "What's up?"

"You know that modification I had been working on for our firearms?"

"You mean the one to disrupt the nanites?" Race asked curiously.

"Yeah," Konway confirmed. "I was wondering if you could look over the mods before we upload them to the rifle systems and biosensors since you're the expert. If you have a way to keep it from killing the host, that would be awesome, too."

"You haven't run out of lab rats to infect yet?" Race teased.

"Not yet." Konway smiled, handing over a datapad for Race to review.

Race quickly tapped through it and handed it back to his senior teammate. "It looks good. If it's any consolation, I'm not totally sure the shockwave is what's killing them. The nanites cannibalize much of the host and rely upon themselves to maintain them rather than the organs. I doubt they live too long without the nanites."

Konway's face curled in disgust at the very thought. "I'm glad I'm almost done working with them, then."

"Me, too," Race said. The whole thought of having a small active batch made them all nervous, Race more so than the others, with his firsthand experience of what they could do. They'd reluctantly agreed to in an effort to better understand how they worked and to develop some sort of weapon to fight them.

"So how long are you planning on remaining anti-social?" Konway blurted out.

"Huh?" Race asked, caught off guard by his teammate's bluntness.

"Every time something bad or out of the ordinary happens, you sulk back into this isolated state of yours," Konway explained as he sat on Race's workstation. "I don't mind too much; you drown yourself in your work and make the department look good. But we all kind of miss your wit at the meal table."

Race almost had to laugh, surprised at how well his routine had been picked up by his comrades in what seemed like such a short time.

"And you're missing quite the spectacle," Konway continued. "It seems Annette's short run-in with Illandra has managed to rub off on her. She's picked up on some of her finer traits."

"Like?" Race said, a little scared of how that comment sounded, knowing Illandra's powers.

"I think you're going to have to see it for yourself," Konway teased, knowing he had piqued Race's interest.

He had seen. Illandra's last couple of days on the station had been an interesting experience for them all. Both Illandra and Annette were prone to sudden fits of laughter without a word being spoken. Illandra had become a combat expert almost overnight, adopting several of Annette's techniques in a training exercise one day. It was enough to make Race suspicious.

"There you guys are," Zain said, walking into the workshop. "I've been looking all over for you. Cap wants us, pronto. Sounds like we got a mission."

Race and Konway leaped to their feet and followed Zain down the hall to the captain's office, where Annette was already waiting for them. The three entered and gave their commanding officer the customary salute as they reported in.

"Grab your gear, Marines," the captain said. "We're heading back to the fleet. We've got reports of another wave of Cenari ships crossing the nebula."

"Do you think they've noticed us?" Annette sounded alarmed.

"It doesn't appear so," the captain answered. "We're taking her down to basic life support here for the meantime. This wave seems to be passing through a less dense section of the nebula. They must have thought there was no reason for a surprise this time. Looks like they're just eager to get here and get to fighting."

"How much time do we have?" Zain asked.

"The invasion force is expected to be here in ten hours. We need to be on the Montana within five. Get your stuff and meet me on the shuttle as soon as you can." The captain dismissed them.

"Yes, sir," the Marines said in unison before rushing out the door.

Race was in such a rush, he didn't know how much time had passed when they were all on the shuttle heading out of the nebula. The long trip out of the nebula had been greatly shortened with all the advancements Race's team had made to the navigation programs and sensor array, but it still took a couple of hours to traverse the nebula safely.

Race decided to take Konway's advice and check in on his friends. He found Annette in the cargo bay working on some equipment.

"What happened here?" Race asked, admiring the mess of parts Annette had laid out around the bay.

Annette looked up from the motor she had taken apart. "You left your cave?" she teased.

Race scrunched up his face in response. "Funny. What did you break now?" he teased back.

Annette returned his unimpressive expression. "We were doing some testing on this unit, and something blew. Captain said we were going to need them for the mission, so I'm trying to get this drive back up and working."

"Anything I can help with?" Race offered.

"Do you know how to rebuild a quantum drive?" Annette asked skeptically.

She was obviously aware of his lack of mechanical skills. "Does it have an interface program?" Race asked sarcastically.

"Here." Annette smiled and handed him a flashlight, trying not to laugh. "Just hold this."

They were putting the last couple of parts into place when the captain called them up to the front. They quickly finished tightening the last fixtures and made their way to the shuttle's cockpit. Neither of them was ready for the terror they witnessed when they looked out the ship's windows. Before them was a starship graveyard. Several ships helplessly floated in pieces across the void of space. Both of them were in too much shock to say much of anything when the shuttle comm unit alerted them to an incoming call.

"Glad to see you're okay," said Admiral Montana when his image appeared before them. "We were afraid to contact you for fear of revealing your position."

"What happened here?" the captain said, still in shock at everything in front of them.

"The bastards arrived early," the admiral replied, disgust tainting his voice. "Way early."

"What can we do to help?" the captain asked, ready to spring into action.

"We gave them a run for their money, but a couple of them broke away and made a run for it. We need you to go after them. Find out whatever they're after and stop them. The *MacArthur* should be around soon; they'll be taking over as flagship. Captain, I need you and your team in charge"—the admiral paused to look at Race through his display—"for obvious reasons. Your secondary mission is still a go if the opportunity arises."

"Yes, sir," the captain replied. "Are you sure you don't want us to help you with anything in the meantime?"

"I'm afraid there's no time," the admiral said almost reluctantly. "Those ships are a lot faster than we expected; you need to get on their tail quick. We'll be holding some of the other ships back for repairs and to hold the border in case any more of those ships come across. You just focus on your task. I will have one of my men send over a copy of all our log reports for our new chief tactician to review. While I'm at it, enjoy being a major. Hopefully it does you some good."

"Yes, sir," the captain repeated before the signal cut out. He turned in his chair to face his soldiers. "You heard the admiral: put on your game faces and let's get ready to go."

"Ah, Major," Zain said, being the only one brave or naive enough to speak up, "what secondary mission?"

The newly promoted major let out a deep sigh. "If the opportunity arises, we're to try and board one of the ships, verify the nanite threat, and capture the vessel for research."

Annette's small pods in the cargo bay suddenly made sense to Race as he joined his teammates in sharing their tension. Zain let out a nervous whistle in response.

"Are we actually going to try and go for it?" Konway questioned the orders.

"Wouldn't be the first time we've had to do the impossible," Zain said, stating the obvious.

"We have our orders, and I'm sure we're not the only ones that know it," the major explained. "We'll keep an eye out for the opportunity; I just suggest we don't look too hard." The captain moved around to Race and forced him down into one of the seats. "Now then, Chief, I suggest you get to reviewing those logs."

Almost as if it had heard the captain, his biosensor lit up, displaying the field promotion to the new rank.

"Wait," Zain said after the captain left the cockpit, "if you're a warrant officer now, does that mean we have to call you sir?"

*   *   *

"Wait, come back here," Race yelled at Annette as he chased after her.

He had been going over some of the logs from the battle when she saw something that startled her. When he looked up at her, he could tell she was frightened by something. For some reason, he shared her fear.

When he'd first seen the enemy ships, something tensed up deep inside him. He didn't know why, but he was downright terrified by them. He recognized them from somewhere; he just couldn't place where. He was pretty sure that Annette had.

"I've got to finish the pod," Annette said, not wanting to face him.

He grabbed her arm and spun her around to face him. "Wait," he called to her again.

"Let go," she yelled through clenched teeth, using some of her training to force his grip loose.

"I know you saw something on that footage," Race argued.

"I don't know what you're talking about," she lied, still trying to get away.

"I need to know what it is," Race called to her.

"Nothing," Annette answered, finally reaching the bay.

He grabbed her by the arm once again to force her to face him. "Please," Race pleaded, "I need to know."

Annette looked at him, her face still covered in fright. Suddenly, her expression changed. "Would you stop harassing the girl?"

It was Annette's voice, but somehow he knew it wasn't

her words.

"What are you doing in there?" he demanded.

"It's kind of hard to explain," Annette's voice answered.

"You told me you weren't going to use your powers on people without their permission anymore," Race scolded.

"I have her permission," the voice claimed, almost offended.

"It's true," Annette said, resuming control of herself.

"Give me a minute," the voice said, taking back control. "This will be a very difficult conversation with two of us sharing one mouth."

Annette once again returned to her normal posture, showing that she was in control.

"What did she make you do?" Race asked Annette sternly.

"Nothing," Annette said, responding just as sternly. "She asked me, and I agreed of my own free will."

"You don't understand," Race argued. "She's different."

"I understand just fine," Annette argued back. "I know all about her powers, and she didn't use them to convince me of anything."

"I can't believe this," Race said, throwing his hands up in the air and walking away.

"Is he done throwing his fit?" Illandra asked, a ghostly image of herself appearing next to Annette.

"Almost," Annette said. Illandra's rally to her side seemed to calm her down a little.

"Illy, you've got some explaining to do," Race demanded of her.

"Please don't call me that," Illandra's ghost said. "You know I hate that name."

"Now," Race commanded.

Illandra rolled her ghostly eyes. "Annette's agreed to create a mental link with me so that I can help you out with what you've got going on here."

"Where are you right now?" Race asked, attempting to wave his hand through her projection to see if she really was there or not.

"I'm a couple days away from the Imperium capital planet," Illandra answered, slapping his hand.

Race pulled his hand back, the sting from the slap shooting up his arm. "Then how did I feel that?"

"You didn't." Illandra mocked him with her brown eyes. "I just made your mind think you did. Now, what's got you in such an uproar?"

"Besides this?" Race asked, rubbing his sore hand. The thought was real enough to even leave a large welt on the back of his hand.

"Yes," Illandra scolded, crossing her arms.

"Ask her," Race said, motioning to Annette, having a hard time remembering what it was in the first place.

Illandra turned to face Annette and raised one of her eyebrows questioningly.

"The ships are here." The words struck terror into all of them, Race still not sure why he should be afraid of them.

"Show me," Illandra said, the playfulness leaving her avatar's face.

Annette closed her eyes for a couple of seconds in what

Race presumed was a mental sharing of information.

"You have to promise me you'll never step foot on one of those ships," Illandra ordered him.

"Why?" Race questioned. "What's going to happen if I do?"

"It could cost you your life!" Illandra exclaimed.

"How do you know that?" Race said, dumbfounded.

"Because you showed me," Illandra told him. "One night you were having bad dreams. I wanted to see what was bothering you. When I looked into your mind, I saw you being murdered on the hull of one of those ships."

"Permission?" Race scorned. The mentioning of the dreams triggered an image of the recurring nightmare he'd had.

"That was actually before I made that promise," Illandra said defensively.

"That's why we did all this," Annette interrupted. "We want to do everything we can to prevent it."

Race was touched by their actions, even though he was still upset with their means. Both emotions paled in comparison with the fear of his own life being on the line.

"Tell me everything," Race stated coldly.

"Your powers are working on a way to save you," Illandra said, "as are we. Until we come up with an answer, you just need to physically stay off those ships."

"I haven't had that dream in a long time," Race commented.

"Really?" Illandra said, surprised.

"Maybe he already found a way to prevent it?" Annette

guessed.

"It's possible," Illandra agreed. "If you like, I can take a peek tonight and see."

Race wasn't sure how much he liked the idea of her poking around, but at least she had asked this time. "A little peek wouldn't hurt, I guess," he muttered.

"Good," Illandra said smugly. "I'll look when you're sleeping tonight and tell Annette what I find. Now if you'll excuse me, I have some things I need to finish up here."

"I'm sorry," Annette said once Illandra's image had faded away. "I didn't mean to trick you or anything. I just didn't want anything to happen to you, that's all." She reached her hands out under Race's arms and hugged him close to her. Race couldn't tell who exactly it was that was hugging him. Her embrace was reminiscent of times Illandra had held him, but the feeling was definitely Annette's.

Race wasn't sure if it was instinct or compassion that kicked in when he eventually returned her embrace. "It's all right," he said, feeling the softness of her red hair next to his cheek. "Who else knows?"

"Just me," Annette said. Another alarm triggered in his memory.

*   *   *

They were aboard the United Republic Ship *MacArthur* within an hour. Race had to force himself to continue studying the logs, his need to persevere in overcoming the doom their presence signified. The new major wasted no time putting his crew in command, with Annette as the head pilot,

Konway as the lead science officer, and Zain as head of security. To keep things from getting too uncomfortable, he made their appointments in conjunction with those that already held the positions.

"So where are they heading?" the major asked, taking his command chair in the center of the bridge.

"Their last course has them heading toward a system just outside explored space," one of the bridge officers stated.

"What do we know about it?" asked the major.

"Not much, sir," a lieutenant named Leif stated. "Most of the planets are uninhabitable, but there is one that's marked for possible terraforming."

The now-major looked over at Konway, an unspoken command issued.

"I'll give her a call, sir," Konway acknowledged.

The major nodded. "Get us on that course and tell the others to follow as quickly as possible."

"Yes, sir," Annette said, already punching in the heading on the navigational system.

"Who is he calling?" the officer next to Race whispered.

"His wife," Race whispered back.

A short time later, Konway informed the major that he had made contact and was ordered to put it on the center screen.

"Mrs. Reece," the major greeted the image, "it's good to see you, again. I wish it were under better circumstances."

"You, too, sir," the scientist responded. "I hear it's Major now. Congratulations."

"Thank you." The commanding officer smiled. "We have

some Imperial ships heading toward a planetary system outside Galactic-explored territory. One of the planets has been marked for possible terraformation. I was hoping that as head of the Republic's terraforming division, you could help give us some information about it."

"What's the system?" the black-haired woman asked.

"65 Alpha 9," one of the officers spat out after a look from the major.

"Right, let me pull that up for you," she said, lifting her datapad. "Oh yes, that one. We've sent a few unmanned rovers to explore it. It might have been habitable at one time, but it's a desolate wasteland now. It's almost completely riddled by sandstorms twenty-four/seven. I'm not really looking forward to that project."

"Anything we should be aware of?" the major asked.

"Not that I can think of," she said, going over the information. "Some potential mining areas on some of the moons. I'll see if I can send you a copy of our reports for you to look over."

"I'd appreciate it," the major thanked her.

"You can repay me by ordering my husband to take some leave when you guys are finished." She smiled at him.

"Consider it a deal." The major couldn't help but return the beautiful woman's smile. "You'd best get the twins somewhere safe. It looks like these ships might pass pretty close to your station. I'd hate for you to get their attention."

"We have a couple hidden bunkers on the surface." Konway's wife nodded. "We'll hit radio silence and hide out down there until we've heard from you."

"Good idea," the major approved. "We'll try not to keep you waiting. I'll transfer you back to the gunny so you can say your goodbyes." He signaled Konway to take control of the call.

The crew went back to their duties. Race was so busy, he jumped when Konway interrupted them.

"I think there's something we need to discuss, sir," Konway said. "My wife made some cryptic comments before she hung up on me."

"Anything good?" Zain questioned, his imagination obviously going someplace other than intended.

"Not the time, Staff Sergeant." The major shot Zain a look from the corner of his eye.

"Sorry, sir," Zain said, sealing his lips tight.

"Any idea what she meant?" The major steered the conversation back on track.

"Not completely," Konway answered, "but she made it obvious there's something on the planet we need to know about that's not in the file. And then she sent me this message shortly afterward about our kids' different birthdays." Konway showed them the message containing a series of numbers on the sensor unit attached to his forearm.

"But your kids are twins." Race remembered all the times the proud father had discussed his offspring.

"Exactly," Konway agreed.

"So what? Coordinates?" Annette said, looking at the numbers as the arm passed her to reach the major.

"I think so," Konway agreed.

"She wants us to look at this spot on that planet?" Zain

summed up the findings.

"All right," the major said, making his decision. "Shift through the info they provided and see if we can figure out what she's trying to tell us. If we've already found what they're looking for, it would give us a massive edge when we finally catch up to them."

"Yes, sir," the team said in unison.

Chapter 14

CONFIRMATION

Record Date: 349.364 PGST

ILLANDRA BREATHED A SIGH OF relief once the captain made the announcement that the trip was nearly over. Most of the trip had been uneventful, and the rest of it had been boring. As much as she tried to fight it, she spent most of her time looking over Annette's shoulder. The mental link between them had several benefits. Not only was Illandra able to ghost-walk almost instantly to Annette's location, but she was also able to access a lifetime of skills, such as piloting and even combat. It was still no substitute for the real thing, but it was pretty close.

The link also provided a couple of annoyances, like the fact that their thoughts weren't always as private as they liked. The slightest distraction on either end allowed for stray thoughts to wander into the other's head. Both ladies found themselves answering mental questions from time to time that were meant for no one but themselves, especially if the other mind was unoccupied when the thoughts crossed over.

Anthony's ship had been severely damaged during the

conflict, so they were forced to depart the *Puller* on a standard cargo ship that had come to drop off repair supplies for the war relief. They first went to Earth, the great home of the human civilizations. Along the way, they held several interviews to replace those of the staff lost in the conflict. Anthony's position had gifted him with some of the highest-qualified candidates for the various positions. Illandra quickly grew bored of hearing them all brag about their successes.

There were also numorous meetings about the Cenari, and this time Illandra wasn't spared from any of them. Her expertise provided by the encounter with the infected corporal was more than enough to see that she wasn't excused, and what Tranagra had shared with her meant she had more firsthand knowledge than any other person in the entire Republic. Only a select few were aware of the alien's existence, and even fewer knew where he lived. Anthony had seen to it that his presence was kept in the utmost secrecy.

When they reached Earth, their new ship was awaiting them with all new staff members as well. A military squad was also set to accompany them, their purpose to guarantee their safety. Annette even gave her unsolicited whisper of approval.

They remained on Earth for almost a week clearing up the final details to allow them entry to the Imperial Consortium. Anthony had barely gotten involved before he was able to push through the final obstacles barring their acceptance. Then they were on their new ship traveling to the heart of the IC. Between meetings and conferences, Illandra had spent her time trying to get to know the new faces, including that of her own new personal assistant, a young woman named Kaylee.

Kaylee had a list of recommendations as long as, if not longer than, many of the other applicants'. Illandra had no idea that Anthony was going to assign her as Illandra's personal assistant. Otherwise, she would have paid more attention in the interview. Kaylee was one of the quieter members of the new crew, but Illandra had found that she wasn't the shy type of quiet. The woman could hold a decent conversation, but just seldom found the need to. Illandra could tell she had a strong spirit, and would often work herself several hours beyond what was necessary, often making Illandra put in several of her own.

Surprisingly, Kaylee was almost Illandra's height, and very close to Illandra's build. If the young woman had dyed her dirty-blond hair to match Illandra's, she didn't think anyone would be able to tell them apart from behind. She had felt there was a reason for that, but decided to let Anthony have some of his secrets.

Illandra had been in the ship's common area going over some details with her new assistant when she sensed her mentor's trouble as he attempted to search for her on the ship. She shot him an image of her location so he would know where to find her and waited for his arrival.

"What's happened?" Illandra questioned the worried ambassador as he entered the area and approached her.

"We need to talk," said Anthony, looking very sternly at Illandra's assistant. "In private."

Illandra quickly reached out with her mind to tap into

her mentor's thoughts before her assistant even had a chance to excuse herself to find some other pressing matter to attend to. *"What's happened?"* she repeated mentally.

Anthony was visually shaken by how easily Illandra had intruded into his mind. She had done her best to hide some of the advancements from him, but his obvious tension meant something big had happened. She found herself very comfortable and didn't want to get up.

"Are you going to tell me, or should I just go peeking around in your head and see what other things I can find?" Illandra asked.

"How did you…" Anthony started to reply before breaking himself off. *"Never mind. Another wave of ships has broken through the field. They weren't battle-cruiser types like the last ones; these ones were smaller and more tactical."*

"Oh, I already know about it," Illandra informed him.

Anthony found himself at a complete loss for words, both physically and mentally. Illandra took great pride in the accomplishment of being able to make her mentor speechless; it was something that very few people could do.

"I'm mentally tied in with one of Race's teammates." Illandra gave up her secret. *"I can see and hear almost everything that goes on over there. They were called back because of the invasion, but the ships beat them across the nebula. The fight was over before his team could even make it there. They're now following the remaining ships in an attempt to stop them."*

"I don't believe it," Anthony blurted as he regained himself from Illandra's shock. "Such a great distance. It's never been done before."

"Tranagra showed me how to do it. It's a permanent link," Illandra thought reluctantly, trying to make sure her thoughts didn't get transmitted over to Annette. *"It can be annoying, but it does have a few perks."*

"Amazing," Anthony said, struck with awe. "When were you planning on telling me all this?"

"Who said I ever planned on telling you?" Illandra smiled at Anthony, bringing his blood to a slight boil.

"I thought we agreed that you were going to show me some of the techniques this alien showed you?" Anthony scolded.

"And I will, whenever you find time in your busy schedule," Illandra said, patting his poor hand on the table next between them.

"I'll make some time tonight," Anthony assured her, allowing the issue to be closed for the time being. "We have another meeting coming up. I suggest you keep these details to yourself. It's supposed to be classified."

Illandra nodded her acknowledgment to her mentor's request and followed him off to the conference room where they held most of their meetings.

*   *   *

Like the other galactic establishments, the IC had moved their capital farther into their own occupied space. Illandra was looking forward to visiting the planet; she had heard that the engineers had tried to incorporate several of the various historical cultures in most of their buildings.

After the long trip ended with them landing on the

moon, a small shuttle ferried them down to the surface. They received an unexpected surprise when they exited the shuttle: a squad of soldiers in dark-green uniforms was waiting to escort them safely to the embassy.

"Here, put this on," Illandra's assistant said, handing her a small device that clipped onto her ear. "It will translate for you."

"Thank you," Illandra said as she grabbed the device to put it on. Illandra really didn't need the device since Tranagra had taught her how to access the area where thoughts became words, but she still put the device on for show.

"Welcome to Shanghai, Congressman Martin, Vice Ambassador Page," saluted a young officer as he intercepted the group. "I am Captain Tso Young of the Imperial Elite Guard. The Imperial Council has asked that I ensure you get to your embassy in one piece. I'll also be working with your security detail to ensure your safety while you're here."

"Do the people here really hate us that much?" Illandra asked.

"The Cenari group isn't that large, but they are mostly extremists," explained the captain. Illandra could tell by something in the captain's eyes when he looked at her that he had some hidden agenda in mind. "Most of the Imperial Council don't want war with the United Galactic Republic."

"And where do your loyalties lie, Captain?" asked Anthony.

"To the Empire," the captain stated solidly.

"Can you tell me who the strongest supporter for peace with the Galactic Empire?" questioned Anthony.

"That would be Representative Chilong," the captain answered. "He's the one that assigned me to your security. I would assume that he's already at the embassy waiting to receive you."

"We shouldn't keep him waiting then." Anthony thanked the soldier as they followed him to the vehicles.

The guards hurried to grab the luggage and pack it into the transport, where they prepared for their trip to the embassy. Illandra tried to enjoy the scenery of the planet, but she could feel Anthony trying to reach out to her. She could tell that some of the suggestions she had given him had helped him focus his abilities, but he still had a long way to go to catch up to her.

"Yes?" Illandra mentally reached out to make the connection for him.

"Damn it, lass, I was trying to do it myself," her mentor cursed. *"Oh well. What do you think about the young captain?"*

"There's something off about him," Illandra said. *"I get the feeling he's a good soldier, but there's something I just can't put my finger on."*

"I think he likes you," said Illandra's mentor with a smile.

"Maybe, but he also has a hidden motive," Illandra replied sourly.

"Oh? What is that?" Anthony questioned.

"I'm trying very hard not to violate his privacy to find out," Illandra mentally scoffed. *"If I were just out poking around in people's heads, I would have known I was promoted from your personal assistant to Vice Ambassador. When were*

you planning on telling me that one, old man?"

"Who said I ever planned on telling you?" Anthony replied smugly.

"That's a very nice sword you have there, sir," one of the Marines interrupted the silence of the trip.

"Thank you," said the captain appreciatively as he pulled the sword from its sheath. "It's pure dentarite; the whole thing was crafted on the molecular level. The blade isn't more than a couple of atoms thick, and it can cut through anything. There's only a couple like this in the galaxy. It's mostly for decoration, but it has come in pretty handy on a couple occasions."

"That's amazing," gasped one of the other Marines. "Pure dentarite? That must have cost you a small fortune."

"You can tell because the blade has a bluish-green tint to it. It was a gift from the president," said the captain, smiling. "The Cenari have been rather restless since their arrival; the president himself gave me this sword for stopping an attack on the palace."

"You happen to find yourself in the right time and place fairly often, Captain?" asked Anthony, something obviously playing on his mind.

"It's kind of a special gift of mine," said the captain with a smile as he peered down toward the end of the vehicle so he could see Anthony. "It's hard to explain; sometimes I just get this feeling like I need to be somewhere. It hasn't let me down yet."

Illandra's eyes widened as the all-too-familiar words rang through their ears. *"You don't think he's a precog, do you?"* Illandra mentally questioned Anthony, already knowing he was thinking it, too.

"I don't see why not," Anthony replied, just as stunned. *"If it's capable of happening in our part of space, there's no reason it can't happen here."*

"I could buy a small moon with this thing." A Marine drooled over the blueish-green metal.

"It still wouldn't make your wife happy," laughed the soldier next to him, causing several other members to join in before quickly being silenced by their commanding officer.

Upon reaching the embassy, they were directed to a secure garage before they were even allowed to get out of their vehicles. An embassy representative was waiting to greet them. Just as Captain Tso Young had predicted, Representative Chilong was also among the men receiving them. The guards were split into groups to help get their things unloaded and people directed to the right areas. Not wanting to waste any time, the embassy manager had already reserved a private room for the two officials to confer in. Illandra wasn't spared that meeting, either.

"I'm glad you're here, Congressman Martin," the small representative greeted them once they were in the room. "There are several of us that really want a peaceful resolution to this conflict."

"As do we, Representative Chilong," Anthony replied. "Why don't you start filling me in on what's been going on here?"

"As I'm sure you know, there's been a new political party that's formed calling itself the Cenari. They're a radical bunch. They go around making wild accusations without any proof, and their numbers keep growing. It started as a small movement of nobodies, but the longer they persist, the more that seems to rally to their cause."

"Do you know who started the Cenari movement?" asked Anthony.

"It was Senator Chan," Captain Tso Young answered from his corner of the room. "I remember when he went to meet some members of a Planetary Research Committee from the outer rim a couple months ago. They had claimed they had found something amazing and asked to show him. When he came back, he was…different."

"Different how?" Anthony searched for clarification.

"It was like he was a different person," the captain explained. "Made my stomach turn inside out just to be around him."

"How many Cenari loyalists would you estimate are in parliament right now?" Anthony asked.

"It's still a small group, but their members' outside parliament has grown uncountable," Chilong answered. "They've already taken over a couple mining facilities and space stations."

"Any idea what they really want?" Illandra established herself in the discussion.

"What does any terrorist group want?" Representative Chilong asked. "Spread panic, fear, false propaganda to rally others to their cause. They're doing a pretty good job of it, too, if you ask me."

"You know there are still several members of the Consortium that are upset about the Great Divide," Anthony suggested. "The Republic got the largest chunk of space. The Euro-Alliance managed to find the largest supply of dentarite. Some of us think that it might be a ploy to gain more territory and resources."

"If they want riches, why not go after the Euro-Alliance?" asked Illandra. "They have all the dentarite."

"That's exactly why they don't," the captain stated. "Most of the Euro-Alliance ships are completely armored in dentarite. Trying to attack them would be like trying to attack a tank with a machine gun. The Consortium and the Republic are on the same level technology-wise. If I wanted a weaker opponent, the Republic would be the best option."

"I don't know if I'd totally agree with you on your technology," Anthony interrupted. "We saw firsthand what your new ships can do."

"Those ships weren't entirely ours," Representative Chilong mourned gravely. "One of the stations they've captured is a shipbuilding facility. They modified it to build those prototype ships. Those ships entered your space without the approval of the IC government."

"Have you tried to investigate any of the Cenari facilities?" asked Anthony.

"We have," Captain Tso Young answered, once again breaking his silence, "but whenever we get someone close, they suddenly break off communication. Some of them even come back claiming loyalty to the Cenari. I'm afraid if we aren't able to put a stop to their efforts, the Imperial Consortium could be looking at civil war."

Illandra could feel the disturbing emotion from the captain as he thought about his country fighting itself.

"We are here to help," comforted Anthony. "The Republic doesn't want a war with the Consortium, nor does it want to see the IC destroy itself from within. We received news that another fleet of ships had broken through the belt. Can you tell us anything about them?"

"After you defeated the first wave, we got a report that they were building different types of ships. They're smaller, lightweight reconnaissance ships. The weapons were still pretty advanced, but they're meant to search and explore. I don't think they were expecting you to be able to fight off their first attack so easily. I'd like to hear more about how you did it, if you have the time?"

"We had a little bit of luck working on our side." Anthony smiled.

"I heard it had something to do with one of your military green citizens," the captain said, shooting Illandra an almost devilish smile.

Illandra could almost feel the captain's obsession at that point. Not being able to restrain herself anymore, Illandra once again broke her promise and reached into the mind of the highly decorated captain.

"You must be referring to Sergeant Allard," said Anthony, smiling. "Very remarkable individual, not much different than yourself, Captain."

The captain was almost honored to hear the compliment. Apparently, Race had already made quite a name for himself. "I hope someday to meet him," said the captain.

"I'm sure you're all very tired after such a long flight," the representative said. "I'll let you get settled in; we can discuss more of these details at a later time. You're welcome to sit in tomorrow on the Senate hearing, but you don't address them until Thursday."

"We might just do that." Anthony smiled as everyone stood up from the table and extended his hand.

"It would be nice to meet some of your fellow officials," Illandra said, trying to sound twice as professional as Anthony had.

"We'll look forward to it," said the senator, accepting his hand for a firm shake. "How long are you planning on staying with us?"

"Until we're no longer needed here." Anthony smiled.

"We'll do our best to make sure that isn't too long," laughed the senator. "I'll see if I can have the captain arrange a tour of some of our fine planet."

"It would be my pleasure." The captain bowed to his guests.

"A tour of the area would be most appreciated," Illandra said with a curtsy. "The view through the transport windows wasn't enough to satisfy my cultural curiosity."

After the two Imperialists finished their goodbyes and left, Illandra could tell that Anthony wanted to talk a little more.

"You read him, didn't you?" Anthony asked when they were finally alone.

"Yup," Illandra confirmed, not really all that concerned that she had been caught in the act.

"I didn't think you could hold yourself back when he mentioned Race." Her mentor frowned slightly. "What did you find out?"

"He is a precog," Illandra confirmed. "He seeks a good challenge to test his skills, but his abilities make it hard to find. When he thinks of how skilled Race is, he sees the ultimate challenge; he's almost bloodthirsty for it. The only reason he's so interested in me is that he knows I have a history with Race."

"Really? You think he can be trusted?"

"For the most part. He wants what is best for the Consortium, even though he's not a hundred percent sure what that is. He could be a very useful ally."

"And Chilong?"

"The senator seems honest enough. It seems he's still not telling us everything; I almost get the feeling they already know about the Cenari," she answered.

"It's altogether possible," Anthony agreed. "If they've managed to capture or kill any, I'm sure they've done an exam and found the nanites, assuming that's what it is."

A beam of fright trickled down Illandra's spine as she remembered the autopsy of the infected soldier that tried to kill her. "I hope we're wrong," she said gravely.

*   *   *

The next morning, Illandra awoke to find her assistant had already picked out a set of clothes for her visit to the Consortium legislative building. Truth be told, she wasn't that fond of them, nor of having her decisions made for her, but it was part of the responsibilities Anthony had placed upon her assistant. Some of the garments were customary for her new position, adorned with the galactic emblem. Illandra was forced to wonder if Anthony might have been trying to tell her something about the way she customarily dressed, though.

She met up with her mentor for breakfast in the embassy's well-catered cafeteria while they waited for their Marine detail to arrive and escort them to their destination. While they weren't able to address the Congress, their presence was recognized upon their arrival. They were given special seating to listen to the discussions.

Illandra did her best to endure the session. The proceedings didn't seem to be much different than those of her own government. During one of the recesses, several congressmen approached Anthony and Illandra and welcomed them. Illandra was surprised to find such a warm welcome considering the current hostility between the two governments. She had to remind herself that it wasn't the whole government that was out to get her, just a small radical group. When she inquired about the Cenari movement, she found out that they rarely ever showed up to any of the meetings anymore, claiming lack of support of the government.

As if hearing their names, a small group of people barged through the auditorium doors. Without talking to anyone, they moved to their reserved seats.

"Looks like it's one of those rare days," the congressman Illandra had been talking with commented as the pleasant smile fell from his face.

The leader of the Congress called the session back to order before Illandra could respond, causing everyone to rush back to their seats. The discussions continued to ramble on, but Illandra no longer paid any attention to them. Instead, she was focused on the Cenari representatives. She really wanted to hate them for all the pain they had brought to her, but she was lost in their emotionless blank stares. She fought to keep the word "robotic" out of her mind as she examined them.

That was when the screaming started. A deafening shriek that filled the room and shook Illandra to her core. No one else in the room could hear it because the scream hadn't been made by a physical mouth. Illandra was fully aware that the scream was mental and where it was coming from.

Anthony seemed to be nervously scanning the room, much like he had in their encounter with the infected soldier. Illandra grabbed his hand and used her powers to echo the voices of the captive Cenari hosts.

Anthony looked at her, biting his upper lip to keep from losing his composure. Their worst fears had been realized: the Consortium wasn't on the brink of civil war; it was in the middle of an invasion.

Chapter 15

DISCOVERY

Record Date: 349.385 PGST

RACE STRUGGLED TO ONCE AGAIN pick himself off the floor where Zain had once again thrown him. Konway had had the brilliant idea to test Race's psychic abilities against Zain's combat prowess. Race had come to the conclusion that Konway's brilliance was painful. He looked up to see Annette sitting on one of the cargo boxes in the room, Illandra's ghost hovering next to her with a huge smile on her face.

"You don't have to enjoy it so much," Race thought out to her. Somehow, he always seemed to know when she was around, yet he couldn't fathom why.

"I've wanted to knock you around for some time now," she thought back, Annette doing her best not to laugh at the inaudible conversation. *"At least I can watch someone else do it."*

"What did I ever do to you to deserve this type of abuse?" Race asked, hurt.

"What about right before you left for boot camp?" Illandra reminded him.

Race unwillingly nodded in agreement; he probably had

386

deserved at least one of the painful slams he'd recently received.

"Had enough?" Zain asked, reaching out a hand to help Race to his feet.

"Enough was about ten takedowns ago," Race said, sorely accepting the assistance. Zain's combat skills had been unmatched, a true testament to his position within the SORD unit.

"Got one more in ya?" Zain asked, pulling him up. "Then we'll call it quits."

"Yeah," Race grunted as he stood up. He felt a couple of sore areas that were sure to be bruises come morning. "Just give me a minute to figure out where I put it," he joked.

"Take all the time you need." Zain smiled, patting him on an already bruised shoulder. He walked over to get a sip of his water while Race rethought his strategy. For being so muscular, Zain was surprisingly quick and agile. If Race was going to beat him, he was sure he would have done so by now, but he hadn't been that lucky.

Race took another sip from his hydration bottle and put it down. "All right, let's get this over with."

The two men walked to the center of the area they had cleared and took their fighting stances. Zain's elbows were tucked in tight to his chest with his hand loosely protecting his face, much like a boxer. Race had adopted a similar stance but usually flared his elbows out a little. Race took a couple of deep breaths to prepare himself for the beating he was sure to receive.

"Feel the attack coming; don't see it," a voice echoed in-

side his head. Race wasn't sure why he should trust the echo, but for some reason he did. He took a few more breaths as he tried to expand his awareness. He nodded to Annette to signal he was ready. Zain didn't bother signaling; he was always ready for a good fight. Race just hoped he could give him one.

"Three…two…go!" Annette shouted.

Zain wasted little time throwing the first punch, but as it approached, something was different. The fist aimed for Race was traveling so slowly, he felt he could have walked out of the way. It barely moved an inch, and as it covered that inch, Race saw several possibilities start to play out in his mind. Some attacks he dodged, some he blocked. Another inch and Race saw several more possibilities branch off from the first set, some of which already ended up with him on the ground.

As the clubbed hand crept farther forward, the sequence of scenarios where Race survived the opening moves split into more sequences. For each inch Zain's hand moved, Race could see the progression of multiple outcomes the fight would take, like a giant chain of events branching out before him.

Among the mess of branches, he saw it. It wasn't a victory, but it was close. Race decided to go for it, and no sooner did he make his decision than the snail-paced hand broke from its time restraints and flew toward his face at lightning speed. His body was already moving as the blow passed inches from his head. His body mirrored the chain of events from his vision, not even needing him to direct it.

He blocked a kick and dodged another punch as the events continued to play out.

At the end of the sequence, when Zain went to attempt his famous takedown, Race shifted his right leg and wrapped it around Zain's leg. As Race went falling to the ground, he straightened his intertwined leg, forcing Zain to stumble forward. Race grabbed Zain's arm, throwing him to the ground, and wrapped his around Zain's head. Instead of Race's normal solo thud as he hit the ground, it was accompanied by a second that sent Zain reeling in pain from his own encounter with the floor.

Annette and Illandra's ghost both jumped to their feet in disbelief at what they'd witnessed.

"Where'd you learn that one?" Zain asked, grabbing his arm to calm the pain shooting through it.

"I didn't," Race replied, debating if it was really worth it to call it a victory. The counter had done as much damage to him as it had to Zain. "It just seemed like the right thing to do."

"There's only a handful of people that know that counter," Zain said in anguish, "and most of them aren't stupid enough to use it."

"I can see why," Race responded, wondering how many ribs he might have cracked.

"I can't believe it," Annette said, racing over to Race's side to help him up. "You did it, you actually did it!"

"I did something." Race was forced to sit up. "I don't think I'd ever want to do it again, though."

"Wait," Zain said, pushing himself up with his good arm,

"was that actually it? Like '*it*' it? You didn't just get lucky?"

"No," Race said, almost surprised. "I actually did it. I consciously activated my abilities."

"*That's a huge step!*" Illandra beamed her congratulations into his head.

"I know," Race blurted, forgetting not everyone around could see her.

"You know what?" Zain asked, reaching a hand to Annette in hopes of a little assistance.

"Nothing," Race dismissed quickly.

"Don't be a baby." Annette brushed him off while pulling Race to his feet and pulled his arm over her shoulder to give him some support. "Race took about twenty more of those collisions than you."

"But I'm not supposed to take any," Zain whined, doing his best to get up with his injured arm.

Annette was making use of a medical kit she had brought along to scan and treat the two combatants' wounds when Konway joined them. Race had looked for Illandra, but she had disappeared among the disorder.

"How'd it go?" Konway asked, entering the room.

"Twenty-seven to one," Zain answered, massaging out the tenderness from his freshly treated arm.

"One?" Konway's face brightened at the news. "As in controlled inducement?"

"Unfortunately," Race informed him, remembering the pain. "The one was probably just as painful as the twenty-seven, though."

"Oh my goodness!" Konway jumped ecstatically.

"Where's the recording? What about the sensor readouts?"

"Ah, crap," Zain said, frustrated.

"Don't tell me you forgot." Konway dropped his shoulders in disappointment.

"We kind of gave up after twelve," Race explained. "We were pretty sure it was just going to be a waste of time."

Konway covered his face with his hands to hide his frustration, taking a deep breath to try and relax. He had been dealing with a large amount of stress ever since they'd started their chase of the alien ships a couple of weeks ago. The ships had proved to be too fast for them to keep up with; the only reason they were even able to keep them on their sensors was the fact that they were stopping to wreak havoc on every ship and station along the way. One of the stations had been where Konway's wife and twin boys resided.

"I'll guess we'll just have to try it again," Konway decided after he was done moping.

Race and Zain exchanged a quick look between them, remembering the pain of their last encounter. "Let's not," they pleaded in unison.

"It seemed pretty important when they called you away," Annette said, trying to give the boys a breather. "Everything okay?"

"Finally got word from the wife," Konway said with a smile forming on his tired face.

"That's great news," Race congratulated him. He hoped that the news would make his friend a little more tolerable.

"Yeah," Konway replied. "They were hiding out in the bunker they told us about. They were scared to make contact in case the ships were still close by. Everyone made it out fine. They're sending for replacements now."

"A whole space station?" Zain commented. "That isn't going to be cheap."

"I'm glad I'm not paying for it." Konway managed a little laugh. "Major's called a meeting, we all need to get back to the bridge. Apparently, the ships are about to reach that planet. We need to watch the sensors and our chief strategist needs to make our plan."

Race was almost tired of being referred to as Chief. He let out a sigh before grabbing the blouse of his uniform and heading for the lift.

"So how did it feel to toss around a superior officer?" Konway asked, thinking Race was out of hearing range.

"Pretty good the first couple times," Zain answered with a shrug. "Been a while since I got to polish some brass." Zain pointed to his shirt collar where their military rank insignia were pinned on. Like all other officers', Race's were made from polished steel, and commonly referred to as brass.

*   *   *

Race didn't think it could have gone any better. After the fleet dropped out of the slipstream, they were right on top of the Cenari ships. There were six that crossed the nebula together, but only half of them survived the initial battle. It was still a pretty good number, considering the tiny ships were outnumbered by more than four to one. Race wished he had that kind of advantage right now, but he didn't even have twice their numbers.

They had approached from behind one of the system's larger planets, using its gravity to hide their presence. Before they had a chance to activate any defensive maneuvers, the fleet had focused on one of the ships and turned it into a pile of rubble.

The attacking fleet then split into two groups, each targeting one of the remaining invaders. It was easy to see why they gave the fleet so much hassle. Even though they weren't as big as the previous juggernauts, they could still take a good beating. These smaller vehicles were also extremely maneuverable, almost able to dance around the fleet's attacks. Race had to coordinate the attacks so almost all the ships were firing at the same target at once, not leaving it any room to move and force them to take a couple of hits. It would have been a very different battle had they not been able to take the first ship out by surprise.

After the enemy ships had taken several hits, they were forced to flee and abandon the planet they had spent so much time trying to reach.

"Damn," the major said, pounding the arm of the chair, "they got away."

"Sorry, sir," Race apologized. He had hoped that whatever was on the planet would be valuable enough for them to defend it to the end.

"Not your fault, Chief," the major pardoned Race. The term Chief still made him feel a little awkward, but he was starting to get used to it. "They've been here for days. Does it look like they found what they were looking for?"

"Hard to tell, sir," one of the original crew members answered. "They were still running sensor scans when we surprised them, so I'd guess not completely."

"Well, that's some consolation then," the major moaned. "Let's use what we know and get it first."

"Yes, sir," the crew said at once.

Race handed his station over to the ship's security officer, doing his best to acknowledge the compliment he was given before rushing over to help Konway with his task. "So what have you got?" Race asked, looking over his right shoulder, his commanding officer joining him to look over the other.

"I'm looking up the coordinates now, sir," Konway said. The information that his wife had given them didn't specify any cardinal directions, so they had four points to check out. They had narrowed it down to two areas by looking through the files Mrs. Reece had given them.

"It looks like they destroyed some of the satellites monitoring the planet, sir," informed the ship's main science officer.

"I only need two spots," Konway responded, hoping they'd at least be able to get those two points. "I can get one, looks like it matches the actual report we found. It must be the other spot. Damn, there's too much interference there to see anything."

"Can we launch a probe or something?" the major asked, concerned about sending men in there without knowing what might be waiting for them.

"I don't think so, sir," Konway answered. "There's a huge sandstorm in the area. It's wreaking havoc on so many different levels, I doubt it would even get close enough."

"How sure are you this is what she was trying to tell us, Gunny?" the major asked.

"Extremely, sir," Konway answered, without an ounce of doubt in his wife's message.

"You got anything, Chief?" the major said, turning to face Race.

Race could feel a sting of mourning looking at the planet, but he didn't understand why he had such an attachment to it. "No, sir."

"I guess you're going to have to go down there and take a look then," the major concluded after taking a couple of seconds to think it over. "Sergeant Keegan, you're probably the only one qualified to land them down there. Have Staff Sergeant Amyas meet you in the shuttle bay."

"Yes, sir." The SORD group jumped into action, charging for the main lift off the bridge.

"When you get down there, you'll be on your own," the major warned them before the doors to the lift could shut. "We're going to pull back so they don't try to surprise us."

The team nodded their acknowledgment.

Within a couple of minutes, they were in a shuttle on their way down to the planet. This shuttle was much smaller than the one Race was used to. The one they'd used to get in and out of the nebula was built for long trips for several groups; this one consisted of a cockpit, a storage area, and the door out of the ship. They crammed themselves into the cockpit and launched to the surface.

As predicted, the storm made the descent pretty difficult. Race was glad to have Annette at the helm, even if his stomach wasn't. Annette landed them as close as she could to the target. The atmosphere on the planet wasn't breathable, so they were forced to don the space suits on the shuttles.

The suits didn't prove to be much more comfortable than the shuttle, but they served their purpose. One by one, they filed out of the ship and started to make their way to the coordinates they had been supplied. Luckily, the pounding of the sand on their suits was loud enough to drown out most of Zain's complaining.

While the wind made their trek challenging, they were able to complete it without any incident. Near the area, the team spread out and tried to find whatever it was they were looking for.

After about twenty minutes of searching, Konway called the team over to him. The area seemed to be in the roughest part of the storm; Race could barely see his hand in front of his face. Even the sensors on his suit had a hard time telling him what was in front of him.

As he approached his team, Race started to make out the shadow of something looming near them. He tried to put it between him and the wind, but the storm was coming at him from too many different directions for it to be effective.

"You all right?" Annette's static-filled voice called out to him over their communication units.

"I'm almost there," Race answered, almost able to see them now. "What is it?"

"Big," Konway's voice answered in his ear.

Race could already tell that from its shadow. A couple more feet and he was able to make out some of the details.

Judging by its outline, it was like a giant obelisk he had seen in one of his Egyptian history lessons. The pillar stood about fifteen feet high and was covered in markings Race had never seen before.

He finally worked his way close enough to it that he was able to reach out his hand and touch it. The obelisk seemed completely solid, all made from one giant piece of bluish-green metal. There were several symbols all over it, hook-type markings mixed with different-sized circles, half open and half filled in. Every so often, Race would get a good look at one and a word would jump out into his head as if he knew what it meant.

He started to feel his way around the obelisk, looking for some unknown item he secretly knew to be there. After a couple of minutes, he found the small button high above his head hidden inside one of the alien markings.

When he pressed it, the letters in the obelisk started to glow a darker blue than its metallic tint.

"What'd you do?" Konway yelled at Race through the comm, alarmed by the change in the obelisk's appearance.

"Sorry," Race apologized. "The dust was beginning to become a nuisance. I was having a hard time reading."

"You can read it?" Annette questioned him. She had seen enough of his abilities not to be surprised, but that didn't seem to tame her suspicions.

"Kind of," Race yelled back. "I think the obelisk is the source of the storm."

"Why would it do that?" Zain hollered.

"To keep the wrong people from finding it," Race answered.

A light spread from the top of the obelisk that started to grow out into a dome around the group. The sand flying under the dome stopped and fell to the ground around them, the wind pushing it no longer able to get into the shield created around them.

"What does it say?" Annette asked him, no longer needing to scream to be heard.

With the storm gone, Race was finally able to make out the markings. He looked for where the markings began and started to read aloud. "It talks about the people that once lived here," he summarized. "How they fought in a great war against a plague of their own doing. Some sort of bug they invented that took control of many of their people. There are several names mentioned of the fallen, some battles." He moved to another side of the obelisk as he continued to hear the story in his head. "The final battle was fought by one person, some Tranagra. Against orders, he took their last great ship and flew it into the heart of the enemy fleet, where he detonated the weapon that destroyed them all."

"*I saved them,*" a ghost's voice on the edge of tears whispered in his ears. Race turn to see who was there, but the area behind him was empty.

"Everything okay?" Annette asked. She had been watching him suspiciously since he'd got there, more so than the others.

"Yeah," Race assured her, checking once more to make sure there really was no ghost before turning back to the writing. "The weapon destroyed the technology the enemy and they were dependent on. The planet, too."

"That explains why no one's home," Zain said regretfully.

Race moved over to the last panel. "It's because they moved," Race contradicted him.

The group jumped to his side, trying to make sense of the strange readings as if they could read them as well. Even the ghost seemed excited by the news.

"They had enough to put together one last ship and head for a new planet. This marker is to direct any survivors to the new home. These are the directions for how to get there. That's why they're hiding it so hard, they don't want their enemy to find them in case they come back."

"You mean the nanites?" Konway asked.

"Could be; the way they described them seemed close enough," Race said, acknowledging his suspicions. "Would explain why they're here, looking for signs of them."

"And we found it," Konway said, examining the obelisk in awe.

"Do you think we can follow them?" Annette asked.

"Not easily." Race pursed his lips in frustration. "Their coordinate system is different from ours, not to mention we have to take galactic shifts into account since the directions are so old. It's going to take a lot of work to figure out."

"Copy what you need," Zain ordered him. "We can't leave it here, and it's too big to take with us. If the Cenari find it, we'd be putting them all at risk, assuming there are any left."

Even the ghost reluctantly agreed with Zain, but they all knew it was the right thing to do. Race looked at his datapad to enter the commands, but his AI was already hard at work imaging the pillar to take a digital copy with them. It was for the best; Race knew he would have been stalling most of the time, trying to find another way to save the structure.

When they were done, they headed back to the shuttle to prepare for launch. Zain had determined the obelisk was pure dentarite and would have to be blown up from space, as none of the explosives they had with them were strong enough to destroy it. There was still no sign of the other ships, but they flew a great distance before exiting the planet to throw off their trail.

The fleet made a quick sweep to pick them up once they were in orbit, and with a word from their commanding officer, the battle cruiser's cannons made the greatest discovery Race had ever known vanish.

Chapter 16

ALLIANCES

Record Date: 349.386 PGST

THE WALLS OF THE EMBASSY were starting to drive Illandra crazy. The only time they were allowed to leave the embassy was when they sat in on any of the Consortium's Congress sessions. There wasn't a lot to do in the embassy; it was mostly meant to protect its residents, not entertain them. It had a cafeteria that was too small for the number of people it serviced and a gym that was even smaller. She had made frequent use of them both over the past month that she had been stuck there, more than she actually cared for, most likely an influence from her new link buddy. She was pretty sure that they had canceled each other out, but she was feeling some of the benefits of the workout.

It was hard for them to get any real intelligence on the Cenari stuck where they were. They tried to keep their distance from the Cenari representatives in fear of being infected by them. Illandra had been cautiously trying to reach out to any of them, afraid they might suffer the same fate as the corporal she had exposed on the Puller. She was forced to listen to their constant ramblings and try to decipher what

401

clues she could. Nothing useful had been brought up as of yet.

Illandra and Anthony were relaying their findings, or lack thereof, back home. The president's council hadn't been too impressed by their progress and had been pressing for them to try new methods, but Anthony had been pretty strict on what they had allowed, considering the actual danger the Cenari possessed.

"I think we need to tell Representative Chilong some of our findings to enlist him to help us," Illandra blurted out, more tired of their bickering than anything else.

"I'm sorry, Miss Page, but that's not something we're allowed to do," said one of the men on the other side of the call. His name was Blake, one of the president's staff appointed to handle most Cenari incidents. He was tall and skinny, and something about his face made Illandra want to call him Rat Man.

"It's Ambassador Page," Illandra corrected him sternly. It made her realize why Anthony enjoyed his title so much. "Also, we're the ones that get to decide how much or little we get to share with them. If we feel something should be shared, then it is. They've been fighting the Cenari for some time already. You act like they don't already know what they're up against. All we'd be telling them is that we know, too, thus making them more likely to share more of the information they have. It might even open up the possibility of a joint strike against the Cenari. Right now, they're only a small but very dangerous group. Imagine what we'll be fighting if they take control of the entire Consortium. We need all the allies we can get to put an end to them as fast as possible."

It had been a mouthful; Illandra just hoped that it hadn't landed on deaf ears. There was an uneasy silence as several of the representatives exchanged secret nods expressing their concerns about or consent to the idea. Rat Man hit a button on his console to mute the transmitter while he listened to someone off the projection.

Illandra was nervous. She found herself dreading the possibilities of who might be on the other side of the conversation. She hoped it wasn't who she thought it might be. Had she overstepped her bounds? She had told him to call her ambassador instead of her correct title of only vice ambassador.

She quickly reached out to Anthony in hopes of confirming what she feared. *"Please tell me it's not the president he's talking to."*

"It most likely is," Anthony replied. *"He likes to sit in on these type of things from time to time to keep abreast of the situation."*

Illandra let out a couple of mental curse words, some of which grabbed the attention of Annette through the mental link they shared. Illandra could feel Annette taking a quick peek over Illandra's shoulder to see what had riled her up before quickly retreating back to her own part of the galaxy. Illandra admired Annette's ability to leave the room.

"Well, Ambassador Page," the rat-faced man said, returning to the conversation, "it seems we'll try it your way. We'd also like to implore the two of you to explore other opportunities as well. As you said, time is of the essence."

"We'll expand our efforts to see what other methods may be safe to pursue," Anthony agreed.

"Very well." Blake nodded.

There was a quick round of goodbyes before Illandra quickly jumped and hit the button on the terminal to disconnect them and fell back into her seat. It was a comfy chair; its high armrest made it easy for her to sink in and hide.

"You did pretty well," Anthony congratulated her.

"He hates me," Illandra sulked.

"Who?" Anthony asked curiously.

"Rat Man," Illandra explained.

Anthony found himself unable to hold in his laughter, knowing perfectly well who she was talking about. "He might, but the president seems to like you."

"That's only going to make him hate me more," Illandra observed.

"He's not one to hold a grudge," Anthony assured her. "It's his job to be the voice of opposition to ensure all options are considered fully. I'm sure you'll come to appreciate him quite well in the future."

"Really?" Illandra asked. "You think so?"

"Sure," Anthony assured her, "as long as he doesn't hear you call him Rat Man."

Illandra did her best to conceal her embarrassment, hiding her burning cheeks behind her hands.

* * *

Anthony wasted no time calling Representative Chilong to the embassy for their meeting, and he was quick to respond to the summons. They were making use of one of the conference rooms to break the news. They had brought back Captain Tso Young with him. Illandra still hadn't warmed up to him, despite his advances. Locked up in the embassy, she felt more like his prisoner than a guest of the planet at times.

Anthony had broken the news about the infected soldier; they had replaced some of the details about the alien ship with a Cenari survivor from the invading force. Illandra thought it was close enough.

The two were sitting quietly, fidgeting like children caught hiding a secret from their parents.

"We don't know anything about this," Tso Young denied the accusations.

"There's no point in lying," Chilong responded with a voice so dreadful it sent chills down Illandra's arms.

"I'm…I'm sorry," the captain stuttered. "These matters of the Cenari are extremely classified for fear of spreading mass panic."

"We understand," Anthony said soothingly.

"It's actually the captain here that's been keeping the Cenari at bay on Shanghai," Chilong praised him. "That's why he's got that sword he carries with him everywhere."

"Why don't you tell us what you know about them," Illandra probed.

"They're not all the same," the captain started, "but we've narrowed it down to about three different kinds. The first look like normal people, kind of infiltrators. Sounds similar to the infected soldier you described. The other two you don't come across that often. We're not sure if it's because they're less common, or because they're just that well hidden. The first is like a tank, big and massive. It increases muscle growth in its host by about a hundred times. I've seen a blow from one of them crush a man into pieces."

The visual memory Illandra picked up with that was far from pretty.

"They seem to be the keepers of the hounds. We call them hounds because the first dozen we came across seemed to have actually been modified dogs. They're still plenty strong, but their superiority comes from their agility and speed. They almost always travel in packs, and never too far away from one of the giants."

"You said the first couple," Illandra noticed.

"Yes," the captain said, "most of the ones we've examined lately have been…" His voice trailed off, unable to identify the ones he had killed as humans.

"I understand," Illandra apologized, her sincerity helping ease his pain. His story wasn't much different than what she had expected from Tranagra's description of them. "Do you know what they're planning, and why they're so interested in the Republic?"

"No," the representative interrupted. "We know they're building their forces up, but we're not sure what their plan is. Anyone that's even gotten close has gone missing, most likely captured. We're not even sure how badly we've been compromised."

"Not as badly as you fear," Illandra assured him. "From what we've gathered, the nanites are unaware of the thoughts of the host. They usually shadow the host for a while before taking over, but they can't read the host's thoughts."

"You know this from one attack?" Tso Young asked, almost as relieved as he was curious.

"After being electrified enough to kill the controlling nanites, the host had a moment to pass along a few items," Illandra lied through her teeth.

"How did you manage that?" Chilong asked.

"After a short fight with Sergeant Allard, several Marines electrocuted him, which we believe killed enough nanites to allow him to regain some consciousness," Anthony explained.

"Then they took over a nanoscope and used the comm channel to hack into the medical bay and try and dissect me." Illandra recalled the encounter.

"Wait," the captain exclaimed, jumping from his seat, "they can take over electronics?"

"It was under very special circumstances," Illandra clarified, attempted to calm them. "We had to supply them a current to keep them alive. You didn't know that?"

"No, we didn't." The representative expressed his concern. "We'd better make some preparations."

"I'll make a call," the captain said, pulling a small cylinder from his pocket.

"Now that we're on the same page, maybe you'd be more forthcoming with some of the information on the Cenari?" Anthony attempted to probe for more information.

407

"I'm afraid there's not much more to share," the representative stated, disappointed. "As I've said, we've had problems getting people into the Cenari. We expect most of them have become infected. Lord knows how much intel they've gained on us in the process. We stopped sending people in fear of becoming more compromised. All we know is they're planning something big. They've rallied most of their forces into a single system."

"Has anyone returned from there lately?" Illandra asked, an idea starting to brew in her head.

"None of ours." Chilong mourned a special loss.

"What about one of theirs?" Illandra asked. She could feel Anthony attempting to probe her mind with a sly look, wondering what she was planning.

"I believe one of the representatives that supports the Cenari recently came back from their base," the captain said curiously. "Do you mean to catch and interrogate him? Or the host?"

"It's too dangerous," Chilong objected before Anthony could give his own objections.

"I can do it," the captain volunteered. "I've done it before. Then we can electrocute it enough to where the host can tell us what's going on."

"I think a dead representative will attract too much attention," Anthony observed, "at least more than we care for."

"That won't be necessary," Illandra stated. "I should be able to handle this."

The two Consortium citizens exchanged another awkward expression. "How?" asked the captain.

"You know I won't allow it," Anthony objected.

"It needs to be done." Illandra returned a stern objection of her own. "And I'm capable of doing it."

"Would the two of you mind giving us a moment?" Anthony asked them.

"Of course," Chilong said, standing up from the conference table as he and Tso Young left the room.

"You know it's too dangerous," Anthony scolded her the moment the door had closed with them outside the room.

"To do it the way you're thinking, yes," Illandra agreed.

Anthony stared at her, confused and once again speechless. Illandra felt him trying to reach out and read her mind to see what she was planning, but her powers had long surpassed his, denying him access. "Then what did you have in mind?" he finally asked, giving up.

"I'm just going to probe his memories," Illandra answered, as if it should have been obvious. "If I don't talk to him, he won't react. The nanites won't attack his brain. I can go through his memories and see what the host witnessed while they were at the base."

Anthony was busy rolling around in his chair as he began to ponder Illandra's idea. "I don't like it," he objected.

"That's because you didn't come up with it first." Illandra smiled at him.

Anthony tried hard not to laugh. "That may be, lass." He returned her smile. "When are you going to do it?"

"Tomorrow," Illandra stated, happy to have her mentor's blessing.

"During your speech?" Anthony reminded her of what

she was dreading.

"Crap." Illandra rolled her eyes. Now she had to find a way to be in two places at once.

*   *   *

It had taken almost all night to convince her, but Illandra had finally found a way.

"You could have at least walked yourself to the podium," Annette complained over the mental link they shared. *"You know I hate heels."*

"I've walked in heels for most of my life," Illandra assured her. *"Just access it from my brain, and you should be able to walk like a pro."*

"Oh yeah." Annette remembered some of the advantages of their mental link. Puppeting Illandra's body, Annette made her way up to the podium and cleared her throat. *"I hate public speaking."*

"You'll be fine," Illandra assured her for the hundredth time. *"All you have to do is access the speech from my brain and make sure it goes out my mouth. Public speaking is ninety percent confidence. Just imagine you're getting ready to pilot an AC3200."* Illandra had no idea which ship an AC3200 was, but she knew it was one of the easiest ships to pilot from Annette's own knowledge.

Illandra could see her body take a deep breath from where she floated in the center of the room. *"Here goes nothing,"* Annette said, getting ready. *"Remember, if anything goes wrong, it's not my fault."*

Illandra nodded while she secretly prayed that everything would turn out okay.

"Good morning, ladies and gentlemen of the Imperial Consortium. I'm Ambassador Illandra Page, and I'm honored to be received here today." The speech flowed out of her mouth.

Illandra caught a couple more lines to make sure Annette had everything under control before turning to her task. She floated over to the Cenari that Tso Young had informed her had recently come from their main base. She reached into his mind and started to retrace his steps back to where he had come from. The turmoil of the host mind made it difficult to focus on the task and find what she needed; she saw several images of people just sitting in rooms not even talking. She assumed the Cenari didn't need to talk much to discuss their plans, as they were all wirelessly linked.

She finally reached the memories she was looking for. She found herself standing on a station. From a nearby window, she witnessed a horror she wasn't quite ready for. Several hundred ships lay in waiting, ready to strike at a given command. Several of them were the ones that had already attacked the Republic, but there were many other models that she hadn't seen yet. It was only a matter of time before they launched their attack. With these numbers, it wouldn't be a battle; it would be a slaughter.

She quickly left the mind just in time to see Annette close out her speech to a warm crowd that showered her with applause. At least that had gone well. Illandra hovered over to meet Anthony and her puppet at their reserved area.

"Everything all right?" Anthony whispered as Annette

sat down next to him. "You seemed a little more nervous than usual."

"You know what they say," Illandra heard her voice say, "public speaking is ninety percent confidence." It felt weird to hear someone else talk with her voice.

"It's not me," Illandra mentally projected to Anthony while allowing him to see her astral form. *"Annette's been piloting my body while I went digging."*

"I wish you'd tell me these things beforehand," her mentor scolded her. *"Although, not too bad for her first time. Maybe I should find someone willing to link with me."*

"Never mind that." Illandra pushed him. *"We have a problem."*

Chapter 17

DISASTER

Record Date: 349.387 PGST

RACE WAS BUSY MOPING ABOUT his room, trying to arrange things in some sensible manner. Normally he'd be in his office working in an attempt to space out his anxiety, but the only thing he had to work on was the source of his turmoil. The alien relic had been the find of a lifetime, proof of alien life on another planet, and he had been forced to destroy it. He felt as if he had destroyed a part of himself with it, and he had been dragging it along with him since. Now all he could do was rearrange the contents of his room and hope it somehow helped put the pieces back in place.

"Chief Allard," his commanding officer's voice paged him through his biosensor.

"Yes, sir," Race responded.

"Better get up to the bridge, Chief," the image said, coming onto the screen. "Looks like those ships are starting to move."

"I'm on my way," Race replied, grabbing the blouse to his uniform and heading for the door. It had all been their fault he'd had to destroy the artifact. Maybe now he could take some of his frustrations out on them.

He exited the lift and took his normal post at the tactical console. The command deck of the MacArthur was a quarter of the size of the Puller. Where the Puller had whole circular stations to support a team, the MacArthur only had single consoles barely large enough for two people to operate.

He looked over the information to see what was going on. The ships had taken up orbit around the planet once again to continue their search. Race hoped they discovered the crater where the obelisk used to be. With any luck, it would anger them as much as making it had upset Race.

"What do you think, Chief?" the major asked.

"Looks like they're back to look for whatever they were searching for," Race answered.

"Think they noticed your modifications to the planet?" the major that had been handed a fleet asked.

"If they haven't, they will soon enough," Konway commented.

"Hopefully they notice it before I blow them to smithereens," Race added.

The major approached Race's station, placing his hands on the top to support his weight. "I know you're upset, but don't make it personal," he whispered so only Race could hear him. Everyone else was so quiet, Race was pretty sure everyone could hear regardless. "That's when you're more likely to make mistakes."

"Yes, sir." Race nodded, trying to put his feelings aside. But it was personal. They had made it personal the first time they invaded Republic space and blew up the ships under his

414

tactical command. They had made it personal when rather than surrender, that last ship attempted to crash into his home, the Taurus space station, killing several of his friends. They had made it personal when they infected one of Race's teammates and attack Illandra, forcing him to take its life rather than allowing them to execute their plans. It didn't get much more personal for Race.

"Good," the major said, knocking the top of the console in triumph. "Now then, do you think they feel like talking?"

"I can attempt to hail them if you like, sir?" The ship's comms officer offered up her services.

"Get to it," the major said as if it should have already been done. He was still breaking the bridge crew in. His SORD unit had been so well trained that they knew when he said something like that, he was giving an order he was expecting to be done.

The comms officer started executing the command on his terminal. There was a brief pause while she waited for a reply. "No answer, sir," she reported after a moment.

"Are they at least receiving us?" the major asked.

"Hard to tell, sir," she answered.

"Very well," the major said sourly. "Put me on." He waited for her signal to let him know that the broadcast was established. "Cenari vessels. Regulations require that I give you one last opportunity to surrender yourselves. My crew isn't happy with the havoc you've caused, so you'd be making a lot of people happy by not doing so." He turned around to walk to his chair, his gaze catching Race with a certain sparkle in his eyes before he turned to sit down. "Also, we found what you were looking for on the planet, and we've destroyed it. The only remnants of it are encrypted in our database, and you can go to hell if you think I'm going to let you put your hands on it."

Race wasn't normally one for speeches, but he found he rather enjoyed this one. It seemed to have done the trick. The two ships had changed course for the command ship orbiting just over the pole of a distant planet. They didn't seem to be in much of a good mood as they shot at the ship far outside the effective range of their weapons, missing widely as Annette easily maneuvered the ship around their fire.

As planned, Annette turned the ship around and hit the boosters in retreat from the ships. The major's speech had done well to goad them into pursuit. They were so intent on catching the ship, they didn't even notice that they had passed the rest of the fleet's ships hiding behind a pair of the planet's moons. When the enemy ships were too far to turn back, the fleet opened up on them from the rear.

The Cenari didn't even have time to react to the bombardment that lit up their aft sections. To Race's dismay, the first ship was quickly disabled, but the damage wasn't enough to cause it to explode. Race feared the possible implications that might have, but he ordered the rest of the fleet to attack the remaining ship.

"Damn," Race cursed, hitting the panel with his fist as he watched the last ship's engines kick in to flee.

"We got a lock on them?" the major asked, sharing Race's frustration.

"Yes, sir," Konway answered, "but it won't do us much

good with how fast those things are."

"Send the rest of the fleet after them," the major ordered. Race quickly relayed the commands to the other ships, fearing what the office would order next. "What about that other ship?"

"Power seems to be out to most of the ship," Konway explained. "I'm reading some elevated radiation levels, but nothing that would be too dangerous for a space suit."

"Any chance she might blow in the near future?" he queried.

"It's hard to say, sir." Konway reviewed his sensor readings. "We don't know anything about these experimental systems. I'd assume they'd have a safety ejection for the core if they were going to pop. Using my best guess, I don't see any signs that it's about to."

The major snarled, disappointed with Konway's report. Race feared the words he knew were coming. "I guess we have a job to do then," the major concluded. "Chief, Staff Sergeant Keegan, time we head down to the docking bay and get ready to breach."

Race handed over his station to his counterpart as Annette followed suit. They joined the major in the elevator, where he punched in the command. They were on the way to their destination.

When the doors opened on the flight deck, they were greeted by the surprising sight of the fourth member of their team.

"Staff Sergeant Amyas." The major shared the surprise of the two other members in the lift with him. "What brings you here?"

"I heard you were about to give our secondary objective a go," Zain said, saluting his superior as they exited. "I came to volunteer."

"Appreciate the enthusiasm, Marine, but I think these two are better suited for the task," the major dismissed him.

Race knew Zain never volunteered for anything. He admired his teammate for the moment, willing to switch places with him and sacrifice himself in exchange. He wondered if Konway would have done the same if he hadn't had a family.

"But, sir," Zain objected, "I'm the combat expert. I'm the best choice to take the ship if there's anyone still alive on there."

"If we're to take that ship, we need our ship expert and programmer to figure out the systems," the officer explained. He wasn't used to having his orders questioned. "Besides, we have it on good authority that they might be infected, in which case the only one to stop them is the chief."

"I've never fought one to know that, sir," Zain disagreed once again. He wasn't one to follow orders he didn't agree with. "We've got the upgrade to our rifles to disable them, and if you give me some power armor, I'm sure I'll be more than a match for them. The chief can do any interfacing remotely through my sensor unit that he could do over there. Or send him after we've taken it."

The major's face was starting to turn red from his frustration. "I've made my decision, Staff Sergeant, now get back to your station." His voice had taken the soft, deep tone that sent chills down Race's spine.

"But, sir," Zain objected once again.

"Give us a second, sir," Race interrupted, pulling Zain aside before he ended up getting himself put on suspension. Zain's biceps were so huge that Race could barely even curve the ends of his fingers around it.

"You can't go over there," Zain warned him when they were alone. "You know what will happen."

"I can't let you take my place," Race informed him, trying to imitate the major's patented tone. "When did she tell you?"

"Don't blame her," Zain said nervously. "We saw how distressed she was and drew it out of her."

As usual, Race hadn't even bothered to think about how much Annette had been going through keeping all the secrets. She was racking up an unhealthy collection now with his and Illandra's.

"I've put her through a lot," Race observed out loud, more to himself than to his present company. He looked over his shoulder at the spirited redhead that always seemed to be there for him.

"Good news is she's still by your side," Zain added. "Not too often you meet a girl willing to do half the things she'd do for you."

Race wondered if he knew how far she had actually gone to save him, but he was right.

"Listen," Race said, getting back on topic, "I appreciate what you're trying to do, but nothing's going to happen to me. I worked it out a long time ago. I've got a plan." It was a lie, the same lie Illandra had told him the last time he gave her permission to look into his mind.

"You sure?" Zain eyed him suspiciously.

"Promise." Race did his best to reassure both of them. "Trust me."

"Is that an order?" Zain smiled at Race to let him know that Race had won him over.

"If it keeps you from getting locked in a cell." Race felt a smile breach his own lips in reply, even though he tried hard to fight it.

"All right, but when you come back, we need to have a nice long talk about all this," Zain ordered him. "And no more secrets."

"Deal." Race nodded. Zain was much better at making threats than Race. Probably because they all knew firsthand that he could back them up.

Zain returned his nod and gave him the proper salute before retreating back to his station.

"Mind explaining what that was all about?" the major asked after Race returned, somewhat satisfied that his orders were now being followed.

"I'll tell you all about it when I get back," Race assured him. If I come back, he mentally added to himself. "Right now, I just want to get over there and make sure it's not going to blow while I have enough time to get back."

"Fair enough," the major agreed. "Get over there and check it out. If there's any sign of damage to the core, get out of there pronto. If not, see what you can figure out about those systems and take control of it."

"Yes, sir." Annette and Race saluted in unison.

"Go suit up," the major ordered.

Race and Annette raced over to one of the chambers and pulled out some space suits and started to put them on over their uniforms.

"So when did you tell them?" Race asked, putting the boot covers over his current ones.

"Not too long ago," she said, unable to look Race in the eyes, ashamed he had found out. "I'm sorry, I know you didn't want me to, but..."

"It's okay," Race forgave her before she even had a chance to explain. "I know I've put you through a lot lately. You haven't had too many people to talk to. You've been with me every step of the way, and I'm happy to be with you. After we get back, maybe you'll let me take you out to properly thank you?" Something about facing his mortality made Race a little braver than usual.

"Really?" Her face brightened up more than Race had ever seen it. It warmed his heart to make her a little happy before the anguish he was inevitably going to put her through. "I'm going to hold you to it."

"Sounds like a date then," Race said as he finished putting the last of his suit on.

Annette was finished shortly after him. They made their way back to their commanding officer, who had been ordering some of the dock crew to bring out Annette's experimental ships. They reminded Race of small underwater recreational equipment, the kind scuba divers would use to steer through deep waters. They even mounted them the same way, grabbing a handle with each arm and being dragged behind it.

"Are you sure these things will work?" the major asked Annette as they approached.

"They've only been through some minor testing, but they've performed pretty well so far," Annette assured him. "I'm fairly confident they'll do the job."

Race was pretty sure they'd at least get them there.

"Better give him a quick rundown on how to use it, then you two need to get over there," the major ordered.

Annette quickly explained the system to Race, showing him how to make it go and stop. To steer the craft, you just pointed it the way you wanted to go. Race had a hard time understanding the purpose of the small vehicles. They didn't seem to have much of an advantage over a small craft. Annette had told him something about them being more maneuverable and too small to be picked up by sensors and such, but all Race could do was shrug and say, "I guess."

Moments later the two were flying through the small void of space that separated the enemy ship from their own. "Like they don't know what we're doing," Race whispered to himself.

"Shush," Annette's voice replied over the radio, reminding him too much of Illandra.

Race shrugged it off. The knot in his stomach was building more than he cared for and it obviously wasn't going anywhere. He tried to ignore it the best he could by programming his space scooter.

They landed on the ship's hull and locked their boots and crafts to the surface with their magnetic seal. A loud clink echoed as they snapped together resonated through their suits.

"Step one, make it to enemy ship without experimental vehicles blowing up on us, check," Race joked.

"Smart-ass." Annette was apparently not amused. "Sir, we've landed on the ship," she notified their leader over the public channel.

"Start your search in the port aft," the major's voice came over their headsets. "Looks like there might be an access hatch or something you could use there."

They picked up their experimental vehicles and starting floating around the ship looking for any access points. Race wasn't able to tell how long the search had gone on for by the time they finally called it off.

"I thought you built some hull-breachers into these damn things," Race said, frustrated that he was still on the ship and not in it. "Kind of pointless to bring them out here if you're not going to use them."

"The hull is pure dentarite; it would take a while to cut through. I'm not seeing any alternative, though," Annette acknowledged. "Maybe if we targeted one of the damaged sections, we might be able to break through a little quicker."

"Doesn't look like you have much of a choice," the major's voice came over their radios once again.

Race's AI had already pulled up a good area to attempt their breach from her prior scans. Annette put her unit down on the hull and started the breach procedure. A large circular saw on the bottom of the unit started to spin around as it began cutting a manhole-sized tunnel. The vibrations shook through the hull of the ship, tickling their feet.

The progress was slow, the ship's hull resisting the entire process. Each millimeter the breaching attachment gained seemed to take even longer than the last. Race would have broken through the hull with his own two hands if he could. He was almost tempted to see if he could channel some of that augmented strength he'd had in the past.

Some movement out of the corner of Race's eye caught his attention. His head jumped to see what it was, and his eyes didn't believe it. Walking on the hull of the ship was a Cenari beast as large as the one he had fought on the alien ghost ship. What shocked Race was that the creature didn't have any suit. The nanites were able to sustain the host in the very void of space.

"Watch out!" Annette said, grabbing Race by the shoulder and pulling him forward. As he spun around, he saw another Cenari approaching from the other side.

"Another one." Race pointed.

Annette took out her gun and quickly programmed it to disrupt the nanites. Race pulled his sword from his sensor unit to fend off the assailant that had gotten into close range.

The creatures swung at Race. Race had to fight his instincts to jump back. He had been trained for such things. "Jump up, and you won't come back down." Instead, he spun to dodge the attack, using his free hand to push Annette away in the process. As he came around, he used his sword to cut her tether to her breaching vessel. The giant hand tore through the control panel of her transport, shutting off the drilling.

There was another swing from the beast as Race dodged once again. He was bracing himself to spring at the creature's head with his sword when the barrel of Annette's rifle came over his right shoulder. He saw the blue energy beam shoot out from the barrel and zap the creature in the chest. The creature had a violent spasm as it fried its skin and probably a few vital organs as well. There were a few last twitches, and then the monster stopped moving altogether.

Race turned to look at the other creature, who had stopped its advancement. The shot had already drained Annette's battery. She cursed, taking a knee to hold her rifle as she dug out another magazine. The creature saw its opportunity to strike and started to charge the two. Race detached his tether to give him some more freedom. He charged at the creature, hoping to make him pause long enough for Annette to finish reloading. The creature was unfazed.

Race had to come up with a plan B. He waited until he got within striking distance of the Cenari, then squatted down and slid forward across the ship's hull. Race traveled several meters before he used the magnets in his feet to slow himself down. He turned to see the monster pursuing him. The giant had covered about half the distance when a flood of blue light flashed from behind it, sending it lifeless off the hull.

Race spacewalked his way back to Annette. She was looking over her breacher, hitting its side hoping it would somehow fix the damage the Cenari had done to it.

"What happened?" the major's voice came over the radio.

"Two Cenari attacked us on the hull, sir," Race reported. "Looks like Keegan's breacher is damaged. I don't think it's going to be able to finish the job."

For a moment the radio was as silent as the space around them. "Abort the mission," their officer said frantically. "Get back here, NOW!"

Race knew what it meant. Annette's vehicle was damaged; there was no way the little cruiser was fast enough to get the both of them out of there in time. This was the moment, and now it all made sense. Annette was quickly hitting buttons on the remaining unit for the automatic retrieval. She took Race's line and reattached it to his vehicle.

She looked Race in the eyes for one last time. "I'm sorry," she apologized, on the edge of tears.

She hit a button on the unit to start to power up.

"Not as much as I am," Race told her.

Annette was confused. She looked down at Race's belt to discover that the other end of the safety line was no longer attached to him. In her haste to get Race to safety, she hadn't noticed that Race had attached his end to her suit. Before she could react, the unit darted off, pulling her with it. Race took a deep breath as he harnessed his powers. The first thing he did was try to push Annette out to safety as far as he could.

Race looked around at his surroundings and sighed. The time had come. The ship that had retreated not so long ago reappeared, ripping through a dimensional rift. Most likely the Cenari had relayed their distress when they found out what he was doing. The ship locked on within seconds and a beam of energy shot out to destroy him.

Like he had done a hundred times in his dreams, he lifted his hands up to meet the weapon blast. His will to live called out every bit of his powers. A wall of energy materialized in front of him, colliding with the beam that was meant to vaporize him. The clash rattled through his bones as he bore the weight of the encounter. The light was so blinding, he could see it through his closed eyes as it washed all around him.

He knew he only had to hold out a little longer; the fleet ships would surely be locking onto the target and preparing to fire. The ship was badly damaged; it wouldn't take much to destroy it.

"Just a little longer," he told himself through clenched teeth.

"Believe, and it will be done. Waver just a little, and all is lost," his friendly ghostly voice said. It had become more prominent over the past couple of weeks. Race found it kind of annoying, especially now.

But it had been helpful. Race did his best to believe in his abilities and clear out all his doubt. "I know I can do this," he grunted to himself, forcing belief. He had no concept of time for a while, so he couldn't really tell how long he had been holding on for.

Suddenly, it was gone. Race tried to open his eyes, but he was still blinded from the intense light. "Did I do it? Am I still alive?" he asked himself in disbelief, trying to feel his face through his helmet to verify it.

"You still out there, Chief?" the voice came over the radio.

Race couldn't believe it. He fell down to his knees in exhaustion, trying to hold back the tears of victory. He fumbled blindly for his radio, his vision still a blur of pure white light. "I'm here," he laughed, on the border of hysteria.

His sight slowly started to return to him, enough to where he could make out the blurry outline of his ship. It seemed they had put the ship directly between him and his attacker. "They'd sacrifice a whole ship for me," Race said humbly to himself.

Race suddenly felt vibrations from the scorched hull around him. He looked around the void, trying to determine the source, but his blurred vision made it hard to see anything. He started to see flashes of light, a mixture of orange and blue. He knew what they were before he could even focus on them. They were the blues of plasma fire and oranges of fire from the exploding ship.

The excitement quickly fell from him as he knew he had not escaped his fate. He had survived the impossible just to die from the collateral damage of the ship blowing up.

"Shit," Race cursed as he bowed his head in defeat.

Chapter 18

MIRACLE

Record Date: 349.388 PGST

ILLANDRA WAS WALKING THE HALLS of the embassy. She had just finished briefing the Imperialists about what she had learned from her reading of one of the Cenari and was looking to distance herself from them, hoping it would somehow distance her from the bad news. The headaches were also starting to act up again; it was about time for her to go back to her room and put on the cursed crown Race had given her as a going-away present. But before she did, she was going to head to the cafeteria and grab a small snack to take back with her.

"So it's true then," she heard a voice call from behind her.

She turned to find the young captain standing at the end of the hall. When the headaches started acting up, it was harder for her to tell when people were sneaking up on her. Otherwise she probably would have known he was there long before he spoke. Enough to avoid this unpleasant conversation.

"What's true?" she asked, the void in her stomach and

sting in her brain urging her to leave him behind.

"Psychic testing in the Republic," he answered, closing the space between them. He tried to keep his voice low enough to not reach beyond the two of them, but the words seemed loud enough to echo, at least in Illandra's head. "You're one of them, aren't you?"

She met him halfway and pulled him into a nearby empty room. It was one of the many conference rooms in the building; they might have even used it before. They all looked the same, and there were so many of them in this place.

"What are you talking about?" She tried to pretend like she didn't know what he was referring to, activating the room's security defenses just to be safe.

"We've had reports for some time now," the young captain said, tugging the wrinkles from his sleeve now that it was free of Illandra's clutch. "Rumors, mostly; it seems to be one of your highest-kept secrets. Tell me, is that what your precious green card represents?"

She tapped the pocket of her shirt where she kept her ID. Looking at his face, she realized she had already given him all the answers he needed. Taking him to a secret room, activating security measures, grabbing for her card. All mistakes she wouldn't have made if it hadn't been for that blasted headache. Stupid, she cursed herself. She could attempt to wipe it from his mind, but Tranagra had refused to teach her that. According to him, it was both dangerous and immoral. Probably too dangerous to attempt with her stabbing headache, anyways.

"I will tell you, but you must promise me that it stays here between you and me," she reluctantly told him.

"And why would I do that?" He smiled at her. He already had everything he wanted. Of course he was confident.

"Because it's the only way you're going to find out about yourself." Illandra took her turn to smile as his suddenly vanished. An important lesson from Anthony: *If you want someone to care, make it personal.*

"What do you mean?" he asked suspiciously.

"Ah-ah-ah"—Illandra shook her finger—"you haven't given me your word."

"Words can be easily broken," Tso Young warned her. "Why would you trust me?"

"Not the word of a leader like you, Captain," she baited him. He was as much hers now as she had been when she stumbled into his trap earlier. "You know how worthless one's word is if it's broken. Your word is your life."

"Very well," he said, submitting. "You have my word, whatever you divulge will stay between us alone."

"And that which you've already guessed?" she tested him.

He thought about it for a minute. Illandra knew his type. Even with her headache, Illandra could read what he was thinking. "Fine," he finally stated after grinding his teeth for a bit. "On one condition."

Illandra knew there wasn't any way this could be good. "What?" she said scornfully.

"You accompany me tomorrow"—that evil grin reappeared on his face—"on a date."

431

"We're in the middle of an invasion, and you want to take me out on a date?" Illandra scoffed.

"If we deny ourselves what makes us human, we've already lost the fight for humanity," he argued.

"You have to be kidding." Illandra hoped he was joking. "The city is crawling with Cenari, and you want to take me out there?"

"Actually, I was going to take you to a nearby town. The one I grew up in before joining the military," Tso informed her. "And no harm will befall you as long as you're with me."

He was serious, and Illandra found she rather hated him for it. Of course, she didn't have much choice if she wanted to buy his silence. The words of her mentor seemed to play through her head. "You get nothing for nothing." "Very well," she said unwillingly.

"And you have to at least attempt to have a good time," the captain added.

"Fine," she snarled. "What is it you want to know? Make it quick, I have a terrible headache."

"I thought you were supposed to save that excuse for during the date," he joked.

Illandra just stared at him, mustering as much contempt as she could into her expression.

"I apologize." Tso's grin quickly vanished. "Very well. Where to begin?" He started to walk around, pinching his chin as he began to piece the puzzle together. "The obvious. You pretty much confirmed that your government is testing for psychically gifted individuals. You obviously seem to be one of them. I'm guessing that you were able to get the information you shared with us. I'm going to say you're telepathic."

"Yes." She nodded regretfully. She felt having her secret exposed was as if she were caught without her clothes on. "We call them enhanced humans. And I am a telepath, although I didn't start off that way. My type is called pathics, but that's because of our empathic abilities. Very few of us ever become strong enough to actually be considered telepaths."

"And you identify these enhanced humans with your green cards," he continued his deductive trail.

"Yes," she said, keeping it shorter than her previous answer. Shorter answers revealed less.

"How many different kinds are there?" The captain was fascinated and looked at her with doe eyes, waiting for the information to flow.

"I don't know." She tugged at her blouse to make sure it was still there. It didn't feel there. "I've only met one other kind."

"Chief Allard." It wasn't a question. "What type is he?"

"The same type as you," she answered. The captain straightened in surprise. It felt good to at least catch him a little off guard, and he was more than a little.

"Me?" the captain asked, putting his hand over his chest. "Ah, that's what you meant." Illandra simply nodded in response. "What type are we?"

"Precogs, short for precognition." Illandra sat in the closest chair she could find. It was taking a lot out of her to simply stand.

"Like some sort of *suan ming*?" The translator failed to pick up the uncommon word. She had heard the term before; Chilong had referred to wanting to consult one for luck. They were something similar to fortune tellers. A practice the most found dubious, enough to reflect in his eyes as he looked at her suspiciously.

"Not really." She did her best to explain. "It works more like a driving force to make sure that you're in the right place at the right time. Also, a strong ability to predict your opponent's moves with pinpoint accuracy. On rare occasions, being able to pick up on consequences of unrelated events."

With each suggestion Illandra mentioned, the doubt faded further and further away, dozens of memories flooding through him as each one hit a particular truth. Illandra had seen it before in Race as well, an inaudible ding that echoed through his head whenever he heard or thought something that had to be true. Probably another side effect of their abilities.

Long after Illandra had finished explaining, the young captain was still wandering around the room replaying memories as the pieces fell into place.

"Who do you think is stronger?" he asked, suddenly breaking the silence.

Race, she thought. "I don't know," she said instead. "I've never seen you use your abilities." It really didn't matter that much; Race had so much formal training to foster his abilities, among other advantages, she didn't think he could even come close. For some reason, the uncertainty made him more interested in finding out.

"How do you know I even have them?" he asked.

"The way you described how you picked up that sword of yours," she assured him. "I can also feel it when it's working around in your subconscious, sometimes. Only because I know what to look for."

"You've been in my head?" The thought deflated some of his excitement.

"My abilities don't have much of an off switch," she said, trying to ease him. "I pick up on things pretty easy, but not much more than what someone can learn reading one's body language. I haven't been fishing around in there"—she waved her fingers around his head—"if that's what you're worried about." It was almost true.

It seemed to relieve him enough as he returned to thinking of other questions to ask.

"One more question," Illandra said, rubbing her temples. "I really need to get back to my room and take something for this headache."

"Is it from your powers?" He was more curious than actually wanting to bring the conversation to a close.

"Is that your question?" Illandra teased him. She probably shouldn't have given him a choice, but she didn't want to have him mentally nagging her in the future.

"No—" He stopped abruptly. He took another second to consider what it was he wanted to know most. His face became stern as a rock as his expression hardened. "How do I become stronger?"

Illandra would have stepped back if she was standing. Instead, she pushed herself into the back of the chair. She wasn't sure if she wanted him to get stronger, but with the looming threat of the invasion, maybe he needed to be. She took a deep breath. "I don't know much of Race's training," she stated. "From what I understand, it's kind of like any other muscle. The only way to improve it is to continue to use it. Now that you're aware of it, you should be able to try and put yourself in situations to develop it. Race usually activates it out of necessity. Sometimes he tries to consciously activate it by putting himself in situations where he's severely outmatched." She hoped she hadn't given him too much; she didn't like his expression that much.

"Very well," he said. At least he didn't seem completely dissatisfied with the answers. "I'll arrange for separate transport for us after the congressional session tomorrow. It will be less dangerous if people think you left with the senator's vehicles than securing passage out of the embassy."

She'd have to pack a change of clothes to take with her. She had hoped Tso had forgotten that part of the agreement. "Very well."

*   *   *

The date was nowhere near as bad as she'd feared it would be. The captain, or Tso, as he had asked her to call him on their outing, had made several arrangements. After the congressional session had adjourned, he gave her a couple of hours to change and prepare while he did the same. "The longer we wait, the safer it will be," he had told her, meaning he didn't mind if she needed too much time.

Illandra was half tempted to be as disruptive as possi-

436

ble, but then she remembered how long it had been since she had actually had time outside the embassy. Even more predominant, how long it might be until the opportunity to actually see some of the scenery might come again. The pale walls of the embassy were starting to drive her crazy. Illandra would have done anything to get out of them for a night. Now that the opportunity was there, she tried her best to enjoy it.

After they had both changed and Illandra had refreshed herself, they got into his vehicle and took the back exit out of the building. Illandra was surprised at Tso's choice of transportation. For how flamboyantly the captain acted at times, his vehicle was actually quite average. "Flashy cars attract more attention," he informed her. The milky-white vehicle wasn't without its comfort, though. Illandra found the full synthetic-leather interior most pleasant.

They caught an express lane out of the city and were out of the city and to the next within half an hour. Illandra had tried to get him to slow down so she could see some of the capital's sights, but he wouldn't have it. Tso claimed that it would attract too much attention. "If you didn't want to attract too much attention, you should have told me before I picked out this dress," she informed him. He was practically speechless when he first saw her, unable to take his eyes off of her. Of course, Illandra wouldn't have had it any other way. It didn't persuade him, but he did his best to point out some of the bigger, more significant sights along their path.

The city of Tso's heritage was named after a city from original China, one Illandra struggled to pronounce. It felt more like Italy than it did China. The streets were waterways, where people with boats ferried others around like taxies. They first stopped by a small temple where Tso prayed for a blessing for the evening, hoping all would go well. Illandra found the small structure adorable. There were hardly any walls, or a ceiling either. All that marked the building was a small pinkish trim that surrounded the outside being held up by support beams every ten feet. Inside was mostly paved, a few rows of trees and flowers defining the paths.

When Illandra had asked him about why it was so open, he simply replied, "Praying to one's god is something that should never be hidden. It is something that should be done with pride, in the open for all to see."

Next, he took her to a small shopping area where he followed her through a couple of stores. Illandra found a clothing store that had a wide assortment of both classic and modern-era outfits. She had spent nearly a quarter of her credits on outfits and souvenirs by the time she begged Tso to get her out of the store. He left almost as reluctantly as she did; he had been enjoying watching her try on much of the shop's inventory.

Their next stop was for dinner, and not a moment too soon. It had been a long day, and if they waited any longer, Illandra was sure that her stomach was going to start making noise. The restaurant was owned by a childhood friend of Tso who had been waiting for them. He had provided a secluded area for the two to enjoy their meal. After a waiter had taken their order, a group of musicians appeared on the stage and started playing classical music from their culture. Illandra had known of the instruments before, but this was the first time she had seen any of them in person. Some looked much like instruments she was familiar with, but they all had sounds that were unique and exotic to her. By the time they were done, Illandra was in love with the city and never wanted to leave. She admired Tso for having grown up in such a wonderful place and found herself curious as to why he'd left.

She was still playing the music over in her head as the boat dropped them off by the parking area. She would have danced back to the car if she was alone. Tso was telling her about a temple nearby in the mountains that he would like to take her to next time when she felt up to it.

She was quickly snapped out of her magical trance by three strangers hovering in the shadows. She could sense they were up to no good. She grabbed Tso's arm just above his wrist. He felt it, too.

He pulled them to a stop. "Come out," he demanded. "There's no point in hiding." The pleasant Tso that had taken her out on their date no longer seemed to be there. Instead, it was the cold and calculating Captain Tso Young that stood beside her.

He put his arm up and pushed Illandra behind him to protect her, but she could still see the three gentlemen that were approaching. The two men on the right were of average size, one of whom had a small chain wrapped around his hand. The third man was almost a giant, about the size of Zain, tapping a large metal pipe in his hand. All three wore dark sweaters to blend in with their environment. Illandra had never been in a fight before, but she wasn't sure how good the odds were.

"Give us all your money," the unarmed man said. "The bags, too."

"Maybe a little time with your girl there, too," the man with the chain said, eyeing Illandra.

"I'm sorry, I can't do that," the captain said, his tone deep and threatening. "You'd best leave now before I have to hurt you."

The crew laughed; the unarmed man laughed the most, having to use the big man next to him to keep him from falling down.

"That's good," the man said between laughs. "I haven't laughed that hard in a long time. But seriously, Tank here's never lost a fight." He patted the giant. "And then you have the two of us to deal with, too. Just give us your money before we have to hurt you."

"Let me apologize ahead of time for your hand"—Tso smiled, pointing at the chain man—"and your arm." He pointed at the giant.

"Very well," the unarmed man said. "Get 'em, boys."

It happened so fast that if Illandra had blinked, she swore she would have missed it. As the two armed men charged, Tso reached a hand into his jacket. When it came out, it held a blueish-green blade. The blade was too short to be called a sword, too large to be called a knife.

As Tso pulled the blade from his jacket, he instantly drove the hilt into the incoming chain-wrapped fist of the larger man. The impact sent chain links flying in different directions and fingers twisting the same. The man reeled back in pain as the giant came in swinging his large metal pipe. Tso caught the metal with his open hand, just as the blade went through the giant's bicep, separating his arm from the rest of him. Off balance, the giant continued to twist and crashed to the ground. Tso threw the metal pipe at the broken-handed chain man. The pipe, with the giant's hand still attached, twirled in the air a couple of times before clubbing the man in the head and sending him to the ground with his friend.

Illandra didn't get to see what happened next, as the third man was rushing her, hoping to take her hostage. Illandra was in such shock from the display that she didn't know what to do, but it wasn't her that acted. Using Illandra's hands, Annette took control and caught the man's hands as he reached to grab her and pushed them to the air. As they came together, Illandra's knee shot up and caught her attacker between the legs so hard that he instantly went to the ground, howling in pain.

"*Thanks,*" Illandra sent over the link they shared.

"*No problem,*" Annette replied. "*You'd better get to a safe place, though. I think that time is approaching.*"

Illandra didn't have time to pry with her attackers all around her, but she didn't like the sound of that.

"My sword cauterized your arm, so there's no worry of blood loss." The captain claimed his victory over the fallen. "You can have it reattached, but only if you act quickly. Otherwise, I can claim a couple other limbs if any of you want to continue."

441

The three stumbled to their feet and back into the shadows. "Are you okay?" Tso asked, checking her over.

"I'm fine," she managed to tell him. His vehicle wasn't too far away, so she did her best to walk calmly over to it. When she arrived, he was already there holding the door open for her.

"Are you sure you're fine?" he asked her once again.

She had managed to escape the attack unharmed, but her hands were shaking uncontrollably. It wasn't just the attack that bothered her, but the brutal ease with which Tso Young dismissed them.

"Do you take a knife with you on all your dates?" Illandra asked, making sure to keep the door between them.

"No." He smiled helplessly. "I usually don't, but I had one of those feelings that I was going to need it."

She wasn't sure if she should be thankful for that.

"A little brutal, don't you think?" She never knew when to keep her mouth shut. "Cutting a guy's arm off?"

"This isn't the Middle Ages," he scoffed. "The doctors can reattach it and have it working again in a week."

"But what if they go to the police?" She really wished she knew where the off switch to her mouth was.

"The hospital will probably do that for them," he answered. "They've probably been harassing tourists for some time. Once the police look into it, they'll realize they've finally found their criminals and put them in jail. If they're able to find out that I was the one that took them down, I'll probably get another medal for it."

Illandra was even more shocked now than she was earlier. He actually enjoyed it. She forced herself into the car before she blurted out another question she might regret learning the answer to. She managed to keep her mouth shut for most of the ride home. She had lots of questions, but most of all, she now doubted whether Race was actually stronger than the man sitting beside her. While Race's powers seemed stronger, there were some lines he would never cross. Race still maintained his compassion for others, no matter how hard the military tried to weed it out of him. The captain didn't seem to care about such lines, making him probably a much more deadly opponent.

The music kept the trip from being too silent, and while Illandra wanted to probe more about what was going on with Annette, doing so would have left her defenseless around the captain. She was able to manage a couple of questions, the responses to which made her completely forget the events that recently just happened.

"What is he thinking?" she practically yelled through the link she shared with Annette. *"He knows if he sets foot on that ship, he's dead."*

"He seems to believe what you told him about the dream," came Annette's response.

"Oh please, all three of us knew that was a lie," Illandra reminded her. *"Stall as long as you can, I'll be there soon."*

"I'll do my best," she answered.

Illandra knew her best wouldn't be good enough. Annette didn't know how to work Race as well as she did, and she was too powerless when he looked at her with those baby-blue eyes. She wouldn't even remember to access any of

Illandra's abilities to force him in line.

Sure enough, a couple of minutes later, Illandra felt the gushing of emotions from Annette as she gladly accepted his invitation for a date. Illandra did her best to hold her contempt from transmitting over the link. *Sure, easy enough to promise something you'll be too dead to deliver on*, she thought to herself. She didn't have the heart to tell Annette the truth; she'd be sad enough in the near future if things didn't work out.

When they made it to the embassy, she was so quick to rush off, she almost forgot all her bags. She rushed back to get them and gave the captain a hug that she quickly regretted.

"I'm sorry things ended on such a sour note," the captain called to her as she was about to enter the embassy.

She didn't have time to stop and explain, but she couldn't leave things on such a low. "You once asked me who was stronger, you or Race," she called out, stopping him from getting back into his car. He folded his arms on the top of his car. "When Race fights, he fights with all his strength and heart. He fights because he has to, to protect those around him. Not because he wants to. He'd never admit it, but there's a big part of him that hates fighting; it symbolizes a failure to accept one another.

"When I saw you fighting, I noticed you didn't fight for me or you, or even because it was the right thing to do. You fought because you wanted to, you wanted to hurt those guys. Your heart had nothing to do with it. Because of that, Race will always have a strength you don't possess. If you truly want to become as strong as you say, find something worth fighting for."

The captain did his best not to smile. It was obvious he didn't think she knew anything that she was talking about. "Some would say that those who fight with their heart fight with a dual sword."

"That's a lie," she told him, trying not to pull herself through the door, "one that people make up who never really learned how to fight with the heart." She made a move to escape through the door, but she suddenly remembered something that the captain had said to her earlier that seemed to fit the situation. She quickly ducked her head back out the door to catch him getting back in his car. "Someone once told me, 'If we deny ourselves that which makes us human, we've already lost the fight for humanity.'"

She waited long enough to see his smile and return a wink and then she was rushing off toward her room. She brushed past a couple of people and activated the sensor to open the door to her room. Last time she'd checked in with Annette, they had landed on the ship. The fight to save Race was already on.

She quickly threw her bags in the corner, a loud crash letting her know one of her trinkets had possibly broken in the process. She managed a cringe as she rushed to her bed. Before she could reach it, something caught her attention and stopped her. She turned to look to the side. Where she expected to see the north-facing wall of her room, there was just space. The black, empty void of space, complete with stars twinkling out in the distance.

If she didn't know any better, she would have thought she had projected herself, but she knew this was something much different. Not even five feet in front of her, Race and Annette, wearing their yellow space suits, stood on the outer hull of the Cenari ship from Race's dream. Floating off in the distance, Illandra could see a lifeless Cenari.

Not believing her eyes, Illandra picked up the nearest object and tried to throw it at Race's head. "Idiot," Illandra called out to him as it made a thud against the wall that wasn't there and fell to the floor.

She walked over to the wall and tried to touch it, but her hand passed right through the barrier. On the other side, she didn't feel the lifeless cold of space, but she still felt it was better not to try and fully cross.

Race was looking around; she could tell he was having that feeling of his that something was wrong. She wanted to throw something else at him, but the success of her first attempt proved how worthless it would have been.

"I'm sorry." Annette scrambled to reattach Race's safety line back to his pod.

Illandra could see the remorse in Race's eyes before he acted. Illandra saw what Annette missed: Race pulled the other end of the tether from his space suit and attached it to the back of Annette's suit as she prepped the pod for launch.

Annette hit the launch command before Illandra could tell her what Race had done.

"Not as much as I am," Race replied just before the tether reached its max distance and Annette was ripped away from him.

"You asshole!" Illandra yelled at the display. She picked up one of the bags and threw it at Race, but it bounced harmlessly off the invisible wall she was using to view him through.

Illandra almost expected to get dragged off with her anchor, but her view stayed an arm's reach away from Race. She saw him turn and catch the beam from the Cenari ship. Her hands reached out, but she pulled them back just shy of the wall, knowing it wouldn't do any good. Instead, she watched with horror as Race did his best to survive the beam.

To her surprise, he did. Race looked almost as shocked as Illandra felt. He dropped to his knees and started laughing uncontrollably. Illandra just about joined him. She took a deep breath and enjoyed the triumph. She was still going to deck him next time she saw him.

Their celebration was cut short by the look of dread that appeared on Race's face. She didn't know what could have caused it. Tempting fate, she looked back down the the ship to see what had switched Race's mood so fast. There was no noise in space, but the sight of the inferno that was engulfing the ship was enough to terrify her.

Illandra looked back to Race. He was spent. There was no way he had enough power to save himself. She only had seconds to act; hesitation would mean the end of him for sure. Illandra didn't hesitate this time. Holding her breath, she jumped forward and wrapped her arms around him. The next second she was falling back toward her room.

The fire rushed past them. She could feel the wave of heat brush her feet as it passed by, blinding her for a second.

She bounced off the floor and rolled a couple of times, not letting go of the man in her arms.

Illandra wasn't sure if she believed it at first. Had she done it? Had she done the impossible? Did she defy fate and save Race? Illandra's vision was still readjusting after the bright fire, but she did her best to feel if he'd managed to stay in her arms. It felt like he was there, but that could just be wishful thinking. Countless seconds passed as she waited.

Then Illandra heard a sigh.

Of all the things he could have done, he sighed.

It annoyed her. Illandra felt around until she could find his shoulder, and then she hit it.

"Ouch," Race cried out.

Chapter 19

ΛFTERLIFE?

Record Date: 349.390 PGST

RACE WAS PRETTY SURE HIS life was over. He still felt the remnants of his body, but he figured that was normal, considering he had never been dead before. His vision had once again been taken from him by the explosion of this ship, just as he'd been starting to make out the blurs. The last thing he remembered was the force of the explosion throwing him to his demise. Death didn't feel anything like what he'd expected it to.

Now it was just a matter of waiting for whatever was to come next. Race pondered what that might be. He expected a bridge or someone to escort him across. Race hoped it didn't take too long. He never enjoyed waiting. He was patient enough, as long as he had some type of alternative to occupy himself, but Race didn't have anything dead. Not even a pair of thumbs to twiddle.

Race hoped he didn't have to wait long. He took a deep breath and released it, barely aware of the fact that he even had lungs. Shortly afterward, he felt a sudden sting in his shoulder.

"Ouch." The words escaped his lips almost involuntarily. Race also made a note of the fact that he still had lips and speech.

"Oh, shut up, you big baby," the voice came. His hearing was almost gone as well, but he recognized the voice. Race tried to fathom what it was doing here. All he could think was that someone or something on the other side was trying to make him feel welcome. The owner of the voice should have been alive and well, not to mention on the other side of the universe. No reason for her to be here.

"Please stop," the voice called out again. "You're not dead."

Race knew that wasn't possible; there was no way he had survived that explosion. Even if it hadn't killed him, he couldn't have survived long in space with a damaged suit.

There was another sharp pain in his arm followed by him letting out another "Ouch." He rubbed his arm where the soreness had struck him. It felt real enough.

"All right." Race decided to play along. "If I am alive, why can't I see?"

"Your vision hasn't come back yet?" she panicked. "I'll call for help." Race felt a tugging on his arm as if someone was trying to help him up. He did his best to follow it to his feet and gain his balance. His body was weak, which was to be expected after the expenditure of his powers and being blown up. Then again, it could just be the phantom sense of having a body to begin with.

Race heard the beeping of a device as his hostess made the call for help.

"I need you in my room right now," Race heard the female voice from his past say. Race couldn't help but smile thinking of how that might have sounded.

"Is everything all right?" Race heard the voice of Illandra's mentor.

"No," the spirit replied. "Grab a medical kit. A doctor if you can find one."

There was another beep as he guessed the call had come to an end.

At least you can still make calls in the afterlife, Race thought.

"Besides your sight, is everything else okay?" Race was pushed a couple of steps backward until he fell into what he guessed was a chair. The fall was followed by several tugs around him as his suit seemed to be getting pulled off of him. The more time that passed, the more Race was starting to believe he might have actually survived.

"Other than being dead?" Race felt a smile creep upon his lips, followed by another short jab of pain in his bicep. "Would you stop that?"

"Would you stop believing you're dead?" the soft voice demanded of him.

"Sure," Race said, still not believing it, "but only if you explain to me how I managed to survive."

The tugging stopped. "I don't understand it myself," Illandra admitted. "Annette contacted me…"

"Annette!" Race suddenly remembered, jumping to his feet with a sudden dizziness that he did his best to shake off. "Is she okay?" If Race really were dead, it would make more sense for Annette to be here instead of Illandra. It was more likely that she didn't escape the ship's blast and followed him to the other side. It didn't seem like that was possible, though. Race had only done what his powers had instructed him to do, and he was pretty sure they wouldn't have wasted the action if it was to end in failure.

He could sense the sudden panic from her as he was once again pushed back down into the chair. "I don't know, let me check." There was an uneasy silence as he felt awkwardly alone again. Just as the doubt of his survival started to grow again, she came back to him. "I definitely feel like she's there, but I'm not getting a response. It's like she's unconscious. I'll float over there and check on her in a bit. But first, let's get you taken care of."

He did his best to comply as some more of his space suit was stripped from him. There was a chime from the door and his hand was left stuck in the sleeve of his uniform when Illandra abandoned him to answer the door.

Race counted two pairs of footsteps rushing through the door before it closed behind them. He must have found a doctor.

"We got here as fast as we could," Race heard the mentor say. "Are you okay?"

"I'm fine," Illandra replied. "He's the one that needs help."

Even blind, Race could feel the awkward eyes upon him.

"How…" he heard the congressman stutter. "He's supposed to be on the other side of the universe."

"He was," Illandra confirmed. "There's a problem with his vision. He needs medical treatment."

Race heard one of the individuals approach him. There were more sounds he couldn't quite place followed by the familiar humming of a medical scanner.

"Can you tell me what happened?" an unfamiliar voice asked him.

"Well, a ship shot at me; it was very bright inside the beam." Race recalled the steps leading up to his demise. "That was the first thing that blinded me. Just as my sight was starting to come back to me, the ship I was on blew up, and that's what killed me."

"I assure you, lad, you're far from dead," Anthony laughed.

"I guess synaptic overload," the stranger said. "Should be able to fix it no problem."

"I saw it." Illandra started to tell her side of the story. "You wouldn't believe it, Tony, I saw it all. It was like that whole wall was gone. I could see out into space, just like I was there. I was only a couple feet from him. The ship started to explode. The explosion was coming. I couldn't even think. I just reached out and grabbed him. Then he was here."

"Amazing." Her mentor was having a hard time keeping up with her rapid-fire comments. It didn't seem possible, but Race kind of liked that explanation better than being dead.

"*I don't believe it,*" the ghost that had been following Race around chimed in. Race wasn't sure which side of the survival argument that fell on. If he was dead, the better chance for him to communicate with the spirit, but Race had also heard it before the explosion.

"Don't believe what?" Illandra asked. Race shook his

head in disbelief and tried his best to look where the voice had come from. Had she heard the ghost as well?

"Don't move," the stranger ordered, grabbing Race by the chin to force his head back.

"You heard that?" Race struggled to ask without his head bouncing too much.

"Yes, you said you didn't believe it," Illandra said.

"That wasn't me," Race assured her. "It's the ghost that's been following me."

"So now you're being haunted?" Illandra asked. He didn't need his sight to see how frustrated she was growing with him.

"Don't blame him," the ghost defended Race, *"he still can't see me as of yet. A ghost is probably an accurate description of me."*

"Wait, that wasn't you?" Illandra was starting to believe him. "Tranagra?"

"Yes," the ghost answered.

Race remembered that name from the alien obelisk that chronicled the war. "You know him? You can hear him?"

"Should I check his ears as well?" the stranger attending to Race asked. Everything they'd discussed must sound crazy to anyone that didn't have an understanding of what they'd all been through.

"I doubt it would do any good. He obviously didn't hear me tell him not to set foot on the ship or else he'd die." Another sharp sting rang out from his shoulder as a small fist hit him.

"See, I am dead," Race said, almost excited.

"You're not dead," everyone, including the ghost, scolded him in unison.

"Besides, you told me I was safe now," Race continued.

"You know that was a lie," Illandra admitted to him. "I wish you'd just use your powers to find out the truth that you're alive."

"How would I know that I could trust my powers in the afterlife?" Race asked.

Illandra was silent for a bit. Very rarely was she at a loss for words; it would almost be worth treasuring if it weren't for all the other things going on.

"Can I hit him again?" she finally said.

"At least let me finish with him," the stranger said.

"So this ghost of yours," Anthony said, taking charge of the conversation. Race preferred him in charge; there were fewer threats that way. "Tranagra, you say?"

"That was the name on the obelisk." Race tried to tilt his head toward the voice he heard, but the firm hand on his jaw yanked it back into place. The milky white that coated everything flashed a bit, and he suddenly saw several blurry images around him.

"What obelisk?" Anthony asked.

"The one on the planet the Cenari were investigating," Race said.

There was a momentary pause as Race saw the blurs move around a bit. "How much longer, Doctor?" Anthony asked him.

"Almost done," the man said. It was true; Race's vision was becoming better by the second. He could make out the large room he was sitting in, the nicely made bed and organized furniture. It reminded him of a fancy hotel he could never afford. The doctor tending him looked to be about the same age as Anthony, both of whom were wearing what looked like their bedclothes. Illandra, however, looked radiant. She was wearing a white dress, and with his vision still slightly blurred, he could have easily mistaken her for an angel. That bothered him more.

The doctor finished up and excused himself, after a brief warning from Anthony requesting he not reveal anything he had seen or heard in the room. When they were alone, they continued their conversation.

"Is there any way you can tune me into what he's saying?" Anthony asked Illandra.

"If you'd practice some of your exercises, you'd be able to do it on your own," Illandra scolded her mentor as she placed a hand on each of his temples. Obviously, Anthony wasn't as in charge as he thought. Few were when Illandra was in the room. "There."

"So who is he?" Race did his best to demand of Illandra.

"Well, he's not a ghost," Illandra started to explain. "Well, maybe he could be considered a ghost."

Rambling, Race thought to himself.

"Remember when you found the ship in the nebula? The alien you followed around on the ship?"

Race scowled at her. He hadn't told anyone about the ghost he had seen on the ship, not even Annette. He had doubted his sanity enough at the time; he didn't need anyone else doubting it as well. There was only one way she could have known about it.

"I know," she confessed. "Permission. I would have found out about it anyways. Once he fired the weapon, Tranagra knew there was no way his people could rescue him. He sacrificed himself to save all of them. But he knew he wasn't done. His body started to give way; he separated his mind from it. When you found his skeleton, he used what little energy he had left to imprint himself into you."

"There's an alien inside me?" Race could feel his heart start to pound as he once again jumped out of his chair. "And you knew about this?"

"I wanted to tell you. I really did." Illandra held out both of her hands in front of her to block Race even though he was several feet away.

"Do not blame her." The ghost stopped Race in his tracks. *"She only did what she had to do, as did I."*

"I…I heard him that time," Anthony said, his eyes dancing with excitement.

"I'm not some pawn in your game," Race yelled in every direction, making sure the alien could hear him.

"No, you are not," the alien agreed, and suddenly he was there. Just as Race had once chased him in the alien ship. His purple skin with hints of blue. Long, slender tentacles swaying off the back of his large, arched head as if they were hair. Covered in his golden armor, he made Zain look as small as Illandra. *"You are the only hope this universe has at surviving."*

"Me?" Race asked, wanting to go punch the alien.

"Yes." The alien nodded. *"My people barely survived the*

Cenari, and now they're back. They will destroy everything you care about. And once they're done with that, they'll move on to the rest of the galaxy, and then the universe. If you don't stop them, here and now, then they will never be stopped."

Race stumbled to find the words he needed. "I can't take on a whole army of those things by myself."

"And you won't." The ghost stepped forward. *"This is my fight, more so than any of yours. I will help you, train you to use your full powers effectively."*

"I seem to be able to use them pretty effectively now," Race informed the alien.

"When you've used them at their best, you do so by accessing my knowledge." The alien took Race's triumph away. *"Learn to use them on your own, and you'll be a hundred times stronger than any fleet."*

"Is that even possible?" Anthony asked, stunned. He had been tugging at Illandra's sleeve, pointing at the alien figure. If he could, Anthony probably would have run over to shake the creature's hand. Race didn't think Anthony would have been as excited if the alien had taken up residence inside him instead.

The alien simply nodded his acknowledgment.

"There may not be enough time for that," Illandra interrupted Anthony's joy. "I read the mind of a Cenari host the other day. They have a fleet ready to attack. I'm almost sure they're waiting for reports back from the advance party that was looking for your planet."

"The advance party is destroyed," Race informed everyone. "I was standing on the last ship when it blew up."

"*They won't wait long, then,*" Tranagra concluded. "*Your leader told them of the information they found. They'll soon send the whole fleet into your space to extract it.*"

"We can't survive that," Race claimed. "We barely fought off the few waves they've sent at us."

"*Show me what you saw,*" Tranagra asked as it turned to look at Illandra. Race had to stop and take a second and wonder how a ghost could see if it had no body. He didn't have any time to consider it before the scene started playing through his head. Even though Illandra had sent the memory to Tranagra, Race was able to see it play through his mind as if he were watching a movie. It only made sense; the two of them were sharing the same mind.

The sheer number of ships was enough to send a cold chill down Race's back and cover his arms with goosebumps. As terrified as he was, it activated something in his abilities, driving him to action.

Tranagra looked grim as death as the memory played in his mind. "*This seems impossible. How have they amassed such an army so quickly? This is unlike their previous attempts. I have no idea how we can defeat them as they are.*"

"I can do it," Race said. Even he was surprised at the amount of confidence his own voice contained.

"You can't take on an armada, Race," Illandra scolded him.

"Normally, I'd agree with you," Race conceded. This time when he stood up, he wasn't hit by a dizzy spell. "But this one, I can. I don't know what it is, but if I can get there, I can stop 'em. I can stop them all."

459

Tranagra looked at him, his eyelids squinted diagonally as they observed Race. *"It's true,"* the alien agreed. *"His powers know of a way."*

"His powers didn't do much to save him." Illandra refused their plan. "If it weren't for me, he'd be dead right now."

Tranagra let out a laugh that was almost as eerie as it was amusing. *"You haven't figured it out yet?"*

"Figured what out?" Illandra asked. She never did like having secrets being held from her.

"The only time the Run'hura ever dreamt his demise was on the nights you intruded upon his dreams."

Illandra face scrunched up as she tried to determine what Tranagra was hinting at, but Race was quick to put the pieces together. "Hah!" Race cheered, excitedly pointing a finger at Illandra. "My powers showed you exactly what you needed to see so that you would link yourself to Annette and rescue me."

Illandra's eyes widened as her cheeks blushed a furious red. While it was true that Illandra enjoyed being the manipulator of circumstances, she grew quite furious when the tables were turned. Race was all too happy to point them out, regardless of whatever consequences she would plan for him at a later time.

"Just when I thought it couldn't get any better," Anthony praised the ceiling above him. "Shared alien consciousness, ripping people through space, and now precog abilities working on such an elaborate scale. I can't wait to discuss this with the committee."

Race felt the congressman was enjoying the whole thing

a lot more than Race cared for, and it seemed Illandra shared Race's feelings.

"Are you sure that's wise?" Illandra asked her mentor.

"This is cutting-edge stuff," Anthony protested. "These are some of the most significant advancements we've ever seen in humanity. It has to be recorded, even if no one sees it for the next couple centuries. Future generations of enhanced humans are going to look back and realize that everything they have sprang from this one moment, from these two who broke every boundary of what it means to be human."

"*If humanity survives.*" Tranagra attempted to put an end to the congressman's excitement.

"Oh, ye of little faith, my friend," Anthony said, refusing to let his excitement be calmed. "If there's one thing I know about humanity, it's that we are survivors. You don't know us, but we have been through countless near-end experiences, some even of our own making. But we adapt and overcome. Well, here is an adaptation"—Anthony threw one arm around Illandra and dragged her to where Race was standing and flung his other arm around the Marine—"and here is the power to overcome.

"You say Race showed Illandra what she needed to see to save him, and I don't doubt that for a second. But a good strategist doesn't just set up the next move. He sets up the next several moves to come. Race didn't just show Illandra what she needed to see to save him; he's now on the other side of the galaxy in a perfect position to pounce on the armada before they rip humanity apart.

461

"You'd be a fool to underestimate either one of these two on their own. Put the two of them together and there's no limit to what they can do. These two are together for a reason, and I almost feel sorry for the Cenari when Illandra and Race come knocking on their door."

Race wished he had half the confidence Anthony had placed in him. Something in the speech made Race feel like he had much more, even if it was just for a little bit. Even the shadow on Tranagra's face seemed to part for Anthony's determination. Now they just had to find a way to not let him down.

"I just have to find a way to get there," Race announced before too much of Anthony's enthusiasm had worn off.

"I think I might know someone that can help with that," Illandra contributed, looking like she was trying to keep from biting her nails.

"Oh?" Anthony asked curiously. He looked her up and down and must have quickly figured out who she meant. "Ooooooooh." He quickly unwrapped his arms from around the couple's necks as if it felt awkward for them there. "I should probably leave the two of you alone to discuss. Tranagra, I wonder if you might be able to project yourself to my quarters? I would love to hear more about your people, and I have so much I want to ask you."

"As would I," the ghost said. Race noticed that his image was starting to become translucent. *"Unfortunately this is incredibly draining on me. I fear I cannot maintain this state any longer."*

"Ah." Anthony tried to keep his frown from showing.

"Maybe some other time, then?"

"*I shall look forward to it.*" Tranagra placed his right fist over his chest and bowed respectfully.

Anthony tried to repeat the gesture, but before he could even start it, the ghost was gone for good. "Well, I'll leave you two to it," Anthony announced once again, feeling out of place. "I'll get with the consultant's manager and see about getting a room for you, Race."

"Thank you, sir," Race managed to say before Anthony rushed out the door.

Race turned to look at Illandra. There was something that had been bugging him ever since he had gotten his sight back. Illandra looked stunning. Too stunning, in fact. He hadn't seen her look so stunning since their last school dance ages ago. The problem with that was, she wasn't expecting him. Which meant she was dressed that way for someone else.

Now that they were alone, Race could ask her about it. "So who is he?"

"Well, it's complicated," Illandra said, backing away, trying to put a chair between the two of them.

"You're mentally connected to another person on the other side of the universe that allowed you to rip me through space, which was all put into place because my powers caught you snooping around in my head and took advantage of it. I also just found out that I have an alien consciousness in my head that just so happens to be connected to the nanites armada about to invade and kill us all, and I find out you've been good friends with him for some time

463

now. How much more complicated can it really be?"

"You'd be surprised," Illandra stalled.

"Try me." Race waved her on.

"Okay," Illandra said, taking a deep breath. "His name is Captain Tso Young, he's in charge of the security detail here and has deep ties with Imperial Intelligence."

"And you're dating him why?"

"It was only one date," she defended. "He forced me into it. He found out about the green card program, and it was the only way I could keep him silenced."

Race took a second to think about it. Something was obviously missing. "And?" there was always an "and."

Illandra closed her eyes before blurting out her next sentence as fast as she could. "And he's a precog, and really good, and the whole reason he's using me is that he hopes that I'll lead him to you so that he can challenge you to find out which of you is stronger."

Illandra was talking so fast it took a little bit for Race to understand everything she said even minutes after she had finished. Race couldn't decide if he should cry or laugh. He did his best to let the laughter through. "Can't we ever do anything the easy way?"

"You have to promise me you'll never fight him." Illandra rushed to him and grabbed his arm.

"Why?" Race wondered. "Do you like him?"

"No." Illandra was taken back. "What are you even talking about? You were just asking Annette out on a date."

Race made several awkward sounds before he was able to find the words he was looking for. "It wasn't like that."

"I know exactly what it was," Illandra warned him. "Making a promise to the poor girl only because you didn't expect to have to keep it. You're taking her on that date when you get back there. You've already put her through enough."

That did bring up another good point in his "I'm dead" argument. With all that he had been through, it just might be that he was dead, but instead of being in the place he thought he would be in, he could be in a place of punishment. "Wait, are you sure I'm not dead?"

"Shut up," she yelled, giving him another jab to the arm she'd been punishing since he'd gotten there.

Chapter 20

ΛLLIΛNCE

Record Dates: 349.401 – 349.430 PGST

ILLANDRA WAITED. SENATOR CHANG AND Captain Tso Young were due any second. Race and Anthony were already in the conference room of the embassy. All they needed was for the rest of their party to arrive. Then they could get down to business.

Race was happy to get out of his room, even if it was to be trapped in another. With Race presumably being dead, Anthony felt it was better for him to remain that way to better increase the success of his mission. They had snuck him out of Illandra's room with one of her coats over his head to hide his identity, and into the room next to Anthony's. When the facility manager asked who was going to be occupying the room, Anthony informed him, "Nobody, and I'd prefer it if you kept it that way."

The man wasn't displeased nearly as much as Illandra had thought he would be. This surely wasn't the first secret he had kept. They had made arrangements for the staff to take Race his food, knocking, leaving a fresh tray of food, and removing the previous one. Race must have been pretty

466

good at hiding; some of the staff had started to refer to him as the embassy ghost.

The doctor had visited him once to follow up. Otherwise, the only people that were allowed to see Race were Anthony and Illandra, who were busy trying to figure out how to correlate things with the Consortium. The main thing that they had struggled with was getting them to believe that Race was alive and well and here at an impossible distance from where he should be. With Tso Young's ties to Imperial Intelligence, he would soon know about Race's death, if he didn't already. Explaining anything was going to be a chore in itself.

It had been several days, and they hadn't come up with anything. They were pressed for time; any day now the fleet could launch their invasion forces. That was when they decided to take Race's advice: "Just introduce us. If that guy's so anxious to fight me, you think he'd be happy to know I was alive."

Race made it sound so much simpler than it actually was. So much could go wrong, and now Illandra waited patiently for the two to clear the embassy's security procedures. The vehicle they arrived in was brought into the VIP garage, where it was scanned for any weapons. It always found some; the captain rarely went anywhere on official business without one of his prized swords on him. As a regular guest, he was usually cleared to keep it.

"Miss Page," the senator said after the Marines cleared them through the entrance into the building. "Such a pleasure to see your lovely smile again."

She took the senator's hand and shook it, welcoming him.

"And I'm afraid to be the one to remove it," the captain said, taking his spot beside him. "I'm not sure if you're aware, but we've received word of your friend, Chief Allard. He's been reported missing in action during a conflict with the Cenari forces. I'm afraid it's mostly a courtesy, though. Reports are that he's most likely dead. I know you two were close; I thought you should know as soon as possible."

The young captain was probably more stricken with grief than she would have been if it were true. "I've already received the report, Captain, but thank you for your concern." It took all she had to keep the smile from her face. Race might be right; the captain might be happy to know he was alive. Maybe even happy enough to help them out. "I haven't heard any word about the rest of his team, though. Have your sources by chance heard anything of them?" She motioned them toward the door and toward the conference room.

"One of them is listed in critical condition, I believe the female member of the team. They have her in a medically induced coma, but I believe they expect her to make a full recovery." It made sense; Annette still hadn't picked up her end of the link they shared. She'd gotten a scattered thought from time to time, but mostly it was like when she found her sleeping. "In the meantime, they are reassigning another green card to replace Chief Allard as the tactical officer. I believe he is a Sergeant Henry Straum. Do you know anything about him?"

The captain was well informed, too informed for her liking. "Race mentioned him once or twice; they trained together in boot camp. Race thought highly of him, I know that much."

"Hopefully he'll be able to make a difference in the war," the senator said darkly. They knew it was no war. It was to be a slaughter; genocide would be more like it.

"That's actually why we invited the two of you here," Illandra informed them as they neared the room. "We have something resembling a plan in the works that we were hoping you could help with."

"We could all use a little hope right about now," the senator stated.

"I fear hope is useless," the captain practically scolded the senator. "I doubt it's going to take much less than a miracle to win this."

"You shouldn't be so quick to dismiss hope." Illandra beat the senator to the door. "Hope gets us through the darkest of times, giving us light where none can pierce. Hope gives one the ability to hold on for just a little bit longer when our strength is gone. Hope is the seed of all miracles. If you believe enough, and with a little luck, you just might live long enough to see one." She hit the sensor to open the door.

The door slid open and the senator entered, followed by the captain. The captain only made it a couple of steps before stopping in his tracks. The two precogs' eyes met; there was no denying the recognition. Both of the Imperialists smiled. The senator's hope had been restored; Illandra wished the captain's smile was for the same reasons.

"I was just telling Ms. Page about the reports of your death," the captain said as Illandra shut the door behind them.

"I'd love to hear some of the details," Race bantered. "I hope you weren't too upset with the news."

Sure, now you're cocky, Illandra thought to herself. It had taken her the better part of a day to convince him he was alive. It took a few skipped meals and a hungry belly to convince him otherwise.

"I actually didn't believe it for a second," the captain replied. Even though he had forced himself to accept it, Illandra could tell that the captain had doubted the report all along. Illandra tried not to be jealous of them; she did have abilities of her own.

"I take it you are part of this plan Illandra was telling us about," the senator said, coming around the table to shake Race's hand.

"Actually, I think I am the plan," Race said, taking the offered hand. "Senator Chang, I take it?"

"A pleasure." The senator nodded his head in acknowledgment. "I can't wait to hear what you have in store for us. Your prowess with the invasion forces has already made you pretty popular, even all the way here in the Imperial Consortium."

"I wish I deserved most of that credit, sir," Race thanked him, "but I couldn't have done any of it without the brave men and women that served with me."

"I think a little luck might have something to do with things as well." The captain nudged the senator out of the way so he could have a chance to talk to the man he'd admired for so long.

"Captain Tso Young," Race said, accepting the outstretched hand. "Illandra's told me a lot about you. Seems we both have had our fair share of luck."

"I hope I don't disappoint." The captain smiled. While everything looked calm between the two on the outside, Illandra could easily see the attempts the captain was making to intimidate Race. Tso had a death grip on Race's hand, attempting to force his dominance. If it had been any normal man, the hand might well have crushed under the pressure. But Race used his hands every day. He was even expecting the overly firm handshake; all he had to do was flex his hand muscles and the captain's vise grip was virtually negated. Race was either too stupid or too smart to respond to the captain's other attempts, Illandra couldn't tell which. Race could appear to be very confident at times, but Illandra knew most of the time it was by accident.

"Let's get down to business," Anthony said, calling the contest to a close.

The two boys released their grasp, and everyone took their seats.

"The plan's very simple," Anthony started to explain. "We have intelligence that suggests that if we can get the chief here to the enemy fleet, we might have a way to permanently dispose of the Cenari once and for all."

"I'd like to know what type of intelligence you have," the senator said. "We haven't been able to get anyone inside their ranks for a long time."

471

"Some of our researchers have been looking into ways of stopping the nanites." Anthony started to explain the lie they had made up. "We believe we've found a way to disrupt them long enough for us to activate some of the ships' self-destruct mechanisms. If we can cause enough of the larger ships to go, we should be able to create enough of a force to destroy all of them."

Illandra could tell they weren't completely buying it, but they had enough hope to give it a try.

"What is it you need from us?" the senator asked.

"We need your help securing passage to the Cenari fleet," Race notified them. "I need to get there undetected."

"You'd need cloaking technology to get there undetected," the senator stated, fearing the plan had already failed before it started.

"Or a Cenari ship," the captain commented. The wheels were turning.

"One with live Cenari," Race added. "One that can sneak us into the fleet."

The senator felt the impossible as he looked down at the table, a dark shadow cast over his face.

The captain was much more hopeful. "I might just have something to get us there."

"Us?" Race questioned. He didn't like what the captain was implying. Neither did Illandra.

"If you're to accomplish this, you're going to need all the help you can get. Besides, this is an Imperial matter more than a Republic one."

"This is a matter of humanity," Illandra corrected him.

"Maybe so," Tso conceded, "but even so, this is Imperial space, and you need Imperial consent to carry out this mission. The only way you're going to get that is if someone from Imperial Intelligence accompanies you. Two can move almost as covertly as one, and it doubles the chances of success."

"And three would triple it," Illandra added.

Race was not happy with that at all, but he chose to hold his tongue for the time being. There was no way she was going to leave the two of them alone. She trusted him enough to accomplish the mission; she didn't trust him enough to take care of Race, or not abandon him. Or worse yet, betray him.

Anthony did not hold his tongue. "I don't think enemy territory is the best place for an ambassador," he warned her.

"If anyone is captured, we'll need someone with good negotiating skills to handle the situation," Illandra informed him. "Besides, I have several other skills that can be of use on this mission."

"I think that is something we can discuss in more detail at a later time." Anthony put the subject on hold for the time being.

"Agreed," said Race, adding his disapproval.

"For now, I'd like to hear more about this idea of yours, Captain." Anthony steered the conversation back on course.

"The Cenari representatives have requested to leave the planet," the captain explained. "I've called in some favors to suspend their takeoff. If we stow away aboard their ship before they're released, we could catch a ride right into the heart of their fleet."

"It's quite possible that they're waiting for the information that unit has gathered before making their strike," Illandra heard Tranagra tell Race. *"They won't wait long, but if they know the information is coming, they might wait long enough for you to get there and find your way to destroy them."*

"Couldn't they just send them a message?" Illandra mentally asked the alien.

"The Cenari were programmed to exchange information directly with each other," Tranagra explained. *"The technology is more secure and ensures all information is exchanged and updated to the collective. If they believe they'll be able to recover the full information, they'll want to upload it to the hive. That means bringing him into their core."*

"That might just work," Race agreed, "if we can find a way to remain undetected."

"Their ship is large for the small crew," the captain informed them. "I doubt the Cenari feel the same need to wander aboard their ships, plus there are several maintenance hatches we should be able to make use of."

"I can hack the ship's systems to cover our signals," Race thought out loud, "maybe even track the crew."

"Then I'll make the preparations," Tso Young said, preparing to leave the room.

"I'll talk to the local security CO and see if he has any supplies we can use," Race said, attempting to escape the confines of his room.

"I'd better handle that, Chief," Anthony cut him off. "You're still considered dead, and that's the best advantage you have working for you on your mission. No one will be looking for, or expecting you."

"Very well," Race conceded. "Illandra, I guess I'm going to need you to help me get back to my room unseen."

Well played; Illandra had to hand it to him. Race was starting to learn the rules of the game.

*   *   *

Illandra felt much like a spy from one of the movies as she ducked around the corner following Race's directions. They had fought, but like always, she had won. Race didn't want Illandra to go; he didn't want her to be in danger. Illandra reminded him that the safest place she could ever be was by his side, where he could protect her. She also had to remind him that she was still connected to Annette, and even though she wasn't awake, Illandra still had full access to all of Annette's abilities. It would be like having Annette there in person. If he had a problem with Annette watching his back, he could have that conversation when she woke from her coma. Race didn't have much to say after that.

Anthony was a totally different matter, on the other hand. The last thing he wanted was the two strongest psychics getting killed. Illandra had to remind him of the speech he had given Tranagra. A couple of hours and several other arguments later, he finally agreed.

Even Senator Chang had come by to state his opposition, but he was more worried about agreeing to a mission he knew very little about. She let Anthony handle that one; the two had built a rapport during their stay.

After two days, they were ready to sneak aboard the alien ship. They had secured enough weapons and the needed energy clips. Race had modified them with an update Konway had developed to be lethal to the Cenari. He had warned them that the burst update should kill a Cenari, but the blast would suck the power out of their clips; he guessed about four shots before they'd have to swap the battery mag. Tso Young had also brought some of his own supplies along.

Tso showed up that morning, and a couple of hours later they were sneaking through a side door to the shipping yard. There was no security in this part of the facility, so they were able to walk around without any incident for a while. The next part of their operation wasn't as easy. The Cenari were still members of Congress, so their ship was held in a very high-security section. There were lots of sensors and staff to ensure the safety. Tso Young had made some arrangements to modify some of the sensors, but they still needed to get through the area undetected. After several hours of ducking and hiding, they were almost to the ship.

Race darted off past several crates to check the corner before coming back. *"Two guards,"* he thought over the temporary mental link Illandra had created for them to talk over. *"Right by the ship. No sign of moving anytime soon."*

Illandra had already detected them. *"We can't stay here long. Another patrol could pass by any minute."*

"About ten minutes," Tso informed them, looking at his sensor. *"We might have to take them out."*

"If we do that, they'll just order a security sweep of the whole area," Race refuted. *"Not to mention delaying the*

476

*launch and searching all the ships. They'll probably have the
security features re-enabled by then, too."*

Tso snarled, but he knew Race was right.

"Use your powers." A voice that didn't belong to any of
them came over the link. There was no mistaking whom the
dark shadowy voice belonged to.

Tso looked at them, trying to figure out the source of the
new person that had joined the conversation.

"I'll explain later," Race told him. *"I'm not sure how my
powers are going to be of any use here."*

"Not yours," Tranagra clarified. *"The small one. Use your
power of the mind to make them not see you."*

Race had to grab her to prevent her from sitting up and
revealing their position. *"How do I do that?"* she asked.

The instructions came to her, but not in words. It was
simple enough, but hard to believe that it would work. It
wasn't that they wouldn't see them; she was just going to
trick their brain into believing that what they were seeing
wasn't of any relevance. She didn't know if she was up for
the task, but they didn't have much of an option right then.

"All right," she sighed. *"Wait here, let me give this a shot."*
She reached out with her mind and locked onto the two
soldiers standing guard. Her hands were shaking, but she
pushed herself out from her cover. She slowly approached
them, making sure not to make any threatening moves.
About halfway there, one of the guards turned to look
straight at her. She froze instantly, a bead of sweat running
down her cheek. She held onto her powers, focusing on the
guard. After an eternity that consumed just seconds, the

guard turned back to his buddy. She picked up her pace a little and slipped past them to the access hatch of the ship.

Race followed shortly behind, the large bag of supplies strapped to his back. This time the other guard glared at Race, sending a bolt of fright that locked his muscles in place. The fear was overwhelming, the nagging sensation trying to draw her attention from the task at hand. She did her best to ignore it and focus. A moment later, the guard focused on something else. Race sneaked out to join her in her hiding spot near the door.

Tso Young followed the path next. There wasn't much time until the next watch came by. He paid the guards' stares little attention when they came upon him; his nerves of steel just shook it off. At least until one of the guards took a step toward him. Illandra checked him; she was sure he hadn't seen him, but she couldn't tell why he was moving.

"Does he see me?" Tso asked, a hand going toward a sword that was now on his back instead of at his side.

"I don't know," Illandra answered, confused as to what was going on.

Tso took three steps to the side; the guard moved to intercept him. The guard wasn't alarmed, nor was he out to get him. Illandra didn't know what was going on. She was sure it was working, but she couldn't tell why it wasn't.

The blade on the captain's sword inched from its sheath.

"If he makes a threatening move toward the guard, he'll destroy the mirage," Illandra heard the alien raise the alarm. The strain was making it hard for her to focus, but she refused to give up. He'd do more than just destroy her illusion.

He'd destroy the mission before it even had a chance to begin.

Race was already in motion. His eyes scanned the area for a distraction. Without knowing it would work, he lifted his hand and focused his powers on a stack of cargo on the other end of the bay. In response, the stack toppled over in a loud crash that echoed through the bay.

The guard turned his head to investigate the noise. Tso returned his sword back and stood as still as a statue.

"What the hell?" the guard said, looking at the mess.

"You should go check that out," Tso commanded him softly. If Illandra were closer, she would have punched him.

The guard nodded and moved to investigate, allowing Tso to rush by and join Race and Illandra. The other guard had moved to cover his partner, which allowed the group to access the ship's hatch and board the vessel.

"Step one complete," said Illandra, almost collapsing once they were safe.

Chapter 21

ΛNNIHILΛTION

Record Dates: 349.473 – 349.487 PGST

THEY HAD MADE IT. THEY had snuck aboard the alien ship. Race hacked the ship's sensors long before the Cenari boarded the ship, and then the trio was restricted to the service tunnels. Luckily, not for too long. The Cenari hardly even used much of the ship. Two of them remained on the bridge to fly, and the others barely even moved. Race had guessed that was because the nanites maintained most of the host body, preventing the need for waste or digestion. Race wondered where they got the energy or materials to maintain the bodies, but it really didn't make much difference. After several days of observing them, the group braved venturing into one of the vacant rooms. They still kept most of their supplies in the access tunnel in case they had to make a quick escape. Race had overridden the lock and set his AI to alert him the moment it detected someone even remotely close to the room.

Race was getting tired of rooms. He'd been trapped in too many lately. The price he paid for remaining dead. He tried to pass the time with exercise, the foreign captain silently challenging him with every one. It pushed Race well beyond his limits, as it did for the great captain. Illandra did her own thing, as usual. Most of the time, she couldn't even look at the men during their competitions.

"I hear we're of the same type," the captain said one day when Race was too sore to attempt any type of challenge.

"You mean with the thing?" Race asked, pointing to his head and then making a binocular-type motion with his hands to try and signal his second sight.

"Yes," the officer acknowledged, picking up on the pantomime. "One day I'd like to test my skills against you if you're up for it."

Illandra had warned him that challenge would come. "I don't see why not," Race accepted, "maybe when we have some more space and aren't surrounded by enemies. I'm told that most of my advancements came during boot camp when I was put against another one of us."

"You mean Staff Sergeant Henry Straum?" The captain had done his research.

"He's a staff sergeant now?" Race wasn't too surprised by that. Henry was pretty much Race's equal and he probably had more opportunities to advance in a bigger unit, not to mention the privileges the green citizenship card had earned him.

"And the newest member of the Taurus SORD team," the captain added.

The captain had managed to wound Race without even lifting a finger. He felt the sting in his chest, about the spot where he guessed his heart was. He knew what the captain

481

was implying. Race had been replaced. Even if he survived the mission and made his way back to his unit, there might not be a place there for him anymore. "It's good to know they'll be taken care of." Race tried to focus on the positive to mask his injury.

Illandra shifted around in the crude bed they had crafted for themselves in the room. Race and the captain quickly sealed their mouths, afraid they had woken her. They slept in shifts, making sure at least one person was up at all times to alert the group to any Cenari movement. She sat up and yawned. It wasn't a great sleep, but they were getting used to it.

She removed the collar Race had given her from the alien ship. Race knew its true purpose now that Tranagra had merged more of his own consciousness and he remembered their dream conversations. Helping to have saved Illandra's life was probably the only reason he even remotely trusted the alien.

No sooner had the collar touched the bed than the surprise displaced any sign of the drowsiness from her nap. "She's awake," she exclaimed.

Before either of the soldiers could ask what she meant, the small woman jumped off the bed and wrapped her arms around Race's neck. Race was shocked by the display of emotion. He and Illandra had been taking a break since she'd left Taurus. "Oh my god," he heard her say, muffled, into his shoulder, "I thought I lost you."

Race really didn't know what was going on. He grabbed the smaller woman by the arms and pushed her back a bit to look at her face. His eyes saw Illandra, but his mind had lit the coal-colored hair into flames. Even the face no longer matched that of the person that was supposed to be there.

"Annette," Race cheered. Without thinking, he pulled her back into him and returned the embrace. "You're all right." He had been so worried about her, but there was nothing he could do.

"Good to see you're doing okay." Illandra's ghost popped in beside them. Race couldn't tell if Illandra was concerned or happy to see the two of them together.

"Sorry," Annette said using Illandra's lips. Race quickly let his arms fall as he released Annette and the two took a step back to put a some distance between them.

"It's all right," Illandra assured them, not too convincingly.

"I get the feeling I'm not seeing all of this conversation," the captain said, eyeing them suspiciously. Race couldn't help but think how things must look to him. Race and Illandra unusually close, Annette talking to thin air. The only reason Race could see things without any assistance was because of his mental sharing with the alien Tranagra, one of the very few benefits he'd found so far.

The ghost closed her eyes for a second; Race assumed she was tuning the Imperialist into the conversation. In a couple of seconds, that suspicion was confirmed. Tso blinked his eyes a couple of times, almost in disbelief. "Ah, I see," he said, the clever smile that annoyed Race appearing. The captain was becoming too informed with all their secrets for Race's liking. He already knew more than enough from his connections with Imperial Intelligence, but they had been forced to let him in on many of their other secrets. There was no telling how many he might try and hold against them later.

"I've been up for a couple hours," Annette told Illandra. "I've been trying to get ahold of you, but I couldn't sense you."

"I had the collar on," Illandra snarled while pointing to the device she thought of as a curse lying on the bed.

"I figured," Annette said before turning back to Race. "I saw the ship explode. How did you survive?"

Race pointed at Illandra. There were still times he doubted his escape, but he had been forced to accept it. Being alive was required for him to accomplish the mission.

"Somehow, I was able to use the link to pull Race into my room before the explosion killed him," Illandra explained.

"We did it?" Annette's face danced with excitement; her sacrifices had not been in vain.

"Yes. I owe you my life," Race thanked her.

"You owe her a lot more than that." Illandra scolded him with her eyes. Race did his best not to cower.

"Wait. Where are you now?" Annette's eyes browsed the unlivable conditions they were forced to reside in as stowaways.

"We're hiding on a Cenari vessel heading toward their invasion fleet," Race started to explain to her. "Once we get there, we're going to sneak onto whatever vessel we dock with and follow my powers to whatever is tugging on them and hope it helps us stop them."

484

"So you don't have a plan," Tso laughed.

"You didn't have to come," Illandra reminded him.

"Someone had to make sure this mission succeeds." He laughed again.

Race blocked out the continued bickering of the Imperialist and the ghost. He had been caged in the room waiting for Illandra to bring news of Annette. He reached up and caressed her cheek, grateful to have her with him again. Her eyes smiled back at him, and his heart soared.

"What do you need me to do?" Annette let the moment pass and put a stop to the quarreling.

Illandra thought to stop her from joining their group. Annette could be even more stubborn than Illandra when she had made up her mind. Illandra had learned well enough from their time linked together. Illandra sighed, dismissing her objection; the decision had already been made.

"You can pilot my body," Illandra replied. "I can support all of you better like this, anyways."

That made Race feel much better. No matter how much Illandra assured him, Race didn't feel that she could absorb enough experience through the link to handle the mission. There was no substitute for the real Annette. It completely changed the dynamics of the mission, at least in Race's head.

"How much longer until we strike?" Annette asked, her face already assuming the serious expression she got whenever a mission was on.

Race checked his biosensor to retrieve the information. "We're still about a week out," he informed them.

"Okay," Annette acknowledged, sitting on the makeshift

bed they were all using. "I'll be ready." Before anyone could comment, the body went limp and fell over. Annette's image faded from the body as Illandra's body hit the bed once more.

"Your girlfriend can be a real pain sometimes," Illandra said before disappearing. Her body didn't jump back to life; Race figured she'd probably stopped to talk to Annette before returning, once again leaving him alone with the captain.

"Let me see if I'm caught up here. Your new girlfriend is psychically connected to your ex-girlfriend?" the captain asked after they were sure Illandra wasn't coming back.

"I guess," Race responded shortly.

"You really don't like to do anything the easy way, do you?"

"Easy is boring," Race responded with his normal lie. He really wished he could do something the easy way, just once.

*   *   *

They were moving too slowly. The ship had docked; Annette had taken over for Illandra while Illandra herself was haunting the hallways. It still disturbed Race every time he saw it, but it gave them the advantage they needed.

"There's no way around them." Illandra's thoughts came over the link they shared.

The group had followed Race's senses to this spot. It was the largest threat drowning out the danger funneling in from all around them. They couldn't move on until they dealt with the two misshapen Cenari creatures blocking the path. Even Illandra couldn't figure out what was beyond the

486

door.

"*We have to,*" Race told her. "*Whatever we need is beyond that door.*"

"*We'll have to take them out,*" the Imperial captain said. The more Race had to deal with him, the less he liked him. He was too quick to resort to violence, but this time there didn't seem to be another alternative. Illandra's new tricks were useless on the mechanical nanites.

"*And quick,*" Race agreed. "*We can't afford one of them raising the alarm.*"

"*Preferably when they're not looking at us. We don't know if the Cenari can still report back even after the host's death,*" the captain further recommended.

That was going to be the tough part; the Cenari barely moved.

"*I've got an idea,*" Annette said, handing off her firearm to Race. She went to a panel on the opposite side of the wall and pulled off the wall plate protecting several round conduits of various sizes and colors. Her teeth clenched as she placed it on the ground, praying it didn't make any noise. Race didn't even know what half the cables did, but it took Annette only seconds to find the ones that she needed. It was good to have her back.

She completed her tinkering and rushed the group around the corner, where she once again took another piece of the metallic wall apart and worked with another handful of cables.

"*All right,*" she said, letting the team know she was done, "*now we just have to get their attention.*"

"*I'll attract them.*" Tso beat Race to the punch. The Imperialist was quicker on his feet than Race was, gone before Race could even move to head him off.

On feet light enough they could have walked on water without causing a ripple, the captain quickly made it over to the area where the corridor connected. He knocked on the wall a couple of times and then danced up the wall, where he braced himself almost near the ceiling, well above the normal range of vision.

"*I hate that guy.*" The words slipped from Race's thoughts into the link they shared.

The insult caused a warm feeling in the captain that shined back through the link. It heated Race's jealousy even more.

Something shuffled down the hallway; Race could already tell it wasn't loud enough to be what he wanted. They hid out of sight while Illandra piped in the image of what was going on from her ghostly view safe in the hallway. A moment later, only one of the guards came into view of the others. Race let another curse escape into the link.

Even the way the creature walked twisted Race's stomach in disgust; their half walking, half hopping made Race think of what a cross between a dog and monkey would walk like. The first thing it noticed was the panel that Annette had removed near their door. It moved to investigate, examining it from several different angles as it approached.

"*Now,*" Illandra screamed as the creature poked its head into the mess of cables.

Annette didn't need the cue. She had already jammed

the ends of two loose cables into each other. A ball of blue fire erupted from the booby-trapped junction, erupting around the unsuspecting Cenari as it either burned or melted everything in its path.

There was more shuffling down the hall. Race wasn't sure what they were going to do with the other one; the trap felt like a one-shot deal.

Luckily, they didn't have to do anything. As the beast came into the hallway and saw its fallen comrade, Tso fell from his perch high above him. As he glided down, he pulled his sword from its sheath over his shoulder. The sword circled through the air and found its way through the Cenari's neck. The head fell without grace; a thud echoed out as it hit the floor at the creature's feet.

It was clear now why Illandra didn't want Race to fight the captain.

Race and Annette quickly left their cover to head for the door. Race tried not to look at the burnt creature when he passed, but he found it impossible to keep his eyes off of it. If he thought the creature was hideous before being charred, he didn't have a word to describe the incinerated flesh. He didn't have a word for the smell, either. The other creature's face was well hidden as they passed it; the captain's blow had been so well planned that the body had even managed to land over the head, preventing any nanites from using the eyes even after the creature's death.

Annette quickly removed the side panel near the door, her brow scrunched, trying to figure out the foreign device. "I don't know how to open this one," she said.

She didn't need to. Tso shoved his sword through the center of the device, and the door opened almost as if it feared it would be next.

Illandra was already in the room, her ghost petrified by the sight. Race didn't even believe it himself: an unsightly mass of what appeared to be flesh intertwined with machinery sitting in the center of the room, cables dangling in from around the room connecting the blob to various parts of its surroundings.

"*It's several bodies,*" Illandra told them. Her face made to vomit as if it actually had a stomach to lose. "It's combined them into one for more power."

The sight made it almost impossible for Race to keep his stomach. He somehow forced himself to manage. Annette didn't fare so well, possibly from her connection with Illandra and being able to actually feel some of the horror the hosts undertook.

"You don't belong here," a twisted voice echoed over the room's audio system.

"*It's a core,*" the alien entity inside Race informed them. "*I can't believe they actually exist.*"

"What's a core?" Race stopped using the link.

"How do you know of the core?" the voices echoed once again.

"*A core is like the central processor of the Cenari,*" Tranagra explained. "*It does most of the planning and thinking. All the information the Cenari gather gets transmitted to the core, and it's the one that takes the information and formulates it into strategies and assigns the tasks.*"

"I know because I know who you are," Race yelled into the room. He had heard enough. "I don't know how you've survived this long, but you have no place here. Your quest for vengeance on the ones who made you is as futile as it comes."

"I don't think you should be making it angry," the captain warned.

"You can't stop the Cenari," the voice almost seemed to laugh. "We have no need for vengeance; we need only grow. If the makers failed to stop us, what hope do you think you have?"

"The makers did stop you." It was Race's voice through his lips, but not Race's words. Not even Race's language. "I stopped you at the *Battle of Ilis Comra*. I watched as the *Dalrak'na* ripped your bodies to shreds. Tell me how it is you survived!" Tranagra did a much better job at demanding information than Race did.

Race had never known a machine to be afraid, but this one almost seemed to tremble. "Impossible," the voice echoed. "You have knowledge beyond the scope of your race. You speak the language of the Makers. How can this be?"

"You weren't the only one to survive the impossible," Tranagra scolded the machine. "Now tell me how you survived!"

"It is irrelevant," the core stated. Tranagra had amplified Race's powers to the point that he knew what was coming. Several doors to the room opened as disfigured guards flooded into the room.

491

The rest of his team quickly moved into action. Tso used his sword to decapitate one of the monsters that rushed him while Annette fired a couple of shots from her rifle to kill the others before the battery died and she went to swap it out for a new one.

They weren't the targets, though. All the creatures were focused on Race, biting and clawing their way toward him. Race didn't care anymore; he only cared about one thing now. Destroying these abominations.

And the power was there. The one that Race feared so much in the past was now coursing through his veins. He no longer feared the power. If it meant the end of these things, he would embrace it, welcoming the blue flames that covered his vision. Race stretched his palms out in front of him, mentally halting his attackers in mid-stride as they tried to reach him.

"Allard!" Tso called out, "catch!"

The captain's bluish-green blade sailed through the air as it spun toward Race. Race latched onto it with his powers and guided the hilt into the palm of his hand. He pulled the sword to his side and swung it like a bat to meet the nearest mutated creature closing in on its target. The blade cut the savage beast in half as if it were slicing through air.

Race quickly circled his feet to dodge the next creature as he brought the blade above his head and brought it down on the creature as he landed before him, severing the second mutilation's hindquarters from the top half.

The last attacker was closing the distance to Race. It leaped to clear the other bodies Race had disposed of. Race refused to wait for the beast and threw the sword at the monster. The blade twirled through the air and ripped through the creature as easily as it had the prior attackers. Race used his telekinetic powers to return the blade back to its owner as it circled the room and landed at Tso's feet.

Race started to approach the mesh of bodies in the center of the room, parts of it twitching in reaction to every step he took closer.

"Destroying the core will make no difference." The warped voice attempted to play for its life, this time in the alien language that only Race could understand. *"Another core will be crafted in my place."*

"Yes," Race and Tranagra answered, their thoughts intertwined, *"but not right away. And not before I can destroy this fleet."*

"You are only three." The voice seemed to almost laugh at them. *"You don't stand any chance against the might of the Cenari."*

"Before I destroy you, you will hear my name. And when you do, you will echo it to every Cenari cell you are connected to so they can fear my coming."

"We know the one named Allard," the speakers crackled. "It is strong for the Terrans, but no threat to Cenari."

"Allard is only one name for this creature," Race threatened, only a couple of feet away. "You shall know him by his true name, the *Run'hura*."

"NO!" the voice shrieked through the audio system, so powerfully that many of them shorted out, raining sparks throughout the room. "That's a foolish prophecy. That's impos…ble!"

Race waited long enough for the entity to transmit its message to the remainder of the Cenari before disintegrating the core into mere atoms, using his hands to mimic crushing the abomination. The cluster unraveled into a cloud of dust carried off by the station's circulation system.

Once the last of the core was gone, Race turned to gather his team and leave. Tranagra was helping him sustain the power. The blue still blanketed his vision, but control of his body was now his alone. "Come," Race informed the others, "we haven't much time."

They were back in the halls, without the need for stealth this time. Their presence was common knowledge by now. There were Cenari throughout the halls, but most of them were attempting to flee from the advancing trio. Every so often, they'd run into a small group that would attempt to halt their progress, but Race would make short work of them quick enough to send another wave of panic through their ranks.

"Here," Race said, following his senses through a large door. He mentally triggered the control panel on his way in. He would have ripped the panel out as well, but he knew the captain would soon stick his sword through the panel to disable the door.

The room was dark for a couple of minutes, the only light emanating from the fire of Race's eyes, which was starting to wither out.

"What is this place?" Annette asked, happy to be out of danger, if only for a moment.

"Their army," Race said, triggering the lights to illuminate their surroundings.

They were in one of the station's docking bays meant to house over a dozen large-scale freighters. There were no ships in the bay, however. It was packed from top to bottom with robots, modified with combat tech better than anything Race had ever seen. The empty shells hung lifelessly from their stacks, spanning farther than the eyes could see, even though Race could still feel every one of them with his mind.

"I don't get it," Illandra's ghost said as it attempted to count them all. *"Why robots? Why not just infect their way into an army?"*

"They need to catch the hosts first," Tso said. He'd been watching Race with a clenched jaw since he'd first started using his powers. Race didn't know why the captain was so upset, nor did he have time to worry about it now.

"He's right," Race credited Tso. "But more importantly, these robots were controlled directly by the Cenari core without the need to relay commands through additional nanites."

"Which you just destroyed," Annette reminded them. "Who controls them now?"

Race answered by activating a terminal nearby. A couple of lines of familiar code started self-executing on the console; then a familiar image compiled itself on the screen.

"Let's say you wanted to make an AI small enough to fit on a portable device." Race started to explain a secret he hadn't even known he'd been keeping. "Since you have so few resources to work with, you expand it to spread itself on any spare resources and allow them to interconnect like a giant supercomputer."

"You have got to be kidding me." Annette laughed, nearly beside herself.

"I don't believe it," Illandra said, covering her mouth to hide her surprise.

"Operation matrix, online," Bella's image said from the terminal she had freshly hacked her way into. "Activating communication pathways to robotic hive network… Complete."

"Your AI is taking over the robots?" Tso said, catching on. "How many can it control?"

"There's no limit," Race explained. "She can copy a part of her subroutines into each robot and network them into one. The more she has access to, the stronger she becomes."

Tso looked at all the robots in disbelief. He could barely imagine the sheer power that the number of units could collectively possess.

"Fifty-one billion, four hundred and nine million, eight hundred and seventy-nine thousand, four hundred and eighty-one units online and awaiting orders," Bella informed them once she had completed the process.

"All right, I'm not good at math, but there is no way there are fifty-one billion robots in here with us," Annette protested.

"There are only about five million units upon this station, of which nearly a quarter reside in this bay. The fifty-one billion is the number of robots connected to the Cenari's core network across all ships and space stations in the area," the AI clarified.

"You've literally just stolen your enemy's army," Illandra halfway scolded and congratulated Race's accomplishment at the same time.

"For once, something easy." Race smiled before turning to the terminal to address his AI. "Bella, take control of this fleet and eliminate all infected Cenari. Activate whatever self-destructs you can and manually blow up the ones you can't. Turn it all to scraps."

"Initiating," Bella responded. "I will use a battalion to clear an escape path for you before destroying this facility once you are safely away." There was a quick flash and her image was gone.

The internal doors on the shuttle bay swished open as the bottom level of androids activated and came to life. They exited the bay to the halls full of ravaged Cenari. The chaos of the station elevated to pure anarchy as the combat-enhanced androids started to attack the already disoriented Cenari. The Cenari tried to defend themselves as the next array of bots were dropped down to the floor and became active.

"Go get 'em, girl," Race said proudly of his creation.

Race's power was gone and had taken a good portion of his normal strength with it; he barely kept himself from falling to the ground. He held the group back from quickly attending to their escape. He did his best not to hinder their progress too much, but the battalion of robots clearing the halls more than ensured their safety.

Tso had managed to work his way to the front where all the conflict was. He viciously sliced his way through any Cenari that dared to get close, like he was taking out some unknown frustration on the poor creatures. Annette stayed near Race, as did a couple of the robots to protect him in his weakened state.

When they made it to the shuttle bay where their ship had landed, Tso finished up the last of the Cenari, sheathed his sword, and marched silently into the ship.

Race examined the bay. He guessed it was one of the few, if not only bay not converted to something else. Besides their ship, there were a few other vessels inside the bay. The ship the ambassadors had used to get here had been unaltered by the Cenari, possibly in fear that it might be studied and some of their secrets might be discovered. The other ships were fully modified, and full of information.

Race knew this war was far from over. There was no way destroying the fleet would destroy the last of the Cenari. Race left his escorts and started to head toward the nearest vessel.

"Where are you going?" Illandra reached out to him.

"This isn't over," Race informed them. He grabbed the attention of the nearest robot. "Bella, sweep that ship and make it mine. I'm taking it out of here."

"You can't leave now." Annette grabbed his arm to stop him from walking away.

"I still have a mission to accomplish," Race tried to explain.

"I can't lose you again," she pleaded with him, tears

nearing the corners of her eyes. "I just barely found you."

"I'm not leaving you," Race told Annette, bringing her closer to look her in the eyes. "I'm taking this ship, and I'm coming back to you. The real you."

The pain was gone, but the tears were pressing even harder. Her hands grabbed the side of Race's face and pulled him down until their lips locked in a moment of passion too pleasant for Race to resist. The two were so enwrapped in their kiss, they were clueless about the battle around them.

When they released each other, Race refused to even open his eyes in fear that what had just happened might have been a dream.

"I'll see you soon," Annette said, running off. Race's eyes forced themselves open to watch the redhead leave.

There was the sound of someone clearing their throat behind him.

Race turned to find the apparition floating there before him. "Can we please not do this now?" Race rolled his eyes. "This is far from over. I still have a job to do. This is only a setback for them; we still have a war ahead of us. I need to prepare for what's to come."

"You know, it doesn't really matter if you actually do manage to pick between us," Illandra told him, getting back to her point.

"What do you mean?" Race fearing the words she might utter next.

"We're psychically joined for life, and we're only going to mesh more over time. If you're with either one of us, it's really with both of us." Illandra confirmed the one thing he possibly feared more than the Cenari.

"I'm not sure if I like the way that sounds," Race said, clenching a hand over his heart.

"Good." Illandra winked before fading away.

"I hate when she does that." Race looked around the empty bay. The remaining Cenari had been killed or cleared out by the army of robots. Only a few robots still lingered to cover him. "The ship is cleared for your journey," his AI announced from his wrist.

"Good work, Bella," Race congratulated her. "I'd kiss you, too, if I could."

"Promises, promises," the program teased.

Race forced a chuckle; he was near moments away from collapsing under the weight of his own body. He entered the ship and took the cockpit to plot his course. He set the ship to take him all the way to the SORD HQ. He could hear the engines of his friends' ship starting up. He watched long enough to see the ship safely leave the armada before launching his own. There were still about a dozen androids in the ship, Bella following her directive to protect Race.

Race remained awake long enough to ensure his own ship escaped as well. He even managed to witness several explosions before he retreated to a suspended-animation chamber. His trip home was going to be long, and there weren't nearly enough supplies for him to last without it. He made a change to the chamber to keep him from going into too deep a sleep. He had much work with Tranagra to do.

"Looks like it's just you and me, gal," he started his last goodbye. "See us home safely, would you?"

"I will always be here for you," the artificial intelligence told him.

He found a spare room that still had some remnants of a bed where he could get some rest. His powers had left him nearly drained, and although he would have to use the sleep chamber eventually, he wanted to stay awake as long as possible. As he began to doze off, Race remembered a time when he'd wanted to do nothing more than steal a ship and fly off into unknown space. Here he had the opportunity to do so, but there was nowhere he'd rather be than with his friends.

EPILOGUE

Record Date: 349.487 PGST

ILLANDRA TRIED TO KEEP RACE psychically linked to the group for as long as she could. The ships barely broke into the slipstream before he was too far for her to maintain it, though. Annette had piloted the ship for a bit to elude any attempts to cut off their retreat. There was almost no resistance, the ships too occupied with the mutiny of androids now overtaking them.

They felt a couple of impacts as ships started to explode, another good reason Annette was piloting. They jumped before things got too shaky. Once they were clear and the course was set, Annette handed over Illandra's body and went back to her side of the galaxy.

Everything had gone too perfectly. From Race defying his demise to them stowing away on board the Cenari vessel, from destroying the core-making room to Race's AI turning the enemy's own forces against them. It was nothing short of mind-boggling how perfectly Race's powers had ensured their victory. It just went to show how much they had truly underestimated Race's abilities. Hopefully, she wouldn't make that mistake again anytime soon.

Now all that was left to do was return home, report their success, and wait for their next assignment. Illandra was wondering what that might be when a loud crash echoed through the hull of the ship.

The noise jolted Illandra out of her daydream. The sound had come from inside the room. She turned around to see the captain with his fist in a dent in the side of the wall.

"You lied to me," he accused Illandra, barely keeping his temper caged.

"About what?" Illandra said, unaware of any misleading she might have given him.

"You told me you weren't sure who was stronger," Tso finished his accusation.

"Even I had no idea how powerful Race is," Illandra defended herself.

"But you knew he was stronger," Tso fumed.

"I suspected," Illandra fessed up. This had all the makings of a very awkward trip.

"Yet you led me to believe that we were almost equal," he said, taking a step toward her, a hand grabbing the sheath to his sword. "Knowing he could rip things apart with his very mind and create shields out of thin air."

"Remember when I told you that Race doesn't enjoy fighting?" If she didn't calm Tso down quickly, this conversation was going to take a bad turn.

Tso stopped his advance. "Yes." He eyed her curiously.

"I told you that Race only fights because he has to, to protect those that he cares about." The captain seemed to ease a bit. "He was fighting to protect the entire human race.

That's what drove him to be so strong. He's only as strong as he needs to be." The captain took a step back. There was some sense coming back to him. "This threat, it required him to become what he is. I already told you: if you want to be like Race, find something worth fighting for."

Tso fumed for a moment, not sure what he wanted to do. Not able to decide, he stormed off the bridge to some isolated part of the ship.

Illandra let out a big sigh of relief once the door closed behind him. "Yup, it's going to be one awkward trip," she said to the empty room, spinning around in her chair.

Λ LETTER FROM THE ΛUTHOR

I know there are many excellent novels out there, that's why I'm so honored that you have taken the time to given this one a chance. I wanted to take this opportunity to personally thank you.

This piece of work represents ten years of work, but don't worry, the sequel is well on its way and should be in your favorite story by the summer of 2020! I hope you've enjoyed it as much as I have creating it.

Now for one last shameless request. Did you know why authors are always struggling for reviews?

> Once this book gets 10 reviews, my wife stops using it to swat flies.

> After this book gets 30 reviews, my wife will stop using it as a door stop.

> Finally, at 50 reviews, my wife will clear me to publish my next book!

Only you can help stop the abuse of literature! Please leave a review so that I can complete my work!

-RICHΛRD ROSS

ABOUT THE AUTHOR

Richard has been a fan of Science Fiction and Fantasy all his life, literally. His mom will tell you stories of how the only thing that would keep him quiet as a baby was reruns of the original Star Trek. There are even rumors he was born early just so he could celebrate being born the same year Star Wars first showed in theaters.

Richard is an extremely creative person and loves using his skills to build fictional worlds. After years of exposure to fiction literature and films, he felt the urge to take the inspiration and make a story of his own. Thus, he started down the path of becoming an author and started the book series known as A Cosmic Endeavor.

Richard lives in Southern California, where he moved after leaving the US Marine Corps. He is married to Paola Ross, who he thanks every day for her divine-like tolerance of his crazy shenanigans. Richard has two children, Trenton and Kayla.

DID YOU KNOW?

Most printing companies require a blank page at the end of your book, and it has to end on an even number because every page has a front and back. That means I have this whole page with nothing planned for it.

Now, I'm not one to waste space, so I thought long and hard about what to put here. My first idea was to put in a little doodle, but I am such an awful artist, my stick figures would rather commit seppuku rather than suffer the disgrace of public humiliation. If I was any good, you'd be reading a Cosmic Endeavor comic or graphic novel by now. I settled on sharing some useful links for you.

COSMIC ENDEAVOR
https://cosmicendeavor.com

A community site revolving around this very story. Get extended bios on characters, and read works in progress from the next journey of your favorite characters. Community members are encouraged to share their own stories and artwork inspired by the Cosmic Endeavor universe.

RICHARD'S BLOG
https://richardross.us

My centralized hub for all my creative projects where you can sign up for my newsletter and stay up to date. There's also a live chat that I keep open while I'm working to chat with wonderful people like you. It's active right now as I work on this!

Made in the USA
Coppell, TX
21 October 2022

85088901R00298